Linda Winstead Jones is a bestselling author of more than fifty romance books in several subgenres—historical, fairy tale, paranormal, contemporary and romantic suspense. She is also a six-time RITA® Award winner, including the 2004 RITA® Award for paranormal romance (writing as Linda Fallon). Linda lives in north Alabama with her husband of fifty-two years. She can be reached via lindawinsteadjones.com.

Linda Winstead Jones
and
Lisa Childs

RAINTREE: ORACLE
AND
CURSED

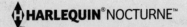
HARLEQUIN® NOCTURNE™

Recycling programs
for this product may
not exist in your area.

ISBN-13: 978-0-373-60126-4

Raintree: Oracle and Cursed

Copyright © 2015 by Harlequin Books S.A.

The publisher acknowledges the copyright holders
of the individual works as follows:

Raintree: Oracle
Copyright © 2015 by Linda Winstead Jones
Cursed
Copyright © 2015 by Lisa Childs-Theeuwes

Printed in U.S.A.

CONTENTS

RAINTREE: ORACLE

Linda Winstead Jones

For Linda Howard, fabulous writer, partner in crime, travel buddy and, most of all, good friend.

Prologue

Autumn in the North Carolina mountains was always special. Even after serving six years as keeper of the Raintree Sanctuary, the beauty of the place and the season was not lost on Echo. The days were cooler now, and she liked that. The leaves on the trees had turned enticing shades of gold, orange and red. These early-morning walks along a wooded trail were for her and her alone. The rest of the day might be spent handling Sanctuary business, but each day began just this way, with a long walk and blessed solitude.

Suddenly her vision dimmed, and an instant later a burst of bright light blinded her. Echo dropped to her knees, hard, then fell forward, grasping at the dirt and small stones on the trail with her fingertips, trying to hold on so the world wouldn't spin out from under her. For a split second she was able to think, and what initially came to her was *I'm too young to have a stroke!*

But then thought was gone, the images bombarded her and she realized this was no stroke.

There was water, lots of it. Icy-cold salt water filled her nose and her mouth; she choked on it. It burned. She could not breathe. The two worlds—hers and theirs—merged. She was prone on a dirt trail on Sanctuary land, holding on for dear life, but she was also *there*. And she was drowning.

The boat was sinking, going down fast. Water rushed in, sweeping people off their feet and away, pushing them under the cold water. The forceful and icy water swirled around her legs, pushing and pulling until she, too, fell and was washed deep into the sea. She screamed, and water filled her lungs.

There were one hundred and three souls on board; she knew that in a way she could not explain. Though she was underwater and for all intents and purposes drowning as so many already were, she heard the panicked cries of those who had not yet been swept under the dark waters. They were all screaming for help, and they were all going to die…

And then it was over.

Echo felt as if she'd been kicked by a mule, but she blinked twice, three times. She caught her breath and rolled onto her back. Her entire body trembled; her knees were weak, and she remained cold. So cold. She wasn't sure how long the vision had lasted. Even though it had seemed like seconds while she'd been caught up in it, she noticed that the sun had moved a bit higher in the sky. The morning was growing warmer.

She didn't sob, but silent tears streamed down her face. Her lower lip bled; she'd either cut it when she fell or had bitten it during the vision.

All her life she'd dreamed of disasters as they were

happening. Sometimes she'd go a few days without a nightmare, but she'd never gone more than a week, maybe eight days, without one. Now and then she might see a disaster before it took place, but not often. Not nearly often enough.

This was new. For the third time in a little over a month, a vision had come to her while she was awake. Each one had stopped her dead in her tracks, had thrown her to the ground—or the floor—and had twisted her body and mind as she suffered along with the victims. She'd always hated the nightmares; she'd dreaded them. But this…this was so much harder. This particular vision had been far more vivid than any of the others, much too real. What if they were getting worse?

If she had not been pulled out of the vision in time, would she have drowned with the others? Would she have died on the trail that had, until a short time ago, been such a place of peace?

As with the other instances she would go back to the house, sit at her computer and try to piece together when and where the disaster was happening. Or had already happened. In her heart she knew that once again she would be too late. Her true curse was that she was *always* too late.

Being keeper of the Raintree Sanctuary—this blessed land that was so special and necessary to her family, her clan—had not been her idea, but she'd done her best to embrace the assignment. She'd left the band she'd loved and quit her waitress job. She didn't miss the job, but she did miss the band and the girls she'd played with. Most of all she missed Sherry, her friend and roommate, a pretty good drummer who'd died in her place. Sherry had been murdered by a psycho Ansara soldier who'd thought she was killing Echo Raintree. A lot had happened six years ago, when the Ansara had attempted to take on the Raintree clan. Changes, upheaval, the beginning of a new era. The end of the evil leadership of the Ansara clan, the beginning of a new Rainsara clan with Mercy, Echo's cousin, the previous keeper of this Sanctuary, at the helm with her husband.

At the time, getting away from it all had seemed like a good enough idea. Some days she could almost forget that the idea hadn't been hers.

Even though she had initially argued a bit—she'd never been a fan of being told what to do—she'd thought being here, living in this safe place, would help her learn to control her ability. Being honest with herself, she admitted that her "control" wasn't just poor, it was nonexistent. Instead of learning, she was getting worse.

The Raintree clan was by far the most successful— and powerful—in the magical world most people had no idea existed. There were other clans, other groups held together by blood and by bond, but none were as old or as organized as the Raintree. Echo's cousin Dante was Dranir, leader of the Raintree clan. With her husband, Judah, cousin Mercy led the closely affiliated Rainsara clan. Gideon was always there to help his siblings, if help was needed. That branch of the family was all amazingly powerful. Why couldn't she control fire, or lightning, or heal the sick and wounded? Why was *this* her so-called gift?

Echo jogged back to the house, breathless and hurting, her knees knocking. It was always possible that this time was different. Maybe she wasn't too late.

By the time she pieced together the clues, the story was on the newsfeed. *Russian Ship Sinks, Search for Survivors Under Way.* Echo's heart dropped. Tears filled her eyes, blurring the words on the computer screen. "There are no survivors," she whispered to the screen, and then, without a second thought, she wiped away her tears, snagged her cell phone off the desk and thumbed her way to the contacts list.

Her cousin picked up on the second ring. "Hi, Echo. What's up?"

Gideon sounded cheerful. He was so happy with his life! Too bad she was about to ruin his day.

"Are you busy?" she asked, as if this were an ordinary call. Her heart pounded; her breath caught in her throat as she suffered second thoughts. This was her family, after all. She loved them; they loved her. She would do anything not to hurt them or cause them distress. *Almost* anything.

"I have a few minutes," Gideon said. "Everything okay there?"

She probably should have called Dante directly, since this was about to be his problem, but she was closer to Gideon. They lived in close proximity and had for years. He was the one she always turned to in times of trouble. Gideon was only a dozen years older than she was, but he was more of a father to her than her real father had ever been. Half the time she never knew where her parents were, and she had learned long ago not to bother them with her troubles. They didn't like it. Her troubles put a damper on their fun.

Besides, cousin or not, Dante scared her a little when he was mad. And this was definitely going to make him mad.

She started with a casual, "How are Hope and the kids?"

"Everybody's fine," Gideon said. "Emma is playing softball this year. Fall ball, they call it. Tournament this weekend. She'd love if it you came to a game." He laughed. "I promise you, softball at this age is absolutely hilarious. It'll be worth the trip."

Unfortunately, hilarity was not in her immediate future. Echo hesitated. She ran a lone, dirty fingernail across the top of her desk. She'd always been a little bit of a rebel, but this…this was going to take real courage. "Any chance Emma is ready to take on her role as caretaker of the Sanctuary?" she asked. After all, Emma was destined to one day take on this job. It was what she'd been born to do.

Gideon's tone changed; she could hear the seriousness over the phone lines, could *feel* it even before he spoke. "She's five years old, so no. Not yet." His voice lowered, making her wonder if there was anyone else around. "Dammit, Echo, she deserves as normal a childhood as we can give her."

Echo paused. She took a deep breath and let it out slowly. No one was going to be happy about this, but what choice did she have?

She'd never had control over her powers of prophesy, and she'd actively fought the empathic powers her cousins insisted she possessed. Powers they said would grow in time. She didn't want to be an empath, didn't want to suffer the feelings of others. She didn't want to be a prophet, either, suffering their disasters, as well, but there wasn't much to be done for that. Was it too much to want control over her *life*? No, it was not. For all she knew the same magic that made this land a safe haven for others in her clan was causing the distressing shift in her abilities.

She had to start somewhere and this was it.

"Call Dante and tell him there's a position to fill," she said, calling on every ounce of bravery she possessed. She took another deep breath. "I quit."

Chapter 1

One year later

Ireland. Echo had always wanted to visit, it was on her short bucket list, and now here she was. This trip was hardly a vacation, though. She was on a mission. She needed help, the kind of help her cousins had tried—and failed—to give her.

The village of Cloughban was well off the beaten path. She'd gotten turned around three times trying to find her way here. The GPS on her phone seemed to think the place didn't exist, but she had a map. An actual paper map that was so old she handled it carefully so as not to tear it along the folds. Still, she'd taken more wrong turns than she cared to admit to. She'd almost given up once, but at this point she couldn't afford surrender.

Echo parked her rental car in a small space beside

the village pub—the Drunken Stone, a name which made no sense at all—exited the vehicle with purpose and walked toward the center of town. It felt good to stretch her legs, as she tried to decide how to proceed from here.

In spite of her troubles, she was instantly charmed. She'd left behind the stifling humidity of a North Carolina autumn heat wave for a cool breeze and...this.

The village might've come right off a postcard. The road was narrow, barely wide enough for two small cars. There wasn't a single building in town taller than two stories high. They were all very old, that was evident in the weathered stone-and-brick walls. The buildings were dull grays and browns, but the doors had been painted bright colors—red, purple, blue and green—and there were flowers everywhere. In window boxes and large tubs along the sidewalk. Hanging near shop entrances, stems loaded with blooms flowing from earthenware pots to the ground. She slowed her step, momentarily caught up in the simple beauty of the place.

The windows of the shops along the main road were all enticing, their offerings tempting. Candy, colorful scarves, hats and jackets, cheeses and wines. Ice cream and coffee. If she stayed here for a while, if she found what she was looking for, that might become her favorite establishment.

The sun was shining, but thanks to an increasingly stiff breeze it was cooler than Echo had expected. She hugged her arms to herself, wishing she'd grabbed her lightweight jacket out of her duffel bag. She didn't want to go back to the car to get it. The walk back would hardly be a long one, but if all went well she might be here for a while, and she needed to be properly equipped for the weather. This trip was not much more than a whim, and in a fit of frustration she'd just thrown a few clothes into her red duffel without giving much thought to the weather. She stopped in front of a boutique with her eye on a dark blue sweater in the window.

How did a store like this survive in a town so small? She supposed the locals had to have a place to shop other than the next town over, but still, through the window the boutique looked to be stuffed to the gills with really nice, upscale merchandise.

Echo stepped into the shop, which was smaller than she'd thought it would be as she'd peeked through the window. Small, but crammed with shelves and racks of colorful clothing. And hats! There was a very interesting collection of hats on a rack at the back of the store. The clerk behind the counter, a middle-aged woman with reddish-blond hair and an easy, wide smile, said, "Hello. Can I help you?" Her accent was lovely, lilting and almost musical. Echo realized *she* was the one with the accent here.

"I saw a beautiful blue sweater in the window."

The woman waved her hand dismissively as she stepped around the counter. "Ah, you don't want that sweater. It's far too expensive and the color is all wrong for you. It's too dark. You'll look best in pastels or jewel tones. Definitely jewel tones." She crossed the small space between the counter and the rack near where Echo stood and grabbed a green sweater. "This one will suit you much better." She lifted the price tag. "And it's on sale. What luck."

The green was a better color for her, she supposed, and who could pass up a sale? Half price. It was meant to be. Echo bought the sweater, which was folded neatly and with great care before being placed in a brown paper bag. Already she was eyeing a raincoat and a matching hat, but she supposed she should wait and see how long she'd be here before she made any more investment.

The cashier cleared her throat and asked, her tone a bit too carefree, "I don't believe we've met. Are you new to Cloughban? Are you visiting a relative or a friend?"

"Just visiting," Echo said simply as she counted out the euros.

"My name is Brigid," the saleslady said. "I hope you'll come back while you're here and look around some more. Do you expect to be here for a while or will yours be a short visit?"

"I don't know yet," Echo said honestly.

"Well, do come again."

"Thank you, Brigid. I'm Echo Raintree, by the way. It's very nice to meet you." She didn't have any idea how long she'd be here, or if she'd need more clothes, but it was a good sign that she'd made a friend right off the bat. She offered her hand for a handshake. Was that the protocol here? It seemed like the right thing to do, and since Brigid took the offered hand for a shake, she figured she wasn't too out of line.

The handshake didn't last long. It was, in fact, oddly brief. Brigid's smile faded.

Echo left the pleasantries behind and got down to business. "Maybe you can help me. I'm looking for a man named Ryder Duncan. Do you by any chance know where I might find him?" Cloughban was a small enough town. Maybe it was one of those places where everyone knew everyone else.

The once-friendly woman's smile faded; the change in her mood was instantaneous and complete. "No, sorry. I can't help you." Brigid's speech was clipped, the crisp words passing through pursed lips. Gone was the wide smile. Her eyes narrowed. "You'd best be on your way. I'm about to close for lunch."

Echo was ushered from the store, all but thrown out as if she were a bum and Brigid a brawny bouncer. In seconds she found herself on the sidewalk, shopping bag in hand and her head spinning from the rejection. All she'd done was mention Ryder Duncan's name!

Duncan was, if her research was correct, a powerful and rare teacher. A professor of magic. A wizard, a sorcerer, a shaman. He was a stray, unaffiliated with the Raintree or the Rainsara or the now-defunct Ansara clan. It wasn't as if you could use Google to search his name and come up with "wizard" but if you knew where to look, and she did, a small amount of information did exist. Not enough to paint an accurate picture, but enough for her to know that she had to at least try to find him. His last known place of residence was here in Cloughban. *White Stone.*

Being keeper of the Sanctuary had put her in control of a vast number of proprietary computer records. After she'd announced her resignation, she'd started her research.

In the past year, her cousins had tried to help her control her abilities so she could live a somewhat normal life. With books, charmed amulets and a number of meditation techniques, they *had* tried. A couple of times she'd actually thought it was working, but the results eventually faded away. Maybe they were too close to her. Maybe she needed to work with someone who was not family.

She hoped.

Echo stopped on the sidewalk and pulled her new sweater from the brown bag. Brigid had been nice enough to cut off all the tags, so all she had to do was pull it on and toss the bag in a nearby trash bin. That done, she glanced around again. Either everyone in this village took lunch at the same time, or there was an impressively fast phone tree and she was being shunned. Closed for Lunch signs were posted on doors and windows. As she walked around the small town square she heard locks being thrown, one after another. Why would an ice cream shop close for lunch? She couldn't be the only person who occasionally opted for an ice cream sundae.

Just as alarming, where were the pedestrians who'd been on the square when she'd walked into the clothing shop? They were all gone. *All.*

Frustrated, she turned about, around and around, looking for a sign of life. Any sign. She saw no one. She could almost swear a gray pall had fallen over the entire town in a matter of seconds. Even the once-bright colors seemed dimmer, though she knew that was impossible. The square no longer resembled the picture on an inviting postcard. Instead, it looked like a place wide-eyed pale children with axes and an appetite for brains might live. Great, just what she needed. She turned toward the rental car, trying to decide what to do. If the very mention of Duncan's name caused this kind of reaction...

No. It was coincidence. Nothing more. With the sale done there was no more reason for the clerk to be friendly. It was lunchtime. Maybe Brigid was hungry. Maybe everyone was hungry! The weather had simply taken a turn. Everything that had happened in the past few minutes was explainable. She'd just have to wait out lunchtime and ask again. Someone else, this time. Someone not so sharp.

She'd almost reached the car when the first drop fell.

If you could call it a drop. Soft Irish rain, more mist than true rain, was cool on her face. It felt good, she had to admit, though she had no desire to be soaked to the skin. Not in this cool weather. She should've bought the raincoat instead of the sweater.

Echo's stomach growled. With the time difference she didn't know what meal her body was asking for, but it was definitely time to eat. Given the way the town square had suddenly become deserted, it would be a waste of time to head back that way. Instead of getting behind the wheel of the rental car she turned left and ducked into the pub with the weird name. The stone building, which didn't have a single first-story window, wasn't exactly what she'd call inviting, but surely the pub served food of some kind. At this point anything would do. Maybe her head would clear once she'd had something to eat.

The Drunken Stone was dimly lit, all dark wood and dark leather and beer advertisements. One table in the far corner was occupied by three older, gray-haired men. Was Ryder Duncan sitting there? Not that any one of them looked like a powerful wizard. She didn't look much like a prophet, so what did appearances mean? Nothing, really.

While she had found mention of Duncan in the Raintree records, there weren't many details. There definitely hadn't been a photo. All she really knew was that he was a teacher, and he lived in—or at least had once lived in—Cloughban.

One of the men actually looked like a garden gnome come to life, with a squished face and a tremendous nose, but he was a bit taller than any gnome she'd ever seen—just a bit—and he didn't wear a pointed hat. The other two were thinnish and looked enough alike to be brothers, or maybe cousins. The similarity was in the nose and the slant of the eyes.

The man behind the bar was not older, gray-haired or gnomelike. He was good-looking, tall and lean with wide shoulders in a snug gray Henley. She'd guess he was in his mid-thirties, just a few years older than she. He had a nice head of thick, dark hair that hung just a little too long. There was a bit of wave in that hair that looked as if it was begging for a woman's fingers to straighten a few misbehaving strands. Adding to the mystery was a leather cord just barely peeking out from the collar of his shirt, and a leather cuff on his right wrist.

He was, in fact, quite nice to look at. Just what she needed.

No, just what she *didn't* need! She had the worst tastes in men. Her romantic history was more tragedy than comedy, and in the past year she had not even dared to get involved with a man. After a lifetime of dealing with her own so-called gift, when it came to men she much preferred those who were unencumbered by magic. She didn't even want them to believe that true magic existed. It would be easier that way. But what if she allowed herself to hook up with a serious boyfriend and had an episode in front of him? How would she explain it away?

"Can I help you?" the too-good-looking barkeep asked.

Considering the reception she'd gotten when she'd initially asked about Duncan, she decided not to go there just yet. She'd passed a lot of nothing on her way to Cloughban. If the bartender was no friendlier than Brigid, it would take her at least an hour to find her way to the next small town. And that was if she didn't get turned around again.

"I'm starving. What do you recommend?"

"I recommend a very nice café in Killarney," he said, his Irish accent not as pronounced as Brigid's had been. And then he continued. "Are you lost, then?"

"No, why do you ask?"

"You're American, and we are far off the beaten path. You won't see a tour bus on the streets of Cloughban."

No tour bus would be able to make it down the narrow, winding road she'd taken to get here, but that was beside the point.

She stepped to the bar and took a stool. No matter what, she was not going all the way to Killarney for lunch! This was a public place—a *pub*—and she was hungry. If the bartender tried to send her away, she'd plant her feet and insist on being served.

Well, it was never a good idea to piss off the people who were going to handle your food, but still…

"I'm looking for someone, but first I really want something to eat. A sandwich should be safe enough. Please," she added as sweetly as she could manage.

He smiled at her, but the smile did not touch his dark eyes. Not Irish eyes, she knew in an instant. Not entirely. There was a bit of Romany in those eyes. Tinker, to those less kind. She shook off the empathic abilities that had been trying to come to the surface in the past several years. Dammit, she didn't want them.

"Safe enough, I suppose," the hunk and a half said in a voice of surrender. He didn't try again to send her to Killarney. "Beer?"

"Tea," she said. "Sugar, no milk." She needed to be completely clearheaded for what was coming, judging by what she'd encountered so far.

* * *

Rye hadn't known who the woman was, not when she'd first walked through the door, but it hadn't taken long for his instincts to kick in and alert him to the trouble she was bringing his way. His instinctive reaction had been to suggest that she lunch far from his humble establishment. For all the good that was going to do. She was a stubborn one; he saw that right off.

She'd been well into the room before he'd realized more precisely who she was. *What* she was. Up close the eyes gave her away. Her brilliant green eyes and the voice that whispered in his head. *Raintree princess.*

Too bad. She was a pretty girl, petite and fair, with soft, pale blond hair cut to hang to her jawline. He didn't normally care for short hair on a woman, but he had to admit, the neck revealed was nicely tempting. Long and pale and flawless. She had amazing eyes, a very nice ass and breasts high and firm and just the right size for his hand.

He'd feed her, but then she had to go. Killarney was likely not far enough away.

Doyle Mullen was working in the kitchen today, as he did six days a week. He cooked, swept and manned the bar when Rye had to step away for a few minutes. His was not a particularly demanding job, but it was one that had to be done. The pub menu was limited. The single laminated page offered ham and cheese sandwiches, chips, vegetable soup and brown bread. There was also fish and chips, but he could not in good conscience recommend them to anyone. Not even her.

After delivering the order to Doyle, Rye returned to the bar and made the tea himself. It gave him the opportunity to turn his back on the Raintree woman for a few minutes. Dammit, he could still feel her eyes on him.

She hadn't said so, not yet, but she was here for him. He felt it as surely as he would feel rain on his face if he were to step outside. The question was, why? What did she want?

Even without the talismans he wore, Rye was not the most powerful psychic in the world, not by a long shot. He had learned as much or more as he'd been born with, learned at the knee of his Romany mother. Sometimes knowledge slammed into him and he knew it was truth. Other truths were muddy, or hidden from him entirely. He'd often thought it would be better to see nothing at all than to be given only the occasional glimpse. It would ease his frustration considerably.

He had other gifts, gifts he kept dampened, but his psychic ability had never been his strength. If he were honest, he'd admit it was often more annoying than helpful.

He delivered the Raintree woman's tea, then went into the kitchen to check on her meal. It was not quite ready, so he waited there until it was. Doyle tried to make conversation but Rye was in no mood to participate. Eventually the cook went silent. No one else came into the pub; he knew without watching the door. No magic was involved in that knowledge. A bell sounded when the front door opened. Usually a shopkeeper or two stopped in for a bowl of stew or a sandwich about this time of day, but so far all was quiet. Because *she* was here.

They knew. Someone among them had realized who she was and the word had spread like wildfire. He wondered if the pretty girl realized that her family name had the power to strike fear into the hearts of others. They would hide from her if they could. If she wasn't careful, someone might do more than hide.

His life here in Cloughban was orderly. Predictable. He liked it that way. More than that, it was necessary. Thanks to an ancient protection spell, stray tourists didn't find their way here. Only those who possessed magic could make their way to this special village. If anyone—tourist or wandering Irishman—was going to get lost, they got lost on another road in another county. But then, the Raintree woman wasn't exactly lost, was she?

When the sandwich was done Rye delivered it as he had the tea, but again, he did not linger. While the Raintree woman ate he left his station at the bar to check on the regulars in the corner. Three grumpy old men who had been a part of this community for as long as anyone could remember. In a town population that was ever changing, these three were constant.

He stood close to the table and crossed his arms across his chest. "Are you fellas ever going to buy anything? Do I have to depend on strangers to wander into the place in order to make a living?" Tully, Nevan and McManus had been fixtures in this pub since long before Rye had taken it over. They'd probably be here long after he was gone.

Nevan, who was short and squat and looked as if his face had been scrunched together by two overly large hands, grinned. Not a pretty sight, considering that the old man was ugly as sin. "There'll be a good enough crowd here tonight, and you know it. You don't need our business in the middle of the day."

His friends agreed with him.

"Maybe I shouldn't open until four, then. I could sleep late if it suited me."

Tully nodded. "That would be fine. I still have a key

to the back door. You haven't changed the locks, have you, son?"

Rye scowled and took a bar towel to empty tables, just so he wouldn't have to face the Raintree woman. If he were lucky, she would eat, pay and leave.

He didn't feel at all lucky today. She was trouble, and in his experience when trouble came for him it never walked away. It usually planted its feet and stayed awhile. He hadn't experienced trouble of her sort for a long time. A very long time.

Her stool scraped across the floor as she pushed it back so she could stand. Coins were carefully counted out and placed on the counter.

And then she walked to the corner. All three old goats smiled at her; he saw that out of the corner of his eye.

"Perhaps you gentlemen can help me," she said.

Rye stifled a snort. They would be instantly charmed. They would tell her whatever she wanted to know. To a point.

"I'm looking for a man," she said.

McManus cackled. "Lucky lass, you've found three."

She smiled. Good Lord. Dimples. "I'm actually looking for a particular man. Ryder Duncan. Do you know him?"

"I do," Tully said in a booming voice. "And so do you, pet."

Rye turned, ready to face the inevitable. Nevan pointed a crooked finger in his direction. The Raintree woman turned around slowly. Maybe she paled a little.

There was no running from it, he supposed.

"I'm Duncan. What the hell do you want?" he asked sharply.

Yes, she definitely paled. She took a deep breath and closed her eyes.

If someone was going to come for him—for the child more likely—why her? She was alone, she was not particularly powerful in that special Raintree way, nor was she physically strong. But she was a woman, and a pretty one at that. Did the Raintree think he was that weak?

More importantly, *did they know*?

Chapter 2

Oh, no. Not him! Echo was no fool. Well, she was occasionally a fool, especially where men were concerned. She already knew it would not be a good idea for her to spend too much time with this one. There had been an instant attraction. Nothing she couldn't handle, of course. He was kind of a jerk but he was a pretty, sexy jerk.

He was also her last chance. She hadn't come all this way to flake out because Ryder Duncan was not at all what she'd expected him to be.

"Maybe we can have a word in private?"

"No need," he said sharply. "You can say whatever you need to say here and now, before you're on your way."

Yes, definitely a jerk. "I'm looking for a…a…" How much could she say in front of the three older men? Duncan wouldn't expect her to know who and what he was, so he wouldn't be worried about what she might say. "A teacher," she finally said. "A trainer."

"For you?" He all but scoffed. His lip curled a little.

She wanted to call him a very bad name and walk out with her head held high. But then what? Where would she go from here? Maybe he wasn't her absolute last chance, but she didn't have a plan B at this moment. She took a deep breath, swallowed her pride and said, "Yes, for me." More swallowing. "I need your help."

He turned and walked toward the bar, calling out as he went, "I don't do that anymore."

The three old men listened closely. They no longer bothered to even pretend to engage in their own conversation. The one on the far end must be hard of hearing, because he leaned over as far as he could, tipping in her direction.

Echo didn't want to say anything that might give her true intent away. It was best to keep magical abilities hidden from those who did not have them. That was a bridge difficult to cross, and anyone who found themselves human in a supernatural world almost always became resentful, in time. In the end, they wanted what they could not have. No ordinary human could ever understand her desire, her *need*, to be rid of all magic.

Gideon's wife, Hope, was the exception to that rule. Ungifted to the bone, with a husband and two little girls who were anything but, she was fine with who she was. More than that, she didn't want magical abilities. She said she had her hands full enough as it was. And she wasn't wrong.

Echo followed Duncan to the bar. Slinking away after one or two rebukes was not her style. "You're too young to be retired. I'll pay you." This was one purchase she would gladly dip into Raintree family money for. "I'll pay you well."

He didn't even bother to turn to look at her, which offered an interesting view. Echo tried not to notice the nicely shaped butt, the way his gray shirt stretched across broad shoulders, the thick, wavy hair.

"I don't need your money, and I certainly don't need the hassle," he said as he rounded the bar.

"But I need…"

From behind long expanse of scarred wood that stretched between them, he turned to look her in the eye. Big hands on the bar, he leaned forward in a way that was unmistakably threatening. His expression alone stopped her words, made them freeze in her throat. "You *need*. You *want*. You have my answer, love, now be on your way."

She lowered her voice, edging toward desperation. She had no idea what might come next if he continued to refuse her. "You don't even know why I'm here, what I need."

He was unmoved. "I don't care."

Echo turned, mustering what little pride she had left to walk out the door before the tears came. She could not speak another word without losing what little control she had left. Dammit, she would not cry in front of that jerk! He wasn't her last chance, couldn't be. There had to be another way.

She just didn't have any idea where to look for it.

Once she was outside, the heavy wooden door closed solidly behind her, the rain began to fall harder. It was still what they'd call a soft rain, but she'd get soaked in the short walk to her car. Just as well that she wait a few minutes. She needed to calm down before she got behind the wheel. And went…and went *where*?

Echo backed against the rock wall of the pub, protected by a small but sufficient overhang above. She leaned there, boneless and shaking with a mixture of anger and frustration. She looked to the right. The square was still deserted, but given the rain that was not unusual. In her mind she continued to ask, *Now what?* No answer came to her. None.

She was lost. Far from home, alone, desperate for help—and lost. Worse than simply turned around, she didn't know where to turn next, didn't know which direction to take. She'd come to Cloughban so sure Ryder Duncan would help her. She hadn't realized how deeply she'd believed him to be her last and only hope. Now what?

"Hello." The small voice from Echo's left-hand side startled her so much she twitched as she turned to glance down. The voice belonged to a child, maybe ten years old, with an impressive head of curly red hair, a smile that would surely light up any room and deep chocolate-brown eyes. As ordinary as she appeared to be, it was definitely odd that in spite of the steady rain, the little girl was not wet.

"Hello," Echo responded. "Who are you?"

The question went unanswered. "You're American," the girl responded. "I can tell by your accent. Sometimes I watch American television."

Yes, she was the one with the accent here. "You're right, I am American." The fact that the girl had come out of nowhere and was oddly dry was the least of her worries. The kid was, at the moment, a welcome distraction. "My name is Echo."

"I *love* that name," the child said with enthusiasm. "My name is Cassidy, but most of my friends at school just call me Cass. I like Cassidy better, but I don't want to tell them. It might hurt their feelings. There's no way to shorten Echo! You're so lucky. No one will ever call you Ech."

In spite of herself, Echo found herself smiling. "While I'm here I'll call you Cassidy, since that's the name you prefer." Again, there was that uncomfortable sensation of being lost and not knowing what came next. Her voice was lower, less steady, as she said, "Though I'm afraid I won't be here much longer." The rain was letting up a bit. It would end soon, and she'd have no reason to stand here and wait. No, not wait, *procrastinate.*

"Yes, you will," Cassidy said. "You're going to be here for a very long time." She seemed sure of herself, but then she was a child, a child who knew nothing about what had brought Echo to this place. Or what—who—was sending her away.

Cassidy leaned toward Echo a little and lowered her voice. "You need to go back inside. He will help you, he's just scared. Only a little scared, but still scared."

For a long moment Echo couldn't speak. How did the kid know about Duncan and his refusal to help? Duh, the child had been listening in somehow. That's why she wasn't wet. Cassidy hadn't appeared out of nowhere; she'd been inside, hiding in a dark corner or behind a booth, and had slipped out of the pub quietly either right before or right after Echo.

"No, I can't stay here."

Cassidy was not at all put off by that statement. "Yes, you can. You will! Besides, you really shouldn't drive in your condition."

"My…"

Echo stopped speaking because Cassidy disap-

peared. The kid didn't run away; she literally vanished
into thin air. Here one second, then poof, gone the next.

Was Cassidy a vision of what would be, like those
Gideon had once had of his eldest daughter? A delusion, brought on by her own frustration? An incredibly
gifted child? She'd never known anyone to be able to
disappear that way.

It was possible the child had not been there in body
at all, but had somehow manifested from a distance.
Or didn't exist at all. Yes, she was right back to delu-
sions. Great.

You shouldn't drive in your condition.

If she had an episode while she was on the road...

It began with a sensation of intense heat. She felt
that heat on her face and in her blood. Instinctively
she raised her hands up to protect her face. Her vision
dimmed, her knees went weak. Echo turned clumsily.
It took all her strength to throw open the pub door. It
didn't matter that Ryder Duncan had sent her away; she
would *not* fall to the wet sidewalk. She would not ex-
pose herself that way.

She lurched into the pub and took four steps before
she fell to her knees. Her last clear look at the here and
now was of Duncan's unhappy face.

Rye was about to ask the Raintree woman what the
hell she was doing back in his pub when she dropped
to her knees. Hard.

"Not now," she whispered.

"Not now what?" he snapped. "If this is some kind
of a trick to get me to change my mind, forget it."

She fell forward, drew in her knees and covered her
head with her hands, drawing herself into a ball. She
shook violently. What the hell?

McManus lifted up slightly and peered over the top of the table to get a better view. "I think she's having a fit."

"Sure looks it," Nevan said.

"Looks like a seizure to me," Tully said.

Nevan chimed in again. "What's the difference between a seizure and a fit?"

"What difference does it make?" Rye dropped beside the Raintree woman, placing a hand on her shoulder. She felt hot, as if she had a fever, and she continued to shake. Hard. Dammit, she'd been fine when she'd left a few minutes ago.

Whatever was going on, she was not faking.

He let loose a stream of foul language that had Tully laughing and Nevan crossing himself. She was light enough, easy to pick off the floor and carry to the back of the public room.

"One of you fetch Doyle from the kitchen and tell him to watch the place for a bit," he said. All three men agreed, without question. Not that he expected any actual customers this afternoon. They knew to steer clear; they would know Raintree was here.

That was why no one but her had come in for lunch. Did Echo know her family name sometimes elicited fear in others of their kind? In the past, Raintree royalty had sometimes been imperious and even dangerous. Not in the past couple hundred years, maybe, but independents remembered their history, they had heard the stories. They came here, more often than not, to be left alone.

Rye dipped down just enough to open the unmarked door at the back of the room. Steep, narrow stairs loomed ahead. He carried the Raintree woman up, into the room where he slept some nights, and lowered her to the unmade bed. Dull afternoon light streamed through the windows.

Already she was cooler, and the trembling was lessening. He backed away from the bed to stand by the door, arms crossed and scowl in place. It had been a long time since he'd had a woman in this bed. Just his luck, she was not there for a pleasant reason.

What the hell did she really want with him? Why was she here? No Raintree, especially not one of the royals, would need his help. None of them would leave the clan looking for a teacher when they were surrounded by some of the most gifted individuals in the world. No, she wanted something else.

Rye hadn't been lying when he'd told her he didn't teach anymore. He no longer had the patience for it, and besides, his attention had to be focused elsewhere. He was also no longer wild about bringing strangers into his circle, even for a few days. The last time, a good four years earlier, things had not ended well. He had to be so careful.

It wasn't long at all before the woman on his bed opened her eyes and looked at him with tear-filled, hope-filled, impossible eyes. Those eyes had a way of cutting through him, of touching him deep down in a way he did not wish to be touched. He knew he was screwed even before she whispered, "Please, make it stop."

Chapter 3

Fire. She hated the visions of fire more than anything else. This one—a true inferno—had taken place in a warehouse of some kind. China, Echo thought. Not that it mattered. The disaster was over. The fire had been waning as she'd fallen to the floor.

She looked at Ryder Duncan as she pulled herself back to the present. Straightening her sweater was as much a nervous gesture as anything else. It was a way to remind herself that this place and time were real. *She* was real, and safe. Unburned, no smoke in her lungs…

As was usual, she felt as if she were caught between a dream and reality, as if she were dreaming that she was awake but wasn't quite there yet. The feeling would pass, she knew, but it usually took several minutes. She clutched the sheet beneath her hands, holding on to this world for dear life.

Her greatest fear was that one day she'd leave this

world behind for much more than a few minutes. What if she stayed within a vision of disaster? Drowning or on fire, caught up in a violent earthquake or a trapped in a war zone. Would she die with those around her? It was that fear that had driven her here, away from her family, away from home and her responsibilities. The only way to handle that fear was to gain enough control so that she knew she'd always come back to herself.

Duncan had been her last sight before the vision, and now he was her first sight after. Even in her distressed state, she could appreciate that annoying as he was, he was a fine sight. Focusing on him allowed her to leave her fears behind. For now.

Normally she was alone when she came out of a vision. She'd always thought that was best. Her dreams of disasters, her visions of pain and suffering, they weren't meant to be shared. Who would want to share them? Still, she had to admit, it was nice to see Duncan's face waiting. Even if he did look pissed.

He was not at all what she'd expected when she'd flown to Ireland. It had been silly of her to expect anything at all! She hadn't been able to find much in the way of detail about him. A mention in a story from ten years before, a second- or thirdhand account. In the real world, the world she lived in, "wizard" didn't necessarily mean an old man with a long gray robe and long white hair and a magical staff. Though that was not impossible…

She sat up, uncomfortable to be on what was obviously his bed but too weak to stand just yet.

He continued their conversation as if there had been no break, no pause for her vision.

"Make what stop?" he asked, his voice cold.

She was probably wasting her time, explaining why

she'd come to him for help. He'd already turned her down flat! But he had asked the question—*make what stop?*—and she knew better than to lie to him. She didn't know exactly what powers he had, what gifts he possessed. He might realize she was lying; he might already know why she had come.

The truth. What else did she have to offer?

"My name is Echo Raintree. I'm called the Raintree prophet, but everyone knows I'm a poor excuse for a prophet." That was her curse, as much as the visions. Always a disappointment, always less than she should be. "My visions come too late. There's never anything I can do to help the people I see and hear…and feel. There was a time when I only saw these horrible things in my dreams, but as you just witnessed that is no longer true." She shivered, then pulled the front of her sweater closed as if that might warm her. "They come all the time now, day and night, without warning, just…" She shuddered. "I don't know what to do."

He did not move closer or drop his arms. Jaw tight, dark eyes cold, he responded. Somehow, his Irish accent was more pronounced than it had been before as he asked, "You want me to train you to be a better prophet?"

Her heart leaped. In the beginning, even just a few moments ago, that had been her plan. But as she lay on his bed, shaking, feeling as if she'd blink and be back in the burning building, she realized she wanted more than control. Much more.

"No. I want the visions gone. I want them wiped away, erased. I want…help. The kind of help only you can offer."

There was an uncomfortably long pause before he responded. "You want a lot," he said without emotion.

"Yes, I do."

Anger flashed in his dark eyes. "Are you telling me there are no Raintrees who can help you?"

Again, she had to stick with the truth. If she lied to him and he found out, there would be hell to pay. One did not try to pull the wool over the eyes of a wizard. "They've tried, but…no luck." Not knowing how much he knew, how much he saw, she had to tell all. "My cousins have attempted to teach me to control the visions. When I asked they said it was impossible to get rid of them entirely." Gideon had refused to even discuss that possibility. "Maybe I'm too close to them, too connected. A st—" She caught herself. "Someone outside the clans seems like a better option, at this point."

He didn't respond for a few drawn-out seconds, and then he said in a lowered voice, "Poor Raintree princess can't get her way at home so she flies across the pond to ask a *stray* for help."

Her chin came up a bit. "I didn't call you a stray." Though she almost had. *Caught.* Echo swung her legs over the edge of the mattress, taking a deep breath in an attempt to regain her strength. If only her knees would stop knocking. It was impossible to be strong when her entire body was weak, shaking, drained. She didn't want Duncan to see her as weak. Not that she should care what he thought of her. She'd never see him again, once she drove away from Cloughban.

Which would probably be very soon. It was looking as if her trip had been a complete waste of time, as if Ryder Duncan was not all he'd been rumored to be. Any decent teacher would see that she needed help and offer it!

"No, not out loud," he said. "But isn't that what you

call those with magic who are unaffiliated with your clans?"

She stood. Anger helped her find her legs. "Okay, fine. I almost called you a stray. Sorry if that offends you. What would you prefer?"

"Independent."

He remained angry; he'd called her a princess with disdain...yes, this trip had been a waste of time. She wanted to run, she wanted to hide from those dark, condemning eyes. "Stray seems more appropriate to me." She walked toward the door he blocked, trying not to let him see how devastating his refusal was. She would not beg!

"Sorry to have bothered you." She thought about the little girl—real or imagined—she'd been talking to before the vision began. Beneath her breath she mumbled, "I guess Cassidy was wrong."

Duncan didn't move away from the door. Echo had to stop a couple of feet short. It was that or physically move him, and given his size and very nice solidness, *that* wasn't going to happen. After a few seconds, she waved her hand in a dismissive gesture. He still did not move. Dammit, did he want her to go or not?

"Cassidy?" he said in a lowered voice.

Echo sighed. "A little girl that was probably all in my head. I saw her, or imagined her, outside the pub right before this latest vision. She said I'd be here for a long time." Wishful thinking, a real child with magic, a new precursor to the visions? She didn't know. Cassidy had obviously been wrong when she'd said that Duncan would help her.

"What did she look like?" he asked.

She wanted out of here before she started to cry. She wanted to walk out with her head high and a smidgen of her dignity intact. A smidgen was all she could hope for at this point. If she stood here too long, neither would happen. "What difference does it make?"

"Indulge me."

Echo backed away a little. Duncan could get under her skin much too easily. Just standing close to him made her shiver. Then again, maybe that was no more than lingering physical weakness thanks to her latest episode. Might as well give him what he wanted so she could boogie on out of here and have her nervous breakdown in private.

"Curly red hair, dark eyes, a few freckles. Maybe ten years old. She was on the sidewalk and then...she wasn't." She didn't feel the need to explain anything more to him.

Instead of ushering her out of the room and down the stairs, Duncan stayed in place. He seemed to be contemplating her. Why? He'd already turned her down. Not once but two or three or four times.

"You give up far too easily, princess. Don't you want to hear my answer?" he asked, and for the first time there was some humor in his voice. Dark humor, but at least a bit of his anger was gone.

"Fine." She crossed her arms, much as he had. "Give me your answer." Maybe it would make him feel better to tell her off before he let her go. Jerk.

"I will not strip away your gifts."

"You wouldn't call this a gift if you had it," she snapped.

He held up a stilling hand. "It's possible—I won't tell you it's not—but it isn't an easy process. There would be a high price to pay. Your cousins were right to dismiss that option if they care for you at all."

Well, *that* was interesting. Apparently what she

wanted most of all was possible. She hadn't been entirely sure. "What kind of price?" No price was too high; she'd do *anything*.

He ignored her. "I can teach you to control your abilities."

Echo sighed. "I've tried, I really have. That's not…"

"Of course it's not what you want," he interrupted. "You're spoiled and undisciplined, and I suspect you have been all your life, *princess*. The gift of prophesy is rare and difficult and precious, and you have squandered it. I will not strip your abilities away, but if you do precisely as I say I will help you learn to master them."

That was what she'd planned to ask for when she'd walked into the pub, but now she realized it was not enough. Duncan would do no more than her cousins had done for her, and that wouldn't do. She'd tried talismans, meditations, exercises. In this case she'd have to face *him* each and every day, and she didn't think she could take it. Besides, she did take a perverse pleasure in being the one to walk away. She'd bet no woman had ever told Duncan no.

"Thanks, but no thanks." This time when she shooed him aside, he moved. She opened the door, started down the long, narrow stairway. Her knees were still shaky, and she had no idea where she'd go from here. Ryder Duncan was not who she'd thought him to be, and she could not, would not, put herself in his hands. One good thing had come out of the encounter. He wouldn't do it, her cousins wouldn't do it, but someone could remove her abilities entirely.

She had almost reached the bottom of the stairs when his soft voice stopped her. "It will only get worse."

She didn't turn to face him, but she listened.

"The pain, the frequency and intensity of the events.

Because you fight it, because you are spoiled and untrained, because you fear your gift rather than embracing it, what's happening will eventually kill you."

After a moment of complete silence, Echo turned and looked up. She didn't know Duncan at all, she didn't even like him much, but she didn't doubt the truth of his words. "You can take it away. You said…"

"I said there was a price you and those who care for you would not wish to pay for such a miracle."

It wasn't what she wanted, but what choice did she have? She had nowhere else to turn. Besides, when he discovered that she could not master this curse no matter how hard she tried, maybe he'd agree to strip it away. No price would be too high.

"When do we start?"

Rye sat at a table with the woman on the other side. The old men had left, and so had Doyle. They were alone, though that would not last. In an hour or so the late-afternoon crowd would start to arrive.

He should've sent Echo Raintree on her way, should've let her go to another part of the world searching for another stray who might be willing to do as she asked. He could've and should've sat back and allowed her to implode. It wasn't as if he had any love for the Raintree clan.

But apparently Cassidy had said Echo would be here for a while. Cassidy was never wrong.

Echo rambled. About her problems, about her struggles with her abilities. There was something about a band, and parents who liked to gad about more than care for their only child. She was tired of seeing horrible things and never being able to do anything to stop them or influence them. He listened, but he was also distracted. Beautiful face, feminine figure, bright eyes. Any man might be understandably distracted.

He knew a bit about control, more than he was willing to share with her or anyone else. It was the reason he clung to routine, one of the reasons he remained in this quiet, enchanted village. The question was, could he *teach* control again? It had been more than four years since he'd taken on a student, and the last time hadn't ended so well. There had been successes in the past, but were even a hundred successes worth the risk of a catastrophic failure?

Finally he interrupted her. "You're stalling."

She looked guilty. Rye had spent so much of his life hiding who and what he was, her easy-to-read expressions were a puzzle to him. The Raintree woman was an open book. How had she survived to this point? He knew she was twenty-nine years old. At one point in her rambling she'd said something about starting a new life at the age of thirty. A life without visions, a life without nightmares.

She was a mere six years younger than he was, but listening to her...it was as if they were not even of the same generation. Their lives to this point had been so very different.

He would help her if he could, but he couldn't promise her a life without nightmares.

"Sorry," she said in a lowered voice. "I didn't mean to go on and on. We need to focus on the future, not the past. How do we begin?" She looked more than a little apprehensive.

"We don't, not yet."

"But you said..."

"I don't know you and you don't know me. Our first step is to get acquainted."

Now the open book was suspicious.

"That doesn't mean I want to get you into bed," he clarified. "Though I imagine nearly every man you've ever met has tried."

"I didn't say I thought..."

"You didn't have to."

She pursed her lips. "I didn't know mind reading was one of your abilities."

He started to say, *It's not*, but kept that piece of knowledge to himself. True, some thoughts jumped out at him on occasion, but it was damned hard work to go around reading the minds of others. It was also potentially dangerous.

But perhaps it would be a good idea to let her believe he could peek into her head at will. Did she not know she was an open book? Did she not realize that everything she thought was written on her pretty face for the world to see?

"So, there's not a file on me back at Raintree headquarters?"

He expected her to laugh at the idea of Raintree headquarters and files on independents, but she didn't. "Not much of one," she admitted. "I didn't have an easy time finding any detailed information on you."

"Good." Before she left he'd find out what—where and how—she had discovered about him, and make sure no one else could follow in her footsteps. He couldn't make it impossible for someone gifted to find him— those with special abilities found their way to Clough-ban all the time—but if there was any kind of a paper or electronic trail it would have to be eliminated.

She straightened her spine. "So, how do we get to know each other?"

"Among the many jobs you've had, have you ever waited tables?"

"Many times. When my band was playing in Wilmington…"

Not that again. "I don't need to know the details," he snapped. "You start tonight, princess." With that, he slid from his seat and stood. He'd spent too much time looking at her. She was starting to get under his skin, and that was the last thing he needed.

She stood, too, more than a little angry. "I've had about enough of that. You can call me Echo or Raintree or pain in the ass, but do *not* call me princess."

"Why not? Isn't that what you are, a Raintree princess?"

Echo lifted her chin in obvious defiance. She'd probably deck him if he told her she was cute when she was mad.

"Some might say so, but that's not who I want to be. I just want… I just want…"

A normal life. A life without pain. Ordinary worries, ordinary dreams. He knew very well what she wanted. "It doesn't matter what you want, love."

"Besides, you make *princess* sound like an insult."

"Maybe it is," he admitted.

She took a step closer, angrier, tense. "And another thing—you can stop interrupting me."

"If you would get to the point in a timely manner, love, I wouldn't need to."

She punched him in the chest. "And *love* is no better than princess. I am not your love. I am not your princess. If you can't call me Echo or Raintree, don't call me anything at all. I'll be happy to answer to *hey, you*."

"As you wish. Be back here ready to work in two hours. You'll need a place to stay. Maeve Quinlan rents out rooms by the week. She should have a vacancy." He gave her directions, which were quick and easy. The Quinlan house was within walking distance, as was everything in Cloughban.

"How long will I need that room?" Echo asked. "One week? Two?"

One week or even two might be manageable, but he was not optimistic about that timeline. What had Cassidy meant by a long time? To an eleven-year-old, a month might be a very long time.

"I haven't any idea." He still wanted to send Echo Raintree on her way, but why fight it?

Like it or not, his daughter was never wrong.

Chapter 4

The rain stopped as suddenly as it had started, leaving Cloughban looking freshly washed, sparkling and clean. Echo drove the short distance to the bed-and-breakfast. It would be an easy enough walk—she could see the two-story house from the pub—but she needed to park her rental car. Duncan had told her there was parking available behind the boardinghouse.

It would cost her a small fortune to keep the rental car indefinitely, but what choice did she have? It would be a day's trip to return the car to the Dublin airport and then get back to town. She didn't know anyone in Cloughban well enough to ask for that kind of favor.

She would've been better off to fly into the Shannon airport, but it wasn't as if she'd taken her time and planned this trip well. The flight to Dublin had been the next with an available seat, and she'd taken it.

Besides, she didn't want to be stuck without an easy

and immediate mode of transport. If things didn't go well she could leave at any time.

Always have an escape route…

Echo carried her bag up the narrow stairway, half listening to her new landlady, who led the way with a sway of her hips and a bright smile she occasionally cast over her shoulder. Maeve Quinlan was fiftyish, tall and pleasant looking with salt-and-pepper hair and a sturdy build. She wore a calf-length skirt in a girlish pink print, a matching blouse and a white cardigan. She could easily pass for a 1950s housewife.

"Breakfast is at seven." Mrs. Quinlan's voice was as bright as her smile. As soon as she'd confirmed Duncan had sent Echo, she'd been much more welcoming. "If you're not an early riser there are always pastries in the kitchen, and you're welcome to help yourself. I make a fabulous lemon blueberry scone." The word *fabulous* was accompanied by an expressive wave of her hand. "Lunch is on your own, but you're welcome to join us for dinner if you'd like. Just be sure to let me know if you'll be here so I can set a place at the table for you. There's nothing sadder than an empty place at the table, is there?" She walked briskly down the second-floor hallway to open the second door on the right. "Here you are, love. I hope the room suits you."

The easy way *love* rolled off the lady's tongue made Echo cringe. Duncan's *love* had probably been meant in much the same way. These people used *love* the way her Southern aunts used *honey*. Anyone and everyone was called *honey*. Great. She'd made a fool out of herself insisting that he not call her *love*.

Well, it wasn't the first time she'd been a fool. Wouldn't be the last.

"It's lovely, Mrs. Quinlan."

Again, that expressive wave of a hand. "Call me Maeve, pet." Before Echo could respond she continued with, "The bath is at the end of the hall. You'll be sharing with Maisy Payne, who's staying in the room next door. She's our new librarian. Not that the Cloughban library is much to brag about, but we do have one. Maisy is a lovely girl. I'm sure the two of you will be the best of friends."

Echo refrained from telling her new landlady that she didn't need or want any new friends. She needed to get what she'd come here for and then get the hell out of town.

Maeve left her new tenant on her own, in her rented room. A small but nicely furnished room that, with any luck, would be home for a short while. Echo stared longingly at the narrow bed that was pushed up against one wall. She dropped her duffel on the floor and plopped down on the bed. Not too hard, not too soft. Just right.

Echo sat there for a moment, bouncing gently. It had been a long day. The longest. She'd slept on the plane, but that had been hours ago! With that in mind she laid back, stretching out. She might as well rest while she could. The time difference was going to be a bear, and the vision of the fire had drained her.

She was here and she'd found Duncan. It was too early to know if she'd get what she needed from him or not, but there was at least a chance. That was more than she'd had yesterday.

The bed was narrow and short, but it was also really comfortable. She'd just close her eyes for a few minutes…she'd take a moment and unwind a bit…

A banging on the door woke her. Disoriented, she noted a couple of things at once. She'd been sleeping hard. It was dark outside and it was completely dark in her new room, until the door flew open and someone switched on the overhead light. Echo's instinct was not to be afraid. Instead, she was annoyed. Who would do such a terrible thing? The light was far too bright. She pulled the pillow over her face to block it.

Someone snatched that pillow away.

"If you're going to work for me, it's best not to be two hours late for your first shift."

Duncan. Of course.

"I fell asleep."

"Thank you for informing me," he said dryly. "I never would've figured that out for myself."

"There's no need to be sarcastic." She opened one eye. Too bad he was such a jerk. He was more than a little cute. No, not cute. Handsome. Sexy. Brooding, like her own Rochester.

Yeah, because every modern woman needed a boyfriend who kept a crazy wife in the attic...

"Can't I start tomorrow?" She yawned and began to stretch again. Then she squealed as Duncan picked her up and slung her over his shoulder. The world spun. How dare he!

"No, you may not," he said as he carried her from the room, slamming the door shut with one foot. "This is exactly what I was talking about when I said you were spoiled and undisciplined. You will be on time. You will do as you are told. You will not be late again!"

"Great. You're one of *those* bosses."

"One who expects his employees to actually do their jobs? Yes!"

She bounced hard as he started down the stairs. Hanging on to the back of his shirt for support was necessary.

"Wait. Wait!" she called as she tightened her grip.

He stopped in the middle of the staircase, and Echo took a deep breath. "Let me wash my face and brush my teeth, maybe throw on a clean shirt." And pee. Not that she would share that detail with *him*.

Duncan turned and carried her up the stairs. He moved more slowly this time, giving her a moment to appreciate the solidness of the body against hers and the tempting wave of his hair. He had a nice neck, she admitted to herself, a strong jaw and broad shoulders. He carried her as if she weighed nothing. It would be beyond foolish to get involved with him, and since he obviously didn't like her much that wasn't a concern. That didn't mean she couldn't appreciate his finer attributes. Not that she would ever admit aloud that he had any.

He placed her on her feet near the door to her room. "You have five minutes."

"Five?" The expression on his face stopped her from saying more. "Fine, five minutes."

And then he tossed a black shirt that had been slung over his shoulder—much as she had been—in her direction. "Wear this."

If she had any objections to wearing the tight black T-shirt with the pub logo on it, she hadn't said a word. He'd realized it was a bit too small when he'd chosen it from the stack of shirts in the storeroom, but it did show off Echo Raintree's fine figure to its best advantage.

The customers didn't complain, either. Every eye of every male in the place, young and old, married and not, followed her as she served drinks and food and brilliant smiles. Complete with dimples.

Yes, she'd done this before. He might think her a fine employee if she hadn't slept through the first two hours of her first shift.

He could've cut her some slack, he supposed. She'd had a long day. He'd been to the States a time or two himself and he knew very well that the trip was a challenging one. He could empathize. To a point.

If he cut her some slack, they'd never be finished. And he wanted to be finished. He wanted to get this done and send her on her way. If she got too curious, as his last student had, she'd have to go. Finished or not, on the verge of an ugly death for a pretty young woman or not, it was a risk he could not, would not, take.

The crowd began to clear out half an hour before closing time. It was a weeknight, after all. Echo cleaned tables without being told. She handled a bar towel like someone who'd done it before. The way she moved was oddly tempting. Graceful but strong. She flowed from one table to another, easy and, at least for now, unworried. Yes, tempting.

He could not afford to be tempted, not by her. If he was ever stupid enough to get involved with a woman again, if he allowed his body's demands to override his brain, it would not be someone with the last name Raintree.

One thing he could say for her. Princess or not, she did not shy away from work.

As the last customer left, Echo walked to the counter and took a stool there, directly across from Rye.

"If I was wearing a shirt this tight at home I'd get a ton of tips. Here? Nada."

"We don't tip."

She pursed her lips in what he assumed was mock displeasure before saying, "So I noticed. I think tipping is a practice that should be instituted ASAP. Barmaids across Ireland would be ecstatic."

In spite of himself, he smiled. Her complaint was

lighthearted, and had been delivered with her own smile.

He didn't allow his smile to last. She was not his friend; she was not going to stay in Cloughban.

"Be here tomorrow at eleven."

"I'll be working a split shift?"

He nodded.

"It's not like you do any business at lunchtime," she argued. "You don't need me."

He glared at her, just a little.

"Fine, fine, I'll be here by eleven."

If tonight's reception to her was any indication, his noontime business was about to pick up. Not that he would tell her that. She might take it as a compliment. As they got to know her, his customers seemed to forget that her last name was Raintree. Most of them, anyway.

"Don't be late."

She headed to the back of the room to grab her sweater. "Never again, boss, I swear. I'll be here early. I'll stay all day. Whatever it takes to convince you that I am not spoiled and undisciplined, I'll do it."

"I'll believe that when I see it. Good night, Raintree."

"Night, boss." She exited by the front door, and when she was gone the pub felt suddenly and completely empty.

Even satellite phones were not entirely secure, but all things considered…there was no other choice.

"There's a Raintree in Cloughban."

After a short pause, the man on the other end of the line asked, "Which one?"

"Echo, the prophet."

The sigh of relief on the other end of the line could be heard from miles away. Hundreds or thousands of miles? That was a mystery. "She's no threat. They worried about her during the conflict with the Ansara, but she was not a factor."

The Raintree clan was always a factor! "I can kill her if you'd like." It was a thrill to watch someone die, and a Raintree! Not just any Raintree, either, but their prophet. The keeper of their Sanctuary. At least, she used to be keeper. What was she now? Why was she here?

"No!" The sharp command left no room for argument. "A suspicious death would only bring in more of them. Just watch, for now. Alert me to any unusual activity."

Too bad.

There was a short pause, then, "Does she know?"

"I don't believe so."

A pause, a gentle hum. "Perhaps she's there to recruit Duncan."

That was a startling thought. Ryder Duncan, part of the Raintree clan? That would be a disaster for all who opposed them. "If you let me kill her..."

Again, "No."

In the past, hundreds of strays had been called to Cloughban. No, not hundreds. Thousands. This place, the stones that fed the energy that surrounded and flooded it, had been here for thousands of years. Maybe longer than anyone knew. Was it possible that Echo had been called here by the power of the stones, as others had? If she knew everything, if she suspected, she would not have come here on her own.

Echo Raintree walked toward the house where she was renting a room. Her stride was slow and easy. Was her presence here really a coincidence? She didn't seem to be on alert, and she *was* here alone. If she knew what was coming, if any of them knew, others would be with her. An army of Raintree would be swarming the countryside.

"Keep an eye on her for now."

"Of course."

The call ended abruptly. It was just business, after all.

Echo walked into the house. A few moments later, the light in a second-floor window came on. She was there. Right there. On her own and unprepared. It would be so easy...

Maybe killing the Raintree woman wasn't approved just yet, but a good scare to make her leave town would probably be seen as clever initiative.

The whisper was caught on the wind that picked up. "I'll be watching."

Chapter 5

Echo walked through the front door of the pub, ready to get to work. Already the place felt a little like home to her. The warm atmosphere, the smell of ale and wood polish, gave a kind of comfortable aura. Ryder Duncan stood behind the bar in his usual place, and he did not look happy. He glanced up, shot some seriously dark eye daggers her way, then shook his head.

The Drunken Stone was a lot busier than it had been yesterday. The same three old men were in what was probably their usual spot, but today four other tables were occupied. At this time of day there was more food and tea being served than cider and beer. It truly was a village gathering place. Every town needed a place like this one.

She dropped her sweater and purse in the back room, then headed toward a grumpy Duncan. "What's up?"

"You're twenty-three minutes late," he said in a sharp voice.

"That's specific." She looked around and saw no clock. He wasn't wearing a watch. One of his things, she imagined.

"What happened to *'I'll be on time, boss'*?"

"I wanted to look around town, and it's not like you do a lot of lunch business."

Duncan swept his hand out to indicate the customers.

"Well, how was I supposed to know?"

"Table four's order is up," he snapped as Doyle walked out of the kitchen.

Echo got to work without delay. Thank goodness the customers were a lot friendlier than her boss. They were a little distant—they didn't treat her as if she were one of their own—but they weren't outwardly rude the way Brigid had been when Echo had mentioned her name.

A couple of them called her *love*, and she did not chastise them. Their intent seemed to be cordial enough. Duncan hadn't called her *love* since she'd told him not to. If he called her anything at all it was Raintree. On his lips, her surname sounded like a curse.

The early lunch crowd was all male, but just after noon three women came in together. It was obvious that they were here to see her. One of the three was Brigid, the woman who'd sold Echo her green sweater before getting all snippy. The way the women glared at her, with interest and more than a touch of antagonism... apparently they didn't get a lot of new people in Clough-ban. Apparently they didn't want new people.

It didn't take any special abilities to tell that these ladies didn't like her. Gideon kept insisting she was a powerful empath, but Echo had fought that curse tooth and nail. Endure the feelings of those around her as well as her own? Experience their hate, love, heartbreak and fear as if it was her own? No, thanks. Whenever she

felt that ability drift to the surface, she did her best to
beat it down.

As she was cleaning up a recently vacated booth, she
heard one woman say to Brigid, "I asked Rye about hiring Shay a few months back, and he said he wasn't busy
enough to take on a waitress. Apparently this Echo has
special skills that my Shay doesn't possess."

The innuendo was so blatant it couldn't even be
called innuendo. It was an out-and-out insult. Echo
considered setting the woman straight, but Duncan insisted that she learn discipline. She supposed letting
something like that slide was the height of discipline.
She'd show him.

While the women waited for their food to be prepared, Echo managed to stay busy elsewhere. She chat-
ted with a couple of customers, and cleaned tables that
didn't really need to be cleaned. When it was ready,
she delivered thick vegetable soup and ham and cheese
sandwiches to the table. She managed to keep a smile on
her face, a smile that was not returned. She even nodded to Brigid, an acknowledgment that they had met.
Echo was no fool. The tight T-shirt had been intended
to appeal to Duncan's male customers. It only seemed
to piss the women off.

It was odd. Yesterday, right after she'd arrived, everything in town had seemed so bright. The flowers,
the shop windows, the people. Brigid wore a nice out-
fit she'd surely gotten at her own shop, but it was a
drab gray green. The other two were dressed plainly;
they wore little or no makeup, and but for plain wedding rings they wore no jewelry, either. If there were
Children of the Corn nearby, she was looking at their
mothers.

The wind picked up. Echo heard it howling around

the building, rattling the door, as she placed a fresh pitcher of water on the table. The wind whistled, danced and howled. The wooden sign that read Drunken Stone, a sign that hung outside near the entrance, clanked loudly against the side of the building. One of the women jumped. The other two ignored the howl and whistle of the wind. Maybe it was normal, for Cloughban. She hadn't been here long enough to know.

They ate, but did not linger afterward. The woman who had mentioned "her Shay" gave Echo one last glare as she walked out the door and into the wind, which caught her dark hair and made it stand straight up for one weird moment.

When the last of the lunchtime customers had left, Echo sat at the bar and faced Duncan. Again.

"Sorry I was late," she said with sincerity. "It won't happen again."

"I'll believe that when I see it."

She couldn't very well argue with him. She *had* been late.

There was so much she wanted to know about the man before her. The questions that filled her head as she looked at him were all personal. *Are you married, boss? Got a girlfriend? I didn't see a gym on my way into town, so how do you keep those muscles? I see Romany in you and I know the Irish are not fans of tinkers, so how did you get here?*

None of those were wise questions, so she said simply, "Tell me about Cloughban."

His response was immediate and rather cool. "Why?"

"I know it's home for you, but to me Cloughban is entirely different from anywhere I've ever lived. It's so far off the beaten path I had a hard time finding it. I kept getting turned around." She couldn't keep looking into his eyes, which were so dark and deep and angry they made her shiver. "I know there are farms nearby—I saw a ton of sheep on the way in—but...why does anyone live here? Why live so far away from everything?"

"You don't see the charm?" Again, his sarcasm.

"Don't get me wrong. It's nice enough, in a *'I want to remove myself from society'* kind of way, but where's the nightlife? What do the people of Cloughban do for fun?"

"Fun?" he asked, as if the concept were a foreign one.

"Music, theater, sports. Good heavens, Duncan, I haven't even found a hint of Wi-Fi anywhere in town." She'd walked around town all morning with her cell phone set to Wi-Fi and held high above her head as she watched for a flicker of a connection. Nada.

"Ah, the internet. I've heard of that."

She gasped, shocked, then almost instantly realized he was pulling her leg. So he did have a sense of humor in there. Somewhere.

"I pretty much figured there would be no cell service here." If she'd planned this trip more carefully, she would've invested in a satellite phone. But she hadn't so she was off the grid, so to speak. "And as I said, no Wi-Fi."

He leaned against the bar, casual but still wound tight. "You live in a world of electronics. We don't. Instead of playing computer games, we play cards or board games. Instead of chatting with people online, we chat with actual living, breathing people. Face-to-face. For escapist entertainment we have books, and storytellers."

"Storytellers?"

"They tell the tales of fairies and leprechauns, of dark magic and light. Nevan is a quite talented *seanachai*. Why do we have need of Wi-Fi?"

"In this day and age it's barbaric to be without it," she said softly.

Duncan smiled. He *did* have a nice smile. Among other attributes. Her heart did a little extraexcited pitter-pat. Wait, no, that was not just her heart.

Damn, this was bad. Why couldn't he be an old white-haired man with stooped shoulders and yellow teeth? Why couldn't Nevan be the local wizard? She'd never be tempted to just sit and look at *him*.

"What about music?" she asked.

"There's music in church on Sunday morning, and on occasion the schoolchildren will put on a show."

She'd seen the quaint two-room schoolhouse as she'd driven into town. Judging by the size of the building and the number of people she'd seen out and about, there probably wouldn't be much more than a dozen children in that school. How good could they be?

Music was essential to life. It was a way to express joy and sorrow. The right song at the right time had the power to lift her spirits even on the worst day. She couldn't live without it, and didn't want to try. Whether listening or singing herself, she *needed* music.

Gathering her courage, she said, "I sing."

Duncan was not impressed. "Many people do. Crazy old Tully sings all the time. He can't carry a tune, though, so don't encourage him."

He wasn't going to make this easy for her. Why had she expected that he would? Everything about Duncan was difficult. "That's not what I mean," she said. "Is there a guitar in this town?"

"Of course there is."

There was no "of course" about it. She could take nothing for granted here.

Echo felt as if she was definitely experiencing some

of the worst days of her life. A difficult and reluctant teacher. An imaginary little girl. No Wi-Fi! She needed music. It was the one thing she was good at that was normal, that required no magic. When she sang she had nothing to hide from the world.

"Tonight, instead of just waiting tables, how about you let me sing for your customers?"

For the first time since she'd met him, Duncan looked genuinely surprised. "Why?"

She leaned slightly over the bar, excited in a way she hadn't been in quite a while. "Trust me, boss."

He leaned toward her. Holy crappola, he smelled like fresh-cut grass and spring rain and *man*. Why did he have to smell good? Why couldn't he stink?

His voice was emotionless as he asked, "When you have a job that includes singing, do you show up on time?"

"Always."

"Then we have a deal." He offered his hand for a shake, and she took it. They shook once, then quickly released. Echo's hand continued to tingle long after he'd let it go. She could still feel his touch as she stepped outside. Must be a wizard thing, she decided as she headed back toward her rented room, a couple of fresh Drunken Stone T-shirts clutched in her hand.

She was almost there when she realized that the wind had died down. It was actually quite a lovely day. Cool, but sunny and clear. She'd teased Duncan about living here, and she did feel as if she'd lost a limb without her phone, but there were moments when she very clearly saw the appeal. It was almost like stepping back in time to the fifties or the sixties. She didn't have to worry about email or phone messages, and she hadn't even turned on the small television in her room.

There was one problem, though. Her cousins would have a fit if she just disappeared without a word. The last thing she needed was Gideon, Mercy, and Dante searching for her. They were busy with their own families, their own hectic lives, but eventually they *would* miss her. She'd be easy enough to follow to a certain point, through the plane ticket and car rental, and she had no doubt that they could find her here if they tried.

She did not want her cousins and Duncan to come face-to-face with her in the middle. No way. Not ever. Her family could and would find her if they put their minds to it. She'd told them she wanted to be on her own for a while, so there was no reason for them to search for her right away, but still…maybe she should make sure.

Echo decided she'd change clothes and then head into town for a few postcards and stamps. She didn't need to say much. A simple "I'm fine, need some time alone" should do the trick.

Rye sat in the rear booth Nevan and his pals usually occupied for a good part of the day, his legs thrust beneath the table. Even they were gone. Echo and Doyle wouldn't be back for a couple of hours; he had the place to himself.

He grasped the small, warm stone in his hand and closed his eyes, and there she was. Echo, a picture in his mind. A picture as clear as if she truly stood before him. She'd changed clothes. She wore jeans still, but now she wore boots and a loose-fitting long-sleeved purple shirt instead of a Drunken Stone T-shirt and comfortable tennis shoes. She smiled at the young man who sold her three postcards. He was smitten. She had no idea.

The smile was real, even though the pain of her gift tormented her. He'd seen her suffer; he knew she was tormented by the visions. Visions that commanded her, when it should be the other way around. Waking nightmares that tore at her very soul. He should not want to help her, should not care. But he did.

He'd tried to help Sybil, hadn't he? He'd seen her suffering and had done everything he could to save her. That attempt to help had ended so very badly... No, he could not let his mind go there, could not relive failures of the past. This time would be different. There would be no personal involvement.

If he failed, if she died, he would be able to move on without feeling as if the entire world had been ripped apart beneath his feet.

So why was he watching her? Why did he sit in a dark corner and use his abilities to spy on her as she engaged in perfectly ordinary activities? She sat at an empty table outside the coffee shop, took a pen from her purse and began to write on the postcards. Three short notes.

Her activities were ordinary—there was nothing for him to be alarmed about—but he did not stop watching, did not release the stone and clear his mind of her even though he knew he should. Echo was nothing like Sybil, not in looks or in temperament. She wasn't like his last student, either, an eager young man who'd wanted much more than he'd initially revealed.

Echo was an open book; she hid nothing from him.

Everyone in Cloughban knew what he was; they knew what he could do. Some of it, anyway. No one knew all, though he was certain a few suspected. Most of them were not entirely normal themselves, though no others had earned the designation *wizard*. Touched with magic, they had been drawn here as his ancestors had been. Some stayed for a year or two and moved on.

Others were lifelong residents. A few came just for a few weeks, curious or needing a short refuge.

Echo asked why anyone would live here, and he had not been able to give her a truthful answer. *Here, I am with my kind. Here, I am safe from prying eyes.* And most importantly, *Here, I feed on the power of the stones.*

He never should've agreed to help her, never should've allowed himself to get caught up in her troubles. It was not too late to remedy that mistake, no matter what Cassidy had told her. Very little in this life was written in stone. *He* was in charge. He could and would change what was, perhaps, meant to be.

All he had to do was tell Echo he'd changed his mind about helping and send her away. All he had to do was look her in the eye and say, "No." Sounded simple enough, but as he watched her from a distance, he wondered if it would be that easy.

Chapter 6

Postcards mailed, Echo walked back toward the Quinlan house. She wondered if she had time for a nap. No, if she overslept and was late for work again, Duncan would kill her!

The white clapboard bed-and-breakfast was as charming as everything else in Cloughban, outside and in. It was well maintained, in spite of its obvious age. The porch, the lace curtains in the downstairs windows, the plain furnishings—everything was spotless. The kitchen was small but functional, as was the dining room. Mrs. Quinlan—there was never any mention of a Mr. Quinlan and Echo didn't feel she knew her landlady well enough to ask—slept in the single downstairs bedroom, while upstairs there were three bedrooms and a shared bath for her paying customers. At the moment, only two of those rooms were occupied. Since Echo and Maisy kept very different hours, they didn't see each other often. Just as well. As far as Echo could see, Maisy had preferred having the second floor to herself.

Maybe she disliked sharing a bathroom.

Maybe she was like those women who'd come into the pub simply to glare at the new woman in town. Maisy was very pretty, tall and dark-haired and definitely a D-cup, so Echo didn't see how she could see one more female in the mix as a threat, but…they were definitely *not* becoming friends.

There were several shelves of books in the downstairs parlor. As she passed by, Echo thought that maybe she'd grab one of those and read awhile. Then again, maybe she'd turn on the television in her room and see if it picked up more than one or two stations.

But, oh, a nap sounded so good. She still hadn't adjusted to the time change.

Echo passed on the book, deciding to check first to see if there was anything on the television. She ran up the stairs, more energetic than she should be, all things considered, and threw open the door to her room. It wasn't locked. What did she have to safeguard?

The first thing she noticed was that her bed had been neatly made. The next thing she saw was a manila envelope propped on her pillow. Maybe Maeve had dropped off the recipe for her scones, which Echo had praised that very morning.

She snatched the envelope off the bed, plopped down in the faded blue wing chair by the window and removed the contents.

Her heart nearly stopped. The single sheet in the envelope was *not* a recipe.

It was a recent photograph of her parents.

Echo had accepted a long time ago—somewhere around the age of nine—that her mother and father were useless in a crisis. They were not great parents and never had been. A child had never been in their plans. They liked to travel, to party at any opportunity. Her father's gifts had never been very strong. He could read minds, when he worked at it. Her mother had been a stray—an independent, Duncan called them—who had the occasional bit of insight into what was to come.

Maybe it wasn't fair to say they were useless. They did love her. Difficult as they were, she'd never doubted that. But they had never really known what to do with a daughter who had nightmares about disasters, a daughter who woke screaming in the night. A daughter who was much more powerful than they had ever been or could ever hope to be.

She knew the photo was recent because her mother's haircut—shared in an email a few weeks back—was new. It looked as if they were in Paris. Yes, that was definitely Paris.

In the photo, the eyes of both her parents had been crossed out, messily and completely, with a ballpoint pen.

Her hands began to shake, her breath would not come. This was a blatant threat to their lives, she understood that much, but why here and why now? Who even knew she was here?

She'd just sent postcards to her cousins insisting that all was well. Postcards they wouldn't receive for days. Maybe weeks, considering where they'd been mailed from. Now this.

For a few long seconds she sat there, horrifying picture grasped in her hands, heart beating so hard she could feel it pounding against her chest as if it wanted to escape. She didn't know what to do. She didn't know who to turn to. One word came to mind, as she began to recover from the shock.

Duncan.

Not only was Echo not late, she was more than an hour early. And she was not dressed for work. She was dressed as she had been that afternoon as she'd wandered about town with that easy smile on her face. For a moment Rye thought she'd shown up early to demand that they begin their lessons. That would be the time to tell her that he'd changed his mind.

No, that wasn't why she was here. Something was wrong. Her face was oddly pale; her hands shook. He wondered if she'd had another vision—or was about to—and then she shook a manila envelope in his direction and said, "I don't know what to do."

She sat in the nearest chair, her legs giving out from under her, and held the envelope up for him to take.

Rye walked slowly toward her. He'd spent the past hour trying to decide how to tell her that he'd made a mistake and she had to go. Now. Tonight. He couldn't afford to care about her troubles, and he sure as hell didn't want to be her knight in shining armor. He was the last man in the world to fill those shoes.

He grabbed the envelope and removed the single sheet inside. It was easy enough to tell that the attractive older woman in the picture was Echo's mother. They favored quite a bit.

"It was on my bed," she said. "Just…sitting there. I thought it was a recipe." She took a couple of deep, too-fast breaths. He worried she was on the verge of hyperventilating. "It's a threat to my parents, right? My cell phone is worthless here. I dug it out of my bag instinctively, then just stared at it for a moment. I can't call anyone, can't send an email or...or..." Her eyes widened. "Police. Are there police here? A constable? A...an inspector?"

"Of course, but..."

She stood, seemingly a bit stronger now that she had a plan. He didn't dare to tell her that the single constable in Cloughban wouldn't know what to do, wouldn't care, wouldn't help at all.

"I have to go," she said. "That's all there is to it. When I get to the next town over I'll call my mom's cell, and I'll call Dante, too. Maybe Gideon. Definitely Gideon." Mercy? No, Mercy was too far away to get immediately involved, though it was possible one or both of her brothers would call her. "I'm not that far from Paris, I can get there in..."

Rye placed his hands on her shoulders. A few hours ago he would've been relieved to hear those words. *I have to go.* He'd had the same thoughts all afternoon. Yes, Echo Raintree had to go. Out of his life, away from Cloughban. Away from Cassidy. Dammit.

"You're not going anywhere." Against his new plans, against his better judgment.

"But I..."

"I have a phone, a landline. You can use it to call whoever you need to call."

"Okay, thank you." She looked up at him, eyes wide, lips full and far too tempting. "I'll do that, but then I have to go."

He knew that was a bad idea. With magic and without, he knew that no matter how unwise it was for her to stay, leaving would be worse. Dammit, she was going to turn his life upside down.

"You're going to stay here," he insisted. "We're not finished."

She shook her head.

His temper got the best of him and he snapped, "You can't tell me the entire Raintree clan can't protect two of their own from whatever or whoever threatens them."

"Oh!" Echo's green eyes shone. Her tense shoulders dropped a little as she relaxed. "If they're on Sanctuary land they'll be fine. Maybe they can take over my old job for a while."

"Your old job?"

She grimaced. "I was keeper of the Raintree Sanctuary."

In his experience, she did not have the discipline to be the keeper of anything. She was a roamer, a butterfly. A princess, not a queen. "You were replaced?"

She wrinkled her nose. "I quit last year and left a few months ago. Dante was very unhappy, but others have filled in since then. My parents can be next in line."

She relaxed; she smiled. "They won't like it, but they'll be safe there." He could almost see her body unwinding. "Everyone else I care about can more than take care of themselves."

Of course they could. *Raintree*.

On occasion Rye had to remind himself that Echo was no normal woman. No lost and mildly gifted stray looking for others like herself, no independent in need of his assistance.

Doyle arrived early tonight, too. He sauntered through the front door, squinted as his eyes adjusted to the dimness of the pub, smiled when he saw Echo. His shoulders squared. Holy God, the woman was trouble. Doyle had been a perfectly steady and reliable employee since coming to town eight months ago. The man was nearing thirty, as Echo was. He was handsome enough to have caught the interest of a handful of women in town, ordinary enough not to cause a stir. Like most of the others in Cloughban, Doyle was different. Telekinesis was his gift. Rye had caught him moving pots about the kitchen a time or two, but he didn't like anyone to watch. Once, when Rye had walked in and caught Doyle playing—or practicing—several pots had wobbled in the air and then hit the floor at once. The stones fed Doyle's gifts, as they fed those of the other independents—strays—in town.

Echo nodded in Doyle's direction. "I have a couple of phone calls to make, but when I'm done can I get a bowl of soup and some brown bread? I think I'm getting addicted to your brown bread."

Doyle beamed. "Aye, lass. I'll get to it."

"Thanks."

Again, she looked up at Rye. "What are you scowling at, boss?"

"I'm not scowling. This way to the phone." He gestured with one hand and she stood. For a moment, a second or two, she stood too close. He could feel her body heat, smell her shampoo, sense the tremendous energy that rolled off her very fine body. She held her breath, and so did he.

Powers he'd tamped down for years shimmered. They danced. A part of himself that he'd buried deep— for good reason—took a breath as it tried to come to life. It took all his control to push it back down again.

He could not afford to allow the wizard he had once been to return. The stones that fed his power, that made Cloughban such a special place, also allowed him to control what he was. What he had once been.

Echo would not like what he had once been.

Walking behind her he pushed down the urge to brush her soft blond hair aside and kiss her neck.

For comfort. For her and for himself. Just because he damned well wanted to know what that tempting neck tasted like.

He had no prophetic gifts; he did not know what the future held. But he knew that, like it or not, he wasn't going to get rid of her anytime soon.

In years past Echo had played for smaller crowds, but not often. She'd admit that in the early days her all-girl band had been, well, a little rough when it came to hitting all the right notes. That had changed with time, but in those first few months they hadn't been able to draw much of a crowd beyond drunk guys who thought it would be hot to hook up with a bass player or a drummer. The band had gotten better and had eventually built a following, but it had taken time.

She'd never performed alone, not until now.

Tonight less than a dozen warm bodies were scattered about the pub. The size of the crowd was a little disappointing. Of course, it was a weeknight. Maybe weekends were livelier.

At least those who were present seemed to like what they were hearing. She didn't have to call on her weak and unwanted empathic abilities to see that. Several customers in the room smiled, a few tapped their feet or patted fingers on a table in time to the music. They all faced the stage and listened.

For tonight Echo sang ballads, love songs, a couple of sappy songs she'd written herself. To really rock out she needed a band behind her. Drums, a bass guitar, an electric piano and amplifiers. At least two *big* amplifiers. One woman and one acoustic guitar made for a quieter, gentler form of entertainment.

What would happen if she had an episode while she

was on the postage-stamp-size stage in the Drunken Stone? She hadn't had to worry about that before, when the visions had only come in her dreams. She hadn't dared to sing in public since her powers had shifted and she never knew when she might be affected. Driving was risk enough, though she'd always told herself she could sense a vision coming on in time to pull to the side of the road. Maybe.

Now, however, she did worry. A little. How was she supposed to live her life if Duncan couldn't help her manage this? Not for the first time, she wondered why his method of ridding her of the ability was so dangerous.

Sometimes she liked to imagine the life she would live without the visions. The people she could meet, the things she could do. No more worry about others finding out who she was and what she could do. No more hiding. It would be worth any risk to live that life.

Echo loved to play the guitar; she loved to sing. The fact that her fingers had already begun to hurt were a clear indication that it had been too long. She'd lost her calluses.

Tonight there were no visions. There was just music and laughter and applause. Even Duncan seemed to enjoy her performance. Doyle came out of the kitchen a time or two to wait tables and lean against the bar to listen to her. He liked her a little, she knew, but he wasn't her type. He was a nice guy. She'd never really gone for nice guys.

That was going to have to change. If she could manage a normal life without visions, without being called a prophet ever again, she'd eventually need a nice guy. The normal package—marriage, commitment, the whole wonderfully humdrum deal—didn't work with the kind of bad boy she was usually attracted to.

Her mind went to her current family. Gideon was in charge of getting her parents to Sanctuary, and she had no doubt about his abilities to do so. The phone call had been tense, to say the least. He'd asked too many questions she couldn't answer.

He'd been pissed to find out where she was; at least he didn't know why she was here.

Halfway through her set, Maisy—the librarian the landlady had been so sure would be a great friend—came in with her good friend Shay. They were both pretty girls. Maisy had very dark brown hair; Shay's was thick and a rich auburn. Dressed in their best—tight sweaters and short skirts and boots—they drew a lot of attention as they walked in.

It took no special powers to realize that neither of these women would ever be a friend to Echo. She got a sharp glance from both girls, then they gave their full piranha-like attention to the bar and the two men there.

Shay had her sights set firmly on Duncan; Maisy smiled coyly at Doyle. The poor guys didn't stand a chance...

Outside the pub, the wind howled with a sudden burst. A few heads turned toward the rattling door. Echo continued to play without a hitch; this was a song she knew well.

Shay leaned over the counter, all but thrusting her breasts at Duncan. Hers were not as impressive as Maisy's, but she didn't have a boyish figure, either. Echo couldn't care less, but really, did the woman have no shame?

The wind picked up and the old building creaked. The wind howled so loudly it drowned out a couple of words of her song. Everyone looked up and back; the door rattled as if an invisible hand was shaking it, trying desperately to get in.

This was a weird town, and Echo had to wonder if someone in the pub, or outside it, was responsible for the sudden wind. Someone who had a gift for manipulating the weather. Someone who could bring the wind and the rain.

Duncan caught her eye, and a voice—*his* voice—whispered in her head.

That someone is you, love.

Chapter 7

"I don't control the weather," Echo said succinctly when she and Rye were finally alone. She'd been about to burst with questions for the past two hours, but she'd held it in until everyone else had left.

"There was little bleedin' control involved, I'll grant you that." She'd come to him in order to master the visions she did not want, and it was clear that she fought natural empathic abilities, as well. Now this? What other surprises were hidden deep in that seemingly delicate body?

The guitar she'd borrowed from him lay abandoned on the small stage; all the customers, as well as Doyle, had gone home. As they'd left, a few had whispered that a fierce storm might be coming.

They were not entirely wrong.

"You were upset to see Maisy flirting with Doyle, I expect, and that…"

"I was not!" Echo snapped defensively.

No, it had not been Doyle. Rye had seen into her mind clearly enough to know better, but she didn't need to know everything he saw or sensed. He didn't like how easily he slipped into her mind, how oddly near her thoughts were to his. The ability to see so much wasn't normal for him, not now. Even before, such connections had been all but impossible.

"Something upset you, and the wind came," he said. "Was it a missed note? An unexpected thought of your parents?"

She leaned back, pursed her lips and then said, "I did think about my parents and wonder how long it would take Gideon to get them to Sanctuary."

"That was likely it, then."

Echo seemed to relax a little. "Maybe there was just a perfectly normal shift in the weather," she argued.

"Wishful thinking, love." The endearment slipped out. *Love.* Maybe she was so upset she'd miss it. "There was nothing normal about that change in the wind."

She narrowed one eye. The expression was likely meant to be fearsome, but it was not. There was not a fearsome bone in her fine body. "By the way, speaking of *not normal*...stay out of my head!"

He remained calm. "You invited me in, or I could not have been there."

"Did not."

Rye leaned back in his chair, thrusting his legs out and trying for a casual pose. He felt anything but relaxed. "You have a gift for song."

"Don't change the subject."

"I'm not. It's time we started your lessons, properly." The sooner it was done, the sooner he could send her away with a clear conscience. "You have a gift for song," he said again, "as you have a gift for other things."

This time, she remained silent.

"Do you burst spontaneously into song without warning? While in the market, or on the street, or sitting in church, do you begin to sing without control?"

She looked confused, and perhaps a little insulted. "Of course not."

He edged forward, placed his elbows on the table between them, and lowered his voice. "It is the same."

She did not hesitate to respond with heat. "It is not at all the…"

"It is the same," he whispered. "As you learn to play the guitar, to hit a certain note with that lovely voice of yours, to sing the right words in the correct sequence. It is very much the same."

She was quiet as she considered his words. "You make it sound so easy."

"No, love, it is not at all easy. Neither is it impossible.

"You are more capable than you realize," he added.

Echo Raintree was beautiful and she possessed incredible talents, but she did not give off an aura of strength. No one would ever see her coming and be afraid. She did not, could not, instill fear with a glance. She was a pretty girl, always lost, always searching for answers. But he saw the strength within her, trapped. Hiding, even from herself.

She fought her strength, denied it. That denial was why she was here now. It was why she was late on occasion, why she ran from the truth of who she was. All her life she'd made light of her abilities, as she'd tried to tamp them down. The result was the mess that sat before him. Echo was definitely a beautiful, out-of-control mess. In order to move on, she would have to not only accept her great abilities, she would have to embrace them.

"I don't feel capable at all," she said. "I feel weak and as if my entire life is out of my control. Not just the visions, but…everything."

She needed a teacher; he had no choice but to become one, for her. One more time. One final student. "The strength is in you. Find it."

Unexpectedly, she reached out a hand and cupped his cheek. The darkness he had buried deep leaped; his body responded to that simple touch. He instinctively jerked away from her touch.

She leaned back, moved away from him. "Sorry. I…" She stood, grabbed her sweater and purse and headed for the exit. "Sometimes I'm a complete moron."

He heard the unspoken end of that thought as she walked through that door without looking back.

Where men are concerned.

It was her day off. She could very easily get into her rental car and drive to a bigger town where she could buy a nice meal, see a movie, shop in a store where she didn't get the evil eye and—miracle of miracles—pick up a cell signal and Wi-Fi on her phone!

Instead, Echo left the boardinghouse and her rental car behind and started walking. Down the road a bit, then easily over a low stone fence and into a green field.

She'd heard that Ireland was an amazing green. The Emerald Isle. It was the kind of visual that couldn't be explained in mere words. Even pictures didn't do it justice. She walked until the boardinghouse was well behind her, allowing her mind to wander as she moved farther away from Cloughban.

It did wander. To songs and visions, to her family and

to friends she hadn't seen in a very long time. It even wandered to Ryder Duncan a time or two. Those annoying thoughts she attempted to push aside, but they always came back.

Duncan was necessary, nothing more. The fact that he was gorgeous and had those great, dark eyes, that he sometimes made her heart beat faster than it should, those were simple distractions. Nothing more.

And, if she were being honest, not so simple.

After she'd been walking twenty minutes or so a strange, thick fog moved in. It carpeted the green fields, hid what might be over the next knoll from her curious eyes.

There were a few odd cottages here and there. Beyond the few primary streets of the village, there were no neighborhoods. No subdivisions. Just small cottages spaced randomly, as if someone had sprinkled them across the countryside with a casual wave of their hand. All the houses she saw looked as if they'd been built a hundred years ago, or more.

In the distance she caught a glimpse of something unexpected. Stones. Lots of them. A few more steps and a shift of the fog and she realized it was—or had been—a structure of some kind. As she drew closer she realized that what she'd spotted had once been a castle. A small castle, but still…a castle. The fog danced around the base of the stones, thick and white. Not much of the castle was left, but a large part of what had once been a tower remained standing. Not very sturdily, but still standing.

What little girl didn't dream of being a princess in a castle? She had, long ago. She'd had her share of plastic tiaras and scratchy princess dresses.

It wasn't until years later that she'd decided being

queen would be much better. Queens answered to no one. They commanded; they did what they wanted to do when they wanted. If a queen ordered a princess to dance until she dropped, the princess would do so.

Wishes aside, she had always been a princess. She danced to a tune that was not her own, and always had.

Echo stopped for a long moment; she stared at the picture before her. Green grass and ancient gray stone, nothing and no one for miles around. This was the Ireland she had always dreamed of. She had the unexpected thought that she could live here. She could stay in this quiet and beautiful place.

No, beautiful as it was, it was not *her* place.

"Hello."

Echo recognized that voice, and then she caught sight of a head of red, curling hair coming out of the fog.

"Cassidy!" Echo said, surprised and pleased. The child was not a hallucination. At least, she didn't think so...

"You found the fairy fort," the redheaded girl said as she drew closer, her figure moving out of the fog and into the light. "Be careful or one might try to hitch a ride home with you."

Echo smiled. "Fairies. This castle is their fort?"

"Don't be silly. The fort is over there." Cassidy pointed to a slightly raised mound not far from the ruins.

"And these..." Oh, she could hardly say it! "Fairies. They're a problem?"

"They're usually quiet and well behaved, as long as you don't disturb them."

It took Echo a moment to realize the child was serious. "I will do my best. What are you doing here?"

"I came to see you, of course."

Echo glanced around her. True, the fog was thick

but…where had the child come from? "How did you know I would be here?"

"I just know things," Cassidy said in a matter-of-fact voice, and then she dipped her chin and looked up at Echo with eyes too old for one so young. "So do you, sometimes."

If Cassidy was a hallucination, she wouldn't feel solid to the touch. Echo took a step toward the girl, intent on placing a hand on her shoulder. Just to be sure. Girl? Ghost? Pure imagination?

Cassidy smiled and took a step back. "He likes you. He likes you a lot."

"Who likes me?"

The little girl giggled, and then said, "You know who."

"I don't…" Echo began. She was almost close enough to touch the child. Almost there. She reached out, slowly, so as not to alarm the kid. Up close Cassidy looked real. She appeared to be solid.

Just as before, Cassidy disappeared without warning. Poof. Gone.

"Dammit!" Echo stomped her foot on the lush, green grass. Then she turned and looked toward the fairy fort. She'd always put fairies in the same classification as the Easter Bunny. Pure fantasy. But there was definitely something odd going on here. Was it possible…?

She shook her head and turned away. No. She would not go there! She'd seen a lot of inexplicable things in her life; she knew magic existed. Magic those who were not a part of her world would dismiss without a second thought. Ghosts, premonitions, elements that could be manipulated with a wave of the hand. Again, she looked toward the mound. She drew the line at fairies. And leprechauns.

At that moment a gentle breeze kicked up. Tall grass around the fairy fort danced as the wind whistled around what was left of the castle.

"No way." Echo turned and headed back toward town. She had a long walk ahead of her, a long walk in which she'd have time to think, and to talk herself out of what she'd seen and heard. A nap, that's what she needed. A nice long nap.

Strange or not, this was a beautiful place. An enchanted land. She'd never seen grass so green or fog so thick. She'd never seen a child—or an adult, for that matter—appear and disappear at will.

As the village ahead came into view, Echo wished she'd had time to ask Cassidy again, "Who likes me?"

It rained for three days straight. Echo couldn't help but wonder if it was her fault. Her mood was definitely gloomy, and if Duncan was right and she'd discovered a new unwanted power in Cloughban...great. Just what she didn't need. She wanted to dampen—or even better, get rid of—the powers she possessed, not pick up another one she didn't know how to control.

The weather was so persistently wet she braved her way to Brigid's shop and bought a dark green raincoat and matching waterproof boots. While the shop owner didn't refuse to sell merchandise to her, she also wasn't the friendly, welcoming woman she'd been before Echo had spoken her name.

She wanted to ask the woman straight out what had happened. Why the change in attitude? But as curious as she was, she didn't see the point. Brigid didn't like Echo. Her friends didn't, either. If she was going to stay here maybe she'd feel compelled to find out what had happened and try to address the issue. But she was temporary here, and it didn't matter.

The rain didn't keep customers out of Duncan's pub. With raincoats and galoshes and umbrellas, they came. Sometimes they came for the beer—and the cider, which Echo much preferred. They gathered to talk, to share stories of their lives.

Sometimes they came to hear her sing.

Her sets were short, the crowds were small. But she sang, and the music soothed her in a way nothing else could. She sang love songs and sad songs, a little country, a little folk, a little new-age stuff. Normally Echo loved to channel Joan Jett, but not without a band behind her. So she settled for the softer stuff.

It was that softer side that was getting a little fixated on Ryder Duncan. *Rye*, most of his friends and customers called him. It was more than his good looks that made him interesting. He had secrets, probably lots of them. Men like him always did. Why no girlfriend? Every single woman in town flirted with him, some more outrageously than others. A few of the married women were just as bold. He kept his distance from them all. He smiled politely; he was never rude—to anyone but her, at least—but there was always a part of himself that he held back.

When she looked hard enough she could almost see the shield he'd built around himself, the shield that kept all those women at a distance. Not just the women, she realized as she watched him speak to a young man who was seated at the bar. His energy was contained, separate, as if he lived in another world and simply observed this one. Why?

Had his heart been broken so badly he didn't dare to love again? Did he have a heart at all?

She needed to stop thinking about Ryder Duncan as anything other than a teacher. For the past several rainy days he had been trying to instruct her in the quiet afternoons when they had the pub to themselves for a couple of hours. He worked with her on learning how to recognize when a vision was coming and how to control it. He insisted that she master the ability instead of allowing it to master her. That sounded good, in theory.

For three days of rain and moping and daydreaming about a slightly surly pub owner, there had been no episodes. There had been no opportunity to practice what she was trying to learn.

Control.

It would help if she actually thought control was possible.

Gideon controlled his abilities, to a certain extent. So did Dante. If not, they'd live in the midst of complete chaos. Their abilities were potentially dangerous. Dante and his fire, Gideon and his lightning. She could not imagine what their lives would be like if their abilities ruled them, rather than the other way around.

Just that afternoon Duncan had asked her, "Are your royal cousins better than you? Stronger? More capable of control?"

When she'd hesitated he'd answered for her.

"No, they are not."

She wished she could believe him.

Echo was about to start the final song of the set when a warning tickle in the back of her brain caught her attention. A niggling feeling, the kind you get when you sense that someone is watching. But this was different. It was deeper; it was a part of her.

It was the warning Duncan had been telling her to keep watch for. A vision was coming, and she did not want that to happen in front of the handful of customers that remained in the pub. Duncan would be able to explain it away, she imagined, whisking her away and telling everyone she had a medical condition, but she needed to learn to handle this on her own. That's why she was here!

It took great effort, but she smiled, set the guitar aside and said good-night. Her fingers trembled; her vision began to turn gray at the edges, taking away her peripheral vision. Her knees went weak. She eased down off the stage carefully, watching her step. One step, then another. *Please, please, not yet.* She headed for the door that opened on the stairway that would lead to the room where Duncan slept. It was her closest escape route—her only chance of getting away from prying eyes before the vision took her.

She heard voices behind her as she placed her hand on the doorknob. They seemed far away, and might as well have been spoken in a foreign language. A few words reached her brain. *Strange girl. Guitar. Another ale. Raintree...*

If she could just get to the bed. Shoot, she'd be satisfied just to make it beyond this door...

And she did. Barely.

Echo closed the door behind her, took two steps—difficult steps, as her legs now felt like lead and her knees shook—and dropped to the stairs. There was just enough control in her fall to keep her from hurting herself.

Forehead resting on one wooden step, hands pressed to another, she closed her eyes and let the vision come. Instead of fighting it, instead of trying to force it down and back, she embraced the scene playing in her head. It was beyond hard to embrace the very thing she'd spent a lifetime fighting, but she took a deep breath and allowed herself to go there, to live in the moment.

Fire, again. God, she hated fire most of all. The heat, the way her lungs burned, the air being sucked away...

But this time there was some semblance of discipline, a sense that she was amid the flames and at the same time not, as if she were having a vivid dream. She made herself survey the scene as if she were truly distanced from it.

She stood in a building—a warehouse, by the looks of it—engulfed in flames. She was at the center; she saw it all. Fire licked at the walls and danced on the ceiling. White-hot fire climbed and danced as if it were a living thing. It looked to her as if the entire building was made of wood that begged to be kindling. The ceilings were high. The walls were awash with graffiti, garish colors in an otherwise colorless place.

In the distance, she heard a faint scream. Who was calling? Where were they? Was she too late again? There was a small explosion, and heat washed over her in a wave that almost threw her to the ground. For a few seconds she had managed to stay in control, but now she could not breathe. She was going to burn; she was going to die here, along with the person she was meant to save...

Suddenly she was not alone. Duncan stood beside her, stoic as ever. Judging by the expression on his face and the easy way he breathed, he was not at all alarmed.

"You're not really near the fire," he said calmly. "You cannot feel the heat."

She knew he was right, but with each second that passed it seemed more real. "I *can* feel it."

He took her shoulders in his big hands and turned her about so she faced him. They were rarely so close.

She had to tilt her head back to see his eyes. Reflections of flames danced there.

"Where are we?" he asked sharply. "*When* are we?"

"I don't know..."

Instead of being frustrated with her failure, he remained calm. "You do, love. It's there." He tapped her forehead with one finger. "It's here."

She closed her eyes and took a deep breath. The air she took into her lungs was cool, fresh, not at all heated. She smelled Duncan, not the fire and smoke that would not, could not, harm her. His scent was pleasant; it was his and his alone. He smelled like man and wood polish and grass. He smelled a little like the beer he served but, as far as she could tell, never consumed.

Again, in the distance, that scream. It sounded like a child.

"You can't do the boy any good if you panic." Finally, he began to show a hint of frustration. Just a hint. *"Where. When?"*

Echo took a deep breath of cool, Duncan-scented air, and with it she drew on his calmness. She searched her own mind deeper than she had before. She wasn't in the warehouse; the fire did not threaten her. She was a watcher, sent here by whatever force had gifted or cursed her with this ability.

"Atlanta," she said. "A Peachtree...something."

"Peachtree what, love?" Duncan whispered.

She came up with an address, could see the street sign and the numbers on the old building. The boy should not be here. There was a skateboard...

"When?"

Again, she went to that new place in her head. It was harder than coming up with an address, much harder, but when she saw the time she laughed. "Not yet. Duncan, the fire has not started yet!"

In an instant the vision disappeared, on a flash of flame and a fading scream. Echo opened her eyes to find that she was still on the stairway. Duncan was beside her, one arm wrapped protectively around her. A wonderfully heavy arm was draped around her waist. A comforting hand pressed against her back. She turned her head; his face was right there and she was so happy…she kissed him.

It was a kiss of joy, a way of celebrating a bit of new-found control and the fact that this time she was not too late. But it *was* a kiss, and as kisses sometimes do, it changed quickly.

Echo was far from a stranger to kisses. Friendly and passionate, impulsively and well-planned…she had been kissed. But this kiss with Duncan swept her away in an instant. He tasted so good; their mouths fit together so well. She forgot fire, she forgot the constant rain; she forgot who she was and why she was here. Only for an instant, but it was an instant that shook her to her core.

Duncan's shield didn't come down, not entirely, but it shimmered. It was weakened. Weakened by her and the kiss he had not expected. She felt that, too.

As a first kiss, it was unplanned but stellar. Heaven above, it was amazing. He smelled good. Their mouths fit together without even a hint of awkwardness. Their bodies aligned perfectly, and if she had her way this moment would never end.

It was Duncan who pulled away, who broke the short but passionate kiss with a curse she could not understand. Gaelic, she supposed. She only knew it was a curse because of his tone.

He cursed, but he did not move away. His body remained close to hers; he held her, still.

When Duncan had joined her he'd closed the door behind him, the door between the stairway and the pub and the people there. Though there were many people close, she and her boss, her teacher, were effectively alone. She could relax here, for a moment or two. She did not have to jump up and make excuses, did not have to explain away what had happened. Not the vision or the kiss.

"Thank you," she said. For the help, for the training, for unexpectedly coming into the vision with her, something she had not known was possible. And yes, for the kiss. In spite of his scowl, she grinned. "I have a phone call to make." She jumped up and ran up the stairs to his room; this was a call she'd prefer to make in private.

She was dialing when she glanced up and out the window and realized that the rain had stopped and the moon shone brightly in a cloudless sky.

Chapter 8

Having realized some real success, Echo approached her next lesson with a renewed purpose. If she could help people, if she could save lives instead of simply watching people suffer and die, then she had no right to wish her abilities away. Duncan seemed to understand that she was determined to be a better student.

He locked the pub doors, front and back. Instead of sitting at a table for their lesson, as he normally did, he moved a few tables aside, clearing the center of the big room. She'd meditated and worked on her focus, and they'd discussed her past troubles and tried to identify clues she'd missed, clues that might help her to identify and improve her gifts.

Looking back, she admitted there had been signs she'd missed. She'd been so determined to deny the visions, she'd blocked all the clues.

A part of her still longed to be normal, but who was she kidding? That wasn't meant to be. She was Raintree.

Echo and her teacher, a man she was much too attracted to for her own good, especially after that kiss, stood face-to-face in the space he'd cleared for this lesson. He stood so close she had to tip her head back in order to look him in the eye. Those eyes were so dark, so intense, she held her breath for a long moment. He would barely have to move in order to put his mouth on hers again.

"Why are we here?" she asked when he remained silent and still for too long.

"You came to me, Raintree. Have you changed your mind?"

Echo shook her head. She didn't mean here in Cloughban; she meant here in the center of the pub. But she didn't argue. She knew damn well he hadn't cleared the floor for a dance.

"Listen," he whispered.

Not to him, she knew that, so she didn't respond. He'd get to the point eventually. He always did.

"There's energy everywhere. Inside us, around us. Between us."

Oh, yes, there was definitely energy between them…

"Don't get distracted," he admonished, as if he'd read her mind. Again.

"You are not a carnival fortune-teller," he continued. "There is no ace up your sleeve, no con man's tricks in your repertoire. You, Echo Raintree, are connected to the energy in this world in a way few, if any, will ever know. You are an oracle, a prophet. A miracle."

"I don't understand what this…"

"Accept who you are, here and now. See and feel the energy around us, and accept yourself not as a small part of it but as its master."

"I'm not the master of anything," she whispered.

"You are," he said. "Whether you like it or not, you are. The question is, will you accept who you are or will you deny it until the uncontrolled energy that's flowing into your body destroys you?"

What choice did she have? None.

Duncan rotated his head as if working a crick out of his neck. He closed his eyes. The muscles in his arms and in his neck visibly tensed.

And Echo was assaulted. Under normal circumstances, she'd dismiss the sudden sensations as nerves or maybe an illness coming on. Her stomach clenched. The hairs on her arms stood up and danced. The assault continued; it grew stronger. Yes, this was what a coming vision felt like.

"Energy," Duncan said. "You can allow it to assault you or you can take control."

"How?"

"Shield yourself. Use your own energy to repel mine."

She tried. Goodness knows she'd been taught how to protect herself against negative energies, but it had never felt like this. She was under attack.

"Try harder," Duncan insisted.

Instead of arguing—her first impulse—Echo did. She tried harder. She strengthened her shield, imagined it thicker, stronger. Impenetrable.

She didn't say a word when she no longer felt the distress of the energies Duncan was sending her way, but he knew. Almost immediately he said, "Good. Now, allow a small amount of the energy in."

"I just managed to block it out."

"You're not controlling the energies, though, you're just protecting yourself."

That was the point, right? Echo took a deep breath. No, simple protection was not the point. Not anymore.

She tried to allow a small stream of energy in, but soon her shields fell and she was once again awash in amazing streams of force that Duncan sent her way.

The attack stopped, and he took a step back. "Not bad," he said in a lowered voice. "But we still have a lot of work to do. We'll try again tomorrow."

Tomorrow. She would be here tomorrow, and the next day, and the next. Why did that knowledge bring a smile to her face?

Rye fingered the leather cord that peeked out from his collar. After a moment he made an adjustment, pushing the cord beneath his shirt so it didn't show. The blessed stone at his throat and the leather cuff on his right wrist never came off. They couldn't. He could fashion a charmed amulet for Echo, but he knew her cousins had tried that and charms hadn't proven sufficient.

Besides, he didn't want her to depend on charms and spells to deal with her abilities. She had to learn. Acceptance had to be step one. Her constant fight against who and what she was had made it impossible for her to take charge.

He knew very well what he was, what he could be.

If he was going to teach control, perhaps he should find some of his own. He didn't possess nearly enough to deal with Echo Raintree, day in and day out. To watch her, to touch her, to step into visions with her so she would not be alone. The kiss had been a colossal mistake, one he dared not repeat.

She'd be here soon for yet another afternoon lesson. After an hour, maybe an hour and a half at most, they

would both be spent. He taught, she learned. They both
worked very hard to ignore the attraction that sparked
between them. Her ability to shield herself was improv-
ing quickly, but she still had trouble controlling the energy around her.

He should've sent Echo away when he could have.
That first day, he should've stood his ground and sent
her packing. Not only did he now care about her more
than he should, she'd been touched by the power of the
stones. He had to finish the job, or she'd leave in worse
shape than she'd been when she'd arrived. They *had*
made progress, as her last vision proved.

She'd called her cousin in North Carolina, Gideon,
the one who was a cop. Gideon made calls of his own
and had saved a young man who'd snuck into an abandoned building to practice his skateboarding skills just
minutes before a quickly spreading electrical fire broke
out.

Rye hadn't told Echo about the stones, and if he had
any choice he wouldn't. They were tempting. Intoxi-
cating. Powerful. And the last thing he needed was a
parade of power-hungry Raintrees marching through
Cloughban. Taking her there would be a last resort.

He had not told her about Cassidy, either, and as far
as he knew they'd not had another encounter. Just as
well. The Raintree *could not* know about his daughter.

For the past five days the sun had shone in Cloughban. Echo had not had another vision, not sleeping or
waking. Considering how they'd been progressing, she
was surprised. Pleased, but surprised.

In addition to working on her ability to control energies, their lessons consisted of honing her concentra-
tion. Through meditation—something at which she did
not excel—and mental exercises, they practiced. Only

through mastery of her mind and body could she ever hope to control her gifts.

One of the most important things for her to accept would be that she could not save everyone. People died every day. She could have vision after vision and not save them all. As she honed her skills her predictions would become more selective.

It had already begun. Perhaps the skateboard boy was destined to do something important with his life. That or an as-yet-to-be-conceived son or daughter or grandchild had an important role to fill in future events. It was impossible to know why he had been chosen, why her vision had led to a second chance for that child. That was something else she'd have to accept—a lack of answers to the many questions still to come.

She had a lot of questions. He heard them, whispers from her mind to his, even though she had not yet found the courage to ask them aloud. She would, in time. *You're supposed to be so powerful; why have I never seen a demonstration? Why do you stay here, in the middle of nowhere? What is it with this town, anyway?* And the one he picked up on almost constantly. *Are you going to kiss me again?*

He'd just as soon send her on her way before he had to answer any of those questions.

She'd grabbed a scone and two cups of strong tea before leaving the boardinghouse, and enjoyed a walk through town. It looked to be another sunny day. Wasn't it supposed to rain all the time in Ireland? Wasn't that why the grass was so green? Maybe Duncan was right and it was all her fault. She was happy, so the sun shone.

She was happy.

It had been such a long time since Echo had been

truly happy that she was almost giddy with it. She didn't even think much about the threat to her parents. Did that make her a bad daughter? No. She knew they were safe on Sanctuary land. Gideon wouldn't let any harm come to them.

Besides, given the way some of the women in town mooned over Duncan, the warning had probably come from some besotted female who saw the American newcomer as a threat. Would it have been all that hard to find a photo of her parents on the internet and do the rest? It did show an amazing bit of commitment that hinted at a serious bunny-boiling-on-the-stove mental issue, but she could think of no other reason for anyone to threaten her.

There had been no hint of danger since that one.

As she walked past the shop where she'd bought her green sweater and the newer raincoat and boots, she experienced a distinct chill. Could Brigid be the one who'd left the disturbing picture? Had she reacted in the extreme because she'd instantly seen Echo as a threat? She was really too old for Duncan. The clerk wasn't old enough to be his mother, but she was certainly old enough to be his mother's slightly younger sister.

Duncan had been teaching her to listen to her instincts rather than fighting them, to accept them as a natural part of herself. It hadn't been easy; she was constantly afraid of another crippling vision. But as she walked into the town square she attempted to let loose the empathic abilities that both Duncan and Gideon insisted she possessed in spades. She opened herself up to the energies around her. Good and bad, strong and weak.

As always, the square was perfectly put together. Flowers bloomed, everything was clean and fresh, every shop window sparkled. Scents from the bakery filled the air, and a few residents who were already out and about nodded and said hello. Echo took a deep breath and opened herself in a way she had always been afraid to do. She reached for energy instead of denying it. She embraced her magic.

She was instantly—but gently—overwhelmed.

Why had she never seen this before? Cloughban was no ordinary town. It wasn't just Duncan who was special. She was surrounded by strays. *Independents.* Most were not very powerful; some had nothing more than what most would call good instincts, or extraordinary good luck. But there were a few, a handful, who were quite gifted.

Mind readers, telekinetics, healers. Shifters! She had never met one, though she'd heard of a distant cousin who had that ability. Fire control, water manipulation... *mind* manipulation.

Cloughban wasn't all that different from the Raintree Sanctuary. These people had been called here, each and every one of them. They had been drawn together, called to a place where their kind could live in peace.

Cassidy, that enchanting little girl, was one of them.

Echo pursed her lips and frowned. She looked around, trying to assign an ability to those villagers she could see. It didn't work that way, not for her at least. The energies swirled and danced, much like the flames she'd seen in her last vision, but she could not single out where those energies belonged.

She was fascinated, but she was also puzzled. Strays didn't congregate, they didn't gather in clusters, didn't populate small towns. At least, she'd never heard of such a thing.

She had one last, strong sense of being surrounded by powerful forces before she purposely shut down.

But not quite soon enough. One last thought filled her head, a truth that would not be denied. Many of these people had come to Cloughban because Ryder Duncan was here. He was their leader, their Dranir as much as Dante had ever been for the Raintree clan.

How had they kept this place a secret for so long?

She should tell someone. Dante, maybe. Mercy? Gideon for sure. In the next instant she knew she wouldn't tell anyone. No one here was a threat to the Raintree clan. These people wanted to live in peace, and she could appreciate that in a way few could. The threat to her parents finally made sense, in a way. Anyone who wanted to be left alone was now a suspect. She was Raintree. Someone, possibly several someones, was afraid she'd bring trouble to their quiet little town.

As she turned toward the pub she experienced a flash of warning, a hint of darkness. Cloughban was not a dark place, but something evil lived here. Her protective shields went up instantly to keep that darkness from touching her. The empathy was new, and when she opened herself she was much too vulnerable. When she reached out again, she did so cautiously.

And got nothing. Whatever evil she'd sensed was gone. No, not gone. That evil hid from her. Whoever possessed that darkness realized she'd touched it, however briefly.

This charming village was a lot weirder than she'd first thought. Weird, but not dangerous. Wherever a number of people gathered, there was some sort of darkness. She'd sensed much more light around her than dark. Besides, Duncan wouldn't let anyone or anything hurt her.

She stopped, glancing back toward the pub. Where had that thought come from? She had no illusions about Ryder Duncan. He might like her well enough, he might kiss like an angel, he might even call her *love* on occasion—an endearment which was no different from a casual *honey* or *dear* or *hey, you*. He was not her protector.

Echo shook her head and continued on. She needed some soap and deodorant, and maybe a chocolate bar. She could learn to seriously love Irish chocolate. The pharmacy was small but well stocked. It had become a regular stop for Echo on her walks into town. With a shopping basket in hand she took her time walking up and down the aisles. She wasn't alone. Two other women carried their own small baskets, and filled them with necessities and luxuries. Like the chocolate. These women did not scorn her the way Brigid had. They even nodded and said hello.

Soon she had everything she needed in her basket. As she approached the counter to pay, her stomach roiled and her vision dimmed. Colors, bright almost to the point of being blinding, danced behind her eyes. The sensation didn't last long, but it was unpleasant. She felt as if a powerful wave of something she could not identify had washed over and through her.

Echo reached for a sturdy shelf and steadied herself as the colors went away and her vision returned. She closed her eyes, hoping for the last bit of nausea to pass. It did, and she felt fine again. Completely normal.

She shook her head and continued on. Well, that was strange! She hoped she hadn't eaten something bad. The odd distress had passed quickly and by the time she stood at the counter with euros in hand, all was well. Nevan walked into the pharmacy. He smiled widely and nodded. If he'd been wearing a hat he surely would've tipped it in her direction.

When Echo walked back onto the square, she shaded her eyes for a moment and smiled widely at the scene before her. What a perfect little town, what an enchanted place. She dropped her hand and headed for the pub with a purposeful walk. Then something struck her.

Hadn't she sensed something bad here not so long ago? Something wrong? Something…dark?

Ridiculous. Cloughban was an ordinary place, the people were ordinary people, and as much as she liked it here, she could not stay much longer.

I've been here long enough. The thought wafted through her head almost as if it wasn't her own but was a whisper from elsewhere. *What a boring town, time to get back home.*

"Ha," she said as she walked into the pub a full fifteen minutes before her appointed time. "I'm early."

Duncan stood behind the bar. It was amazing how much she liked to look at him, how pleasant it was to simply stare and admire. There was much to admire. Had she just been thinking about leaving Cloughban? No. Not yet. The thoughts of leaving town flew out of her mind as quickly as they had entered.

"Second time this week," he said. "Are you ill?"

Echo remembered the bout of nausea in the pharmacy, then dismissed it. "No, I'm fine." More than fine, really. As she looked at Duncan one thought was foremost in her mind. *When are you going to kiss me again?*

When are you going to kiss me again?

The answer to that unasked question should be *never*. But damn, there was something irresistible about Echo Raintree. Rye was no longer certain he could finish what he'd begun without throwing her across the nearest table and…

Her expression changed; she took a step back. She even uttered a low, "Whoa. Too fast."

Rye instantly threw up a mental wall; dammit, he had to keep the woman out of his brain! She blinked, shook her head, and he realized that the image they'd shared had happened so quickly, so unexpectedly, that she actually believed the thought was her own.

Instead of being horrified, she actually gave in to a small, secret smile that spoke volumes. She wanted him as much as he wanted her. The only difference was, she had no idea how dangerous a deepening connection between them might be. For her.

As powerful as she was—and lack of control aside, she was quite powerful—she could be more. The weather power that revealed her mood, her ability to see into his mind, her clear empathic abilities. If he didn't know better he'd think she was like him. A sponge. A receptor.

A dangerous creature.

The two of them together could rule the world. Or burn it down around them.

"Echo…" Should he send her away or embrace her? Teach or shun? Pull her to him or make sure there were always thousands of miles between them?

Doyle burst through the front door, startling Rye, and Echo, too. Echo glanced at her coworker, obviously annoyed to be interrupted. Annoyed and relieved.

"I hear the town council called a meeting for tonight," Doyle said as he slipped off his coat.

Rye gave his full attention to the cook. It was probably a good thing they'd been interrupted, and still…he was hardly grateful for it. "Yes, I was informed earlier."

"What's up?" Doyle asked, then he glanced Echo's way and winked at her.

Rye was being perfectly honest when he said, "I'm not sure." He should be more curious. The town council rarely called unscheduled meetings.

Doyle laughed as he headed for the kitchen. "Shouldn't you know?"

"I suppose I should, but I don't." He could guess, though. There was a Raintree in town, and she appeared to be settling in.

"You're a poor excuse for a mayor," Doyle teased as he disappeared through swinging doors that separated the main room from the kitchen.

Echo blinked. She withdrew from him, more than a little. "Mayor?"

Chapter 9

Duncan sat across the table from her, looking grumpy. He was more than a little annoyed that she hadn't learned to bring on a vision of the future at will.

"I can't force it, *Mayor* Duncan." And she wouldn't want to. The goal—her purpose in coming here—was fewer episodes, not more. She didn't want to learn how to bring them on; she just wanted to control the ones that were going to come whether she liked it or not.

"Let's get out of here." Duncan stood, grabbed her hand and pulled her to her feet. He didn't head for the front entrance, but to the rear door. It opened onto a perfectly ordinary alleyway, she knew. Now and then he made her take out the trash. Around the corner there sat a small, rusty-red car that had seen better days. If Duncan ever left town, maybe that was the car he drove. Did he ever leave town? Shoot, did he ever leave the pub?

Apparently so. He walked around the car, then turned down a narrow street. He continued to hold her hand.

The air was not as cool as it had been earlier that morning. It was perfect. Cool but not cold, sun shining, an occasional gentle breeze. They passed a man working in his garden. Nevan, she saw as he lifted his head and then his hand. When she'd first seen him she'd thought him the ugliest man she'd ever seen, but now… not so much. He was a lovely man, not pretty or handsome in any way, but kind and funny. She waved back. So did Duncan.

He still did not release her hand.

The village was so small, once they'd walked beyond two rows of houses they were, for all intents and purposes, out of town. She had walked this route before, on that afternoon she'd found castle ruins and a fairy fort.

Duncan didn't lead her in the exact same direction she'd taken that day. Instead, he walked a bit more to the west, though he didn't go far before stopping and sitting on a gentle green knoll. She sat beside him, and instantly realized why he'd chosen this spot.

The view was like one from a picture postcard. This was the Ireland so many tourists longed to see, but rarely did. The grass was a brilliant green, the sky clear and bright. In the distance a sprinkling of thatched-roof cottages sat. There was no rhyme or reason to the way they were organized, not that she could tell.

She'd come here looking for help, and she'd found it. What she had not come here looking for, what she had not expected, were these intense moments of what could only be called peace. Peace at a bone-deep level. Complete, soul-brightening *peace*. The sensation never lasted long, but…it was enough. That sensation of peace was like a tonic, like finding beauty where you least expected it and being gently overwhelmed.

Echo now realized that she had never known true peace before coming to Cloughban.

Duncan finally released her hand. Reluctantly, it seemed. Maybe that sensed reluctance was wishful thinking on her part. Maybe he'd only taken her hand to make sure she followed obediently.

It hadn't taken him long to realize that obedience had never been her strong suit, she knew that much.

She looked at him, studied his profile for a moment and then she asked, "What do you want?"

He didn't dare to answer her question honestly. *I want you in my bed. I want you gone. I want my life not to be turned upside down by a woman I cannot ever have.*

For years he'd been perfectly happy to live single and alone. He had his pub, he had his daughter. It was foolish—and impossible—for him to want anything or anyone else.

"I needed to get out of the pub for a bit," he said simply. "It's a nice day. We might as well enjoy it."

Echo relaxed visibly, her shoulders easing. She smiled. "I had begun to think you never left the pub." She pointed to a cottage in the distance. "Is one of these houses yours, or do you live above the business?"

No matter how much he liked her, he couldn't let her in. Couldn't trust her, couldn't invite her to be a part of his life. Not even a small one.

"Where do *you* live?" he asked. "When you're not traveling the world in search of wizards, where do you lay your head?"

She looked at him, obviously realizing he'd changed the subject. Bless her, she let it slide. "All over. I lay my head in a small apartment in Wilmington, North

Carolina. In a big house on Raintree Sanctuary land. In the guest room in Gideon's house on the beach. With friends, when I need it."

"Which one of those felt most like home to you?" He wanted to be able to picture her somewhere specific after she left. Why? He could not say. Echo on the beach, in the mountains, in a small room in a crowded building...

She turned her head, looked away, and he knew what her answer would be. Did everyone read her so well, or only him?

"None," she whispered. "I guess that's what I've been searching for all this time. A place that truly feels like home." She shook off the mood and looked to him. "Is the pub truly home for you?"

"Cloughban is home," he said, attempting to be honest with her without saying too much.

"It's good, to know where you belong." She bit her bottom lip, continued to look away from him. Did she think he'd see too much in those green eyes? "Do you believe my problems will be easier to solve when I find my place in the world? Or do I have to find this control you insist I need before I can discover home?"

He didn't answer. He didn't know how.

Echo was beyond annoyed. Every resident of Cloughban above the age of fifteen was packed into the Drunken Stone, but *she* wasn't welcome.

She'd enjoyed her afternoon walk with Duncan. It had been easy, relaxing. Afterward they'd returned to the pub. She felt as if something had happened between them, but she couldn't put her finger on what exactly. He hadn't kissed her again, and he hadn't held her hand on their walk back to the pub. Right before they reached the pub's rear entrance he'd told her—rather abruptly, she thought—that he'd see her tomorrow. Normally she'd be thrilled with an unexpected night to herself, but this time, today, she didn't *want* the night off. She wanted to know what the residents of Cloughban talked about at a town meeting.

Why did she think it might be her?

She had the house to herself. Her landlady and the only other resident were both down the street at the meeting. It was not her imagination that Maisy had smirked at Echo as she'd walked out the door. As a nonresident, she was not welcome at their town meeting. What the hell could they have to hide? What sort of politics might go on here that would require secrecy? Was banning an observer from their town meeting even legal?

Echo, whose entire life could be classified as weird, decided Cloughban had to be the weirdest place on earth. Almost impossible to find, no cell service, no Wi-Fi, Children of the Corn…though come to think of it, the kids she'd actually seen around town seemed pretty normal. Some of their parents, not so much.

She hadn't seen Cassidy since that day she'd run across the tumbled stones of what had once been a castle. And a fairy fort. To be honest she only rarely thought about the child, as if their two meetings had been no more than a dream. Their first meeting had been the day Duncan had changed his mind about taking her on as a student. Echo had been desperate, panicked, had suffered a horrible vision. It had been such a long day and such a strange encounter, she could almost believe the child was a figment of her imagination. Or maybe a ghost like the ones Gideon saw. She'd seemed so real at the time.

When they'd met at the castle...her mind had been drifting. She'd been vulnerable.

If she had dormant empathic powers and maybe even a way to affect the weather with her moods, could there be another unexplained ability? Like manifesting a dream out of thin air? Dammit, she'd come here looking for less magic in her life, not more!

Having the house to herself should've led to going to bed early, or watching TV, or raiding the kitchen. Instead of indulging in any of those things, Echo found herself nervously rummaging around the parlor, scanning the bookshelves for something to read.

While there were a few fairly new—as in less than twenty years old—mysteries on the shelf, most of the books were ancient. Leather bound and clothbound, spines cracked and fading, pages yellowing but surprisingly sturdy. Echo removed a couple of history books, leafed through carefully, then returned the books to their proper places. As she leafed through she noted dates and names that meant nothing to her, political references and legal opinions. Yawn. Nothing caught her fancy.

Until she deciphered a faded, almost-illegible title on the spine of an old, thin book. *The History of Cloughban.* She squinted at the author's name. Alsaindar *Duncan.*

That answered, in part, her question about why Duncan—*her* Duncan—lived here. It was home. His ancestors came from Cloughban. There was a blood connection. Roots.

She very carefully removed the book from the shelf. It was heavier than she'd expected. With easy fingers, she opened the book to the title page.

The History of Cloughban by Alsaindar Duncan. Beneath the title was a drawing of a big, standing rock, a stone that pointed toward the sky. She touched the page, readied to turn it wondering what she'd find. For some reason this book excited her. Her mouth went dry, her stomach flipped and her heart rate increased. Silly of her to react this way. It was just a book. She started to flip that first page...

The door flew open and a child—perhaps twelve years old or so—came rushing into the room. His reddish brown hair was shaggy and mussed, and his face was flushed. He'd been running. Slick as could be, he reached up and snagged the book from her hand.

"You'll not be needing this now, miss," he said breathlessly.

And then he was gone, the front door slamming behind him.

What the...?

She felt a bit ill, as if she'd eaten something bad, but she recognized the sensation as...wrong. Unnatural. Magical. She could see the book in her head, could *see* that title page. And then it started to fade away and she knew that in a moment the memory would be gone.

Her heart pounded with a new and disturbing realization. This had happened before. Recently. In the town square. No, in the pharmacy. Someone was messing with her memories. Or at least they were trying to.

Control. Duncan had done his best to teach her to harness that control. She did so now. Echo closed her eyes and concentrated, as he had taught her. All this time she'd thought the lessons had been wasted, that she was getting no stronger, but as she reached for control she realized that was not true.

She *would not* forget the book or the boy. She pictured them both as if they were still in the room; she fought to hold on to what had just happened. Her knees wobbled and her mind spun with the effort it took to keep that memory…and then the threat was gone, and the memory remained hers.

She did not bother to try to control the cold wind as she left the house and walked toward the Drunken Stone. They couldn't keep her out. They couldn't mess with her memories. Someone would, by God, explain to her what was going on!

Echo expected that her entrance would cause a commotion, but she was wrong. Every solemn face in the room was turned to the door before she opened it. They'd been waiting for her. Not a word was spoken until Nevan, the gnome, spoke from his usual seat at the corner table.

"Told you so!"

There was a hush on the heels of Nevan's statement, but it didn't last long. Voices rose, some angry, others merely confused. Rye demanded calm. He called for everyone to settle down, but his voice was not loud enough. A few men moved closer to Echo. They were not a threat, not yet, but like it or not a threat was coming. Rye left his post behind the bar—no one was drinking tonight—and jumped onto the small stage. This time when he demanded quiet, the crowd obeyed.

It would be a waste of time to run Echo out of the pub before continuing with the meeting. She'd see; she'd know. Every day she grew stronger. He should've sent her away that first day, should've ignored Cassidy's prediction and his need to make sure the Raintree had not come for her, but he had not and now it was too late. He cared about her. Their instructions were not done; he could not dismiss the threat she seemed to have forgotten about; he did not trust these people, his people, not to harm her. They were protective. Of their home, their lives, the stones—of Cassidy.

"I know what some of you think." He locked his gaze on a confused Echo. "You think the Raintree woman has come for one of us, that she will bring more of her clan here and destroy this…this…" There was no better word. "This sanctuary. You're wrong. Echo is not our enemy. She's one of us, for a short time. She has come here for the peace Cloughban can offer those like us. Nothing more, nothing less. I believe that to be true. No, I *know* it."

One kiss, a shared visual or two…it wasn't much, but he and Echo were connected in a way he had not expected. As he'd faced a crowd tonight—half of them angry, the other half merely confused—he'd come to the unwelcome realization that he would protect her at all costs.

Almost all costs.

"The meeting is over," he declared. "Your worries are for nothing, I promise."

That was a hollow promise, as empty as the freshly washed glasses that hung behind the bar. Life was worry, and had been since his child had come into this world.

It took several minutes, but the crowd did disperse. Most of the townsfolk walked around and well clear of Echo, who moved forward slowly until she stood stock-still in the middle of the room. She stared at him even as Nevan, the last to leave, gave her a comforting pat on the shoulder and muttered, "I tried to help you, lass. You're on your own now."

When they were finally alone, she said, "I believe some explanations are in order."

"Can it wait until tomorrow?"

The expression on her face was one of frustration and anger, and those emotions came through in her voice. "No, I don't think it can."

He wanted more time to think, time to prepare his words carefully. "It's a long story, and it's getting late."

She wasn't going to budge. He added determination to the list of easily read expressions on her pretty face. "Take your time. I've got all night."

He left the stage, walked silently toward her.

"First of all, what the hell is the deal with the book I found…"

Rye lifted one hand and the book, which had been sitting on Nevan's table, flew into his hand. Echo gasped, and her eyes—greener than ever on this night—went wide. She knew he was a wizard, knew he had powers. But he had been very careful not to use them in front of her, until now.

"There are secrets here you are not meant to know."

"Then why am I here?" Her expression softened a bit. "Very little in life can be written off to coincidence, you know it as well as I do. Do you believe it's simple coincidence that I traveled halfway around the world to find you?"

No. No, he did not. "That is the question of the hour, isn't it?"

Rye stopped when he was so close to Echo that he could smell her, feel her body heat. He'd wanted her since she'd walked into his pub. He'd dreamed of her, fantasized about having her even though he knew…

Echo shook her head. "Let's take this slowly, one thing at a time." She pointed. "That's just a history book that was, as far as I can tell, written by one of your ancestors. Why on earth would it be snatched from my hand as if it contained the secrets of the universe? Secrets I am not to be privy to apparently."

"It's complicated."

Anger flared to life again. "No shit, Sherlock!" She took a deep, calming breath. "Give me something. Throw me a bone, tell me…tell me…tell me *something*."

Something. Maybe he could talk his way around this by sharing a small detail, or two. "My family have always been guardians, of a sort."

"Guardians of *what*?" she asked, frustrated.

Like it or not, the time to tell her about the stone circle would come soon enough. Not tonight. If he had his way he would never tell her about Cassidy. "Cloughban. You know it's a different kind of place. You know the people here are not ordinary. They are…like me. Like you. They're afraid you'll ruin what we've found here. Peace. A place we can be ourselves. A home for many strays."

"Independents." She looked up at him, wondering, confused, wanting something more. "Nothing about my life has ever been ordinary," she whispered.

"Or mine," he confessed.

"This morning, in town…" She wrinkled her nose and closed her eyes. "I swear, there was something. Something I can't quite put my finger on." She opened her eyes and looked directly into his. "I do remember thinking that you would never let anything or anyone hurt me."

A thought much too much like his own.

The pub was quiet; they were alone. The attraction that had always danced between them intensified. There was power here, a power he had tried very hard to ignore.

Rye cupped Echo's cheek in his hand. "You cannot stay here, not forever."

"I know that. This is not my home."

"No, it's not. And I suspect some of the people here will not make the coming days easy for you."

Her expression was relaxed now, soft and tempting. "My life has never been easy, either."

Easy. Who had an easy life? Not him, not his daughter...not the woman who stood before him. Life was not meant to be easy. "You should probably leave tomorrow."

"I probably should." She drifted closer to him, rested her cheek against his chest. "But easy or not, I'm not finished here. I know it to the depths of my soul."

He threaded his fingers through her hair, held her close.

No, she was not finished with him, and like it or not he was not finished with her.

Chapter 10

The kiss was not like the first. It was deeper, more profound. It was a kiss to wipe away the rest of the world. While Duncan held her, while he pressed his lips to hers, Echo didn't think about being a poor excuse for a prophet, stolen memories, villagers who didn't want her here, magic.

This was real. She wanted Duncan and he wanted her. His arms encircled her and held her close, so close she could feel the evidence of his arousal pressing against her. If the kiss didn't tell her well enough that he wanted her, that did.

She wanted him here...now. On the bar, on a table, on the floor...

"No," he whispered as he pulled his mouth from hers.

No? *No?* Not the word she wanted to hear.

"Not here," he whispered.

Not here was not the same as a flat out no. *Not here*

she could accept. "You've been peeking into my head again," she said without anger.

"Sometimes I can't help but see." He kissed her again, quickly. Urgently. "Please tell me you're…"

She didn't give him time to finish. "On the pill. Yes." Not that she'd had any need for birth control in a very long time. Two things kept her taking the pill. One, she was optimistic. She wanted a man in her life, and if the right one fell into her lap—so to speak—she wanted to be prepared. Two, she didn't want children. Not ever. Any child of hers would be Raintree. Any child she brought into this world would have some kind of ability. Maybe it would be something lovely and manageable, a true gift. Then again, maybe a child of hers would be tortured, as she had been.

Duncan swept her off her feet. It wasn't the first time he'd carried her. It wasn't even the second time. This was, however, by far the most pleasant. She draped her arms around his neck as he carried her to the back of the room and up the stairs. Quickly. With purpose.

"I think I wanted you the first time I walked into your pub," she said. "I didn't want to want you. You were so annoying." She did something she'd wanted to do since that first day. She ran her fingers through his hair. "You were annoying and prickly," she said without heat.

"While you have always been a ray of sunshine," he countered with humor.

It was a valid argument, but at this moment she really didn't want to discuss her persistent distress.

"Why did we wait so long?" she asked. So many wasted days, so many lonely nights, when she could've been, *should've* been, here.

He carried her into his dark bedroom. Moonlight streamed through the window, lighting it just enough.

When Duncan put Echo on her feet he did so gently, as if he was afraid she might break. She was no sooner standing on her own than he began to undress her. Shirt over her head, bra unsnapped and discarded with a flick of his hand. That done, he stopped to lavish attention on her breasts, touching, kissing, sucking, until her knees went weak.

She loved the way he touched her, the way he made her feel a part of something more. Something better than she'd realized was possible.

Enough, she thought. *I will come before either of us is completely undressed.*

And this is bad because...

"Get out of my head," she said without anger. "I want tonight to be..." What she'd always wanted, what she'd craved all her life. "Ordinary. Normal. Just your body and mine."

He didn't whisper in her ear or in her mind. Instead, he finished the job of undressing her, placed her in the center of his bed and very quickly removed his own clothing.

He looked fine clothed, but naked he was magnificent. Hard, muscled, just a little bit hairy. He did not remove the stone at his neck or the leather band on his wrist, but she supposed that was hardly necessary.

As he came toward her, moonlight lit his chest and she saw the jagged, ugly scar there, much too close to his heart. It hurt her to know that he had been hurt; she was saddened to know that he'd suffered such pain. She'd have to ask him about that scar later. At the moment she had more important things on her mind, and she did not want to be distracted by pains of the past.

Bodies entangled as if they had been made for each other, he kissed her again. And again. He kissed her mouth, her throat, her breasts. Echo spread her thighs to cradle him there. Almost touching. *Almost.* She ached to have him inside her; she didn't want to wait another second. If he made her wait she was going to scream.

Then he was there, guiding himself into her, moving gently. Too gently. She'd waited for this for a long time. Forever. This was no time for trepidation, no time for second thoughts. She placed her mouth close to his ear, kissed the warm skin just beneath and then whispered, "More. Now."

He groaned and did as she asked, pushing deep, thrusting hard and fast until she shattered. She might be embarrassed about coming so fast if he hadn't been right behind her,

Next time would be slower. Next time they would savor their coming together. And yes, she knew without doubt that there would be a next time.

Now and then he called her *love.* She wanted to believe there was a kind of love between them. Temporary, unexpected, just two unattached people who understood each other finding and enjoying each other for a while. Could she call that love? Why not?

"That was amazing," she said. Not at all what she'd had in mind when she'd stormed across the street to confront him, but definitely amazing. She had forgotten everything while they'd made love. All her worries, all her questions…gone. Temporarily. Unpleasant thoughts had already begun to creep back into her head.

Duncan was rumored to be very powerful. He certainly had more abilities than she knew about. Was this a simple distraction? No, not simple, not simple at all, but still a distraction.

"Did you do something to me?"

"I believe I did," he said, his voice light. "If you've already forgotten, then I didn't do it very well."

"No, Duncan. I'm serious. Was there anything…unnatural…?"

He kissed her to silence her question, then pulled away slightly and said, "No magic was involved, at least not on my end of things. And if you're going to share my bed, perhaps you should call me Rye."

"Can't," she said with a sigh.

"Why not?"

"Rye is a bread. Come to think of it, Duncan is a doughnut. I really can't handle all those carbs." She pressed her body to his. Already she wanted him again. It was going to be a long night. "Can I call you Ryder?" It was the name she'd known him as before they'd met, a name no one else called him. At least, not that she'd ever heard.

"You can call me anything you'd like, love."

Love, again. She knew this wasn't the kind of love she was looking for. A forever, ordinary, romantic kind of love. But for tonight, it would do. It would more than do.

The Raintree woman should've left the pub long ago, should've returned to her room at the boardinghouse. Alone. Instead, she remained in the pub. More likely above stairs with Rye.

It was so unfair. Why had he never looked at her that way? What did Echo have that she did not? She wasn't prettier, certainly wasn't sexier.

More powerful? Yes. For now.

Invulnerable?

No.

She hated her instructions to wait. Hated them! If she made Echo's death look like an accident, her body would be shipped home and no Raintree would ever come to Cloughban again. By the time they got suspicious and thought to do so it would be too late. Far too late.

Her last two calls to her employer—not the town council who paid her to keep up their pathetic library but the man who'd hired her to be a part of the first wave of his long-planned invasion—had gone unanswered. He should've at the very least seen that she'd called and call her back. Maybe he was on his way. Maybe he was already here, somewhere.

She knew he was close, and had been for a while. A couple of hours away, at most, and perhaps not even that far. Waiting had been difficult for him, but he'd insisted that everything be just right, including the time of year, the phase of the moon and—most important—the age of the girl. At the moment, she was prime.

Had he seen that a Raintree would arrive just as his plan was coming together? Again, maybe. He wasn't as powerful as he thought himself to be, but he planned to be much stronger very soon. She wasn't sure he'd get that chance. If she had her way he would not, but for now... for now she would continue to play the obedient soldier.

Maisy imagined herself comforting Rye when Echo was dead. She imagined herself taking her place in his bed, making him do whatever she commanded.

Most of all, she imagined herself queen.

Echo slept sprawled across his bed. Naked, beautiful, sated...his, for now.

It was not long after dawn, hours before the pub

would open, when Rye pulled on a pair of jeans and headed downstairs to make a pot of coffee. Sleeping with Echo had not been the smartest move he'd ever made, but he didn't regret it. It had been a long time, a very long time…

"Hello."

He jumped at the sound of Cassidy's voice, spun to face her. She stood near the bar, still dressed in her nightgown. The one her grandmother had made for her. It was old-fashioned and worn, and Cassidy swore it was the most comfortable nightgown ever. She would soon outgrow it. The hem hung well above her ankles. Last year it had almost touched the floor.

"Honey, I told you to stay out of sight while the Raintree woman is here."

"Echo." Cassidy smiled. "Her name is Echo, not 'the Raintree woman.' I like her. Is she going to be my new mother?"

"No." Echo could not stay here. It would be too dangerous—for him, for Cassidy, for every resident of Cloughban.

"Then why is she upstairs in your room?" Long red hair still tangled from sleep, Cassidy looked up as if she could see through the ceiling.

"She's a friend, that's all. A friend who isn't going to stay in Cloughban much longer."

"Oh. I like her, and I thought she might stay for a long time. But now I hope she leaves soon."

"Why?" Had Cassidy seen something? Had she sensed a danger?

Cassidy shrugged her shoulders. "I'm tired of staying home all the time. It's boring."

Rye relaxed. "Your grandmother takes good care of you."

"She does, but I miss my friends. I miss you, Da."
She stuck out her tongue, then said, "I used to see you
almost every day, for breakfast or for tea, or right after
school. Now you're here all the time. You don't want
Echo to know you even have a daughter."

"It's for your own good." He sounded like a father
with those words.

"That's silly." Cassidy's face shifted, was suddenly
older—much older—than her eleven years. She looked
wiser, and far too powerful. She'd seen something, felt
something, that made her thoughts shift. "It's okay to
be the good guy, Da. You don't have to be alone. You
don't have to be who you once were."

He wished, as he had many times in the past, that he
could protect Cassidy from knowing who and what he
had been. He wanted to protect her from the past, a past
long before her birth. What he'd done…it was behind
him, well behind, but he could not erase it.

Rye wanted to give his daughter a hug, but if he
reached for her his arms would go through her as if
she were made of mist. Cassidy was not here. She was
in the cottage she and her grandmother called home.
That cottage was not far from Cloughban, but it was
far enough away to keep her safe.

"It won't be much longer, I promise."

"I really would like a new mother someday," Cassidy said, and then she was gone. She didn't fade away,
she just disappeared.

He liked Echo more than he should. Last night had
been great, and he was realist enough to accept that
they weren't done.

But no matter how much he liked her, how much he
wanted her, she couldn't stay.

If the Raintree found out about Cassidy, they would

take her away. She was too powerful, too unpredictable. He had never known or even heard of anyone who could do the things Cassidy could do. They'd lock her away, study her or use her as a weapon. He didn't trust them; he didn't trust them at all.

And that meant he couldn't trust Echo. Much as he wanted to, he could not afford to trust her.

Chapter 11

Echo woke warm and happy, and sore. Holy cow, Duncan knew what he was doing in the bedroom.

Ryder, not Duncan. A name no one but she called him, a name that suited him. She liked the way it rolled off her tongue. *Ryder*.

She'd only been awake a few minutes when he came into the room with a tray. She sat up as he presented the tray for her inspection. Breakfast in bed. Eggs over easy, toasted brown bread, marmalade, both coffee and tea. No one had ever brought her breakfast in bed before!

"Hungry?" he asked.

"Starving." He placed the tray on the bed near her. She looked over and up to him. "You're wearing pants." She made that sound like the accusation it was. Damned if she didn't want him again.

"I make it a point not to cook naked." He sat on the edge of the bed. Close. Not close enough.

"I suppose you do have to protect yourself." For a moment she focused on the scar on his chest, a scar that looked nastier by morning light than it had by moonlight. She wanted to ask him about it, but not now. She also wanted to ask him about the amulet at his throat and the leather wristband, but she recognized both as being protective in nature. He had not removed either last night.

The real question was, what did a man like Ryder Duncan need to be protected from?

Echo took a cup of coffee and a piece of toast, leaning over the tray as she took a bite so as not to get crumbs in his bed. She wasn't shy about being naked in front of him. In fact, it felt like the most natural thing in the world. He didn't eat, but he did drink a cup of coffee. Maybe he'd eaten downstairs. Once she started eating, she realized that she really was starving.

When she was finished, she leaned away from the tray and asked, "So, do we have to keep this a secret? Do we have to pretend in front of everyone else?"

Ryder gave her question a few seconds of thought before responding. "No. Someone, probably several someones, would know, anyway."

Of course. "Because this is not an ordinary town."

"Not at all."

She should've seen it all along, should've felt it, but she had not. "Is everyone here…different?"

He hesitated. "Not everyone. There are a few spouses and children who are not gifted."

"The little girl I saw my first day here!" Echo sat up straighter, on alert. "I saw her again last week when I was walking, and…she told me about fairy forts." Both memories seemed dreamlike. Were they real? They seemed so, but something was off.

"Sometimes I actually forget about her, and that's not normal. The memory just fades away. It always comes back, though, like I'm remembering a dream or someone I haven't seen since I was a child."

Ryder didn't say anything, but his jaw got tighter, his eyes more distant.

"She told me I would stay," Echo continued. "I thought she was a delusion, a fantasy, because she just disappeared. I mean *literally disappeared.* Cassidy. She said her friends call her Cass but she prefers Cassidy." She looked up into a stony face. "Do you know her? Surely you know *everyone* around here, Mayor Duncan." She smiled. Ryder definitely did *not* fit her mental image of a small-town mayor.

His hesitation was minor, but she noticed. She noticed everything about him, and had since day one. His voice was perfectly even when he said, "Never heard of her, love. She probably was a delusion, as you say."

Ryder took the tray and moved it to the top of the dresser by the door. The tray out of the way, he kicked the door shut, gently but firmly, and then he removed his jeans to join her in the bed. The mattress dipped and creaked, and she rolled into him. It was the most natural thing in the world to drift together. He held her close; she held him. Just like that, she dismissed everything from her mind but Ryder.

"Do you know what I dreamed last night?" she whispered.

"No." His lips found her shoulder and rested there for a long moment.

She sighed in deep contentment. "Nothing. Nothing at all. It's been days since I had a vision, sleeping or awake."

"You've gone days before without a vision."

"Yes, but there's something different this time."

He threw one long leg over her hip, capturing her in the nicest way. "And what's that?"

She whispered, truthfully and with joy, "I am not afraid."

Walsh paced in his room, a too-small, too-shabby rented room, which was not much more than an hour from Cloughban. He didn't dare move any closer until it was time. Just a few more days, and he'd never be forced to sleep in such an ordinary place again. He'd have anything and everything he wanted. He was so close. Years of planning, and he was so close he could taste it. *Almost. Almost.* It was a shame that Rye Duncan knew his face so well. Walsh wanted to watch every step of his plan; he wanted to be a part of it from beginning to end. When this was all over, would he have the ability to watch without being seen? To be invisible, or to shift into something—or someone—else? He could hardly wait to find out.

He'd be a part of it soon enough. The Raintree woman was a fly in the ointment, but she wasn't much of a worry. She was a girl of limited powers, despite her surname.

Just a girl, not an oracle to be feared.

The knock on his door should not have surprised him, but it did. His number-one soldier was early for their meeting.

Walsh invited the man in, but he shook his head and said, "Not here."

His older brother—half brother, and that half did make a difference—was a suspicious man. Walsh was careful, as well, but he wasn't paranoid. Still, until things were settled it was best to humor this man he had relied upon as the plan came together.

They walked around the building, into a deserted field. The grass that grew so high all but disguised a long-deserted famine graveyard. Walsh felt as if a ghost were walking up his spine, but his brother didn't seem to be bothered at all.

The man who walked in step beside him finally said, "I think we should move up the timeline. We need to move now, *tonight*."

Walsh tried to be patient, he truly did, but this man and the woman, they were not as reliable as he had initially thought them to be. When this was over... Well, when this was over he would need them still, for a while. But if all went well, he would not need them for very long. "No. We're not changing the plan now."

"Why not?"

Walsh had been very careful about what information he shared. He only had two soldiers in Cloughban. One was family. The other had shared his bed on several occasions. The others—those headed this way very soon—were pawns he had no qualms about sacrificing.

His brother was anxious. Until now, Walsh had kept much of his plan to himself. They were so close to success, so very close. Perhaps he could afford to explain why the wait had been necessary. It wouldn't do for things to be set into motion too soon.

The girl was of the proper age for optimum transference. He'd waited for this. He'd waited four long years. Four years of research, careful planning and waiting.

"The cycle of the moon must be just right for the incantation to work," Walsh explained. "The girl is the right age, and soon the moon will be full. Days, we are down to mere *days*."

"Days."

"On the three nights when the moon is fullest, the time to take her will be perfect. Be patient, brother. Our rewards will be great."

He would rule. His brother would be his right-hand man. His woman would have everything she'd ever wanted, and more.

And he would bring his mother's people, the once-powerful Ansara, back. When his army was strong enough, he'd wipe every Raintree off the planet.

Some might argue that he was not true Ansara, that they had been wiped out when the Raintree had defeated them, six years earlier. True, his mother had been adopted; she'd had no true Ansara blood in her veins. But in Walsh's heart the Ansara survived through him. He was the last, but he would soon rebuild what had once been a powerful clan.

The grass was waist-high where his brother came to a stop and turned to face him. "You have the incantation with you?"

"Of course." The words were few, the language ancient. But they were powerful words. Beyond powerful.

His brother smiled. It was a smile much like his own; it was their father's smile. Their father had been gone for years.

Walsh didn't see the knife until it was too late. The fact that his brother's hands were visible and empty and relaxed meant nothing. The blade appeared from behind him. It flew through thin air, twisting and turning, rising up to slice across Walsh's throat.

His last thought was, *This was not part of the plan*... and then...

Betrayal.

* * *

Echo climbed into her own bed, burrowed under the covers and closed her eyes. She was so exhausted she'd thought sleep would come instantly...but it didn't.

Her life had been a series of disasters. There had been good moments, too. Family, friends, making music. But disasters had always been a part of her life. She would willingly admit that more than a few of those had been of her own making. Other disasters had been seen and experienced through dreams and visions.

Her curse. Her gift.

Why did she never see anything nice of the future? Why did she never see happiness and joy?

She went to sleep on that thought, and dreamed.

She dreamed of green fields, fairy forts and children. Not her children, certainly, since she did not plan to have any of her own. Maybe these were her cousins' children.

No, Emma was not here, and neither was Maddy. She saw no sign of Dante's kids, or Mercy's. These children were...

Hers. Hers and Ryder's. There were blonde girls and dark-headed boys. They danced around some strange stones that glimmered with amazing energy. The fairies were there, sparkling like stars that had fallen near to the ground.

She didn't want kids, never had, and with good reason. But as she watched these children her heart filled with a love she had never imagined possible. These little people lit the world with a new light. She loved them with a bone-deep mother's love.

Echo realized she was in a dream. Not a vision, not a premonition, just a dream. In case there was some grain of truth here, she attempted to see...how many kids? There seemed to be a lot of them, but she couldn't tell. Maybe what she saw were the same children again and again. Children at different ages, at different stages of their lives.

Suddenly Ryder was with her. She couldn't see him but he stood behind her. She felt him there. As with the running children, that feeling was bone-deep. Love. Not infatuation, not lust. Love. She had never known such a deep love could be real.

His arms went around her; he pulled her back against his solid body, and she settled there.

He whispered in her ear. *This is a possible future. It is not set in stone, not a surety, just a possibility. There are many possibilities.*

His arms tightened around her. He picked her up, off her feet, and spun her around.

And she found herself facing a graveyard, looking at a row of headstones. Ryder Duncan was there.

So was Echo Raintree.

Chapter 12

Rye walked across deserted green fields. It was a path he'd walked many times in past years. Echo had gone back to her rented room to catch a nap between shifts. He had a million things to do, but he needed to see his daughter in the flesh.

The thatched-roof cottage that had been Cassidy's home for her entire life sat on an emerald-green hill an easy half hour's walk from Cloughban. The cottage was small but sturdy, a safe home for a very special girl and her grandmother.

When Cassidy was older and had better control over her abilities, maybe she and Bryna could move to town. Until then, until she'd made it safely through puberty, he didn't dare it. It was a risk enough to allow her to see anyone other than him and his mother-in-law, but he knew complete isolation would not be good for her.

She normally went to school, but had not been lately.

Everyone in town was determined to protect Cassidy from the Raintree. His daughter had friends, but even though those friends all had gifts, they were not in the same class as Cassidy. Not even close. They were gifted. She was exceptional.

The villagers were also determined to protect the stones, which was the reason the book about Cloughban had been snatched from Echo's hand. It was a shared fear that the stones would be discovered. That others, gifted and not, would flock here in droves. That the roads would be widened to allow for buses filled with foreign visitors to gawk and stare, to touch and take photographs. The very idea was a nightmare to those who had found peace in this village.

The stones were sacred. They were not meant to be a tourist attraction.

Bryna knew he was coming; she always did. Rye got the evil eye as he walked through the front door. That was the norm, too. He couldn't blame her.

Cassidy ran toward him; she threw herself into his arms. "Da!" she said in an excited voice. "I've missed you."

Neither of them mentioned the early-morning visit. Bryna did not approve of Cassidy's out-of-body excursions. Neither did he—they were potentially dangerous—but that was a talk they'd have in private. Later.

Bryna didn't miss much, but her granddaughter had the ability to hide whatever she wished to hide.

Cassidy grinned at her grandmother without letting Rye go. "Da has a girlfriend. She's very pretty."

"It isn't polite to snoop into other people's thoughts," Bryna said sourly.

"But, Granny, sometimes I can't help it. Sometimes the thoughts just scream at me."

True, Rye thought as he watched the two of them interact. Echo's thoughts were so strong, so clear. Were his own the same? He hoped not.

Bryna's expression softened. "I know, *ma chroi*, but you must try."

Cassidy nodded and turned her attention back to Rye. "Can we go for a walk? Can we visit the stones?"

Rye nodded. "Fetch your jumper. It's nippy out."

Cassidy nodded and ran for her room, and that's when Bryna turned her hard attention on Rye.

"A girlfriend, eh?"

Their past had been difficult, that was inescapable, but love for Cassidy brought them together and kept them together. The past was the past; Cassidy was the future. "It's nothing serious," he said. "Just a fling."

Bryna scoffed. "Well, that's too bad. It's past time you moved on. Sybil's been gone nine years. That's long enough for you to be alone. More than long enough. A woman would be good for you, I imagine."

Anxious to change the subject, Rye said, "What about you? Your husband has been gone many more than nine years."

She almost smiled. The corners of her mouth twitched. "James McManus calls on me now and again, usually while Cassidy is at school." A snort followed that statement. "Which means I have not seen him lately. The Raintree lass has put a damper on my love life."

Love life? "He *calls* on you?"

Bryna lifted her chin. "That's all you need to know."

And more than he needed or wanted to know.

The conversation ended when Cassidy appeared,

wearing sweater and boots and shouting, "Let's go, Da, let's go!"

Rye's heart swelled when he looked at his daughter. He had never known a love like it and never would again. She was his world, his reason for existing. She was also the reason Echo Raintree could not stay in Cloughban.

The thought of a coffee and pastry from the shop on the square drew Echo out of her rented room. She looked at the pub as she walked past and wondered what Ryder was doing at this moment. He should be taking a nap. She should be sleeping herself!

She'd tried to go back to sleep after she'd awakened from her disturbing dream, she really had, but her mind had been spinning and sleep would not come.

She was tempted to check the door to the pub to see if it was locked, maybe climb the stairs and slip into Ryder's bed...

No. It was not the time to be impulsive. She'd been impulsive all her life! This thing with Ryder was happening too fast, and she needed to think. Right now she was wrapped up in emotion, almost giddy with what she'd found. Emotion would only hold her for so long. Before this went any further, she needed to examine the pros and cons.

She did her very best to dismiss the dream she'd had. It had not been a premonition; it had not been a glimpse into the future. It had just been a normal, ordinary, particularly vivid dream. So, pros and cons in the real world...

She liked Ryder.

He lived in Ireland, which was a very long way from North Carolina.

They were definitely physically compatible.

He was a stray, and while she did not know the extent of his magic, she did understand that the normal life she craved couldn't possibly happen with him.

He kissed like an angel.

He was bossy and had no tolerance for employees who were, on occasion, late.

The sex was fantastic.

What if he wanted children?

Okay, now she was definitely getting ahead of herself. She blamed the dream. A dream of children in one future and her own headstone—beside Ryder's— in another. She still wasn't sure which aspect was more terrifying.

It was a nice day, sunny and warmer than she'd expected when she'd set out. What was she doing thinking about a future with Ryder Duncan? They'd had one very nice night. She'd needed that—the pleasure, the connection, the escape. Maybe that's all it was, all it would ever be. Physical. Fun. Sex for the sake of sex and nothing else. She really needed to get the thought that they might have a future out of her head before he peeked into it and saw too much. She didn't want to send him running. Not yet.

She ordered her coffee and a pastry that was about the size of a baby's head, collected her purchases with a smile and stepped out of the small shop to sit at an outdoor table. There were quite a few people out and about today, walking, shopping, visiting.

A number of the residents of Cloughban knew her. Most of them—maybe all—had been in the pub last night. Some had been in the pub a time or two to hear her sing. On this beautiful day, a few passersby nodded and said hello. Some just glared at her suspiciously as they passed.

She now knew that most of the residents of Clough-ban were like her and her family. Special. Gifted. Cursed. She had seen little evidence of their gifts, but then they'd been hiding their true natures from her. They'd been protecting themselves, and this place.

One couple she'd never met before offered a hesitant "Good afternoon." They both had pronounced German accents. While most of the residents were obviously Irish, it occurred to her that the small town in the back of beyond, a place that should not be a mecca for international tourists given how difficult it had been to find, had a number of foreign residents. Bertrand was obviously French, and Michael's accent was more British than Irish. There were others, customers at the pub, who were definitely not originally from here.

Why had she never noticed this before?

Because someone instructed you, in an entirely magical way, not to.

The voice in the back of her head spoke the truth, and she knew it. Why? Why would the residents of Cloughban bother to hide so much from her? She was Raintree, magic was an everyday part of her life. She would never judge, or try to take advantage, or point and whisper…

The timing was terrible, but there it was—that tickle at the back of her brain that warned her another vision was coming. She left her unfinished coffee and pastry sitting on the small round table and started walking toward the pub. After a few seconds she began to walk faster, then she jogged. Desperate, hurried, she caught a glimpse of herself in the boutique window, but did not look inside to see if Brigid was watching. It would

be best if no one saw her and wondered what had her
in such a rush.

If they knew what she was, would they judge? Take
advantage? Point and whisper?

At the moment there was only one important question: Did she have time to make it to Ryder before she
lost all control?

Her vision began to go gray around the edges. She
could see the path ahead of her, and nothing more. She
kept her eyes on the side of the building she hoped to—
needed to—reach before it was too late. Jogging wasn't
going to get her there soon enough. She began to run.
Faster, harder. A month ago, she could not have made
it this far; her lessons must be helping, at least a little.

By the time she reached the door to the Drunken
Stone her body was more numb than not and she could
barely see at all. She remained in control, for now, but
barely. The entire world was going gray; there was no
sound but the rush of blood through her veins.

She tugged hard, but the door was locked. She
knocked, pounded, called Ryder's name. *Come on, Duncan*, she thought, trying to send him a message. *Wake
up. Answer the damn door!*

She couldn't wait any longer, and she didn't want to
collapse here, at the door. Someone might see, someone *would* see, and she was far too vulnerable while
she was in the midst of a vision. Stumbling, she made
her way around the corner, behind the far side of the
building where she wouldn't be seen by those walking
the square. Completely numb, entirely out of control,
she sank to her knees and allowed the vision to take her.

Cold. It was so cold. Within the vision, she stood and
looked around her. Front, back, all around. She didn't

recognize where she was. Panic wouldn't help her now! Deep breath. Control.

She was in a field, Ireland green, she understood, even though in this world, in this time and place, it was night. She stopped, lifted her head and focused on the scene ahead. It continued to form, taking shape as she watched.

There were stones in the near-distance, stones that were tall and gray and powerful. Incredibly powerful. They were not haphazardly arranged, but formed a circle. An almost-perfect circle, she knew even though she saw the stones from the side, not from above. One of them, the largest stone, was the one she'd glimpsed in the pages of a very old book. A book she had not been allowed to read.

In the center of the circle of stones stood a dark figure. As the scene continued to unfold, it remained maddeningly unclear. She couldn't see a face, just a tall, dark, indistinct shape.

Mists danced and then converged, finally allowing her to see more. That dark form held a knife in one hand and a child in the other.

Cassidy.

Snow began to fall. Fat, white flakes that dropped silently from a cold sky as Echo began to run toward the stone circle. As in a nightmare, she ran as hard as she could but moved no closer. How could she help the child if she couldn't reach her? Ryder had joined her in a vision once; he'd helped her. Could she help this little girl here and now?

Hair wild, eyes unnaturally wide, Cassidy looked directly at Echo and said, in a whisper that sent a fog of warm breath into the cold air, "Save me."

For the first time ever, Echo felt herself being pulled

out of the vision before she was ready to go. She fought to stay, to see more. To reach Cassidy. Where was she? When? Already she knew she was not too late. This had not happened, was not going to happen immediately. The event was so far out it might not happen at all if she did what needed to be done. How could she know which steps would lead to Cassidy's safety? What was she supposed to do?

Echo heard a new noise—quickly approaching footsteps—and realized she was no longer alone. She turned her head and there was Ryder, running, running, then screaming. Snow fell so fast and thick now it was like a curtain that threatened to hide the details of this vision from her.

Cassidy screamed, her high-pitched voice cutting through it all. "Da!"

Ryder ran hard, but he could not run fast enough. He lifted a hand to his throat, tore the leather cord so that the stone that always rested there flew away. Through the falling snow, the stone spun. It was gone. Ryder changed...

Echo's eyes popped open and there he was. Ryder Duncan in the flesh, leaning over her, calling her name. He looked worried. His hair was mussed and he was sweating and breathing heavily as if he'd been running as he had in her vision. Her breath came hard and fast, her heart was pounding, she was still cold—but her thoughts were focused on one truth.

He'd lied to her, more than once. He'd kept secrets. How many, she had no way of knowing.

As he helped her to her feet she pushed away her earlier, silly list of pros and cons. He tried to hold her close but she slipped away and said, without looking him in the eye, "You lied to me. Cassidy is your daughter."

Chapter 13

Echo refused to look directly at him. He reached for her, tried to gently force her to face him, but she slipped away. He'd been so scared to find her on the ground, shaking and moaning while caught in a vision. He'd been attempting to join her, as he had once before, when she'd opened her eyes.

Now she stood with her arms crossed and her back to him, her voice so soft he had to strain to her. She said, "Cassidy's in danger."

Rye's heart jumped in his chest. "What do you mean? I just left her." He spun around, ready to run back the way he'd come.

A gentle hand on his arm stilled him. He stopped, turned. She faced him now, but she was stoic, almost withdrawn. He tried to touch her mind, and found he could not. Because she was closed to him or because he had been shocked to hear her warning?

"Not now," she said. "It happens after the weather turns cold. In my... I was..." She shook her head as if to clear it. "It began to snow. There was a man...or a woman. I couldn't see clearly. Whoever the robed figure was, they had Cassidy trapped in the middle of a strange stone circle."

"Trapped? Trapped how?"

"She was being threatened with a knife."

It was his worst nightmare, that he wouldn't be able to protect her.

"She asked for my help, but I...I couldn't get to her." Echo took a deep, stilling breath and then she looked him straight in the eye. "Why didn't you tell me? I asked you specifically about Cassidy, and you told me you didn't know her. You let me think she was a product of my own imagination."

He'd done more than that. He'd tried to make her forget his daughter. He'd gone into her mind and tried to gently push all thoughts of Cassidy out of it. That particular spell hadn't taken. Because Echo was too strong or because Cassidy had interfered? She did like Echo, for some reason.

How could he explain that he'd been protecting his daughter from Echo's family? He didn't think they would harm her, but they were Raintree and they thought that when it came to those of their kind—the magically gifted—they had free rein. They might want to make her a part of their clan. They might want to study Cassidy; they'd almost surely want to take her away until they were sure she was no danger to them or to others. And if they determined that she was a danger...

His daughter was the magical equivalent of a nuclear bomb. In the wrong hands, she could do a lot of damage. What had happened to the last clan they'd deemed a threat? The Ansara had been wiped out. No, those who called themselves Ansara, who had the blood of that powerful family, had been either killed or *absorbed* into the Raintree clan.

"I see," Echo said in a lowered voice.

"Stop peeking into my head." Why could she see his thoughts when just now hers had been closed to him? His own panic, he supposed. Or else, as he'd suspected, she was now protecting herself from him.

"I can't help it," she said. "It's not all the time, thank goodness, but sometimes it's like you're inside my head whether I want you there or not. There have been times when it was pleasant enough to peek into your head, but…it hurts to hear so very clearly that you don't trust me."

"That's not true. I don't trust your *family*," he clarified.

"Same difference," she said, then she dropped her hand and walked away. She was headed for the boardinghouse, across the street and down a short distance. She didn't run, but there was purpose in her step.

If he didn't stop her she'd climb into her rental car and drive to the airport and be gone. In so many ways that would be for the best. He'd wished for her to go; he'd realized that his life would not be simple again until she was out of it.

In other ways, her leaving would be a terrible loss.

There were others here in Cloughban who could see the future. None were as powerful as Echo, none were called prophet. Still, with their help and with the information he already had to go on he could save Cassidy without her.

But dammit, he didn't want to.

"Stop!" he said in a voice that would carry without being too commanding. He didn't follow her into the street, he didn't chase after her. He knew Echo well enough to understand that if he attempted to physically restrain her she'd just run farther and faster. "Don't leave. Stay."

She turned, but did not backtrack. Her expression was one of determination. There was no weakness there. No softness. No love.

"Don't get sentimental on me, Duncan. It was just sex. There are plenty of other women in Cloughban who would be more than happy to warm your bed. No wonder someone tried to scare me out of town by threatening my family. Someone saw this happening. They saw us. But there is no *us*, is there?"

"I'm not asking you to stay for me," Rye said, his voice rough. On a deep and undeniable level, he knew it had to be her. She was necessary; she was here in Cloughban for a reason. "I'm asking you to help me save my daughter."

Before coming to Cloughban she'd never tried to bring on a vision. It wasn't like she enjoyed them, or could control who or what she'd see. All her life she'd done everything possible to get rid of them, and there had never been any hint of control. What Ryder was asking her to do was impossible. Since she'd arrived he'd been trying to get her to purposely take a glimpse into the future. So far, she'd had no luck.

Of course, she'd also thought it was impossible for her to have a vision about an event that wouldn't take place for days or even weeks. It might be months before there was snow in Cloughban. Snow was not a usual occurrence in Ireland, though it wasn't impossible to get a few flakes, Ryder had said.

What she'd seen had been a full-on winter storm.

They sat at the back corner table, where the trio of old men normally sat. Ryder took her hand, and she grudgingly allowed him to have it.

"The reason you have such a problem controlling your abilities is simple enough, love."

"Don't call me *love*," she snapped. It was impossible to love someone you did not trust.

He sighed and continued. "Fear. Fear colors every vision you experience. Before, during and after, you are afraid. As a result, the visions rule you—you don't rule them."

"I can't…"

"No fear, Echo. *No fear.* You are in control. Past, present, future, you have the ability to see it all if you try. If you wish. If you embrace the visions without fear, then you will control them, not the other way around."

After all this time, didn't he understand her at all? "You wouldn't say that if you'd lived your entire life reliving disasters, seeing and feeling people suffer and die, never being strong enough or fast enough to save them."

He ignored her argument. He clasped her hand tight when she attempted to withdraw it from his. How was she supposed to run away when he held her so? She should not have turned. She should've gone on to the boardinghouse, packed her duffel bag and lit out without looking back.

But she had not.

"What do you wish to see?" Ryder asked. "Where do you want to go? Reach for it. I will help you."

Still weak from the vision of Cassidy, she closed her

eyes. Danger was coming for Cassidy, but at this moment it was Ryder Duncan she wanted to see. Who was he, really? What did he hide from her, other than his daughter and a complete lack of trust?

She did as he asked; she reached for what she wanted with everything she had inside. Instead of fighting her gift she embraced it. For as long as she could remember, she'd approached her ability as if it were a separate entity from herself. A cancerous growth. A parasite. She now knew that wasn't true. It was as much a part of her as the color of her eyes or her love for music.

For a moment, at least, she ruled her gift instead of the other way around. Echo was, at long last, in control. She saw a door ahead, a door she wished to step through. She placed her hand on a cold doorknob. She turned it; she pushed the heavy door open so she could step into a room she had never seen before.

Instead of seeing the present or the future, she went back in time. A scene formed before her, much as the vision of Cassidy had such a short time ago.

Ryder hadn't changed much, but she could tell he was younger. Maybe not much more than twenty. Twenty-five. The scene before her was colorless, gray. The images around Ryder were indistinct, while he remained crystal clear.

As was the knife in his hand and the woman he stabbed through the heart.

Chapter 14

Echo snatched her hand from his and slid out of the booth.

"I can explain," Rye said.

She wasn't surprised that he'd seen what she'd seen. Just like in the vision of the Atlanta fire, he'd been with her, observing.

"I bet you can," she said without slowing her stride. When she was near the door, she stopped, turning to face him. He wanted to chase her but he stayed seated because he knew if he stood she'd bolt from the pub. He didn't want this conversation to take place on the street, where others might hear. How did he look to her from that vantage point? Innocent? No. He wondered if she saw that he had no regrets.

"Who was she?" Echo asked. "Someone who was a threat to you?" *Someone like me?*

No, he had no regrets. Still looking her in the eye, still seated, he said, "She was my wife. Cassidy's mother. Her name was Sybil."

Echo went pale; she took a long step back so that her spine was pressed against the door. She was ready to make a run for it; she was terrified of him and he hated knowing he was the cause of the fear in her eyes. The past was the past, and he'd done his best to leave it there. Unexamined. Unexplained.

He'd never bothered to explain himself to anyone. Had thought he never would. Echo was just a distraction, a bit of fun. He had never fooled himself into thinking that they might have more. He was who he was, and she…she was Raintree. She was also, perhaps, his only chance to identify the threat to Cassidy before it was too late.

As he watched, Echo relaxed. He could see it, feel it. She didn't like what she'd seen—she'd been shocked by it—but she knew him. She accepted him in a way no one else ever had. After she'd taken a moment to think about what she'd seen, she was no longer afraid.

Maybe she should be.

"Did she give you that scar on your chest?" she asked. "Is that why you killed her?"

The truth. Nothing but the ugly truth. "Yes and no. She did stab me, minutes before I killed her, but that's not why I did what I did."

"Why, then?" He saw the flicker of hope in her eyes. She wanted to believe the best of him, but was having a difficult time of it. He couldn't blame her.

Rye stood slowly. He took a step toward Echo, one single long step. She didn't run. He didn't dare get too close, though. She was still uncertain. She wanted to believe in him, but she'd seen a bit of his past that he'd tried, for nine years, to deny. To forget.

"Do you remember how I told you that your powers could be removed but there would be a high price to pay?" He didn't give her a chance to respond. "After Cassidy was born, Sybil begged me to strip away her powers. She controlled fire, but like you she was afraid of her ability and sometimes it got out of control. When Cassidy was nine months old Sybil accidentally burned her. It was a small burn, but the baby screamed and then Sybil screamed." He still heard those screams in his nightmares. Both of them, a nightmare in stereo.

"We were both young, too young to be proper parents, but we did try. What had happened scared us. Terrified us, to be honest. I agreed to strip away Sybil's abilities. I knew it wouldn't be easy. I realized there were risks, but…" He looked at her; she had to know.

"I believed we had no choice, so I did as she asked. I did it for Cassidy, because a child deserves to have a mother who can hold her without fear of what might come of a close embrace." He had tried to shove the memory to the back of his mind, but it came roaring back in vivid detail. "We conducted the ceremony under the full moon, at the right time of night." And in the center of the stone circle, though he wasn't ready to tell her that much.

"It worked, the spell was successful. But as I warned you when you asked me to remove your abilities, there was a cost." A high cost, one he had never expected. "More than her powers were taken. After that night, Sybil was never the same. She no longer controlled fire. She could no longer hurt her child with a touch. But her personality was entirely different, and her memories were muddled. She knew me, but she didn't love me anymore. She was often confused about the smallest things, and the baby…"

He took a deep breath so he could continue. "Cassidy was always special. When she was less than a year old, her favorite toys would drift across the room into her arms. Music, lullabies, drifted out of thin air. Sometimes when she cried, it would rain. In the house." He had been so confused. So…young and lost and alone. To have a daughter who revealed her abilities so young, and so strongly, had turned his life upside down. "Sybil became jealous of the baby. She also missed her own abilities, felt empty without them." The combination had been a deadly one.

The truth. The dark truth he had tried for so long to shove to the back of his mind. "When Cassidy was two, Sybil attempted to take the child's powers for herself. The spell she found and attempted to use required the sacrificial death of her own daughter." He didn't tell her that he'd found them just in time, that Sybil had stabbed him when he'd interfered and then she'd gone for Cassidy.

He didn't tell Echo that he'd spun Sybil around and carried her into the next room of their small cottage before driving the knife through her heart, because he didn't want Cassidy to see her mother die that way. As close as he and Echo were, as easily as her thoughts touched his, perhaps he didn't have to. He tried so hard not to think about that night, not to remember the pain. Did she see?

"If I had to do it again, I would," he said so she would know that he had no regrets.

Echo walked toward him, and he knew her well enough, saw into her strongly enough, to see that her anger and shock had faded. She was no longer afraid of him. She understood in a way no one else ever had. For that alone, he could love her.

She walked into his arms, tipped her face up and kissed him. Gently, tenderly. With love. Her fingers found the scar on his chest and she caressed it through the shirt he wore.

"You still don't trust me," she whispered.

"I don't trust anyone but my daughter," he said honestly.

His statement didn't anger her, didn't hurt her feelings. "I won't tell my cousins or anyone else about Cassidy, I promise you. And I won't tell them about the stones, either."

He grimaced. This was the price he paid for letting her into his heart, into his mind. "You saw them through me?"

"I did." She pressed a warm palm to his chest, directly over the scar. "There are many stone circles in the world. Yours is just one of them. It's a very powerful place. I suppose it's the reason so many gifted people live in Cloughban."

Why lie? She would know. "Yes."

"Do the stones feed your abilities?"

"Yes," he said, waiting for the next question. "They also help me with my own control. I know that sounds odd, that they can make my abilities stronger and at the same time allow me to find that control, but that's the way it's always been."

She leaned in, sharing her body heat, showing him in every way that her short-lived fear was gone. He liked having her there more than he should. No matter how close they were, no matter how connected... she could not stay.

"What exactly are your abilities?" she asked. "You're more than a teacher and a mayor. More than a barkeep and a concerned father. What can you do?"

He sighed before looking deep into her amazing green eyes. "Everything."

* * *

Everything? Impossible. That kind of power would drive anyone insane. But it did explain why he was called wizard, why people traveled from far and wide for his instructions.

Ryder shook his head slowly. "Except out-of-body travel. That's one thing Cassidy can do that I can't."

Out-of-body travel! That explained so much about the two times she'd seen Cassidy. The girl had been there in spirit only. Fascinating...

"The stone and the wristband you wear." Echo waved a finger at her own throat. "They help?"

"They dampen."

Dante and Gideon had worn such talismans; they had fashioned the same for her on more than one occasion. But she knew no one who wore dampening cures constantly. It simply wasn't natural. The power of the objects always—well, almost always—faded with time.

"In my vision, I saw you rip away the stone and toss it aside."

"No," Ryder said sharply. He tensed along the length of his body. "That was wrong. It had to be wrong."

She would admit that since the scene had taken her so far in the future, nothing was certain. Still...

Her mind was spinning; this was almost too much information to take in. *Everything?* What did that mean?

"Last night," Echo began tentatively, "did you... Was it...?"

"Last night was just us."

She relaxed. No matter what had happened to this point, she believed him. "So you haven't used your woowoo on me?"

"I didn't say that."

She sighed and stepped away. As much as she loved

being close to him, as much as she loved holding on, she couldn't let her emotions make her accept anything and everything. Crap!

"Explain, please."

He looked guiltier than he had as he'd explained how he'd killed his wife. "I've influenced you to forget a few things you've seen here. That's all."

"That's *all*?" Her feeling that something was off about this town, the way she had somehow missed the large number of foreigners, the way she occasionally forgot Cassidy. It all made sense now. He'd been poking around in her brain! That was unforgivable. "If you've been playing with my memories, how can I even know what's real?"

"My influence has been minor, I promise you."

Echo crossed her arms, adopting a pose that said, *Stay where you are, buster.* She needed to think about this. She didn't know many people who had the ability to push or remove thoughts from another's mind. It was a rare ability, and there was an unspoken rule about using that ability on friends and family.

She had the distinct feeling Ryder Duncan cared very little for unspoken rules. She calmed herself with the knowledge that he had been protecting his daughter. His daughter and his home. Cassidy didn't need protection from her, but…he hadn't known that.

Echo allowed herself to relax a bit. If Ryder was right about what he could do, he could've made her leave Cloughban at any time. She would've climbed into her rental car and hit the road believing it was her own idea. He could've sent her away and wiped the memory of this place, and him, from her mind. But he hadn't.

"Don't worry," he said. "I'm all but dormant."

All but. That was nonspecific. And insufficient. He

had enough power to join her in a vision, to affect her memories, to send the Cloughban history book flying into his hand. She wouldn't call that dormant, but those talismans were dampening something. *Everything*, he said. How was that possible?

"Why are you *'all but dormant'*?" she whispered.

For the first time since this strange conversation had begun, he looked angry. At her? At life? It was impossible to tell.

"Because I choose to be," he snapped. "The control you need, the mastery over your abilities, there's a reason some come to me to learn. I learned long ago that too much power is not a good thing. Not for me, and certainly not for my daughter. She needs a father, not a resident wizard so enamored of his own powers that he can't…"

"Can't what?" she asked when he faltered.

"Can't love. Not a child, not a woman. The old saying about absolute power corrupting absolutely? It can be true."

Was it true of Ryder? Had he been corrupted?

"Yes," he whispered.

"Get out of my head."

"I can't."

"Use your damned control! You keep telling me how easy it is, use it now!"

"I never said it was easy, and where you're concerned it's damned near impossible."

They couldn't be connected, not like this. He was everything she didn't want! Wanting him physically, enjoying each other in his bed, that was one thing. But to be connected, mind to mind, soul to soul… No. She would never be free of the magical world if she fell in love with a wizard who was damned mayor of a damned enchanted town filled with damned strays!

"Independents," he whispered.

She knew! Somehow the damned Raintree woman knew.

What was the old saying? It's better to ask forgiveness than to ask permission? She would make no more phone calls. She'd not ask for guidance. The time for action was now. Tonight.

Maisy collected her special knife from its hiding place at the back of her dresser drawer. She wadded up the ceremonial robe and stuffed it into an oversize purse. The robe wasn't necessary, but she liked it. When she'd tried it on she'd felt so powerful...so much more powerful than she'd ever been. Her abilities were annoyingly minor. Why have magical powers if they were going to be so insignificant she could barely qualify for a sideshow?

Her father had been able to control all the elements. With a wave of his hand he could control water, fire, earth and wind. Unfortunately, he'd married a woman with no magic at all. He'd spent most of his life hiding who and what he was from the woman he loved.

Maisy had been fifteen when her own abilities had come to life. She'd been shocked, though to be honest there wasn't much about her abilities to inspire fear or amazement. She could control water, to a minor degree. Dishwater in a sink, drinking water in a glass, a narrow stream if she worked very hard.

Bathwater.

After her mother had drowned in the bath, with a little help from Maisy, everything had changed. She'd thought without a mortal woman to influence her powerful father, they could travel the world. He could teach her, train her to be what he was. Powerful. It had worked, for a while. He had tried to train her, for a while.

Unfortunately, he'd eventually figured out what Maisy had done and had been horrified. She'd had no choice but to kill him, too. Her father had always preferred showers to baths, and she'd never been able to figure out how to drown someone in a shower, so she'd taken care of him with a knife. A knife she'd kept near her ever since. It was special. The knife had sentimental value.

After that, Maisy had been on her own for a time, and then she'd found Walsh. He was convinced they'd been drawn together by the powers of the universe, that like called to like. Maybe he was right. Like her, he was hungry for more than he had in his life. More power. More of everything. And he had a plan to get what he wanted.

She couldn't afford to be stopped on her way out of town. Once she had the enhanced powers it didn't matter what everyone knew. They'd all bow to her. Walsh intended to name his clan Ansara, after his mother's people. He intended to call others like him, like her, to Cloughban and take over the village and the surrounding land. People would come, of that she had no doubt. Would they care if they were led by a man who called himself Ansara or would they be satisfied with a woman named Payne? She doubted they would care at all. The Payne clan did have a certain ring to it. Why go back when it was possible to move forward instead?

Walsh intended to take the girl's power for himself, and she had allowed him to go on believing. Why would he think for a minute that she'd stand back and allow him to reap the benefits of this operation, when she'd been the one to do all the work? He wasn't *that* good in bed. No man was. Still, sleep with a man and he became gullible enough to believe anything he was told. That was her experience, anyway.

He couldn't come into Cloughban yet because too many people remembered him from his last visit. Years ago he'd come to Rye for help, as so many before him had done. Walsh had been born with some gifts, but like Maisy he wanted more. Much more. When he'd found out about the girl he'd instantly begun to wonder how he could use her.

It had taken him years to find the spell that would kill Cassidy Duncan and transfer all her powers to the one who wielded the knife. It had taken her just a few weeks to find that spell among his things. She'd searched his room while he slept—drugged just a little bit—and had finally discovered what she needed hidden under the false bottom of a dresser drawer.

He'd actually hidden the most powerful words she could imagine in his sock drawer. What a moron.

When this was over, Walsh Ansara would be answering to her, not the other way around. He could lick her boots and do her bidding, say "Yes, ma'am" when she passed along her instructions. She'd always wanted a lackey, or two. Or a hundred.

If Walsh didn't give her everything she asked for, she'd dispose of him with her newfound powers. She wouldn't need bathwater or a stream. She might rip his heart out or burn him alive. And then…oh, what a life she could have!

In Maisy's fantasies, Rye became the man he'd once been. Dark. Powerful. Heartless. Few here knew who he'd been, what he'd done, but she knew. Walsh knew, too, and he'd been foolish enough to share the information with her. Together she and Rye would rule Cloughban until the new Payne clan grew stronger—thanks to the stones, and thanks to her—and then they'd move beyond this small, insignificant town.

Walsh had used the Ansara name to call a few dark strays to him. His strays were nothing special, nothing at all to write home about. They were far from fierce. But they would do, for now.

Maisy dialed the sat phone again. Why hadn't Walsh been answering his phone? He had to be anxious; they were hours away from the end of his plan. Mere hours!

Chapter 15

Rye never closed the Drunken Stone on a weeknight, but tonight he hung a Closed Until Further Notice sign on the front door and locked it. He called Doyle and told him to take a couple weeks of paid leave. His chief cook and bottle washer didn't seem to mind taking an unexpected bit of time off, though he had sounded surprised.

Of course he was surprised. Everyone would be. Other than Sundays, he could not recall a time when he'd shut the doors to his business.

Alone with Echo, one kiss led to another. And another. They ended up in his bed. Their place. The only place he had known real peace in a very long time. She offered pleasure and comfort. She offered her body, her mind and her soul. Here, in the dark, they could forget everything for a few precious minutes.

He loved her. He couldn't tell her so, couldn't offer her a life here. But he loved her. That was an unexpected awareness he fought hard to hide. He pushed it down, shoved it back. If she saw or sensed his feelings for her she was wise enough—or kind enough—not to mention them. Like him, she had to realize that their relationship, no matter how deep it might go, was temporary.

Curled in his arms, naked and sweating and sated, she sighed. All they had was now, this moment. It wouldn't last. He'd loved Sybil at one time, and look how that had turned out.

"I need a shower in the worst way," Echo said as she disengaged, slowly and reluctantly leaving him and heading for the small attached bathroom. She flipped on the light, illuminating herself. She was picture perfect, nude and shapely and relaxed.

Maybe she wanted some company in that shower.

He joined her under the hot water, scrubbed her back, let her scrub his. He hadn't had many really nice moments in the past few years. Hell, in his entire life. This was one. This was a moment to remember, a memory he'd call back after she was gone.

"I need to try to bring on another vision," Echo said. Water ran down her body, pooled at her feet. "I've never been able to do that, but I am stronger now, and the more we know about what's going to happen…" She shook her head. The tips of her hair were wet, her body gleamed. "I need to figure out how we can save Cassidy. There must be something we can do!"

Echo's vision of a danger to Cassidy was one of the future. He wanted to agree with her that, given the timeline, surely circumstances could be changed. If they could determine a date and a time, they could make sure Cassidy was properly protected. Nothing about the future was certain.

Snow. They wouldn't see snow for months, unless

a freak weather system of some kind moved in. They rarely saw snow here at all.

A shiver walked up his spine. Echo smiled up at him. "If you help me..." she began, and then she went silent. Her smile faded away as she asked, "What's wrong?"

Echo had an untrained and uncontrollable effect on the weather. When she was sad, it rained. When she was happy the skies were clear blue.

Sometimes. Nothing about that particular power was defined. It was new and unpredictable.

Was it possible she could make it snow? What emotion would bring on that kind of weather?

"We have to go," he said, taking her hand and leading her from the shower.

"What's wrong?" she asked again.

Rye threw her a towel and began to dry his body with another. "It was cold, you said, there was snow. But was it a natural snow?"

Echo paled as she read his thoughts. She, too, dried her body vigorously. "Oh, hell, I don't know."

"In your vision, what was Cassidy wearing?"

Echo closed her eyes for a moment, thinking back, searching her memory. Her eyes popped open and she tossed her towel aside, rushing into the bedroom to grab her clothes and start pulling them on with efficiency. As Rye did the same, she described the dress his daughter had been wearing in the vision. Pink-and-yellow flowers, old-fashioned, short sleeves.

It was the same dress she'd been wearing when he'd left her.

Cassidy's first niggle of warning came too late. Her da had warned her, time and again, not to rely on the knowing. She might see things about other people, but when it came to herself and those she loved most dearly, there was a veil. Granny said no one on this earth was meant to know too much about their own path, not the good or the bad.

Someone knocked loudly. Cassidy, who had been reading in her room, stood slowly. She started to call out, "Don't answer!" but she was too late. Her grandmother opened the door.

Cassidy glanced at the window. She could escape by that route, perhaps, but then what? Whoever had come for her had Granny. Granny was old. She didn't have many powers, and she had none that would offer any self-defense. If the person who had come for Cassidy didn't find her, would they take their anger out on Granny?

By the time she decided to go out the window and get help, it was, again, too late. She'd hesitated too long! The door to Cassidy's room opened slowly. *Please be Granny. Please be Granny!* It was not Granny, of course. It was *her*. The woman standing there smiled.

Cassidy remained strong. Crying and begging would not help. Not with this one. She lifted her head and said, in an almost-even voice, "I did not expect you."

"Good." Maisy smiled. "I love the element of surprise. It makes life so much more interesting." Her eyes scanned the room, quickly, efficiently, and then she turned those scary eyes back on Cassidy. "Give me any trouble, and I'll kill your grandmother." She delivered the threat with that weird smile in place and an ordinary tone in her voice. As if she were saying, *I think you'd like this book.* "Then the people I'm working with will go after your friends. The brown-headed boy who always needs a haircut—you like him a lot, don't you?"

Brody! She wouldn't dare...no, she would. She

would, without a second thought. Librarians were not supposed to be evil! It was just wrong.

"I won't give you any trouble," Cassidy said. If she was going to, it's not like she would tell. The librarian said she liked surprises...

"Good. Then the old woman should be fine."

"What about my da?" Cassidy asked.

"We won't hurt your da." Maisy stepped closer.

Instinctively, Cassidy leaned away. The librarian's shields dropped, and her aura changed. Black. There was so much black!

Leaning down, placing her face too close to Cassidy's, the librarian finished with, "Your da's going to become one of us."

They ran. Echo had immediately offered her car, but Ryder insisted the way the roads twisted around to get to the cottage, running—even walking—would be faster.

They ran. His legs were longer than hers so he pulled ahead easily, but she pumped her legs harder in an attempt to keep him in sight. More than once she offered a silent thanks to spin class. Maybe she should've gone to more...

They ran. Echo was too soon breathless, but she didn't stop. Ryder drew ahead of her, but he never left her sight.

She'd barely had time to be angry with Ryder for not telling her the truth about Cassidy, but considering what she'd seen in the vision it was hard to blame him. He was a father protecting his daughter. She could argue that Cassidy didn't need to be protected from her or her Raintree family, but Ryder didn't know that.

She lost sight of him for a moment when he crested a

small hill. What if she went over that hill and he was no-where in sight? How would she know where to go? She topped the hill and there he was, farther ahead than he had been before. Lights from a small cottage glimmered directly before her. The front door stood wide-open. It was a nice enough evening, not too hot or too cold, but somehow she knew the open door was not normal.

Echo reached the cottage a few minutes after Ryder. He knelt beside a woman who was lying on the floor in an unnatural position. As she watched, he cradled her head and lifted it carefully. The woman was still alive, but a deep gash in her head was bleeding badly.

Ryder glanced back at Echo. She could see the pain in his eyes, the anger. "It was Maisy who took my daughter. Help me find her."

Maisy? The librarian? That was wrong on so many levels. Echo shook her head. "How can I do that?" It wasn't near cold enough to snow, and even if she could control the weather with her emotions, it was hardly a gift she'd honed.

Without rising, he offered his hand. She took it.

What she saw in his frantic and disjointed thoughts made her jerk away from him.

"Don't," she whispered.

"That's not what I asked you to see. Where's Cassidy? Where's my daughter!"

"I don't know."

"Is she safe?"

It was the older woman on the floor who said as she tried to sit up, "Cassidy is fine, for now. You will not see her again until the first night of the full moon. To-morrow night."

"I can't leave her with that woman for a full day!"

Ryder shouted. The rafters shook, but the injured woman was unmoved.

"It does not matter what you do or say, you will not see her until that time." The woman grimaced. "Maisy will not harm her until then. She wants…she wants…" Pain and terror filled the woman's eyes. "She wants what Sybil wanted, and she is willing to do…the same."

Echo realized that this woman was Sybil's mother, Cassidy's grandmother. She cared for and loved the child her own daughter had tried to kill. She held the hand of the man who had killed that daughter.

The injured woman continued. "You must find a way to save Cassidy without…" Suspicious eyes cut to Echo. "Without doing what you think must be done."

"There's no need to talk in circles around me," Echo said. "I saw more than enough when I took Ryder's hand."

She didn't want to think about what she'd seen, what might be.

Ryder without control, without the talismans that kept him, as he said, dampened.

Without the stone at his neck and the leather band at his wrist, Ryder Duncan was a monster.

Chapter 16

Rye called Bryna's gentleman friend to collect and care for her. He refused to tell McManus anything about what had happened, and so did Bryna. Fortunately, the old man was accustomed to keeping secrets, and did not balk when others protected their own.

It was odd to see the man he normally knew as one of three friends who drank together and told bad jokes and argued about politics in this position. McManus held Bryna's hand. He comforted her, and did not press to know more as he helped her pack a small bag. He walked out the front door with that bag in one hand and Bryna's arm caught in the other.

There was no sound of an engine after they'd disappeared from view. They would walk. McManus's little cottage was not far away.

With Bryna in good hands, Rye was free to concentrate on his daughter and her kidnapper. Was Maisy working alone, or did she have an accomplice? Or two, or twenty? He didn't know what he was up against, and he did not dare ask anyone in Cloughban for help. He would have trusted Maisy, if Bryna hadn't told him what she'd done. Why hadn't he seen the danger for himself? What other truths hid from him?

He fingered the stone that lay heavy at his throat. Once he removed the talismans he'd know without doubt whom he could trust. He would see all.

Echo stood silently near the door. Poised to run? He couldn't blame her. This was not her mess, not her concern. Bryna and McManus were long gone when he finally looked squarely at her and said, "Go."

She shook her head. Stubborn woman.

"I don't need you," he insisted.

"Yes, you do."

He was going to have to be blunt with her. Could he lie well enough to fool her? He tried. "I don't want you here."

Again she answered softly, "Yes, you do."

He'd been so afraid of the Raintree coming in and taking his daughter, he'd missed the signs of betrayal under his nose. His own people. A Cloughban resident, someone he knew, had made his worst fear come true.

He didn't think for a moment that Maisy was working alone. She wasn't that smart, or that powerful.

If she took Cassidy's abilities, she'd be more than powerful enough.

"I have to stop her, no matter what. I will sacrifice myself." His voice was sharp when he added, "I will sacrifice you if I have to. If I think for even a moment that it will help to offer you up, I won't hesitate. You're Raintree, after all. A prophet, and more. If they would take you in exchange for Cassidy, I would hand you over without a second thought."

Instead of running out the door as she should've, Echo walked toward him, took his hand and sat on the love seat. She drew him down beside her, and he let her. She was warm, soft, much calmer than he was.

It wasn't *her* daughter in the hands of a traitor.

"Of course you would," she said in an even voice. "I'd expect nothing less from a father who loves his child dearly."

"I should look for Cassidy tonight, no matter what Bryna says." He said the words, but he did not stand.

Echo's response was clear and too damn calm. "You won't find her."

He looked at her, this small, pretty, deceptively powerful woman who had come into his life and blown it apart. Everything in his life had been just fine, before she'd shown up. Was she a part of this?

You know I'm not.

Her words were clear. In his head, a whisper no one else could hear. He responded in kind.

I should do something. Anything.

She's fine. She's unharmed and she is not afraid. Cassidy is strong, like you.

You can't be sure.

I am.

With that the connection was broken. Echo leaned into him, placed her head on his shoulder.

Why couldn't he establish a mental connection with Cassidy the way he had with Echo? He could if he...

Echo's hand closed over his, drew it down from his throat and the stone there. He thought she would try to convince him that it wasn't necessary that he undo all he'd done. He thought she'd plead with him not to go to that dark place.

Instead, she simply whispered, "Not yet."

Echo had dozed on the love seat, curled against Ryder. She was almost positive he had not slept at all.

"Did you dream?" he asked as she came awake.

"Yes."

"Did you dream of Cassidy?" His voice was so stoic it was almost dead, and that scared her.

"I did, but I saw nothing new." Just another horrifying dream of snow and a sharp blade and Ryder becoming something dark. She could not make herself see anything beyond that point. Maybe because what had happened beyond that point had not yet been determined. She patted his hand, noting as she did that he continued to wear the leather wrist band. She glanced up. He wore the stone at his neck, as well. She didn't really need to look. When they were gone she would know it. She'd see and feel it. "You should sleep."

"No, I should not." He turned his head and looked down at her. "Go. Go now. Take your rental car and drive to Shannon, and get on the next plane to the States."

It was tempting. She'd be lying if she said it wasn't. The girl she had once been would've done just that without being told. She would've washed her hands of this family that wasn't hers, of this trouble that wasn't hers, and in a matter of hours she'd be on a plane headed out of here.

That girl had never known love. The woman she had become did. Funny, she'd always thought love would be all flowers and beauty and fun. Tra-la-la, love songs all around. Ha. So far, it was anything but.

"You need me here," she insisted.

"I don't need you or anyone else."

Her feelings should be hurt, but she understood Ryder's pain. More than that, she felt it. For once, experiencing the pain of another didn't make her want to run and hide. "Someone has to make it snow," she said lightly.

"I can make it snow, once I've...once I remove the talismans."

She experienced yet another pain. He should never have to make that decision, should never have to become someone he'd left behind years ago in order to save his child. That old Ryder...that wasn't a man she ever wanted to meet.

But saying that now wouldn't make things any better. She kissed Ryder on the cheek, surprising him, and then she released his hand and jumped up. "I hope there are eggs. That's pretty much all I know how to cook."

"I'm not hungry."

"You'll eat," she said confidently.

The kitchen was small but very well organized, and there were indeed eggs. Some kind of thin ham, too. She wished she knew how to make scones, but she didn't. Eggs and ham would have to do. Maybe there was some leftover bread she could toast. Echo didn't bother to look up when she realized Ryder had followed her into the kitchen. He stood in the doorway and watched her.

"Don't argue with me," she said. "In my vision it's snowing when you take that thing off. To my knowledge, I've never been wrong. Unless you can make it snow now, before you..." Change? Transform? Go dark? She wasn't sure what to call it. "Well, you know. Unless you can do it now, then I'll still be around tonight."

"My mother was a Gypsy."

Echo turned to face him then, and though it was hard, she smiled. "I know. I saw the look in you the day we met."

He did not look surprised. To be honest, his expression remained so blank it was impossible to tell if he felt anything at all. "My father took a lot of grief for marrying her, rather than one of their own, but I suppose he loved her. One of my earliest memories is of her teaching me a spell. I didn't have quite enough power to suit her, so she supplemented my mental powers through her own kind of magic. I could control all the elements by the time I was eight. The way her face lit up when I did something extraordinary...I lived for those moments.

"Unfortunately for her, I didn't remain a child who was willing to perform for his mother's approval. I studied on my own, and I grew stronger every day." He caught and held her eye. "I can shift into any animal, make you see and believe anything I wish you to see and believe. A little snow? All it would take is a snap of my fingers."

"What happened?"

"Why do you assume something happened?"

"Because if everything was hunky-dory, I doubt you would have gone to the bother to suppress all those abilities."

The moment of silence that followed that statement was almost palpable. He was deciding what to tell her, how much, how little. With a push she might be able to see for herself, but she wanted him to tell her. She wanted him to trust her.

Finally, he spoke. "You know the saying about absolute power corrupting absolutely?"

She nodded.

"It's true," he said in a lowered voice. "The people

around you seem less than human, because they're so weak. It doesn't matter if someone gets hurt, and if someone dares to get in your way, you'll squash them like a bug. They won't be missed."

It was a bleak picture, one he painted too well. "Who died?"

"More than one," he whispered.

She turned to look at him, gave him her full attention. She should be horrified, but she was not. This was Ryder. He loved his daughter and would do anything for her. Echo was almost convinced that he loved her, too. Almost. He was not a man who could kill people because they got in his way.

"Tell me," she whispered. *Tell me everything.*

For a long moment he remained silent, and she thought he might not say another word. He was torn. Tormented. She could say, *Never mind*, or push him to go on, but instead she simply waited. He would get there in his own time, or he would not.

Finally, he spoke. "Before I married Sybil, I left Cloughban to work for a man who promised me money and power and women. Everything a young man wants and needs." Was that a smile? No, it was a grimace that offered her a glimpse of the man he had once been. "All I had to do was help him get rid of a few men who stood in his way. Bad men all, but that doesn't matter, does it? I killed them. We took their ill-gotten gains."

"How many?" she whispered.

"Three."

"How old were you?"

"Nineteen."

So young. So damned young. It was hard to imagine Ryder as a teenager. Even harder to see him as vulnerable and easy to manipulate. Obviously that's what had happened. She didn't expect that he'd been an angel, but he hadn't been a devil, either. He'd been twisted. Used.

"Where was your family?" Why hadn't they helped him? Saved him?

"My parents were both dead. I lived with my uncle, my father's brother." Ryder's jaw hardened, and so did his eyes. "He was never able to handle me. My uncle was not what you'd call a powerful man. He was an empath, but nowhere near as strong as you."

She nodded. He'd been basically alone. "What happened to this man who hired you?" she asked. "Where is he now?"

Ryder glanced down, then up again to look her in the eye. "I killed him. In all fairness, he was trying to kill me at the time."

"And since then..."

"I returned to Cloughban, determined to leave that life behind." Ryder was wound so tight, she suspected this story did not have a happy ending. "I came home and went to work for my uncle. He owned the pub back then. I tried to make up for the difficulties I had caused him. Most of all, I tried to leave all the darkness behind me and embrace a simpler life."

Out of all that, one word stood out. "Tried?"

Ryder shrugged, and again he looked away from her. "I was still...who I was. Drunk on power, able to do and have and be anything I wished to be. After a few months my uncle and I started fighting again. I was planning to leave Cloughban, to move to a place where no one knew me, where I could truly start over. But then I met Sybil and I stayed here for her. She was beautiful and funny, and she loved me. I thought I loved her, the way a young man will. I did love her, for a while."

She should not feel even an inkling of jealousy over

a dead woman, but what Echo felt at that moment was definitely jealousy. He had loved her...

"That almost sounds like the end, but I'm pretty sure it's not."

His jaw tightened, his eyes went hard. Dark. "No, it was not the end. My uncle was the last of the Duncans, other than myself. He didn't like Sybil. Looking back, maybe he saw what she would become. We'll never know." His hands clenched into fists. Was it a trick of the light that the wide leather band on his right wrist shimmered? Maybe. Maybe not. "When I told him I was marrying her, we argued. He forbade the marriage. I shouted in indignant rage. His heart exploded in his chest as every lightbulb in the pub exploded."

She could see it too well, almost as if she'd been there. His uncle, the empath, had absorbed all that rage and it had killed him. "It was an accident."

"Was it? He wasn't like the others I'd killed. He wasn't a bad man who'd profited from the suffering of others. He was standing in the way of what I wanted, and he died. Sybil and I had planned to leave Clough-ban, to travel after the marriage. This is no place for a powerful wizard. We were thinking London, maybe Paris. With my powers we could make a fortune in no time, and if anyone got in my way...well, their hearts could explode, too."

Much as she cared for him now, she would not have liked the boy he had been. Ambitious, power hungry, willing to kill... "But you stayed."

"I had no choice. I was the last of the Duncans, destined to be keeper of the stones and leader of these people."

"And this?" She waved a finger at her own throat.

He touched the stone, which rested just beneath the

collar of his gray shirt. "I made these talismans for myself the day Cassidy was born. I had tried for a while to simply keep my abilities in check, but all too often I was tempted to use them. They're like a drug. The more I use them, the more I want to use them. Why not? Why let such talent go to waste?"

Echo tried to keep her voice light, even while inside she felt anything but. "So, it was like walking to work when you had a Ferrari parked in your garage."

"I suppose."

She turned her back to Ryder and whipped the eggs vigorously, putting all her frustration and anger into working the eggs into a frothy mixture. She didn't want him to go dark, didn't want him to be without those protective talismans. But she'd seen it; she'd seen him become the man who was willing to kill.

She had to ask, "So, why not save Cassidy and then put the protective shields back on again?"

He didn't say anything until the long moment of silence intrigued her and she turned to face him again. Then, while she was looking into his dark eyes, he told her the truth.

"I'm afraid I won't want to."

Chapter 17

The librarian was being very nice to her, but Cassidy wasn't fooled. Even though her ability to know what was coming didn't extend to herself, she understood that Maisy was not her friend. No matter how much she smiled her creepy smile.

Maisy had come to the school. She had visited at least once a week, smiling and talking about wonderful stories of adventure and family and animals. She'd recommended books from the town library, and Cassidy had loved some of those books! How could someone who loved books be evil? It didn't seem right. How had she fooled everyone? Someone should've known, but somehow she'd hidden all that black in her aura too well. The town librarian was like a villain out of one of the books she recommended.

In books, the good guys always won, but this was real life, and Cassidy was not so sure that's how it would end.

Twice Cassidy had attempted to travel out of body to tell her da where she was, but Maisy must've put shields around the room to keep her contained. She could manage some defense if it came to that, but she was weakened here. She couldn't even read the librarian's mind, not even a little bit. Besides, Maisy said a friend had her grandmother and would kill her if she didn't cooperate. She'd also threatened her good friend Brody *specifically*. It was impossible to know if she was telling the truth or not, but Cassidy wouldn't gamble with her family or friends.

Her da had always warned her that not everyone in the world was her friend, that there were evil people out there who would love to use the powers she'd been born with for their own selfish reasons if they got the chance. Cassidy had always nodded and said she understood, but she hadn't, not really. Not until now.

Maisy brought her a hot ham sandwich and a glass of water at what must be lunchtime. Cassidy tried again to peek into the woman's mind, but like the room it was shielded. She pushed a bit and got nothing. So she simply asked, "What are you going to do to me?"

"Don't worry about it, dear," Maisy said in a weirdly friendly voice. "After tonight you won't have to worry about anything at all."

Well, that was good news… Wait, no, it wasn't!

Her da and Granny didn't think she remembered what her own mother had attempted so long ago. Even though Cassidy had only been two years old at the time, she did have a memory of that night. It was vague, pictures without words, but over time she'd come to understand.

Her mother had tried to kill her so she could take her

abilities. A knife, a few powerful words. Blood spilled.
She knew from the few occasions Granny had spoken about her daughter, Sybil, that at that time she'd
not been right in the head. Duh. No mother who was
right in the head would kill her own daughter, not for
any reason.

Maisy, the librarian, was not her mother. Neither was
she quite right in the head.

Echo tried to get Ryder to eat and sleep, but he would
do neither. He did eat a few bites of egg early in the
day, but he'd had to choke those down and did not care
to try again. His worry poured from him in waves that
almost knocked her down.

She felt his worry to the bone because she loved him.
Maybe she had loved him all along, and that was why
he'd been so damned annoying in those early days. She
didn't want to fall in love with someone like him. Not
just a man who possessed his own magic, but a man
who was surrounded by it. Magic wasn't just a part of
his life, it *was* his life.

As far as her dream man list went, he ticked none
of the boxes. Well, the physical ones, yes—he was tall,
dark and handsome—but in addition to his own abilities he had a daughter who was an extremely powerful
child. Echo had decided a long time ago that she didn't
want kids of her own. What if she was no better a parent than her own? What if her child suffered as she had
suffered? She sure didn't want a hand in raising someone else's gifted child. Especially not one like Cassidy,
who would need constant guidance.

Did that make her a bad person? She didn't think so.

She had a list. Ryder and his daughter did not meet any of her requirements.

Except that he was beautiful and they were compatible in bed. And he made her heart beat fast and hard. She wanted to be with him, to be a part of his life. She wanted to take away his pain even if that meant taking it on herself. Dammit, love didn't pay any attention at all to her lists!

Even Cassidy was adorable, loving and sweet. It wasn't her fault she was special.

Echo had seen the darkness in Ryder when he'd invited her in and she'd touched his hand and his mind. When he was all powerful he cared for no one and nothing. He was ruthless. He was dangerous. He was a man who would do anything in order to get what he wanted.

Great. Another bad boy. All this time she'd planned to find herself a decent, nice man who didn't even believe in prophets.

Coming here had shown her a new side of herself, and she knew now that the abilities she possessed could not be denied. She couldn't wish or work them away. All she could hope for was to learn to control them.

She'd never wished for more magical abilities, but at this moment, she did. More than anything, she wanted to take away Ryder's pain.

He sat in the small living room, staring into space, staring at nothing and no one. She'd tried to bring on a vision, had tried to find Cassidy for him, but it wasn't working. The power she'd wished so hard to be rid of was being stubborn.

She sat beside him. His body stiffened. He withdrew from her physically and mentally. Echo was persistent.

Some might call it stubborn, but she knew what she wanted and she wasn't going to back down. She leaned into Ryder and placed her hand on his chest.

What this moment called for was a rush of optimism. "When this is done, I think the three of us deserve a vacation," she said. "Where do you want to go?"

He didn't answer.

She wasn't about to give up so easily. "Where would Cassidy like to go?"

"Cassidy would like to go to Disney World," Ryder said in a lifeless voice.

"I haven't been in years. We should…"

"I can't take Cassidy away from Cloughban until she's older and in complete control of her abilities."

"Maybe you could bind her with talismans, as you've done for yourself. Just for a week or two. It could work."

"Maybe. Maybe not. You don't know what she's capable of." Ryder looked down at her. "You don't know what I'm capable of."

Now was not the time or place to tell him that she loved him. Later, when all was well. When Cassidy was safe and home again, when Maisy had been taken care of, one way or another. Did Ryder know? Did he feel her love? She tried to peek into his head, but could not. Not because there was nothing to see, but because he was hiding his thoughts from her.

Rye couldn't sleep. The day had passed so excruciatingly slowly he began to think that somehow time had stopped, that this was a nightmare from which he would never escape. His worst fears were coming to pass. Cassidy was in danger, and he couldn't help her.

But the minutes did tick past. He saw it in the clock,

and in the movement of the sun. His time would come; he would be there for Cassidy. More than once he tried to send Echo away, but she refused to go.

He didn't want her to see what he would become in order to save his daughter. He didn't want her around if he couldn't manage to rein in the darkness once Cassidy was safe. What he had been, unleashed, might never be dampened again. Those powers had been bottled up so long, he did not know what to expect when the talismans were removed.

If he couldn't save his daughter, he knew he would never be right again. If she died, if Maisy succeeded, he would have no reason to return.

A time or two Echo had tried to peek into his mind, but he blocked her. It wasn't easy, but neither was it impossible. Eventually she stopped trying.

It was a warm day, all too slowly turning into a warm evening. It was far too warm for snow. Was it possible that Echo's vision—which had been much farther in the future than her normal episodes—was not entirely correct? That vision was all he had to go on. The stones, snow, Maisy and Cassidy at the center of it all.

Where would Echo be as he ran toward his daughter, tearing off the talismans as he raced through falling snow? Ahead of him? Behind him? She hadn't said. Maybe she didn't know.

He stood in the open doorway of the cottage and watched the sun set. Soon, but not soon enough, it would begin. And end.

He heard and felt Echo approach long before she placed a gentle hand on his back. "When it's done, come back to me."

He knew very well that she wasn't talking about a physical return.

"I don't know that I can." After being restrained for so long, would dampening that part of himself be possible? It wouldn't be easy. A part of him would rejoice at the return of power. A part of him would fight to remain, after being smothered for so long.

"Do it for Cassidy." She drifted closer. He felt her heat, felt her emotion. "Do it for me."

Darkness fell while they stood in the doorway waiting. Waiting. He knew what he had to do.

"I will do nothing for you, Raintree. I don't care for you at all," he said, his voice low and cold. "I never did."

She didn't believe him, not right away.

"You're pretty enough, you were handy, and to be honest when I need release it's best not to get involved with a local girl who might be foolish enough to think a night or two in my bed means something more. Face it, you needed to get laid as much as I did. Did you really think it was anything more than that?"

Her hand fell away.

He'd blocked his mind from her, but she was an empath. She'd sense his emotions no matter how hard he tried to hide them. So he thought of Sybil and how she'd tried to kill her own daughter. He thought of Maisy, and what he'd do to her when he got his hands on her. She was going to burn for taking Cassidy. She would suffer before she died.

He filled his heart with hate for those two women. He embraced the darkness that was a part of him— long buried or not—until there was no love in his heart.

"You were convenient, Raintree. Pretty, willing and temporary." He turned to look at her. "For God's sake, go away."

She didn't say a word, but he felt the temps drop. She

believed him. Cold air swirled around him, and around her, as her heart broke.

Beyond the doorway where they stood, side by side but no longer together, it began to snow.

Chapter 18

Echo walked away from the cottage. She walked, and then she ran. She wasn't wanted here. What an idiot she'd been! Thank goodness she hadn't told Ryder that she loved him. He probably would've laughed at her.

She'd been so sure he felt more, but...her empathic abilities were new. Maybe she had felt what he'd wanted her to feel so she'd...

Those thoughts had to go, before they stopped her in her tracks. Focus on the positive, if there was any. She'd accomplished all she'd come here to do. She had learned some control, could now recognize when a vision was coming. No more dropping to the ground without warning. She'd also learned some control within those visions. Maybe she'd no longer feel as if she were right there in the disaster, but could remain an observer. An observer who could help, if the timing was right.

That was all well and good, but it didn't make her feel any better.

She'd walked from the cottage Ryder had left, too, headed in another direction. Toward the stones, she assumed. She had not been brave enough to see if he glanced back toward her. He was focused on saving his daughter, as he should be.

Echo was freezing, and it was her own fault. She had brought on the cold, the snow. Snow and frozen rain fell in fits and starts. She hugged herself in an attempt to keep warm. Now she knew what emotion could bring on snow.

Heartbreak. Desolation. The complete loss of hope.

Cassidy popped into her path, not five feet ahead. Echo stumbled to a halt, her heart almost bursting out of her chest.

"Where are you going?" Cassidy asked harshly.

"Home, I guess."

"No!"

She wanted to hug the little girl, to offer some kind of comfort, but Cassidy wasn't really here. Not in body, anyway. Echo understood that much now. "Your father will save you."

"I know he will." Cassidy rolled her eyes in that maddening way young girls do. "But who's going to save *him*? That's your job. I can't do everything myself!"

For a moment, the snow stopped. The cold remained, but it was not so sharp and cutting. "Why didn't you come to us this way earlier? Why didn't you show yourself to your father? If you'd told us where you were…"

"I couldn't," Cassidy said, clearly exasperated. "Maisy had a spell on the room. I couldn't do *anything*."

"Where are you now?"

"Almost to the stones. Da's coming, I can feel him, but…I need you, too. I need you to save him, if you can, if you…"

And then Cassidy was gone, without warning. Without even finishing her sentence. That couldn't be good.

Echo had never been to the stone circle before, didn't even know what direction to take to get there. Ryder had headed east when he'd left the cottage, but that was not nearly specific enough. There were miles and miles of wide-open fields, and many gentle hills that hid what lay ahead.

Echo closed her eyes. She reached for the source of power, for Cassidy...for Ryder. When she opened her eyes she was surprised to see a trail of flickering lights low to the ground. Twinkling, dancing, yellow and blue and pink and lavender, they lit the way.

For a moment, Echo held her breath. Fairies? Oh, hell, no. Must be Cassidy's doing.

It didn't matter who—or what—lit the way. She had to find her way to the stones. To Ryder. Echo began to run. The flickering lights in her path broke apart as she ran through them, then flew ahead to keep the line going. As far as she could see, those twinkling lights lit her way.

Maybe Ryder didn't want her. Maybe he would never again be the man she'd fallen in love with.

But she was meant to be there, to help. To save him, if she could. If he would allow it.

Was she wasting her time trying to find him? There had been no love in Ryder when he'd left the cottage to save his daughter. No love, no hope at all. All she'd sensed from him was disdain for her and a dark determination. Still, she had to try. Cassidy needed all the help she could get. Echo ran, and once again snow began to fall.

The sight was just as Echo had described it. The stone circle, the snow, Maisy and Cassidy.

Maisy wore a dark ceremonial robe with a deep hood. She held a knife in her right hand. Cassidy was close to her, much too close. The knife was raised in the air, ready to swing.

He was not close enough, not yet.

Rye shouted; he roared as he stripped the leather cuff from his wrist. That was enough to wash him in a touch of forgotten power. It felt good, better than anything he could remember. He yanked the stone from his throat and tossed it aside, and the remainder of his long-locked-away powers returned. They rushed through him fast and sure. He'd been asleep for years, and now he was awake. He'd been sleepwalking; he'd been weak. He was weak no more.

Rye saw nothing but Maisy as he ran, moving faster than he should be able to. Seeing everything around and before him sharper, *clearer*, as if until now his life had been out of focus. She heard him, turned, smiled widely.

In the blink of an eye, he took on some of the powers of a panther. More speed, more lithe strength. His teeth became fangs, his hands claws. Maisy, who had been momentarily entranced, lost her smile. Perhaps she knew that he intended to rip her to pieces.

She turned and the knife she held swung down and into Cassidy.

No!

The knife swung not into Cassidy but *through* her. His daughter was playing out of body again. *Good girl.*

Maisy had no more time. Rye slammed into the evil woman at full force; he grabbed her arms and pushed her out of the circle and away from his daughter before knocking her to the ground. She landed on her back, hard, losing her breath for a moment. Once she'd recovered she looked up at him, wide-eyed and looking like a bleedin' librarian, not an evil witch.

How dare she threaten his daughter!

Prone, vulnerable, she dared to speak. "We could be good together, Rye. You and me, and Cassidy. We can be a family like no other. Look at you," she whispered. "Half animal, half man, all dark power and so, so beautiful."

He barely listened. The woman on the ground was nothing. She was no one. Without warning she swung the knife she continued to hold in one pale hand, aiming for his ankle, trying to bring him down.

She wasn't fast enough. Not nearly fast enough. With one swipe at her throat with a hand that still possessed the claws of the animal she'd admired, Maisy was dead. The knife she'd managed to hold on to all that time dropped to the ground. The silver soaked up the power of the nearby stones; the blade shimmered, it danced and then it went dark. Dead. As dead as the woman.

Rye resumed his complete human form with a minimum of effort. No more fangs, no more claws. The power he had reclaimed remained, rushing through his blood. For the first time in years, he felt alive.

The snow stopped, but flakes had gathered on Maisy's face and on her dark robe. Dead she looked… surprised.

He'd wanted her to suffer for what she'd done, but her death had come too quick, too easy. Not satisfied simply to kill the woman who had dared to threaten his daughter, Rye waved his fingers and sent a stream of white-hot flame at her body. Fire lit the night, illuminated the landscape before and around him. It took only seconds for the traitor to burn to ash.

With a twist of his hand he lifted the ash from the

ground, creating a small whirlwind. He sent the dancing ash high, propelled it into the night sky until there was literally nothing left of Maisy.

Rye turned back to the circle. An alarmed Cassidy—not really Cassidy—disappeared.

Where was she? Close? Far? He knew she could manifest from a goodly distance, but she couldn't have gone too far. Maisy wouldn't have had her eyes off the prize for more than a few seconds. He returned to the center of the stone circle and turned about. Twice. His eyes scanned the shadows, the darkness. In an angry panic, he called her name. Nothing. No Cassidy.

He'd scared her; he'd revealed a part of himself that had been hidden for all her life. Taking a deep breath, reaching for calm, he commanded his daughter to show herself. Warily, she stepped out from behind the tallest stone.

"Da?" she asked, her voice trembling.

His daughter was so powerful, so amazingly special. Why had he kept her hidden away in this place? Together they could have anything, do anything. Money, power…what else was there worth having?

Love.

That thought was not his own.

He turned to watch Echo approach. He'd let his guard down and she'd slipped into his head. Again. Raintree bitch. She made him weak. She wanted him to be the shell of a man he'd been for so many years. He'd never again limit himself that way. Why had he ever allowed himself to be so weak?

"I thought I told you to go," he growled.

"You did. I started to obey, I really did try. To be honest I've never been very good at obeying. I had to make sure Cassidy was all right."

With a power he'd all but forgotten racing through his blood, Rye realized that Echo was a threat. She was, perhaps, the only person who stood between him and everything the darkness wanted.

"She's fine, as you can see. Go."

"No."

"I'll rip out your throat," he said in a calm voice. "I've done that once tonight and now I have a taste for it. Will you die as quickly and easily as Maisy did?"

She should be terrified, but she was not. Echo looked past him; she looked to Cassidy. "Your granny is coming to get you."

"She's close. I see her," Cassidy said too softly.

"Run to meet her. I'll take care of your da."

Rye watched his daughter run away. She was scared of him, but that wouldn't last. When she realized what they could do together, what they could have...

Echo walked into the circle. She was powerful, too, but what she possessed was nothing next to him and his daughter. He could not allow her to get in his way.

"If you know what's good for you, you'll turn around," he warned.

"I've never been very good at knowing what's good for me, either." She smiled. Smiled!

"You asked me once, more than once, to take away your powers. I can do that, here and now." That act would wipe away who she was, perhaps even her memory of him and her idea that she should be here. It would remove any hint they were connected. The way the power was washing through him, he'd likely kill her in the process, or at the very least leave her brain-dead.

She walked up to him, placed a hand against his chest as she so often had. Her palm rested against the scar too near his heart.

Rye reminded himself that the last woman he'd loved had tried to kill him. Had almost succeeded. This one was as much of a threat as Sybil had been. Perhaps more of a threat.

"I can do it," he said. "I can take it all away."

She responded, still far too calm, "Whatever you think is best, love."

He placed the palm of his right hand against her temple.

His eyes were wrong, and she still couldn't see into his mind the way she once had. She felt his emotions, though, and they were strong. Hate, fear, ambition, lust and somewhere, buried deep, love. He'd done his best to deny that love earlier, but she saw it now. She felt it.

"I love you," Echo whispered.

"You're a fool."

"Am I? I don't think so, not anymore. I think maybe love is the only thing worth living for." And dying for, she supposed. Not that she wanted to die.

The hand that had been pressed to her temple dropped away.

"I'll show you what you think is love, Raintree." Ryder was rough as he pulled her shirt over her head. She lifted her arms to assist him. "Sex, that's all it is. You could be replaced by any woman, and I could be replaced by any man. Did you really think there was more to it than that?"

"Yes." She knew there was more. "I love you."

"You fooled yourself into thinking you love the man I used to be."

"The man you still are."

He unfastened her jeans and pushed them down. She kicked off her shoes and stepped out of them.

She stood naked in the center of the stone circle that gave Cloughban—White Stone—its name. By day the stones themselves would be an ordinary gray, but by the light of the full moon they were gleaming white. She felt the energy in the stones, in the ground, in the air. It was good energy, white magic. The only darkness here was within Ryder.

"I love you," she said again.

"Stop saying that!"

"Why? They're just words, unless you give them meaning with your heart as I have." She leaned into Ryder, went up on her toes and kissed him gently.

He stiffened, but he did not move away.

The stone circle sat upon an unimpressive plot of land with a pond to the north and a field to the west. It was far from any cottage, and on this night it was far from prying eyes. Anyone touched with magic would sense the danger here. They would sense the danger Ryder had become and stay away. She was the only one around who didn't have the sense to flee.

Most people didn't realize that Stonehenge wasn't the only stone circle in the world. Not by a long shot. It was just the most well-known. The Cloughban stones were smaller, but the circle here was just as ancient and every bit as powerful.

The clouds that had brought the snow drifted away, broke up to reveal the dark sky above filled only with countless stars and a bright full moon.

Lightning danced on Ryder's fingertips, fire flickered along his arms and in a circle around their feet. The heart of a panther beat within his chest. He could rip her apart as he had Maisy, but he wouldn't. She believed that with all her heart.

"You might not admit yet that you love me, but you do want me."

He didn't deny it.

"I knew you were trouble from the moment I saw you." Echo kept her voice low, even though there was no one around to hear. "I walked into the pub, took one look at you and almost gave up then and there."

"You should have."

"I'm glad I didn't." She slipped her hand beneath his shirt, pushed it high, helped him remove it. Then she moved her hands to his jeans. He didn't fight her efforts. In fact, he helped.

Soon Ryder was as naked as she was. He laid her on the ground, roughly, but not as roughly as she'd thought he might.

"I love you," she whispered.

"You're a damned broken record," he growled. "This is not love." With that he was inside her, pushing, claiming. He moved fast and hard, without a hint of gentleness. She welcomed him, cradled him, offered softness and love where he believed there was none.

The breeze that washed over her was warm and smelled of the ocean. *Impossible.* That was the scent of home…and a very real indication that *this* was now home. Ireland, Cloughban…Ryder.

"Deny it all you want, love," she said. "I'm yours. You're mine."

At that, he did slow. His entire body relaxed. Echo closed her eyes and tilted her head when he moved his mouth to her neck and kissed there. They were still one, still joined, but now there was more. He was as warm as she was. Warmer. The darkness was still there, but it stepped back. It faded. For her…just for her.

The world didn't stop, not entirely, but it slowed

down. There was only him, and her, and the way they fit together. And pleasure. Oh, yes, there was pleasure, sharper and deeper than any she had ever known. When she tried to tell Ryder again that she loved him, the words were all but unintelligible.

She climaxed quickly, too quickly, screaming as she lost all control.

And then he came with her, and on the fading waves of her own climax visions not her own filled her swimming head.

Fire.

Illusion.

Lightning.

The snarl of an animal.

Darkness.

And beneath it all, light.

Chapter 19

He fought. In his mind, his heart, in the blood that rushed through his veins. Rye was at war with himself. A few minutes ago his life, his plans, had seemed so simple. All he needed was Cassidy. Together they would have anything and everything they wanted...

Now, still inside her, still a part of her, he wanted Echo, too. He wouldn't call this love; he didn't believe in love, but he did want her.

Naked, entangled in the center of the stones, he said, "Come with us. You, me, Cassidy... We can have it all."

She sighed; her warm chest rose and fell. "You're an idiot. You already have it all."

He shouldn't allow her to talk to him that way, but... he let the infraction slide. For now. So much had happened in such a short time. He was free. Cassidy was safe. Echo was here. His. Knowing who he was and what he'd done, she still offered herself to him. Body, heart and soul.

He rolled away. Touching her was a weakness. "We have nothing, not yet," he said. "In time, we can rule the world."

She laughed. Laughed! Then she rose and looked at him. Naked and beautiful in the moonlight, flushed with pleasure, she was tempting. Still. Again.

Her smile remained as she said, "You know, in comic books and movies villains always want to rule the world. But really, what do they expect to do with it once it's theirs? Ruling the world just sounds like a lot of trouble to me. One problem after another."

He pushed her down, pinned her wrists to the ground and asked harshly, "What do you want?"

In spite of her vulnerable position, she smiled at him with what she thought was love.

"Easy," she said. "I want you. I want music and, one day, I want babies. I didn't think I wanted kids at all. Even earlier today… But I've changed my mind. Life is so short, so fragile." She sighed and said again, "I want babies. I want to laugh and make love and occasionally just sit back to watch a particularly beautiful sunset. I normally miss the sunrise, but I'm sure they're beautiful, too. Maybe I can learn to get up early enough to see it now and then."

That was ridiculous. Small and unimaginative. "You can have anything."

Her smile faded. "Anything?"

"Yes!"

"Love me."

Rye rolled away and grabbed his pants. What she wanted was impossible.

"Well, you did say anything," she said as she reached for her own clothes.

Pants on, Rye sat in the center of the stone circle

and closed his eyes. The darkness he had reclaimed remained, but it was touched with something new. Something he did not want. It was Echo and Cassidy; it was this place of white magic. What he felt, what interfered, was warmth in a cold world. He pushed the warmth down, shook it off as he might an annoying insect.

Echo was dressed when she said, her tone serious, "I suppose what you're experiencing now is very much like what a heroin addict goes through when they fall off the wagon. The rush is everything, and you don't want to give it up. You have to think about what you must sacrifice in order to keep on experiencing that rush."

Cassidy... There had been a time when he would've done anything for his daughter. And now Echo...

He couldn't love her. It would complicate everything.

"Like any addict," she continued, "I suspect this will lead to an early death for you if you don't...let it go."

"Most likely," he admitted.

"Lock the dark away," she whispered. "Give it up, put the darkness to sleep again." And then, once more, "I love you, Ryder."

He stood and ran.

Echo followed Ryder, running as fast as she could. It didn't take her long to realize where he was headed.

Perhaps he wasn't beyond hope, after all.

By the time she reached the cottage, he was already inside. The front door stood open, so she walked in. Ran in. She wasn't sure what she would find.

On the far end of the living area, Cassidy stood with her grandmother on one side and James McManus on the other. All three looked terrified.

Cassidy's eyes jumped to Echo, and she said, in a child's terrified voice, "That is not my da!"

"Of course I'm your da," Ryder said without emotion.

Cassidy shook her head, and again she looked to Echo for help. "He's still in there, but he's weak. He's fighting, fighting." She took a deep breath. This little girl who could see so much, do so much…she was scared. "The curse is trying to take over, and if it does…"

"God help us all," McManus said in a lowered voice.

Ryder lifted a hand and began to wave it in the older man's direction, but when Cassidy threw herself in front of McManus, Ryder's hand dropped. Slowly. Echo found hope in that instinctive decision. The man she loved would not hurt his daughter.

"There's no curse," he said, flexing the fingers of his right hand as if he wondered why he'd lowered it.

Cassidy argued, "There *is* a curse. Echo sees it, too. Don't you? Please tell me you see it."

Echo walked around Ryder, studying him, wondering what Cassidy saw in him that she had not. The abilities she'd tried so hard to bury drifted to the surface, and with some effort she suddenly saw—sensed, felt—what the child had seen right away.

The powers Ryder had been born with were there, but they were buried deep beneath unnatural abilities that had been poured into him a very long time ago. Poured by his mother, who Ryder had admitted gave him more magic than he'd been born with. She had not taught her young son, Echo realized, she'd changed him. The magic she'd worked hadn't been good or healing. Instead, it was as if she had cursed him. She'd forced this darkness upon him. He hadn't been made to carry that much power and so it had warped him. Perhaps she'd thought she was doing him a favor…

Some favor. She'd made her son a Jekyll and Hyde.

Had his soul been in constant battle since then? Light against dark—innate abilities fighting against a powerful curse.

She had so often thought of her own abilities as a curse, but this…this was a true curse.

Echo placed a hand on Ryder's arm hoping for more insight, but he quickly shook her off. He turned dark eyes to her, and she saw the battle. Another being, a dark one, had been created when his mother had cursed him. Had she realized what she was doing?

"Curses can be broken," she whispered. Ryder wouldn't need talismans to hold back the curse, not if it was removed entirely. That was the only good she saw in this, the only positive development. He had not been born with dark magic; it had been forced upon him.

"What if I don't want this particular curse broken, Raintree?"

She placed her hand on his arm again, and this time she wouldn't allow him to shake her off. "My name is Echo, and you love me."

The smile he gave her was cruel. "No, I don't."

He said he didn't love her, but after that initial attempt at distancing himself from her—which she'd handled easily—he didn't move away or push her back. Something within him liked her touch. Still holding his arm, she closed her eyes and tried to concentrate, tried to identify more. When? How? What could she do to help? She gave it everything she had, but it was not enough.

Until Cassidy took her free hand and squeezed.

At the child's touch, power rushed into Echo. It was the kind of power that could easily knock a woman off her feet, but Echo remained standing. She was strong; she was determined. Ryder's arm was cold and hard beneath one palm; Cassidy's warm, soft hand was in the other. Cassidy's touch fed Echo. It empowered her.

Images filled Echo's head, while a sharp pain filled her heart. She saw beyond the darkness and strength she'd found before in the man she loved. She saw a boy, the boy Ryder had once been. Hair too long, eyes too dark and filled with pain...she would have recognized him anywhere. Anytime.

He had not asked for this, had not sought it.

Yes, the curse could be broken, but only Ryder's mother, the woman who had cast the dark spell, knew how. And she was long dead.

She didn't have to tell Ryder what she saw. He slipped into her head the way he sometimes did, but more completely than before. It would be difficult to hide anything from him now. She was going to have to try...

"Even if I wanted to go back to the man I was, and I do not, it's impossible."

"Maybe not," Echo said as she dropped her hand and stepped away from Ryder. Cassidy's hand remained in hers. She gave the child's small hand a little squeeze, an offer of comfort, of hope.

Ryder closed his eyes. She could see the struggle in him. "I can't..."

"You can!" she insisted.

He opened his eyes and looked at her, and in a flash she saw a hint of the man she loved. For a split second she saw who he was, who he might one day be again. It was not too late.

"I can't," he said again, but then he added, "Not yet. Maisy wasn't working alone. This isn't over. I need every advantage I have..."

"This is not an advantage!" she argued.

He would not be swayed. "Look into the future,

Raintree prophet," he said in an unkind tone, and the man she'd glimpsed was once again gone. "I can't save Cassidy if I'm weak."

"You're not weak," she argued.

"Look, if you can. If you have honed your powers at all while you've been here, you'll see and know, as I do, that without this curse the men who are coming to Cloughban will win." This time he took her hand, and he squeezed tight. Too tight. She thought her bones might break if he continued to squeeze so hard.

She did see, and for a moment her heart stopped. They were gone. They were supposed to be gone! She knew who was coming for Cloughban, who was coming for the stones and the power, for the sanctuary. A name popped into her head as if it were a flashing neon sign, and in that instant she knew who was coming for Cassidy.

As Ryder released her hand, she stepped back and gasped, "Ansara."

Rye walked slowly back toward town. Echo was in his wake, silent—for once—but refusing to give up. He'd told her to stay at the cottage with Cassidy and the others, but she'd refused. Refused to stay behind, refused to be protected. Why did he care if she was protected or not?

He'd placed a spell on the cottage and the people inside, hiding them from prying eyes, keeping them safe. He didn't care about the others, but deep inside he did care about his daughter. Not because she was his daughter, his blood, his child, but because she was so incredibly powerful she might one day be of use to him.

Echo had thought the evil and power-hungry Ansara clan to be no more. Foolish. One had survived. Over the years that single surviving Ansara had brought strays into the fold. Strays like Maisy. They'd begun to build a new clan, one independent at a time. What sorts of promises had been made? Power, certainly. Money. Revenge. Possessing Cloughban would be the final step. They'd have the stones, the magic, the people. And Cassidy. No matter what, they could not have Cassidy.

He could simply take his daughter and go. Screw the town and the people in it. The Ansara could have them.

But a part of him, the weak part he could not yet shake, still cared. With his old powers coming back and trying to take control, he felt like two very different people occupying the same body. He'd managed a balance before, but his dark side had been sleeping so long it was stronger than before. More determined to survive. To win.

That part of him was angry, and determined not to be denied again.

The back of the pub was in sight when Echo said, "Two days."

"I'm aware," he snapped.

"In two days the Ansara will march into Cloughban and if we don't do something they'll take it."

"Go, then. Get into your rental car, drive to the airport and go home."

"No," she said softly.

"Why not? This is not your battle to fight!"

"It is my battle, dammit! Do you think I like it? Do you think I like admitting that this is home now? I don't, but it is." She didn't sound happy about the fact. "All my life I've searched for home. Not Raintree home, not Gideon's home, not a place to crash for a while. *My* home. And finally, I find it on the other side of the world. No Wi-Fi, no Walmart, no movie theater or bowling alley or…hell, anything!"

"Then go," he said again. "Find another home, one with your bleedin' Wi-Fi."

She sighed. He did not turn to look at her.

"It doesn't work that way, and you know it." Her voice was slightly calmer than it had been. "Besides, faults aside, this is the most beautiful and peaceful place I've ever been."

Rye snorted. "Peaceful?"

"Well, normally. Maybe not this week, but…all in all. The important thing is, I belong here. I feel like I've spent my entire life taking one small step after another for the specific purpose of finding Cloughban. And you," she added in a more determined voice.

He needed to be just as determined as she was. Colder. Surer. "This is not your home, and what we have is nothing more than lust."

"Bullshit!" she said as she ran forward to pull up alongside him. "Empath here, remember? A part of you does love me."

She was silent for a few moments after that. Silent and thoughtful. Finally she said, "Two days is not enough time."

"To get ready for the Ansara?"

She didn't answer, not out loud, but he heard her thoughts more clearly than ever.

To make you love me. Jerk.

Chapter 20

Ryder didn't invite her into the pub, but he didn't push her away when she followed him inside, either. Empathic abilities were not required to see that he was a man at war with himself, that since removing the protective talismans he'd been light and evil wrapped in one package.

Her Ryder was a father, a lover, a leader and protector. He was what he had been born to be—a guardian. Guardian of the stones, of his child, of Cloughban… even of her.

He was also a killer. Ryder had killed years ago, and he'd killed again tonight. Did it matter that those lives he'd taken had been dark ones? She couldn't—wouldn't—say. She did understand that with his own darkness flowing free again he was power hungry and slightly sociopathic. *Slightly?* Who was she kidding…?

In spite of all that, there remained deep inside a part

of him a man who was willing to do anything for those he loved. For her. For Cassidy. She looked at him with loving eyes and so easily saw the man he had been as well as the man he was now, at this moment. She saw the good and bad.

It sounded like a fairy tale, she realized that, but in her heart she was certain that love could save Ryder. No, not save. *Guide*. He was going to have to save himself. Love could push back the dark and feed the light. *Her* love. It wasn't enough that she loved him, he had to love her back.

Then they could handle the Ansara, and after that, the cure. The removal of the curse.

Unfortunately, Ryder was right about one thing. He needed every power he possessed to win in a battle against the coming invasion. Dark and light. The Ansara had never been known for fighting fair. She wished she could see more of the future, that she could bring on one of the visions she'd been trying so hard to shake for good.

As they climbed the stairs to his living quarters— she right behind him, he not looking back—Ryder told her, in the crudest terms possible, what he would do to her if she was foolish enough to crawl into bed with him. Her quick response was a simple "Fine." If she ran now, if she allowed him to scare her away, the man she loved would truly be lost.

And so would she. He needed her, but this was not a one-sided relationship. She needed him, too. All her life she'd been lost, in one way or another. She'd been dissatisfied with her lot in life, rootless, wandering. For as long as she could remember she'd been searching for a better place, a better life. Now she understood that her better life was here.

He didn't bother to switch on the light, but it wasn't necessary. Bright moonlight shone through the window. There were shadows here, but not complete darkness. She could see him; he could see her.

By the side of his bed, Echo calmly removed her clothes. All of them. Ryder, standing just a few feet away, watched closely. Eyes dark, hands clenched, he tensed. He remained at war with himself, a war that seemed to cause him physical pain as well as mental anguish. She supposed that would continue until one side or another won. Until he was her Ryder again, or... the other.

She wanted her Ryder back, no matter what the cost.

When she was naked she looked at him. And waited. Eyes never leaving her, he removed his own clothes methodically and tossed them aside. His body was fine, and even in the midst of crisis she could appreciate it. The length, the shape, the muscles, even the erection, which told her that no matter what he said he did want her. Physically, at least.

He took a few steps to join her, wrapped his strong arms around her and without warning threw her onto the bed. She bounced, and then surprised him with a laugh. There wasn't much light in the room, but there was enough for her to see the shifting emotions on his face.

"Maybe I don't want you anymore," he said. "I'm sick and tired of you and your problems and your cloying, needy obsession."

She ignored his words and pointed. "You don't *look* like you're tired of me."

"Any woman would do," he said as he crawled into the bed, spread her thighs and touched her.

"I don't think so," she whispered as he thrust into her.

His emotions battled even as he made love to her. She felt it all when he was inside her. Hot and cold, love and hate, power and loss. Most of all, she felt the pain this war within him brought to life. Not physical pain, but a pain of the soul. A pain of the heart. She soothed him with her body, with her hands in his hair, with the love he refused to acknowledge. Soon he slowed his movements, he relaxed. He flowed into and out of her in an almost dreamlike way that was more than she could bear. This was beauty amid darkness, pleasure amid pain. She didn't want it to end.

As long as they were together, truly together, the darkness could not win. She wouldn't allow it. Couldn't. In this place, in this time, joined body and soul, there was no room for evil. It was pushed aside, shoved into a small dark corner where it was forced to cower, to wait. For a while, at least, for a few precious minutes, he was *her* Ryder. A man who loved his family, his people and her.

Stay with me forever.

I don't know that I can...

As long as they could stay here, stay connected, remain one, he was safe. She was safe. But he began to move faster and so did she. Bodies ruled, not brains and hearts.

It had to end, her body and his insisted.

Echo was in the stone circle; she was in his bed; she was nowhere and everywhere. He filled her, stroked her, brought her to a beautiful edge where she stayed as long as she could. As long as her body would allow. She crested, cried out, held on while the orgasm racked her body. Ryder was right behind her.

And at the moment it was Ryder. *Her* Ryder.

"I still love you," she whispered.

"For God's sake, stop it."

"Stop loving you or just stop saying it?"

"Both." He rolled away.

"No on both counts," she said as she left the bed and headed for the bathroom. She cleaned herself with a warm washcloth, returned to the bed and crawled beneath the covers beside Ryder. When he turned away from her she curled up against his back searching for warmth and connection. Her fingers danced along his spine.

There would be no more snow, not on her account. It was time for her to be strong, to stick to her guns. She knew what she wanted, what she'd been searching for all her life, and she wasn't about to walk away.

"Go home," Ryder insisted in a low, gruff voice.

Echo answered honestly, and in a tone that left no room for argument.

"I am home."

How could Echo sleep with him knowing who he was? She knew very well what he had been and what he could be again. She'd seen it, had peeked inside his dark past. She saw, felt, even experienced, things even he had forgotten, and yet she remained here. She trusted him enough to sleep.

When Echo relaxed completely into his spine and settled into easy, even breathing, Rye moved away from her. Carefully, so as not to wake her. He should leave the bed, leave her be, get away from her influence. Instead, he settled in and watched.

She was beautiful. More than beautiful, she was the embodiment of good, of everything he was not. Echo was beautiful inside and out, an angel to his devil. Light to the dark that was trying so hard to win.

He'd been right to sense the danger when she'd first walked into his pub.

He watched her sleep for a while, then he nodded off himself. It was not a restful sleep. His dreams were vivid and disjointed, and they felt so damned real.

When he woke the sun had risen. Echo was awake, still naked, still beautiful. She was watching him as he had watched her last night for a while.

"If you tell me again that you love me, I'll break something."

She laughed and rolled out of bed. "In that case I'll restrain myself."

"Thank you."

"For now," she added. How could there be humor in her voice? Why was she not running from him? This was not her home to defend, not her family to protect. And yet she stayed.

As he watched her gather her clothes, Rye had the thought that when he and Cassidy left Cloughban, Echo could go with them. Cassidy would need a woman to take care of her. She was only eleven, after all, and there would be many difficult years before she was an adult and could get by on her own. During her early teenage years she'd become volatile and overly emotional, and her powers would be unpredictable. Help would be a good thing. Female help would be best.

Rye accepted that he needed his daughter with him—she possessed so much power, and there was still more to come—but that didn't mean he wanted to be her caretaker. Echo would serve a real purpose, and it wasn't as if he didn't like having her in his bed.

It was the perfect plan. Echo could take care of Cassidy by day and him by night.

She wasn't shy about walking around the room

naked. He got hard, watching her. Did she know what she was doing to him? Of course she did. Tease. She was using him, manipulating him. He'd show her, and this time he wouldn't be so gentle...

"Go," he said, fighting the darker urges.

"I told you, I'm not..." she began as she turned to face him. She stopped when she saw him. Her easy smile faded. Whether it was her empathic ability or simple female instinct, she recognized that at the moment he was more dark than light. "I could use a shower and a change of clothes," she said. "Maybe I'll run back to my room at the boardinghouse for a little while." She dressed quickly, more efficient than he'd ever seen her. "I have a phone call to make first. I'll use the phone in the kitchen, if that's okay with you."

"Just leave," he said, and then he turned his back to her.

He had another thought as the door to his room opened and closed. He should leave Cloughban on his own. Alone. A child and a woman would be too damn much trouble, no matter how powerful either of them might be.

Echo was a real danger to the man he needed to become.

Cassidy frowned into her porridge. That man who looked like her da but was really only part of her da had done something to her. He'd said it was for her own protection, but she couldn't travel out of body to check on him and Echo.

She couldn't complain to her granny or to Mr. McManus. Her grandmother had long ago forbidden her to use that power. Granny said it was rude to pop in on people unexpected and unannounced. She was also afraid that at some point Cassidy might not be able to return to herself, that she'd be stuck in two places unable to become one again. Cassidy knew that would never happen, and at the moment she wasn't at all worried about being rude. This was different! This was important!

"Don't worry, dear," Granny said from a short distance away. "Everything is going to be all right."

Cassidy looked up. Her granny did know some things, but she didn't see all, not the way Cassidy did. "You don't know that. I don't even know that!" She *should* know, but there was a lot that had to happen before she could be sure.

Sometimes the immediate future was set in stone, but usually a series of decisions led to any outcome. It was the reason so many visions of the future came right before they happened. While some events to come were meant to be, those instances were rare. The right decision at the right moment—or the wrong decision at the wrong moment—could change everything.

Her da's protection spell had done more than take away her ability to travel at will. All her powers were dampened. Some were sleeping entirely. Was that a side effect of the spell he'd cast to keep her from visiting, or had he purposely bound her this way?

At the moment she knew only one thing with any certainty: no one but Echo Raintree could save her da from the curse that threatened him.

Showered and dressed, Echo walked toward the town square with coffee and pastries on her mind. She wasn't quite ready to return to Ryder. The expression on his face as she'd left him a couple hours ago…that look had scared her. What if her plan didn't work?

It had to work. She couldn't allow for failure. How could she find so much in him and then lose him to a curse that was more than thirty years old? Ryder's mother... She knew women who had issues with their mothers-in-law, but those mothers-in-law were usually alive.

Echo caught a glimpse of her reflection in the boutique window, and then she noted Brigid beyond. The red-haired woman stared, *glared*, without trying to hide her hatred.

No, not hatred, Echo realized. Fear.

Was Brigid in on the plan? Had she been working with the Ansara all this time?

Forgetting her coffee and sweets for a moment, Echo walked into the shop. A bell overhead heralded her arrival, but it wasn't like her entrance was a surprise. Brigid continued to stare. The eyes were hard, the mouth set, but yes—that was fear.

"Why?" Echo asked. "What are you afraid of?"

"I'm not afraid," Brigid snapped.

Echo pointed a waggling finger at her own head. "Empath. Might not like it, might not want it, but don't lie to me about your feelings."

Brigid took a small step back and lowered her eyes.

Echo sighed. It had not been her intention to cow the woman! "I know more about this village than I did on my first day here. A lot of things make sense to me now, but you—what are your abilities? Why did you go cold when I mentioned my name my first day here?"

Brigid lifted her head and looked bravely at Echo. "I'm a healer. Nothing spectacular like my grandmother, but I do have some skills. I also see glimpses of the future but that's not a strong power. It comes and goes."

"What was it?" she asked in a lowered voice. "What did you see?"

"I remember what Rye was like before. Before Cassidy, before…before Sybil." Brigid clasped her hands together. "When you said your name I saw that Rye return. Darker than before. More dangerous. I thought you'd come here to bring back the man he used to be." She lifted her chin, still afraid but reaching for bravery. "From what I hear, you've succeeded."

Echo shook her head. "I'm here to bring him from the darkness, not pull him into it."

"Why should I believe that?" Brigid snapped. "He's been fine for years. Years! He's a good mayor, a good father. A good friend to some. You show up and within weeks…" She shook her head. "Several in town felt the shift last night. Some of our most sensitive empaths felt the darkness return. Are you trying to convince me that it's not your fault?" Braver than she had been before, Brigid stepped around the counter.

"It's not my fault," Echo said in a calm voice. Brigid wasn't a bad person. She hadn't seen Echo as a romantic threat. She'd seen her as a threat to her friend. As many residents had. Shay. Those who glared. They hadn't hated her; they'd been afraid for Ryder.

"Did you try to scare me out of town?"

Brigid's expression of confusion was a genuine one. "No. Of course not!"

So, someone else had seen the threat, as Brigid had, and left that note. Or else it had been Maisy. Maisy, all along.

"If you want to know what happened, come to the pub tonight. Seven o'clock. Spread the word." After all, she and Ryder couldn't very well defeat the Ansara on their own.

"Why should I?" Brigid asked, her anger rising. "You're here, Rye has changed just as I saw that he would. Why should I or anyone else show up for your... your explanations."

"Because Ryder needs you. He needs you all."

Echo turned and walked toward the door, but Brigid stopped her with a short sentence.

"You're wrong."

Echo spun around. "He does need you, I swear. The others, too. I can't do this alone!"

"Not about that." Brigid was paler than before, and her eyes were wide and watery. "They're not who you think they are."

"Who's not who...?"

"I don't know," Brigid whispered.

Suddenly, Echo did.

Chapter 21

Rye glared into the crowd. These were his people. His friends, new and old. A few of them had known him all his life. Others were temporary residents of Cloughban, gifted independents looking for a place to rest for a year or two or ten. Tonight they were afraid of him. All of them were colored with fear. To the animal that rested inside him, they smelled of it.

They were right to be afraid.

But they were here, here at Echo's invitation. She'd told him they would come, that they knew he was changed but they still cared about him.

Fools, all.

If the dark side was in complete control, he wouldn't bother to warn the people of Cloughban about the planned Ansara attack. They were here, gathered as they had for so many town meetings, but that didn't mean he had to participate. There were enough psychics in the group to make sense of what was to come.

He could leave. Now, tonight. He'd take Cassidy—
and maybe Echo—and go, leaving the village to be
taken by the Ansara. Even if they knew what was coming, they wouldn't be able to put up much of a fight. He
looked around from his perch on the stage. These were
gentle people, people hiding from a world that didn't
accept who and what they were. They were shopkeep-
ers, farmers, wives and husbands and grandparents.

The pub was as full as it had ever been as night fell.
The faces around him were solemn and afraid. The villagers were here, but no one came too near him. No one
but Echo, who sat on the edge of the stage just a couple
of feet away. She refused to acknowledge her fear, even
though he felt it on and in her.

She wasn't afraid of him, she was afraid *for* him.

He explained as best he could, in as few words as
possible. Ansara. The stones. This place. "The invaders will arrive tomorrow afternoon, likely near night-
fall," he said in a calm voice. "I suspect they will bring
weapons of magic as well as weapons of more ordinary
destruction. We have to be prepared for anything."

He was silent as they talked among themselves for
a few minutes. All of them were glad to have the opportunity to turn away, to look elsewhere for a while.
When they looked at his face they saw the dark. Some
saw more deeply than others.

No. They see both, and they are afraid for you.

Of me.

For you.

He looked at Echo while around him the townspeople
talked about where to put the children and the elders
who were unable to fight. They discussed defenses,
weaponry, and arranged for the drugstore to be pre-

pared to house the injured, while the two healers in the area treated them.

His anger got the best of him and he pushed into her head with, *Why are you still here?*

She remained calm. *You know why. I'd say it aloud but I don't want you to break anything. Or anyone.*

It was Maeve Quinlin who bravely approached Rye and asked, in a tremulous voice, "I must tell you, I'm worried about Maisy. I haven't seen her since yesterday afternoon. Do you think one of these Ansara persons abducted her?"

Rye felt no guilt when he answered, "Maisy is dead."

Maeve's shock was clear on her face. "Are you sure? What happened?"

The truth, always. He hadn't wanted to tell all, but it had been foolish of him to think this part of the truth could wait. "I killed her myself."

Many in the crowd gasped. A few edged toward the door.

He didn't owe anyone an explanation, but he needed these people to fight with him. For him. No, for themselves. "She was one of them," he said. "I caught her attempting to sacrifice my daughter."

"No!" Maeve said. "I don't believe that. Maisy was a good girl."

No one had any reason to believe him, not today, but they did believe Echo when she said, "I'm afraid it's true. I saw Maisy raise a knife to Cassidy. I'm sorry, Maeve, but she was not the woman you all believed her to be."

"Cassidy? Is she all right?" someone from the back of the room asked.

"She's fine," Echo said with a tempered smile. "Scared, but unharmed."

"What about McManus?" Nevan asked nervously. "He should be here."

It was Rye who answered before Echo could. "He's unharmed." Trapped in the cottage with Bryna and Cassidy, invisible to any eye but his own, but alive and kicking.

The question Rye had been waiting for came, again from a coward who was hidden by other bodies. "What happened to you?" It would not be difficult to reveal the person who asked that question, but Rye didn't bother. One brave soul had merely asked what everyone else was thinking.

"Some of you remember what I was like before," he said. "I'm back."

"It's temporary!" Echo interjected. "We'll remove the curse after we take care of...of...those who are coming."

"Curse?" Doyle asked.

Doyle hadn't been here before Cassidy was born. He had never seen the man Rye could be. There were few lifelong residents of Cloughban. People came and went. They got what they were coming for—peace or instruction or respite—and then they often moved on. But a few had known him all his life. They'd witnessed his dark power. Did they see that it was worse now for being denied for so long?

The true man he was—and perhaps could be again—rose to the surface for a moment. He looked to Doyle. It was an effort, but he forced the words out.

"If she can't remove the curse, kill me."

Echo ran everyone out of the pub and locked the door behind them. A solemn Doyle had been the last to leave. That done, she spun on Ryder.

"Kill you? Have you lost your mind?"

The man she loved, the man who would die to protect her and Cassidy and the people of this town, was no longer at the surface. "He can try. They can all try. You saw what I did to Maisy." Ryder—not Ryder—smirked. "Maybe he'll try to brain me with a flying pot."

She was not amused. "I told you, I have a plan," she said. "It might take some time…"

"We don't have time," he responded. "I suspect the heat of the battle that's coming will force out what's left of the man you want me to be." He narrowed his eyes. "You have done a remarkable job of shielding this plan from me. I can normally see your thoughts so well. What is it that you don't want me to know?"

Echo lifted her chin. She wanted to trust him, but… she couldn't. Not yet. "I'm not going to take the chance that your less-pleasant half will decide to put an end to it before I even get started."

"Not many people can hide anything from me."

He pushed, a little. Echo felt that push through her entire body. It was like fighting an ocean wave or a strong gust of wind on a stormy day. She pushed back, calling on every ounce of power she possessed. This had to work! It simply had to. She'd gladly share her idea with the man she loved, but if he knew would the other try to stop her?

It was surprisingly easy to think of the man before her as two separate beings. One was the man she loved, the man she would do anything for. The other had been created by the curse, and was doing his best to take over. For now, both men inhabited the same body, but that wouldn't last much longer. One would win. The other would die.

"Was it like this before?" she asked.

He knew exactly what it was she wanted to know.

"Was I a Jekyll and Hyde?" She didn't like the smirk that followed. "Not always, but as I became stronger my presence became more clear to others. Most of the decisions he made were mine, not his own. I was weeks, perhaps even days, away from casting the other out when he put the restraints on me."

He took a few steps closer to her. "I was sleeping when he killed his wife, so don't believe for a moment that the man you think you love is an angel. He's far from it."

"He had no choice," she whispered.

"Didn't he?" The man she began to think of as Dark Ryder reached out to touch her cheek. "He liked it," he whispered. "He liked the rush of taking a life, the blood, the look in his wife's eyes as she left this earth. He'd grown tired of the woman who was, to be honest, a whiny bitch." Broad shoulders shrugged, eyes darkened. "She asked him to take away her abilities and he did, and then she went nuts because she didn't have her abilities. Just like a woman, never satisfied with what she has. She was a lot like you, and you're going to come to the same end."

"Ryder won't hurt me," she insisted in a low whisper.

"Not yet," he conceded. "But when I'm in complete control no one will be able to stop me. Soon the time will come for you to make a choice. Join Cassidy and me when we leave, or die." He leaned down and placed cold lips on her throat. She could back away, she could move, but she knew that her presence was the only thing keeping the man she loved awake.

His arms slipped around her; he held her close. Echo reached deep within herself, searching for every bit of magic she possessed. She needed to see into the future to know how to save him. And herself.

But the future was not yet set. It was fluid, ever shifting. She could see so many possibilities, dark and light, swirling together. In one future she was successful in casting out the darkness of the curse. Ryder, *her* Ryder, was saved. The intruders were defeated and Cloughban was once more a safe haven for those like her. Like Ryder and Cassidy and all the rest.

In another possible future she saved Ryder too soon. He faced the invaders weakened, lost. Those who called themselves Ansara but were not won and they both died ugly. She couldn't help but think of the tombstones in her dream.

In another possible future she made her move too late. She could not save her Ryder no matter how she tried. The darkness won, and while a battle raged around them he drove a knife through her heart with a smile on his face and left town while Cloughban burned.

One chance out of three. Not exactly as discouraging as the odds of winning the lottery, but she did wish they were more in her favor. She'd never been able to see her own future; that wasn't the way it worked. Was that why she had no clearer picture? Or was it simply that what was to come would not be set until they made the decisions that led to it? Either way, she was all but blinded to what might happen.

She wanted to tell someone, anyone, what Brigid had helped her to discern not long ago. Those who were coming were not Ansara; they had simply taken the name as their own. Maybe they'd chosen it because in the past the Ansara clan had had such a savage reputation. Did it matter? Would being called by a different name make them any less fearsome?

The people of this village needed to be afraid. They needed to be prepared for fearsome.

Echo knew she could go, as Ryder had suggested often in the past few hours. Without her here odds were Ryder would be happy to leave Cloughban to the invaders, take his daughter and start his own new life elsewhere. A life of dark magic, of decadence and excess. He would use his own dark powers as well as his gifted child to get what he wanted.

It was more than worry about Cassidy that made Echo accept that she could not leave.

Without Ryder, *her* Ryder, she didn't have a life worth going back to.

"Run," he whispered in her ear. Was that her Ryder talking, or was it the other? *Both.* An order or a plea? Had he managed a glimpse into the mind she was working so hard to shield from him?

She wrapped her arms around his neck and kissed the side of his neck. He was so cold, so hard. So lost. She whispered back, her lips near his ear.

"No."

Chapter 22

It was the clap of thunder that woke Rye from a deep sleep. He sat up in bed, and for a moment, a few precious seconds, he forgot where he was. He forgot who he was. All he remembered was Echo.

Everything that had happened in the past two days came rushing back, filling his head and his heart with pain.

Then the darkness he'd unleashed came rushing back, as well.

For the moment they shared the same mind, the same body. Two separate beings, two personalities, two distinct souls. Eventually one of them would have to go. He wasn't yet sure which one it would be.

Echo was curled up against his side. She should've run yesterday, when she'd had the chance. Now it was too late.

Again, a clap of thunder. Lightning flashed. The

storm outside his window was not at all natural. He felt it deep down.

Had it begun? Echo had seen the Ansara attack happening by the light of day, and it was not yet dawn. Her visions were sometimes late, but she was—as far as he knew—never *wrong*.

She stirred with the third clap, and as he had she jumped up.

"He's here."

"Who's here?" It was annoying to have to ask. She'd done a good job of hiding her thoughts from him, protecting them in a way no one else had ever been able to do.

She narrowed her eyes as she looked at him. "Which one are you?"

He began to answer truthfully. Both. But she didn't wait for his response.

"Never mind," she said as she hopped from the bed and grabbed her clothes. She looked at him as she dressed quickly. "Even if you're mostly my Ryder at the moment, the other will also hear and know, and...not yet. Sorry." She threw open the door. "Soon, I promise!"

Echo ran out of the room and down the stairs. Rye dressed more slowly than she had before following her. He didn't know what she'd planned, but the energy of his surroundings had changed somehow. He felt a current flowing through him. Power. Electricity.

He found Echo standing in the middle of the street, in front of the pub. The sun had not yet risen, but he could not say the skies were dark. There was a blue cast to everything, and it spread as far as the eye could see. The storm, which was unusual for the area, had drawn out others, as well. Those who lived along this main road were coming out of their homes to look to the east.

Blue lightning started near the ground and traveled up in powerful streams of electricity that lit the sky. Thunder followed, rumbling with unnatural power. It was beautiful and frightening and unnatural.

And Echo smiled.

A man was walking along the road, cursing and shooting sparks as he went. Rye would've known this man anywhere, even if Echo hadn't started running toward him with a joyfully shouted, "Gideon!"

"What the hell?" Gideon shouted as she drew closer to him. Electricity danced along his arms. He must've come straight from work. He'd left his suit jacket and tie behind somewhere, but wore black trousers and a white dress shirt, as well as his badge and gun. Her cousin was a homicide detective. A homicide detective who could talk to the ghosts of victims. That gave him a decided advantage.

He lit the early morning in an unnatural way, and she soon saw his wife, Hope, well behind him. She was no longer a detective—she stayed home with their two girls these days—but she wore a gun, too.

They must have come over on Dante's private jet and landed at a private airfield. That would explain their early arrival and the firearms. They had not come through customs…

Gideon snapped, "My rental car died two miles back. What the hell is going on here? I haven't been out of control like this since I was fourteen!"

She ignored the electrical sparks and threw herself at him. The air around him buzzed. It tickled her all over, but she knew Gideon's powers would not hurt her. He would never allow it. She had never been so glad to see him! He was her best, last, *only* hope.

"There's a very strong stone circle in the area," she explained as she let him go and stepped back. "Like Stonehenge but…not Stonehenge."

Echo released her cousin and smiled at Hope.

Gideon's wife was not a member of any magical clan and she was not a stray. Unlike the rest of the family, she had no abilities at all. Well, she had abilities, just not supernatural ones. She was a whiz at keeping her husband and two magically gifted daughters on the straight and narrow.

Knowing what was causing the influx of energy helped Gideon to control the excess electricity that flowed through his body. Thunder and lightning ceased, but he retained an unnatural blue glow. She resisted telling him that he looked as if he'd eaten a neon sign for breakfast.

"We have an audience," he said, nodding his chin to indicate the growing crowd behind her.

Echo glanced over her shoulder. Sure enough, twenty or more villagers stood behind her. At least none of them carried pitchforks and torches.

"It's all right," she said, raising her voice so all could hear. "This is my cousin Gideon."

The murmur that followed was not one of relief. Like her, Gideon was Raintree. Until she'd come here, she'd had no idea her family was so intensely disliked by some strays. No, *disliked* was the wrong word. They were distrusted. That was going to have to change, and fast.

"Come on inside," she said, taking Gideon's arm as Hope drew up beside him. "We have some serious catching up to do."

Cassidy stood at her bedroom window and watched the lightning. Twice she had tried to leave the cottage, but her da's magic still kept her trapped here. She didn't like it. It was not good magic, not at all! Neither did Mr. McManus, who had complained for hours before finally falling asleep on the sofa.

Granny, on the other hand, was perfectly content to wait out whatever was happening. They were safe here. Nothing could touch them; they were invisible to the outside world. Cassidy could not relax, no matter how often her granny advised her to do just that. Too much was undecided. Maybe they were safe at the moment, but would they remain safe?

What if something happened to her da and they were trapped here forever? What would become of them? Would they starve? Go crazy? Would they simply fade away?

The lightning ceased, though in the distance where Cloughban stood a strange blue glow continued, as if a huge and unnatural light shone there. Eventually that faded, too.

She knew something bad was coming, and she wanted to help. She *could* help! If only her da would let her.

Her da but not her da.

The sky changed again, but this time it was the rising sun that lit the sky.

This was the day. Cloughban was about to be under siege.

And she'd never had the chance to warn her da or Echo that Maisy had not been the only spy in Cloughban.

Gideon shook his head. Again. "I don't call spirits back to earth. It's dangerous, for them and for us. When ghosts come to me it is their choice, not mine."

Echo tried to argue. "I know, but…"

"Once a spirit has moved on, it's extremely difficult for them to travel to us. And then, getting back where they're supposed to be is even harder. I will not trap a spirit here, not even to save your friend."

Friend. Ryder was so much more than a friend, but that argument wasn't going to sway Gideon.

After being introduced, Gideon and Ryder had parted as if they could not stand to be in the same room. Maybe they couldn't. She was more sensitive to energy than she'd ever been, and her cousin and the man she loved mixed like oil and water. Did Dark Ryder realize what a danger Gideon was to his existence?

Hope had gladly taken up Echo's offer of her bed in the boardinghouse. She and Gideon had had a long night, after an already long day. The girls were with their grandmother—Hope's mother—probably being spoiled horribly. Every little girl deserved to be spoiled now and then.

Echo lowered her voice as she made her argument. "Ryder's mother cast this…this curse on him, trying to make him more powerful. Maybe her intentions were good, maybe she was trying to help, but her spell almost killed him." It very well could kill the man she loved. Today, tomorrow…he could not bear this for much longer.

Gideon attempted to be reasonable. "Why not just let me make another talisman to hold the powers in check?"

Echo shook her head. "We're beyond that." Well beyond. Dark Ryder would sleep no more. He would live and rule the body he possessed, or he would die. If he lived, the man she loved would disappear. The body would survive but the soul, the essence of him…that would be gone for good. "There's going to be an attack..." She'd explained this already.

Again, Gideon shook his head. "There can't possibly be enough of the Ansara left to mount an attack."

She explained what she'd discovered, that those who were coming were not true Ansara, but independents who had taken on that name. Like her, he didn't think that distinction made much of a difference.

"How many do you think it would take to run over this village?" This wasn't a mecca for the most powerful of strays. Most of the people here had just enough magic in their blood to make them different. Enough to make them long for others of their kind and the comfort of the stones.

His expression went dark. "Not many, if the people here are not prepared. But you're here and you have prepared them."

It was the change in Gideon's posture that told Echo Ryder had entered the room, coming through the door behind her. Her cousin was angry and suspicious. She could tell by the way his fingers curled that if Ryder made one wrong move he'd be on the receiving end of a powerful bolt of lightning.

That hand soon dropped.

"She's here," Gideon whispered.

Echo stood. "Ryder's mother? She came without being called?"

"Not exactly. She's been here all along. She's attached herself to her son." He frowned. "And she won't leave until I fix her mistakes. Great. Just great."

Rye had found himself in control long enough to allow Echo to duct tape him to a chair. Without his help an entire roll of duct tape wouldn't be enough to restrain his other half, but if he could hang on for a while longer it would suffice. He thought of his daughter; he thought of Echo sleeping in his bed. He fought for his very life, for Cassidy and for Echo.

Gideon Raintree looked like an insane man, pacing the room and talking to himself. More than once he ran his hands through his hair, making it stand on end at one point. He continued to occasionally glow blue and…hell, there was no other word for it. *Sparkle.* But he wasn't insane, and he wasn't talking to himself. He was carrying on a conversation with Rye's mother. The Gypsy who had cursed him before she died.

"Sorry is not good enough!" Gideon shouted to an empty space behind Rye. After a short pause he continued in a slightly lower voice. "Well, it was a curse, not a gift, and now see where we are."

Another pause, then, "Tell him yourself."

Echo had been watching, silent and pensive, as her cousin did his thing. Now she spoke up.

"Does she know how to remove it?"

Gideon looked at her. "Yes."

She took a deep breath. "Can it wait until after we take care of the attackers who are coming?"

Gideon threw his hands into the air, frustrated and angry. "Really?"

It was Rye who answered. "This town needs me. It needs the power this curse has given me if we're to win."

"What happens when the cursed part of you decides it might like being aligned with the invaders? What happens when you switch sides in the middle of the battle?"

Rye wanted to argue that wouldn't happen, but he couldn't. Not if he were being entirely honest. He didn't know what his dark side might do.

If Gideon removed the curse, and with it Rye's enhanced abilities, could they still win the battle?

Did he want to take the chance that he might turn on his friends and neighbors, or worse, his family?

"Can you ask her if she also cursed my daughter?" From beyond the grave, or through him, somehow, but…anything was possible.

Gideon shook his head. "No. Your mother saw a gifted child of her blood, and she thought it was you. She wanted to help you along, that's why she did what she did. But that child she saw wasn't you, it was her granddaughter." His head snapped to the side. "All these sorries are not making things any better!"

He waved a hand at Rye. "So, without the curse what are your abilities? What would you bring to the party?"

Rye answered honestly. "I don't know. I was so young when my mother started working with me…I don't know."

Again, Gideon looked into an empty space and listened for a moment, and then he mumbled, "Great. That's just great." He turned eyes a brilliant green, so much like Echo's, to Rye and said, "Nothing. According to your mother, without the curse you have no special abilities at all."

Chapter 23

"Do we dare to wait?" Echo asked. The word still echoed in her head. *Nothing.* All the talismans had done, for the past eleven years, was keep the curse in check. She'd been so sure she'd sensed his own... But no, not if the ghost was telling the truth. The abilities Ryder had called upon since Cassidy's birth were bits and pieces of his mother's curse seeping through.

Gideon shook his head. "I don't think we can afford to wait. How long do we have?"

"An hour, maybe two." The invaders were coming. They were moving closer and closer. She felt them coming, in a strange rush in her blood, in the small hairs on her arms standing up. She felt the shifting energies, and still she could not predict the outcome.

"If I don't do it now," Gideon said, "I might not get another chance."

Winning was almost a given, with Ryder at top form.

If he were mortal? Without any power at all? Not so much. Echo said as much, mumbling under her breath as she weighed the pros and cons.

"Hey," Hope snapped. "Not having a woowoo power doesn't make a person helpless, you know. Jeez." Well rested after a nice, long nap in Echo's bed, she looked pumped and ready to fight. "I'll give him one of my guns."

Echo looked at Hope. "You brought more than one?"

"You said the *A*-word. Ansara. I would have brought an arsenal if I'd thought I could get away with it."

"I've never handled a firearm," Ryder said. "I don't think I have time to learn…"

His head was thrown back, his entire body tensed. Dark Ryder was fighting to the surface. The duct tape would not contain him much longer.

No matter what, her Ryder had to survive. To allow the dark into the world, to let the curse kill the man she loved and free the other…

Echo looked at Gideon. "Do it," she whispered. "Do it now. We won't have another chance."

Her track record as a prophet was less than stellar, but Gideon trusted her. He trusted her now.

Hope stood behind her husband, her gun drawn as he placed a glowing hand on Ryder's forehead. Echo wondered if it hurt, if there was heat in that hand, but Ryder didn't pull back or even flinch.

After a long moment Gideon looked at Echo. "She says you need to say the words. Because you love him, it has to be you." She saw the puzzlement in his eyes. He probably wondered if Ryder was another one of her crushes, a fling, an infatuation. Now was not the time to explain that this was so much more.

She had been prepared to watch, to step back and

let Gideon fix what was broken, but that was not to be.
Echo nodded, and in a low and soft voice she repeated
the strange words her cousin directed her to say.

That's when Ryder screamed. He jerked his head
around to look directly at her, to glare at her. She could
see the pain in his eyes; she could feel it. Those dark
eyes she had come to love were touched with Gideon's
electricity as if the lightning lived there, inside him.
Did it burn? Was it terrible?

"Help me," he whispered.

Instinctively, Echo stuttered, the strange words uncomfortable on her tongue. She hesitated, choked on
the words. She hadn't realized that removing the curse
would hurt him so. The pain was too much! There had
to be another way! But Hope said in her no-nonsense
voice, "It's a trick, Echo. I can see it from here."

Ryder snapped his head around and growled at Hope,
who only adjusted her aim a bit.

The words Gideon whispered, words Echo repeated
carefully, were Romany. Carpathian Romany. She didn't
know the language, didn't even realize there were different variations, but listening, speaking each word
carefully…she simply knew. This was Ryder's mother's
language, a language of power. The language she had
used to cast the curse and the one required to remove it.

Ryder truly was in pain, but it wasn't her Ryder, it
was the other. It was the darkness created by a curse
which had been cast to instill powers that never should
have been. As she spoke the strange words, the darkness and the curse died. A little at a time. Her Ryder
hurt, too, as something that had been a part of him for
almost his entire life was ripped away.

Would he love her after? Would he be so changed
that there was nothing left of the man she loved? He had

warned her that removing her own powers would damage her forever. They had damaged his wife, Cassidy's mother, beyond repair. Was this the same?

No, the powers now being removed were not a part of him. They had been added, forced, poured into a soul unprepared for such magic.

He screamed, an unnatural scream that made every glass in the pub ring. One bottle of whiskey exploded. Then another. The chairs shook slightly, as if Cloughban were experiencing a minor earthquake.

Echo stuttered again and then she whispered, "I love you." Her words were too soft for anyone to hear over the screams, but Ryder heard somehow. He looked at her. Into her.

Save me.

That's what I'm trying to do.

You're killing me...

Would they still be able to communicate this way when he was stripped of the curse? All her life she'd wanted a normal man, a man with no magical abilities, but if they could no longer touch each other this way... she would miss it.

But there was no other way. She didn't want to ever peek into the mind of Dark Ryder, and she did not want him in her own mind. What could he, would he, do there if he had free rein?

No matter what the cost, they had to strip away the darkness. To see the man she loved entirely gone would break her heart. If the darkness won and her Ryder disappeared, it might snow in Cloughban until the end of time.

Gideon placed his free hand over Ryder's heart and directed Echo to say a few more words. She did.

Ryder's head snapped back. His body bucked and

then he went still. His head rotated slowly and then dropped forward; his shoulders and arms went slack. Gideon backed away.

"Is it done?" Echo asked.

"I think so." Gideon looked at a far corner and nodded in acknowledgment of the ghost. "She won't leave until he wakes up and we know for sure."

Echo took a knife and began to cut away the duct tape that held Ryder.

"Shouldn't we wait until he wakes up and we know if the spell, you know, took?" Hope asked.

"No," Echo responded sharply. "We need him, dark or light." She lifted her head to look Gideon in the eye. "They're coming."

Rye opened his eyes slowly. Wiggled his fingers as the world around him came into focus. He felt hungover, only half-present. For a long moment, no one else in the pub realized he was awake. They were making plans, gathering others to fight with them.

He tried to listen in, attempted to peek into the minds of those around him. They could block him, and had, but if they didn't realize he was listening why would they bother?

He heard nothing. Saw nothing. He reached for a vision of the battle to come; he tried to identify the dark magic he knew was coming their way. Again, nothing. He lifted his hand and attempted to start a small fire on his palm, something which had, until now, been child's play.

Nothing.

Without the curse, he was no wizard. He wasn't even a mildly talented stray or a slightly gifted independent.

He was an ordinary human, and in the coming battle he would serve no useful purpose at all.

Echo saw—or sensed—that he was awake and she ran to him. "Ryder, how do you feel? Are you…?"

He lifted his head and looked at her. She paled, and for a moment he believed she was disappointed to see that he was just a man. She'd fallen in love with a wizard and now he was *nothing*. In a town like Cloughban, he was less than nothing.

And then she whispered, "Thank God it's you." She leaned down and kissed him briefly, too briefly, taking him by surprise. That kiss was warmth in a cold world, a moment of peace and, yes, love.

"We don't have much time," she said as she pulled away from him. "They're coming, they're close. As far as I can see, there are only half a dozen of them or so. They still think they'll catch us unaware, which is foolish considering where they're headed, so I believe we'll be…"

"Echo," Rye interrupted. "I'm…" *Powerless, worthless, empty.*

She placed a hand on his shoulder. "I know."

He found a way to continue. "The spell I cast on the cottage, the one to hide and protect Cassidy."

She paled as she finished his thought for him. "It fell when we removed the curse."

Cassidy glanced out her bedroom window, bored with her book, bored with being stuck inside for so many hours. Days! Well, a day and a half. It seemed like longer. She had never realized how much she liked the freedom to come and go as she pleased, even when she didn't *physically* come and go.

The figure walking toward the cottage was one she

knew well, though she had never seen him here in her home. He never came out to the cottage, never visited. She blinked. Strained to see. Why was he walking straight for the front door when he shouldn't be able to see the cottage at all?

At that moment he spotted her in the window. He smiled and waved.

Cassidy had never been able to see her own future, but that smile made her shiver. There was something wrong about it, something evil. It was like her da as he had been in the past couple of days, but without the influence of the good man he had always been deep down.

For a second, a horrifying second, the face coming toward her shifted into an ugly, skeleton-like image. Hollow eyes. Gruesome grin.

She ran from her room, into the main room where Granny sat with her friend. "Don't open the door!" she shouted, but it was too late.

Doyle didn't knock. He blew the door off its hinges with a burst of fire and walked inside through a puff of black smoke.

Rye ran. Echo had offered to come with him, but he'd refused her and taken off at full speed. There was no way she could catch up with him, even if she tried. Just as well. She'd be needed in town.

Had his mother cursed him because she'd realized early on that he had no powers? What a disappointment he must've been, for her to take such steps. Had the curse affected him physically? Was that why Cassidy was so powerful?

Was she still powerful, or had her gifts disappeared with his own?

There was no way to be sure until he was with her again.

Within a matter of days he'd gone from a wizard so powerful his gifts had to be dampened, to the dark man he had once been, to an ordinary man who could not help his daughter or the woman he loved when they needed him. They should've left him as he was, dark and lost. At least then the people he loved, the only people in the world he cared about, would be safe.

But would they have been safe from him?

Suddenly Cassidy was beside him, running unnaturally fast in order to keep up with him. Cassidy, not in the flesh but traveling out of body. Her feet did not touch the ground. The wind created by their speed made her red curls fly back. Her presence was proof that his spell had indeed fallen.

"Doyle killed Mr. McManus!" she shouted. Tears streamed down her face. "He says he's going to kill Granny, too, if I don't...if I don't..." And then she was gone. As quickly as she'd appeared, she disappeared.

Doyle. For all Rye's so-called gifts, he had never seen it. Neither had Echo, or anyone else in town. His cook—much more than a cook apparently—must've called upon a powerful shielding charm or spell to last this long without anyone realizing what he was up to.

Rye ran faster, pushing himself to the limit, wishing he had the powers of a wizard—dark or light—to help him save his daughter. He ran as fast as he could, but he had no idea if he was anywhere near fast enough.

Chapter 24

"They're here," Echo whispered as two long black SUVs raced into town. Maybe their prophet—if they had one—was as substandard as she was. As substandard as she had been, anyway, before taking lessons from Ryder. Didn't they know what they were up against? Didn't one of them see that they were riding into a town that was well prepared for their arrival?

Maybe they knew but didn't care. That was a scary thought.

Standing near the door to the pub, she tried to reach out to Ryder. *Where are you? How are you? What's happening? They're here.* Her efforts were wasted. Since Gideon had broken the curse, she'd been unable to touch Ryder's mind at all. She was effectively blind where he was concerned. Their connection was gone. She missed it, more than she'd imagined she could.

What did it matter at this moment? They had to survive this attack before she could worry about Ryder and Cassidy.

The people of Cloughban had varying gifts, and widely varying degrees of strength. Most were not very powerful. None were what could be called warriors. Warriors or not, all adults under the age of seventy were on the street, armed in one way or another. With sticks, swords, knives and flexed fingers, they were ready to fight for their home.

Echo was ready to fight, too.

Did the invaders want the independents, the stones or Cassidy? Odds were they wanted all three. There was power here, there was strength. For a clan looking to begin anew, there was likely no better place on the planet.

The people here were prepared to defend all. Themselves, the stones, a little girl like no other...

Hope had her gun and Gideon's, one in each hand. In this situation, Gideon didn't need a firearm. Blue lightning danced on his skin as he prepared.

The vehicles stopped, one after another. Doors opened simultaneously as six...no, *seven*...people stepped out. Three women, four men. All were dressed entirely in black. Three were wearing sunglasses, which had to be for effect only since clouds shielded the late afternoon sun. They carried swords and guns of their own. Echo saw no evidence of fire or lightning, but that could come once the fight began.

A tall brunette woman with a severely short hairstyle took the lead. She had to be close to six feet tall! One of the three wearing sunglasses, she was obviously in charge. The other six formed a flank behind her, marking her as their leader, but it was her demeanor, her fearlessness, that told Echo she was leading the pack.

"Seven against…fifty? Sixty?" The tall woman's smile was at odds with her words as she surveyed the crowd. "It seems the numbers are against us, but in this situation numbers mean nothing. Can we talk? You people don't know what you're fighting against." She raised her voice; it all but boomed down the street. "Become Ansara, join us. Be a part of resurrecting a powerful clan that was wrongly eliminated years ago." She turned her head slowly and pinned her eyes on Gideon. "By the Raintree. Have they come to take you, too? Please tell me you haven't all bought into their goody-goody facade."

The crowd was restless. They murmured to one another, they shuffled their feet and a few took uncertain steps back. There were doubts among them.

"They're not Ansara," Echo said in a voice loud enough for all to hear. "They're impostors." She took a deep breath. "Wannabes. They are no stronger, no more capable, than any one of you." She glanced around her. "Any one of *us*."

Shay stood next to her mother; they were dressed in plain, loose clothing that left them room to maneuver, and sturdy low-heeled boots that would allow them to run. And kick. They each held what could only be called a club. Hefty clubs, at that.

The girl who had been Maisy's friend, who had coveted Echo's job at the pub, who had made it clear that she didn't like the newcomer much, caught Echo's eye and nodded once. Echo had no idea what Shay's powers were, but at this moment it didn't matter. That nod was an acknowledgment. Soldier to soldier. *Let's kick some ass.*

As if he were in on the silent exchange—and perhaps he was—Nevan, who carried no weapon that Echo could see, raised his voice as he surveyed the crowd. "Avoid killing the bastards if you can. This is sacred land, and the spilling of blood will darken and weaken the stones. There's been enough blood spilled of late." Then he, too, nodded to Echo.

She took a deep breath and stepped forward, moving closer to the woman who led the attack. Echo was no leader, never had been. She'd always been content to be a soldier, not a general. A princess, not a queen. For the most part, she did as she was told. But in a way she had never expected, these were her people. They needed guidance, with Ryder changed. Changed and, more importantly, not here.

"Go while you can," Echo said in a commanding voice, facing the woman who seemed, at the moment, to stand a full foot taller than she.

Gideon lifted one hand and an alarming ball of lightning danced on his palm. It was a warning, nothing more.

"You've lost the day," Echo said, loudly enough for everyone on the street to hear. "The people of Cloughban have no wish to align with you or with the Raintree. They're independent and will remain so. Leave. No one has to die today."

Behind the leader, the other six prepared to do battle. Guns and swords were raised. She saw no evidence of powers among them. At least, none that could be used in a fight. Echo allowed her empathic abilities to come to life. She reached out, trying to ascertain what dangers these invaders would offer. Fire, lightning, balls of energy.

Nothing. This new clan was so weak they were all but powerless. No wonder they wanted the stones—and these people and Cassidy—so badly!

A short, dark-haired man standing behind and to the left of the tall woman fired the first shot. The bullet missed its intended mark—Gideon—and grazed the arm of the young man who had sold Echo ice cream and coffee on several occasions. He fell. The crowd swarmed forward.

Echo took one step forward, two, ready to engage the invaders. Like Gideon, she had the ability to produce a ball of energy that would disable any attacker. Before she could even produce a twinkling of energy, that newly identified feeling niggled at the back of her brain.

"No," she whispered, stopping her forward progress. Not now! She needed to fight, to play a part in saving this village that had become her home. An important part. These people were her friends and neighbors; she was a part of the community.

But she couldn't fight like this, no matter how much she wanted to do just that. She dropped her hand and backed away, moving closer to the pub, realizing she'd be trampled if she stayed in the street. She'd never been able to stop an oncoming vision.

Her knees gave out, and she sat with her back against the pub door. The people of Cloughban—Ryder's neighbors and friends, *her* neighbors and friends—defended their home with honor. Shay knew how to swing that club. She was stronger than she looked. Echo saw two of the townspeople go down, then watched as Maeve Quinlan hit one of the men in black over the head with an iron skillet. Brigid had kneeled to tend one of the fallen, the boy who had been shot, and Nevan…Nevan had lightning like Gideon. Echo smiled as the old man began to glow, more green than blue but just as powerful and sparkly…and then she was gone.

* * *

Gideon hit the leader of the Ansara invaders in the center of her chest with a bolt of lightning. Not enough to kill her. *Probably* not enough to kill her. She flew back and landed hard on the road, hitting the ground with an oomph. Her sunglasses flew off. She stayed down.

Echo was slumped on the sidewalk. Damned bad timing for a vision. At least she'd had the good sense to move out of the way before she'd been incapacitated.

As he fought, he kept one eye on Hope. She'd been through this before, during the final battle between the Raintree and the Ansara. As one of the invaders swung his sword at an elderly man wielding a long stick, Hope took aim and fired. A good shot, she hit what she'd aimed at. The man in black's shoulder. The old man gave a nod of appreciation in her direction before lifting his stick again and going to the aid of a friend.

Gideon stepped back, out of the midst of the fight. His side was winning; the people defended themselves well. There didn't have to be a massacre in order for the people of Cloughban to win. This was a magical place, thanks to the nearby stones Echo had told him about. As the old man had warned, bloodshed here would seep into the ground and touch the place with a new and unwanted darkness. The people of Cloughban needed to win, had to win, and it was inevitable that many would be wounded and some might die. But there could be no slaughter here.

Light fed good power; evil fed the dark. He could only imagine how bad it would be for the stones of Cloughban to be touched with evil.

One by one, the invaders went down easily. Wounded, not killed, they fell. A couple of them would recover, stand and fight again, but most just slunk away, edging toward their vehicles.

Watching, no longer participating, Gideon experienced a tickle of warning. The invaders were surrendering much too easily. It occurred to him that they could not have hoped to win. None of them, not one, fought with magic. No fire, no balls of energy, no lightning other than his own and the occasional burst of green lightning from the incredibly ugly old man. As battles went, this one was almost amusing. Almost.

The people who had come here to take this village were not trained fighters. They were dressed for the part, and they were armed, but once they began to fight they got in one another's way, tripped over their own feet. The people of Cloughban were not much better.

Gideon stepped back; he lifted a hand to call Hope to his side. The villagers were winning handily. They needed no Raintree assistance. Hope began to make her way toward him.

All but two of the invaders were down when Echo struggled to her feet. Unsteady, she leaned against the pub door as she called his name.

She tried to shout at him but her words were garbled and weak.

Gideon turned his back on the fight and stepped in her direction. "What?"

Her voice was louder as she said, "This is just a distraction. He's going for Cassidy!"

Hope called Gideon's name, a sharp warning, just as something hit the back of his head. He fell, he heard a gunshot and all went dark.

Bryna sat on the sofa next to her gentleman friend who, Rye was happy to see, was very much alive. After the initial attack McManus had been unconscious for a while. Cassidy had thought him dead, but he remained among the living.

For now.

Doyle. All this time, the traitor had been right under his nose. Rye hadn't seen the deception, hadn't even suspected. Echo hadn't seen it, either, which meant that Doyle's abilities were much more than an unsteady bit of telekinesis. Flying pots and an impressive gift for blocking. Judging by a lingering odor in the room and singe marks on the door, he also controlled fire, to some extent. An inborn gift or a one-time trick? It was impossible to know at this point.

Whatever gifts he possessed, they weren't enough to satisfy him. Doyle wanted Cassidy. He wanted her powers, the same amazing abilities Maisy had tried to take.

Rye stood in the center of the main room where he'd watched his daughter grow up. From an infant, to a toddler, to a curious child. Soon she would be a young woman. God above, she deserved to be a young woman. A grown woman. A mother to her own children one day. A grandmother who warned her own grandchild against using potentially dangerous magic.

He wanted to rush to her, to take her into his arms, but he didn't dare to move while Doyle held a knife to Cassidy's slender, pale, *vulnerable* throat.

Curse or no curse, powerful or powerless, he was Cassidy's father; he loved her. He would do whatever was necessary to save her, even if it was the last thing he did.

"What do you want?" Rye asked. His voice was rough and unsteady. "Let her go, and I'll give you anything. Anything at all."

Doyle looked and sounded downright cocky as he

answered, "My brother and I decided that we want what you have, and what you have can be had through her, thanks to a very old spell Walsh discovered."

Power. Magic. The ability to have anything his heart desired with a snap of his fingers. Doyle was not without considerable magic of his own, but he wanted more. He wanted it all.

"Brother?"

The man who held a knife to Cassidy's throat smiled. "You knew my brother well. You taught him, for a while. He was your last student, before Echo Raintree came along to revive your teaching career. That's why I had to be the one to come here, to make the arrangements on this end."

It took no magic for Rye to understand. His student Walsh, the one who had expressed an unhealthy interest in Cassidy and what she could do. Knowing that Walsh and Doyle were related he could see a minor resemblance. In the nose, in the shape of the mouth. He saw too late.

He had to keep Doyle occupied until he figured out a way to disarm him without hurting Cassidy. If he talked awhile, if his arm and hand relaxed. Would he be fast enough to move in and take that knife if Doyle got sloppy?

"You're Ansara?" Rye asked, taking a half step forward.

"Yes and no. Walsh, my late brother, could claim a tenuous connection through his mother," Doyle said with a weird hint of humor. "She died young, so my father, our father, took him in. We both secretly took the Ansara name a few years back. There's power in a name."

One word stuck with Rye, out of all that. "Late?"

Instead of relaxing, Doyle's grip on the knife tightened. "Walsh and I had a disagreement over how we should proceed here. I had to remove him from the equation."

So, Doyle had already killed—his own brother—and would not hesitate to do so again.

Rye lifted his hand, palm forward. He was ready to beg, to plead. He'd do anything...

Doyle shifted the knife he held on Cassidy so that it pressed against her skin. "Use any of your magic on me, and I'll kill her here and now."

Rye dropped his hand. For a long moment, he didn't respond. For all his abilities, Doyle didn't see that he had no powers? Cassidy knew—he could see it in her eyes—but she said nothing to give him away. They had even spoken of the curse...though Doyle had not been around to hear details of the curse or its removal.

"Tell me what you plan to do," Rye said. "This spell Walsh discovered...is it the same one Maisy attempted?"

Doyle nodded. "Ungrateful bitch. She knew Cassidy was meant for me, not for her. I'm glad you took care of her."

The dark man he had been had ripped out Maisy's throat and then set her on fire. Cassidy had been there, but how much had she seen? He prayed she had not seen much.

"Maisy is nothing but ash now," Rye said.

Doyle nodded his head. "Thanks for that."

"I don't understand." Rye took another small step forward. "What kind of spell is this exactly?"

Doyle noticed Rye's forward movement this time. He nodded his head and motioned for Rye to move back. Reluctantly, he did so.

When Rye had taken two steps back, Doyle answered his question. "The spell takes everything a person is, all abilities and strengths, and transfers it to another. In this instance, Cassidy's powers will transfer to me."

Rye's heart was pounding so hard Doyle had to be able to hear it. Everyone had to be able to hear. He had to stall; he had to find a way to stop Doyle before it was too late. "Maisy had a knife. A special knife. I took it. It's in my room above the pub."

"Blood has to be spilled," Doyle admitted, "but I don't need any special knife. Maisy just liked that one. I think it belonged to her father. Or a sister." He shrugged, as if Maisy and her knife were of no consequence. As if the words he spoke were just ordinary words.

"Blood," Rye repeated in a lowered voice.

"Yes, blood," Doyle said carelessly. "That doesn't mean Cassidy has to die. I don't have to take it all."

Cassidy's lips moved, but she made no sound. *Liar.*

"That's good to hear," Rye said, trying to hide his panic at Cassidy's silent, single word. "The stones... Does the spell have to take place there?"

"It's preferred," Doyle admitted. "Not necessary, but there is a better chance of success. It's more likely that all abilities will transfer if the words are spoken there." His eyes narrowed. "Don't think I won't kill her here and now if you give me any trouble. Wait, let me have the powers I need and when it's all done you can have her back. I can't say she'll be unharmed, but she will be alive."

Liar.

He had to stall, had to find a way to move Doyle away from Cassidy. With that knife at her throat, a sudden, impulsive attack was possible. Doyle might prefer to kill her in the stone circle, but he'd kill her here and now if he felt he had no choice.

Rye had never felt so helpless, had never wished so hard for the powers he'd taken for granted.

Doyle wanted power. He wanted it badly enough to kill his own brother, as well as an innocent child. He craved what the darker side of Rye had wanted.

Everything.

Rye asked as calmly as he could, "Why her? Why not me?"

Doyle smiled. "Nice try, boss. Let's face it, you have a lot of abilities and I wouldn't mind having them." The expression on his face said, *Maybe one day I will.* No, he didn't realize that Rye had lost his powers; he still had not seen that truth. "She's more powerful than you are. More powerful than anyone, I expect."

Rye had always understood that Cassidy's abilities would put her in danger, would make her attractive to those who wanted what she had. Power beyond imagining. He'd always thought he could keep her safe at least until adulthood. No child should be threatened like this, and Cassidy...she was a sweet girl, untainted, generous. Filled with love. He loved her. He would die for her if he had to.

"That's true, she is more powerful than I am," Rye said. "But the kind of power that flows through Cassidy's veins doesn't come without a price. There's the issue of control, the very real possibility that the magic will rule you instead of the other way around." He knew that too well, since it had almost happened to him.

"That's a problem I can handle," Doyle said, but Rye saw his doubts.

Now was the time. A shift in the conversation, a suggestion... "If you take my abilities you can keep her, control her and have it all. You can have everything."

"You're offering?" Doyle snapped.

Yes. Hell, yes. He'd do anything, so in the midst of lies and deceit he spoke the truth. "I love my daughter. Promise me you'll let her live, promise me you won't hurt her, and you'll get no fight from me."

Doyle hesitated. He shifted his feet almost nervously. One swipe of that knife and Cassidy would be gone. Just *gone*.

Rye snapped, "Have I used my powers to fight you?"

"No." Again, he saw Doyle's indecision. "But only because I have a knife to her throat."

True enough. If the move wouldn't put Cassidy in danger, he would have wrestled Doyle to the ground already. "Maybe I'm hoping that once you take all I am into yourself you'll love her as I do. Maybe I hope more of me than my magic will affect you. I want my daughter to live, to be taken care of. She can give you everything if only you care for her."

The knife at Cassidy's throat wavered, moving slightly away from her skin. "I've never seen much to speak of out of you. How do I know you have abilities I want?"

He'd been afraid this might happen. Doyle wanted a demonstration, and Rye was without magic. "You want the man I used to be. Ask anyone in Cloughban about the man I was a dozen years ago or so. I've kept my abilities dampened for a very long time with talismans. You saw them, the wristband and the stone at my throat. They're gone now." It was all gone. "Without those safeguards I can do anything Cassidy can, and more. My abilities are fully developed—they are not the gifts of a child. What power do you wish to see? I have them all."

One eyebrow rose slightly. "We'll start with something easy. Fire?"

The cold fireplace was instantly filled with flame.

"I have control of all the elements," Rye said. As if on cue, a strong wind whipped around the cottage, whistling, screaming like a wounded animal. It died suddenly and completely a moment later.

"Telekinesis?"

"Like you?" A lamp, a book and a cup of tea floated around the room so smoothly not a drop of the tea was spilled.

All three items returned to their proper places. Cassidy didn't twitch, didn't so much as wiggle her little finger. There was no way for Doyle to know that she'd been the one to provide the demonstrations.

The man who had been a valued employee for eight months gave the idea some thought. Rye began to sweat. What if he turned down the offer? What if he still wanted Cassidy?

Without magic, could he save his daughter?

"We'll do it at the stone circle," Doyle finally said, edging toward the door. "If I don't like what I become after I kill you I'll continue as planned, with the girl."

At least he was no longer lying about his intentions. Someone would die in the stone circle, and Doyle would become a formidable force in the magical world.

"Fine." Rye followed.

He thought of Echo, wished he could reach out to her as he once had. But he was not the man she'd fallen in love with, and he was on his own.

At this moment, nothing mattered but Cassidy.

Chapter 25

Echo ran. Others had heard her words and followed, but they'd fallen far behind. She'd never run so fast. She'd never had reason to.

Gideon was hurt, but not seriously. She hadn't had time to stop and tend to him, not after what she'd seen in the vision that had taken place as the people of Cloughban had fought for their home. Brigid had nodded at Echo, had all but dismissed her as she knelt down to tend to Gideon's head. The final act of the last standing invading soldier—a short blonde with ears too big for her head—had been to conk Gideon on the back of the head with the iron skillet she'd taken from Maeve. Hope had stayed with her husband and the healer, and with an annoyed Maeve, who'd angrily snatched her skillet back from the wounded soldier. Gideon would be fine; he was being well cared for.

Echo's place was with Ryder and Cassidy. Now and

forever. They were her family as much as Gideon. She'd traveled around the world to find them…

The attack on Cloughban had been nothing but a distraction. She'd seen it in her vision, a vision which had once again come too late. Doyle. Doyle! She had never suspected him, not for a moment. The attackers had distracted the entire town from the real purpose on this day. Taking Cassidy.

She saw everything now. The pieces of the puzzle had finally come together. When he'd hired the soldiers to attack Cloughban, Doyle had promised them the magic they lacked. Four of them possessed a minor ability, three were entirely without magic. He'd promised to make them all Ansara wizards in his new order, to make them his trusted council when he ruled the magical world. Lies, all lies.

Doyle was desperate to rebuild what had once been a powerful, and evil, clan. With himself as Dranir.

He wanted Cassidy, wanted her amazing abilities for himself, but in Echo's most recent vision it had not been Cassidy Doyle stabbed; it had been Ryder. The knife had slipped into his body. She'd felt his pain as if it were her own, had felt the warmth of his blood flowing out and down his body.

It started to snow again, fat flakes and icy bits of sleet falling in spurts. Around her, ahead of her, behind. She couldn't help it, couldn't stop it. The air turned frosty as big white flakes fell to the bright green grass and hung there for a moment before melting away.

She ran for what seemed like a very long time… had she missed it? Had she somehow passed the stone circle? The air turned colder, and the snow that fell did not melt away quickly. It clung to grass and rocks. Was she headed in the right direction? Was she *too late*? The sun had set. Soon it would be dark. She had no chance of finding Ryder and Cassidy once that happened.

Suddenly the way was lit with those sparkling lights she'd seen once before. Pink and yellow and blue and lavender, those colorful lights twinkled against the snow in a slightly waving line that canted to the left. She could see that line all the way to the crest of the next hill. Fairies? Maybe, maybe not. Whatever they were, they had led her to the stones once before. She followed their lead.

The lights danced around her feet, broke apart and moved ahead as she ran. "Please take me to them," she whispered, not knowing if whatever created the lights could hear her and understand. If she didn't find Ryder and Cassidy, if she found them too late…how would she survive? They were hers. Hers to protect. Hers to save on this cold night.

She crested a gentle hill and finally, *finally*, saw the stones ahead. Tall and majestic and shimmering with power, they called to her in a way they had not before. She ran harder, all her focus on the stones. A few seconds later she saw the three standing there. Ryder and Doyle. Cassidy, standing close but not too close.

Doyle held his knife against Ryder's side. Distracted by the unexpected and unnatural snow, he tipped his head and looked up. A few flakes landed on his face and he smiled. She read his lips as he looked at Ryder and asked, "You?"

"Yes," Ryder answered. She was close enough to hear his voice when he added, "Get this over with. Do it now."

Doyle chanted a few words she did not understand— so few words, not enough, not long enough, *not enough time*—and then the knife plunged deeply into Ryder's body. Ryder fell; he dropped to the ground. Echo screamed. Cassidy screamed. The earth shook.

Just as in her vision, Echo felt the blade as if it had punctured her skin as well as Ryder's, but she didn't stop running. She didn't even slow down. The sparkling lights that had led her here disappeared. They didn't fade away; they were just suddenly *gone*.

Alerted by her scream, Doyle turned around and looked at her. And smiled. Murderer. Traitor.

What had once been snow gathering on the ground and falling from the sky turned to ice. It fell, hard and sharp. The frozen pellets that quickly covered the ground began to grow. Ice crept up around Doyle's feet. Ryder, prone on the ground, was not touched by the ice, not at first. Doyle was the target. In a matter of seconds a thick sheet of ice covered his shoes, then climbed up his ankles like frozen kudzu, a cold vine that trapped him in place. The ground around him began to turn white as the ice edged toward Ryder's body.

Doyle looked at the blood on his hands, he looked at a fallen Ryder and then—puzzled—he glanced down at his frozen feet. The knife in his hand waved about in an almost-wild manner.

Echo ran into the circle and dropped beside Ryder. There was so much blood. It soaked his shirt and ran onto the ground, bright red against the white snow and ice. He was already so pale; his eyes were weak. So soon, so quick, he was almost gone.

"He's all that I am now," Ryder whispered, and then his eyes drifted closed. "He is all that I was when I walked into this circle for the last time."

Echo rose and faced Doyle, who was flailing about as if he were on fire. The ice had reached his knees, and just beyond. The knife he'd used to stab Ryder fell from his hand, clinked against the hard ice at his feet. Trapped as he was in ice, he could not bend over to retrieve it.

"I don't feel any different, and I can't do anything," he said. The ice continued to grow. "What the hell? How do I make it stop?" There was panic in his voice, in his movements. "It's damn cold, and I don't like it."

"You did not take all that Ryder is," Echo said angrily, "no matter what you thought your blasted spell would do. He's a good man with love in his heart. He cares about people, cares about this town and the people in it. You can't take that. You can't become what you're not."

Ice climbed high on Doyle's thighs. He was solidly frozen in place. "I just wanted his magic!" he shouted. "I don't want to be tied down by caring about people or places, and love…love just makes you weak."

Her heart was breaking, and still, Echo smiled. She flicked a finger against the hard ice on the side of Doyle's leg. "Weak? Who's weak now?"

Frustrated, he shouted, "I just wanted his abilities. I wanted to be a wizard."

"Unfortunately for you, Ryder doesn't have any abilities, not anymore."

Doyle frowned. Again, he waved one hand like a bad magician trying to make a rabbit appear out of thin air. He knitted his brow, moved his hands while he still could. How long before he was completely encased in ice? "I don't even have my own powers anymore!" He turned toward Cassidy, who stood—pale and shaking with the cold and the shock—several feet away. "Come here, girl. Hand me my knife! I command you!" Cassidy didn't move, and once again Doyle tried to use his old abilities, the ones he'd been born with. He looked down at his knife and squinted as he attempted to make it rise. Nothing happened.

Half a dozen townspeople swarmed into the circle. Echo had not heard them coming. Her attention had been entirely on the three she'd come here to find. Suddenly, the others were there. Behind her, beside her. One kicked the knife away. It skittered over ice and into the soft grass, where it stopped. Another, and then another, attempted to knock Doyle to the ground. After a couple of tries the ice cracked and shattered, and given the way Doyle screamed a few of his bones did the same. The ice had been quite sturdy, Echo would admit. Ice born out of pain and heartbreak.

Nevan placed a heavy booted foot on Doyle's chest and said, "I never liked you, and your vegetable soup is no better than dirty dishwater." With just a few glances, those with abilities gathered the power of the circle and erased knowledge of the spell from Doyle. He'd never be able to try to steal another's power.

With Doyle surrounded and no longer a threat, Cassidy ran to her father. Since others were seeing to a wounded and powerless Doyle, Echo joined the young girl. Together they bracketed the unconscious man they loved.

"I don't suppose healing is one of your abilities," Echo said. Ryder was alive and breathing, but barely. If he was going to die, wouldn't she know? Wouldn't she see or feel it? Maybe. Maybe not. Brigid was tending to the wounded in town, and by her own admission she was a minor healer. Ryder needed more than minor healing. He'd never survive the trip to town.

Cassidy looked at Echo with big, sad eyes. She was scared, and rightly so. So much responsibility rested in her young hands. "I don't know," she whispered. "I never tried to heal anyone before."

Echo took one of the girl's cold hands and squeezed, and she whispered as the snow stopped falling, "Now is the time to try."

By the time Gideon and Hope arrived at the stone circle, led there by a couple of tired and bruised townspeople, the worst was over. Doyle had been taken into custody by the town constable, the one who had green lightning in his fingertips. Nevan, Gideon heard the man called. Echo and a young girl—older than Emma but not by much—were hunched over Ryder Duncan's body.

Hope kept stride with him, and had since they'd left Cloughban behind. "I knew when I married you that our life would never be dull."

"A battle every five to ten years should keep things lively."

She sighed. "Lively is overrated. Dammit, I don't want the girls to fight battles, not ever."

Neither did he, but the occasional battle came with the territory. He, his wife, their girls…they would forever hide a large part of themselves from the rest of the world. They would, on occasion, have to fight for what was right.

This particular battle hadn't been much of a challenge—though he did have a nasty bump on the head. And a headache.

For now, part of his job as a father was to make sure his daughters didn't know too much about the dark side of magic. He didn't even want them to know there were battles in the world. They'd find out soon enough.

He glanced around. "Why the hell is there snow?"

* * *

Rye opened his eyes. Echo and Cassidy leaned over him, their faces beautiful and near, and…worried. Behind and well above them, the moon peeked out from behind a cloud. He wished it were the sun instead of the moon. He was so damn cold.

He'd realized Echo was close when the snow had started to fall, but he had imagined she'd arrive too late to help him. It had been a relief to know that she'd be here for Cassidy. Someone had to be here for Cassidy.

The low murmur of many voices drifted to him, but he paid no attention to them. He was entirely focused on the faces of the two women he loved.

"Am I dead?" he asked.

Echo smiled and shook her head. In spite of the smile, there were tears in her eyes. "Your daughter healed you."

"I did," Cassidy said. Her grin was wider, fuller. Older somehow. "It was hard, but I did it!" There were no tears for his gifted daughter. She'd likely never doubted for a moment that he could save her from Doyle. She smiled at Echo. "I'm so glad you got here in time. Did the fairies lead you here again?"

"Yes," Echo said suspiciously. "How did you know?"

Cassidy giggled. "Silly, there are no fairies anymore. That was me. They were pretty lights meant to lead you where you needed to go." She glanced over her shoulder before Echo could respond. "Granny and Mr. McManus are here!" She jumped up and ran, and he heard her shout, "Granny! Guess what I did!"

Echo placed her head on his chest, as if checking for a heartbeat. He put a hand in her hair and held on. Maybe Cassidy had healed him, but he wasn't quite ready to move.

"I'm so cold," he whispered in her ear.

"Sorry," she responded just as softly. "That was me."

Snow and ice beneath his fingers, beneath his entire body. Yes, that was her.

"I convinced Doyle to take my powers instead of Cassidy's, and he did."

"You don't have any powers," Echo said without lifting her head.

"Now neither does he, I assume." His hand settled in her hair, held her to him.

"He's not very happy about that turn of events," she said. She was so warm, so soft and so very much…his.

"I suppose not. Doyle was after supreme power. He was willing to sacrifice anyone and anything to have it all, and he came away with nothing." Rye realized that he had always relied on his abilities, even when they'd been dampened. Now what? He didn't know who he was, *what* he was. Unless he, like Doyle, was now nothing.

"Not nothing," Echo whispered.

Great. She could still see into his head, he just couldn't see into hers.

A town like Cloughban needed a mayor who was one of them. An independent, a gifted person. Cassidy needed someone who truly understood what she was facing to guide her. And Echo…Echo Raintree deserved better than an ordinary man.

"I've always wanted an ordinary man," she whispered.

He didn't believe her.

Gideon and his wife arrived to put an end to the conversation, and Rye found the strength to sit up, dislodging Echo in the process.

All his life, he'd experienced a surge of energy when

he was amid the stones. He'd felt the power here as if it were a physical thing. Today, he felt nothing.

Gideon Raintree was another matter. Lightning danced on his skin, and he could not stand still. His wife laughed at him lovingly as he moved back, out of the circle.

Rye looked at Echo and said, "Believe it or not, I'm glad your cousin is here."

"Me, too."

Their reasons were likely not the same. Rye gathered all his courage to say, in a calm and detached voice, "He can take you home."

Chapter 26

"Of course I have a room free!" Maeve Quinlan said as she climbed the stairs to the second floor. Showered and changed, hair fixed and makeup applied, she looked very little like the woman who had wielded an iron skillet as an effective weapon just a few hours earlier. "Not Maisy's room," she added in a tight voice. "I am shocked, shocked, I tell you, to think that she would… well, we won't discuss that unpleasantness."

Echo trailed behind, allowing Maeve, Gideon and Hope to go ahead of her.

"I will not give you her room," the landlady said forcefully. "There's no telling what kind of negative energies might be present there. Until the room is thoroughly cleaned in every way, no one can stay there." She tsked. "I imagine I'll have to sage the entire house to clear it of dark energies. That Doyle stayed here for a few nights before he rented his house out by the Conor place. Yet another reason to give the house a good, thorough cleaning."

The residents of Cloughban had never flaunted their gifts. Not in her presence, at least. Echo didn't know what most of them were capable of. What were Maeve's gifts? Beyond making killer scones.

The landlady turned, glanced past Gideon and Hope and said in a sweet voice, "I'm a witch, dear. Just your ordinary, everyday witch."

Echo sighed. A witch as well as a mind reader apparently. This was not an easy town to keep secrets in. How had Doyle and Maisy done it?

Maeve answered that thought. "Oh, they were much better at hiding their feelings and thoughts than you have ever been. If you stay awhile, I'd be happy to help you with that."

Would she be here for a while?

"I don't know, dear. I'm a mind reader, not a psychic."

Hope snapped, "Whatever you two are doing, stop it."

Gideon cast a censuring glance Echo's way. "We're all tired. Let's get some sleep and we'll head out in the morning."

Would she head out in the morning? Was this her last night in Cloughban?

Maeve escorted Gideon and Hope to a room at the end of the hall. Hope turned and hugged Echo tightly. There was love in that hug. They both needed it at the moment.

"Does it ever stop?" Hope whispered.

"No," Echo said, the word not much more than a breath. There would always be bad people who wanted to use those who had paranormal abilities for their own

profit or entertainment. And for someone like Cassidy...
how could Ryder keep her safe from a world filled with
people who would either hate her or crave her for the
abilities with which she'd been born?

Gideon lifted a hand and gave her a tired wave instead of a hug. She returned the gesture. He'd always
treated her like a little sister, had always protected her.
He kept her safe, counseled her, scared away inappropri-
ate boyfriends. But she was a grown woman now, and
he couldn't protect her from everything and everyone.
Though she imagined he would try if given the chance.

He had a family to take care of now. Hope and Emma
and Maddy. If she ever needed him he'd come running,
but it was time for her to make her own way. She needed
to learn to save herself.

The door to their room closed. She imagined they'd
both be asleep in five minutes, or less. Echo glanced at
the door to her own room. With the exception of finding the threat to her parents there—Maisy's doing, she
now knew—it had been a good home, for a while, with
a comfortable bed. She was exhausted. She could use
ten or twelve hours of sleep.

An unpleasant thought slipped into her head. Had
that been Doyle's room when he'd stayed here? Was she
sleeping in the same bed he had, under the same roof?
Did she look out of the same window at night? The idea
made her shiver. Still, she needed sleep...

She also needed Ryder, the man who had made it
very clear that he didn't want or need her.

"Men rarely know what they want or need until we
tell them, dear," Maeve said as she headed downstairs.

Echo watched her go. Witch. Mind reader. If she
stayed here, if she became a part of this town, she'd be

in for a life of surprises. If she stayed she'd be asking for everything she'd come here to rid herself of.

Maeve reached the end of the staircase and turned about to head toward the kitchen. Two steps, and she was no longer in view. If she was still able to read Echo's thoughts, there was no longer any indication.

For what seemed like a long time Echo stood at the top of the stairs. This was an important decision, perhaps the most important of her life. Run and hide or fight? Take the easy way out or take what she really wanted?

She'd gotten what she came here for. While she had not rid herself of the visions they were now more manageable. She could sense when one was coming on, and she was much more in control while in the visions. Control was possible. She still had more to learn, but maybe she'd make a decent prophet, after all.

The weather issue was, she suspected, connected to the stones. Once she was away from this place—*if* she was away from this place—that ability would probably fade. Probably. She hoped so! Her worry on that front came and went quickly. If she went home with a new power, she'd learn to control it as she had learned to control the visions.

The enhanced empathic ability would likely remain. She wasn't sure she liked that one much, but like the rest there wasn't much to be done for it. She'd manage. She'd study and train and one way or another she'd make it work.

The question was, would that happen here or in North Carolina? Would she continue to learn and study with Ryder or without him?

Rye had tried to convince Echo to leave Cloughban immediately—now, tonight—but she was nothing if not stubborn. If he could see into her mind the way he once had, give her a little push, convince her in a subtle, magical way that she didn't like him all that much...

But he couldn't.

Not a full hour ago, Echo had grudgingly returned to the boardinghouse that had been her home for the past few weeks. She'd made it clear she wanted to stay with him. He'd made it clear that he didn't want her here. Everyone who had participated in the day's events was exhausted, mentally and physically. She needed sleep and so did her Raintree cousins.

He needed sleep, too, but the way he felt right now... it might be weeks before he slept again.

Rye felt oddly empty without his abilities. Even dampened as they'd been for years, they'd been substantial. To be without them was like losing a sense, suddenly being blind or losing the ability to smell or taste.

Given the chance, he would change nothing. Better that he be blind than for the world to have to deal with what he might have become.

Screw the world. He would give up everything so Echo and Cassidy wouldn't have to deal with what he would have become.

Doyle, who called himself the last Ansara, was now powerless. Cassidy was safe, at least for now. For the next several years Rye would devote himself to being a father. He would teach only her if he could. Could a man with no power instruct someone like her? He would try. He would try with everything he had.

He'd continue to run the pub. He'd continue to be mayor if the people of Cloughban wanted him to do so. If they wanted someone like them, someone who was special, he would willingly step aside.

And he would do it all alone. He would not tie Echo

down in this remote place. He would not tie her to the ordinary man he had become.

She had so much to offer the world; she deserved the chance to make her mark. To be a powerhouse in the magical world. Raintree princess. No, Raintree *queen*.

Yes, he should sleep. Not just for hours, but for days. The pub was closed. He was exhausted. His daughter had healed him; he would carry no long-lasting scar from Doyle's attack, but the wound had drained him in a way that could not be healed with a gifted touch. He needed rest, and yet his mind would not be still.

Cassidy had gone home with her grandmother. Rye had a choice. He could try to sleep above stairs or he could go to bed in his own room in that cottage.

Instead of doing either, he wiped down the bar in an almost-automatic manner as his mind spun with what-ifs and what-nows. Yes, he needed rest, but sleep would not come for a while.

When the door opened, he jumped. It would take some getting used to, not sensing when that door would open. Not knowing what was on her mind.

"Echo," he said. "Did you forget something?"

"Yes."

"What?"

She walked toward the bar, and him, much as she had that first day. He'd seen trouble in her then. He saw trouble now.

"You," she said.

He should've locked the door after she'd left here with her cousins. He should've locked the place up and gone to the cottage with Bryna and Cassidy.

No, that would be the coward's way. Best to handle this cleanly.

"Go away, Raintree. Your time here is done."

She was not scared. Was she ever? Small and seemingly frail, she was one of the bravest women he had ever known. She didn't back down. "Don't tell me we don't have something special."

If he lied to her would she know? Was their connection completely severed? Earlier she'd been able to see into his head, but he'd been blind to hers. That mental link…was it entirely gone?

In case she could see more than she should, he stuck with the truth. "Perhaps we did have something special at one time, but we are both different now." She was stronger; he was weaker.

"We're not different, not deep down where it counts." She walked behind the bar. Walked into him, wrapping her arms around his waist and laying her head on his chest. She was warm and soft; she was everything he had thought never to know.

There were a million reasons for them not to be together, but he didn't want to argue with her. Not now. He didn't want to talk at all.

He grabbed the hem of her T-shirt and inched it up slowly. She shifted away from him, just a bit, to allow him to pull her clothing over her head. With a few more moves she stood before him completely and wondrously naked. Fine from the top of her head to her toes. Perfection inside and out.

"No fair," she whispered as she began to work the zipper on his jeans. "I am naked and you are not."

He needed her. One last time.

She slipped her hand inside his unzipped pants; he wrapped his arms around her and picked her up, dislodging that hand, making her laugh. He loved her laugh; it was too rare, too precious.

He carried her around the bar, to a table in the middle of the room. She'd had this fantasy once—*they'd* shared this fantasy—before they'd become lovers. Before they'd even kissed. He laid her on the table, spread her thighs, freed his erection and followed her down and down.

And into her.

This connection they had not lost. It was heaven on earth, real and unreal. It was truth and magic. He lost himself in her, body and soul. He claimed her, used her, gave to her. For a few precious minutes the world went away, and it took all their troubles with it. Nothing mattered but this. Nothing mattered but her.

She wasn't like any other woman he'd ever known. Echo Raintree was a gift. A gift he couldn't keep, but one he would always remember and hold close to his heart. Ah, he'd realized she was trouble the moment she'd walked in the door…

His trouble. His woman. His heart.

She shattered beneath him, crying out softly as her inner muscles clenched and unclenched around him. Her response sent him over the edge. He was no longer capable of thought, no longer capable of anything but *this*.

Warm and satisfied and exhausted to the bone, he held her. He'd never expected to feel this way about any woman, had never expected to love this way. She could be home, his home, in a way he had never known. Peace, in a way he had never expected. Here in Cloughban, on her blessed Sanctuary land, in the desert or the mountains or in any city in the world…

Reality returned too quickly. He could not afford to lose himself in her, could not afford to make her everything.

Echo reached up, touched his hair and whispered, "I love you, Ryder." She closed her eyes and sighed. Judging by the expression on her face, she thought all was well. She thought…

Hell, he had no idea what she was thinking.

He withdrew, stood, straightened his pants. She was the vulnerable one at this moment. Naked, sated, still lying on the table flushed with pleasure and what she thought was love.

There was only one thing he could say in response to her heartfelt *I love you*.

"You're fired."

Cassidy woke in her own bed, in her own home, with a smile on her face. She should go to school today. She really wanted to see all her friends again! There was no more reason to hide out. Not from Echo! A quick glance at the clock told her it was too late to get to school anywhere near on time. After yesterday, it was likely no one would be there, anyway.

Tomorrow would be soon enough.

She smelled Granny's porridge, and bacon and eggs, and suddenly she was starving.

Cassidy jumped from the bed and ran into the kitchen on bare feet. Granny was awake and had been for a while, by the look of it. She was dressed and her hair was gathered in a neat bun.

"Is Mr. McManus joining us for breakfast?" Cassidy asked. There was a lot of food on the table.

"No, dear. Perhaps we'll see him later today. I suspect he's sleeping late, as you did."

"Lots of people are sleeping late today!" In her nightgown, her own hair curling wildly in all directions, Cassidy ate twice as much as she usually ate for breakfast. She ate it twice as fast, too. Either the healing or the scare had worked up quite an appetite!

A small, sudden knowing robbed some of her happiness. Her da wasn't sleeping. He hadn't slept much at all last night...

"I need to see Da." Suddenly she knew he needed her. Not just as a ghostlike vision popping in to say hello, but in the flesh. He needed a hug.

Granny shook a finger. "I've warned you about those visits..."

Cassidy stood and ran toward her room. "I need to *really* see him. I can find my way to town," she added in a louder voice as she began to gather her clothes. "You don't need to come along if you don't want to."

By the time Cassidy was dressed, Granny was ready to go. She wore a rather stern expression, along with her favorite walking shoes.

"Child, what are we going to do about that father of yours?" Granny asked as they walked out the front door. That door still smelled of smoke and it hung a little crooked. It could be fixed, though. Everything that had been damaged yesterday could be fixed. Everything.

Cassidy skipped ahead. "I haven't decided yet," she called. She only knew her da *still* needed help.

Echo had never been able to see her own future, and had never really cared to. If what was coming was good, it was much more fun to be surprised. If it was bad and could not be changed, why would she want to know?

But as Gideon—garbed in a protective talisman that allowed him to drive without killing the car's electronics—drove her rental car toward the airfield where a private jet waited, she closed her eyes and attempted to see what might lie ahead for her. Something, anything. A clue, please.

How could she find and lose love so quickly? How

could Ryder send her away? She knew he loved her, and she loved him. With or without magic. Wizard or ordinary man, he was hers.

He'd all but kicked her out of Cloughban. He'd even officially fired her and made her return her Drunken Stone T-shirts. She'd been naked at the time. Naked and in love and so sure they would be together forever.

Since Ryder didn't want to see her again, he'd asked her to leave those T-shirts on the sidewalk outside the pub on her way out of town.

She'd kept one. It was packed in her duffel bag. A part of her hoped he'd change his mind and come after her, maybe with that missing T-shirt as an excuse, but she didn't hold out much hope.

Would she live the rest of her life waiting for Ryder to show up and admit that he'd made the worst mistake of his life when he'd let her go?

Somewhere up ahead, Hope drove the rental car she and Gideon had left on the side of the road on their way into Cloughban. After a couple of days away from Gideon, it had started easily enough. Hope had volunteered to drive, saying she could use a little quiet time. Maybe she'd realized that Echo and Gideon needed to talk. Alone.

They had been on the road almost half an hour before he spoke. Right back to business, dammit. "So, are you going back to the Sanctuary?"

"I suppose."

"Don't be so enthusiastic," he said dryly. "You did a good job there. You're needed and wanted. Just...don't make it snow in July. We don't need the attention."

If her heart was broken now and forever, would it snow when she thought of Ryder? Maybe. Maybe not.

Away from the stones her abilities would be different. Maybe less, maybe more, but definitely different.

"It's just...being keeper of Sanctuary was always temporary in my mind," she confessed. "I was a place holder for Emma. I know, she has years before it'll be time for her to take that job, but still...it was never me. That job was never *mine*." Was that what she'd always been looking for? Something that was meant to be hers?

"What is yours?" Gideon asked, and somehow he sounded both kindly concerned and incredibly frustrated.

She had to be honest. "I don't know."

He sighed. Gideon was such a guy, not really good at the touchy-feely stuff. But he did care. She knew that. Even if he was sometimes maddening, like a big brother or overly protective father would be.

"I use my abilities to help people," he said. "Dead people, yeah, but the dead are people, too. Kind of."

"Is this supposed to be helping?" Echo asked sourly. He was trying, and she grudgingly gave him credit for that, but she was pretty frustrated herself at the moment.

"Dammit, let me finish," he said. "I tried to quit, after Hope and I got married, but this is what I do. I find murderers and take them off the streets. Hope misses it. When the kids are in school she'll probably come back. They won't allow us to partner up again. It'll be a struggle, but we'll make it work because it's who we are."

"It'll be a while before that happens," Echo said absently.

"What?" Gideon sounded confused and put out. "Madison is four and a half. She'll be in kindergarten next year..."

"But what about the boy?" Echo asked.

Gideon looked at her and she looked at him. Green

eyes met in silence. They were both surprised by her words.

"Boy?" he asked after a few moments.

There had been no vision, no crippling experience that took her elsewhere, but she knew. A boy. "In eight and a half months or so," she said. "Yes."

"Hope hasn't said a word…"

"She doesn't know! Jeez, Gideon, the *eight and a half months* should've been a clue." Another Raintree baby. Maybe one with Gideon's powers, his amazing abilities. He had never said he wanted a son. He loved his daughters, doted on them, even. But he'd be thrilled…

"How many?" he asked in a voice filled with something much like terror. "We just planned on the two, but apparently we… I swear, we're careful… Never mind, we don't need to go into that." He blushed just a little. "Okay, tell me. Lay it on the line, cuz. How many kids are Hope and I going to have?"

Echo managed to laugh. "I don't know. This is life, Gideon. Be surprised now and then. Have eight kids if it suits you."

"*Eight?* Bite your tongue. Hope would kill me. Shit! She's going to insist I get clipped, I just know it."

Echo laughed. No, Gideon would not be happy when Hope insisted that he have a vasectomy but in the end he'd do it. And he'd grumble about it. A lot.

They were silent for a long moment. Gideon was probably thinking about the changes a new baby would bring to their lives. Maybe he was thinking about having a son. About baseball and football and fixing old cars.

Did Ryder want a son one day? He loved Cassidy, she knew that, but…was it enough? Did he long for more?

"Back to the matter at hand," Gideon said, all business once again. "Who are you, dammit? Where do you belong? No one can tell you, you have to *feel* it."

Feel it. She'd been feeling all her life. Good and bad, traumatic and ecstatic. On occasion she tried to block it all out, but she did know how to feel.

"I want to sing," she said softly. "I want to make music."

Gideon nodded. "Good. That's a start. What kind of music? Where?"

The answer was crystal clear, but it wasn't going to be easy. Was anything worthwhile ever easy? Wasn't what she wanted and who she was deep inside worth fighting for?

She turned to look at her cousin, studying his profile for a few seconds before she said, in the most commanding voice she could muster, "Turn the car around."

Rye looked toward the table where he'd laid Echo down last night. He wasn't sure he could ever allow anyone to sit at that table again. It was his. Hers. Theirs. He glanced at the stage where Echo had played and sang on so many nights. The space had never looked so empty to him before.

He'd lied to her about never having music in the pub. There were a couple of decent local bands that performed almost every weekend. One played traditional Irish music, while the other dabbled in soft rock. He'd paid them to back off while she'd been here because he wanted to listen to her sing. He wanted to watch her light up as she sat on that stage with a guitar in her hands.

Last night he'd been so sure he was making the right decision in sending her away, but now...he didn't know what came next. He didn't belong here, not when the powers he'd possessed had been stripped away. What if he made them uncomfortable, and they stopped coming to the pub altogether?

It wasn't as if he had many choices. He couldn't take Cassidy out into the world, not with puberty and the chaos that would bring to someone so incredibly gifted on the horizon. Her place was here. Somehow, he'd have to make it work. For her.

The pub remained closed. No one felt like celebrating at the moment. Even the grumpy trio of old men who were here six days a week was steering clear of the place. Nevan had called in reinforcements and rid himself of Doyle and his seven hired guns. They were all in a jail cell somewhere. Rye didn't know where, and he didn't care. The soldiers would receive treatment for their minor wounds and then they'd have their minds cleared of recent memories before they were dropped off in a big city somewhere in the world. Each of them in a different city, a different country.

Doyle was another matter. His memories had been removed, as well, but he would never go free. Nevan's word that the man who'd tried to kill Cassidy would never leave his lonely prison was good enough for Rye.

Some of Cloughban's own had been injured, others were shaken up by the invasion. This was supposed to be a place of safety, of isolation. Soon enough some would need to commiserate, and what better place than the village pub.

The Drunken Stone would come to life again, but it would never be the same.

He needed to find a new cook.

Maybe a waitress.

He'd get a band back for the weekend, but...no, it wouldn't be the same.

Cassidy, who was not allowed in the pub under normal circumstances, sat with her grandmother in the corner booth. He'd been surprised to see them, but he was also glad of the company. He didn't need to sit here and feel sorry for himself.

Bryna looked tired, worn out to the bone. Cassidy had bounced back more quickly than any of the adults. Kids were like that. Rye hoped she could forget what had happened to her in the past few days, but he suspected she would not.

"Da, I'm very disappointed in you," Cassidy said in a put-on grown-up voice.

There were so many reasons for her to be disappointed, but he suspected he knew what hers were. The most magically gifted being in the world, and her father was...

"Not that," she said with childish disdain.

"It's rude to read people without their permission."

"I can't help it," she said. "You're all but shouting. I don't mind that you don't have powers. Inside now you're all blues and greens and lovely yellows. Before there were black spots, but those are gone. You don't want the black spots, Da. Besides, there are still some little powers in you, some little powers that have been with you since you were born. When you recover from the curse, they'll come back to you."

Little powers. Great. His mother had not been satisfied with little powers. Would anyone else be? Would he?

He ignored that part and said, "True, I don't want black spots. So tell me, why are you disappointed?"

She slipped out of the booth and headed his way. "You let Echo go."

He hoped with all his heart that Cassidy's ability to

see and understand didn't apply to *every* aspect of his life. If she peeked into things that she did not understand, she gave no indication. She was normally not shy about asking questions, so he continued to hope.

"What was I supposed to do?" he asked. "I know you like her, but she doesn't belong here."

"She *does*. Echo *does* belong here."

He had thought so, at one time. "If she belonged here she'd be here. That's the way the universe works."

Bryna scoffed, stood and headed for the rear door. "Poppycock," she said in a clear, loud voice. "Do you think the universe is going to do everything for you? The Raintree girl came to you. Of all the places in the world she might've gone in her wanderings, she ended up here. It's up to you to keep her." She snorted. "I need a nice long walk and a nap. Fix it." The door slammed behind her.

Alone with his daughter, Rye tried to remember why he'd sent Echo away. His life was in shambles; he was not who he'd always believed himself to be.

He still didn't want her family to overrun the town, but considering Gideon's reaction to the stones, he doubted that would be a problem.

Cassidy smiled. "I made Echo believe in fairies. She wasn't sure, at first, but I made her believe. I conjured some pretty lights to guide her to the stones, and she wanted to believe they were fairies. She knows better now, but I should really apologize. I told her it was me but I didn't say I was sorry. I can't apologize if she's not here."

"Do you see her future?" he asked. "Do you see Echo?" He wanted to know that she was safe and happy. Even if she wasn't safe and happy with him.

Cassidy shook her head. "Not anymore. She's too close to me now. She's a part of my circle."

It was frustrating. He wanted to know! "How can that be? You barely know her."

Cassidy shrugged, accepting in a way that only a child can be. "When I first met her, I thought she'd stay. I even had a weird thought that she was…the Oracle of Cloughban. Have we ever had our own oracle? What is an oracle exactly? I should've asked Granny. She'd know."

Oracle of Cloughban? No. Echo wouldn't come back.

"Your head is too full," Cassidy argued.

"I'm a grown-up. That happens sometimes."

Cassidy sighed and gave him a look of pure female indignation. Oh, hell, she was growing up too fast. "It's simple, Da. It's so, so simple. Clear your head and focus on what's important. Do you love her?"

"What are you grouching about?" Echo asked. "You're taking a private plane home. It's not like you're going to miss your flight. I know Hope will have to wait a bit at the airfield, but it won't be too long."

"It's not that," he grumbled.

"Then what?"

Gideon's lips tightened and his eyes narrowed, and then he said, "I have a feeling I won't see you again for a long time."

Echo glanced at her cousin's profile. She'd miss him, too, but this was her place. This was her life. "We'll visit, and you can bring the family here for a vacation."

Assuming Ryder allowed her to stay.

Who was she kidding? He didn't get to allow her anything. She'd stay. She was a grown woman who could live wherever she wanted to. The immediate plan

was to settle in and hound him until he admitted that
he loved her and could not live without her. That might
not be easy, but it wasn't impossible, either. She would
fight for him if she had to.

She wasn't a fighter. Never had been. But maybe
she just hadn't run across anything worth fighting for.
Until now.

"Make sure to stock up on dampening talismans before you come again," she advised.

"Don't worry, I will." He sounded no happier than
he had before.

Besides, Cassidy wanted to go to Disney World...

The road was barely wide enough for the rental car.
Gideon cursed when he spotted the dust on the winding
road, up ahead, around the bend. One of them would
have to pull off for the other to pass. Even then, it would
be a tight fit.

But before they turned the bend, Echo knew that
wouldn't be a problem. That was Ryder up ahead, and
he was coming for her.

She wouldn't have to fight, after all.

In her head she saw a flash of an unusual rusty-red
color. It was the color of the old car she'd seen parked
behind the pub.

Echo whispered to Gideon, "Stop."

He did, and then he turned to her, alert in a way only
a cop can be. "What's wrong? Are you having an episode? About to? What...?"

"I'll get out here. This is a wide enough spot for you
to turn around if you're very careful."

She leaned over the console and kissed him on the
cheek. "You really do have to come back. I can't wait
to see Emma and Cassidy together."

He paled, as if that thought had never occurred to him. "Good Lord…"

"We need to start planning a big family reunion. Your kids, Mercy's, Dante's, the whole crew." Look out, world…

Echo collected her bag from the backseat, stepped aside and watched Gideon make his turn, and then she stood in the middle of the road waiting for the rest of her life to begin.

Maybe his magic was gone, but they remained connected in a primal way. To the soul, to the bone. In body and spirit. No one could ever take that from them.

He was coming for her, and apparently he wasn't alone. Along the road, close to the ground, sparkling lights in many pastel colors appeared. They weren't leading her to the stones, not this time. They were leading her home.

I love you, Ryder.

Suddenly her head was filled with his voice. *Love you, too.*

He'd heard her, understood and responded. He was not entirely without magic, after all.

Feet planted far apart and steady, duffel bag in hand, she whispered to the road—and the lights—ahead, "Come and get me."

* * * * *

Lisa Childs writes paranormal and contemporary romance for Harlequin. She lives on thirty acres in Michigan with her two daughters, a talkative Siamese and a long-haired Chihuahua who thinks she's a rottweiler. Lisa loves hearing from readers, who can contact her through her website, lisachilds.com, or snail-mail address, PO Box 139, Marne, MI 49435.

CURSED

Lisa Childs

With great appreciation to
Tara Gavin and Ann Leslie Tuttle
for letting me share Maria's story
and revisit the Witch Hunt series.

Thank you!

Prologue

Europe, 1655

Strong hands closed over her shoulders, shaking her awake. Elena Durikken blinked her eyes open, but the darkness remained thick, impenetrable.

"Child, awaken. Quickly."

"Mama?" She blinked again, bringing a shadow into focus. A shadow with long curly hair. "Mama."

"Rise up. Hurry. You have to go." Her mother's hands dragged back the blankets, letting the cold air steal across Elena's skin.

"Go? Where are we going?" She couldn't remember being awake in such blackness before. Usually a fire flickered in the hearth, the dying embers casting a glow over their small home. Or her mother burned candles, chanting to herself as she fixed her potions from the dried herbs and flowers strung from the rafters.

"Only you, child. You must go alone." Mama's words, the final way she spoke, chilled Elena more than the cold night air.

"Mama…" Tears stung her eyes and ran down her face.

"There's no time. They will come soon. For me. And if you are still here, they will take you, too."

"Mama, you are scaring me." It was not the first time. She had scared Elena many times before, with the things she saw, the things she *knew* were coming before they ever happened.

Like the fire.

"Is this…is this because of the fire, Mama?"

Mama didn't answer, just pulled a cape over Elena's head, lifting the hood over her hair. Then she slid Elena's feet into her boots, lacing them up as if she were a small dependent child, not a thirteen-year-old girl she was sending alone into the night. Mama pressed the neck of a satchel against Elena's palm. "Ration the food and water. Keep to the woods, child. Run. Keep running…"

"How can they blame you for the fire?" she cried. "You warned them."

Even before the sky had darkened or the wind had picked up, her mother had told them the storm was coming. That the lightning would strike in the night, while the women slept. And that they would die in a horrible fire. Mama had seen it all happen…

Elena didn't know how her mother's visions worked, but she knew that Mama was always right. More tears fell from her eyes. "You asked them to leave."

But the woman of the house, along with her sister-in-law, whose family was staying with her, had thought that with the men away for work, Mama was tricking them. That she, a desperate woman raising a child alone, would rob their deserted house. She'd been trying to save their lives.

Mama shook her head, her hair swirling around her shoulders. "The villagers think I cast a spell. That I brought the lightning."

Elena had heard the frightened murmurs and seen the downward glances as her mother walked through the village. Everyone thought her a witch because of the potions she made. But when the townspeople were sick, they came to Mama for help even though they feared her. How could they think she would do them harm? "No, Mama..."

"No. The only spell cast is upon me, child. These visions I see, I have no control over them," she said. "And I have no control over what will happen now. I need you to go. To run. And keep running, Elena. Never stop. Or they will catch you."

Elena threw her arms around her mother's neck, more scared than she had ever been. Even though she heard no one, saw no light in the blackness outside her window, she knew her mama was right. They were coming for her. The men who'd returned, who'd found their wives, sisters and daughters dead, burned.

"Come with me, Mama," Elena beseeched her, holding tight.

"No, child. 'Tis too late for me to fight my fate, but you can. You can run." She closed her arms around Elena, clutching her tight for just a moment before thrusting her away. "Now go!"

Tears blinded Elena as much as the darkness. She'd just turned toward the ladder leading down from the loft when Mama caught her hand, squeezing Elena's fingers around the soft velvet satchel. "Do not lose the charms."

Elena's heart contracted. "You gave me the charms?"

"They will keep you safe."

"How?" Elena asked in a breathless whisper.

"They hold great power, child."

"You need them." Elena did not know from where they had come, but Mama had never removed the three charms from the leather thong tied around her wrist. Until now.

Mama shook her head. "I cannot keep them. They are yours, to pass to your children. To remember who and what we are."

Witches.

Mama did not say it, but Elena knew. She shivered.

"Go now, child," Mama urged. "Go before it is too late for us both." She expelled a ragged breath of air, then pleaded, "Do not forget…"

Elena hugged her mother again, pressing her face tight against her, breathing in the scent of lavender and sandalwood incense. The paradox that was her mama, the scent by which she would always remember her. "I will never forget. Never!"

"I know, child. You have it, too. The curse. The gift. Whatever it be."

"No, Mama…" She didn't want to be what her mother was; she didn't want to be a witch.

"You have it, too," Mama insisted. "I see the power you have, much stronger than any of mine. *He* would see it as well, and want to destroy you." Before Elena could ask of whom her mother spoke, the woman pushed her away, her voice quavering with urgency as she shouted, "You have to go!"

Elena fumbled with the satchel as she scrambled down the ladder, running as much from her mother's words as her warning. She didn't want the curse, what-

ever the mystical power was. She didn't want to flee,
either. But her mama's fear stole into her heart, forcing her to run.

Keep to the woods.

She did, cringing as twigs and underbrush snapped
beneath the worn soles of her old boots. She ran for
so long that her lungs burned and sweat dried on her
skin, both heating and chilling her. She'd gone a long
way before turning and looking back toward her house.

She knew she'd gone too far, too deep into the woods
to see it clearly with her eyes. So, like Mama, she must
have seen it with her mind. The fire.

Burning.

The woman in the middle of it, screaming, crying
out for God to forgive them. Pain tore at Elena, burning,
crippling. She dropped to her knees, wrapping her arms
around her middle, trying to hold in the agony. Trying
to shut out the image in her head. She crouched there for
a long while, her mama's screams ringing in her ears.

Behind her, brush rustled, the blackness shattered by
the glow of a lantern. Oh, God, they'd found her already.

The glow fell across her face and that of the boy who
held the lantern. Thomas McGregor. He wasn't much
older than she, but he'd gone to work with his father
and uncles, leaving his mother, sisters, aunt and cousins behind…to burn alive.

As they'd burned her mother. "No…"

"I was sent to find you. To bring you back," he said,
his voice choked as tears ran down his face. Tears for
his family or for her?

Her mother had seen this, had tried to fight this fate
for her daughter, the same fate that had just taken her
life.

"You hate me?" she asked.

He shook his head, and something flickered in his eyes with the lantern light. Something she had seen before when she'd caught him staring at her. "No, Elena."

"But you wish me harm? I had nothing to do with your loss." Nor did her mother, but they had killed her. Smoke swept into the woods, too far from the fire to be real, and in the middle of the haze hovered a woman. Elena's mother.

"I have to bring you back," Thomas said, his hand trembling as he reached for her, his fingers closing over her arm.

The charms will keep you safe.

Had her mother's ghost spoken or was it only Elena's memory? Regardless, she reached in the pocket of her cape and held the satchel tight. Heat emanated through the thick velvet, warming her palm. As if she'd stepped into Thomas's mind, she read his thoughts and saw the daydreams he had had of the two of them. "Thomas, you do not wish me harm."

"But Papa…"

Other memories played through Elena's mind, her mother's memories. She shuddered, reeling under the impact of knowledge she was too young to understand. "Your papa is a bad man," she whispered. "Come with me, Thomas. We will run together."

He shook his head. "He would find us. He would kill us both."

Because of what she'd seen, she knew he spoke the truth. Eli McGregor would kill anyone who got between him and what he wanted.

"Thomas, please…"

His fingers tightened on her arm as if he were about to drag her off. Elena clutched the satchel so close the jagged little metal pieces cut her palm through the velvet.

He sighed as if a great battle waged inside him. "I

cannot give you to him. Go, Elena. You are lost to me."
But when she turned to leave, he caught her hand as her
mother had, shaking as he pressed something against
her bloody palm. "Take my mother's locket."

To remember him? To remember what his family had
done to hers? She would want no reminders. But her
fingers closed over the metal, warm from the heat of
his skin. She couldn't refuse. Not when he had spared
her life.

"Use it for barter, if need be, to get as far away from
here as you can. My father has sworn vengeance on all
your mother's relatives and descendants. He says he
will let no witch live."

"I am not a witch." She whispered the lie, closing
her eyes to the luminous image of her mother's ghost.

"He will kill you," Thomas whispered back.

She knew he spoke the truth. Like her mother, she
could now see her fate. But unlike her mother, she
wouldn't wait for Eli McGregor to come for her. She
turned to leave again, then twirled back, moved closer
to Thomas and pressed her lips against his cheek, cold
and wet from his tears.

"Godspeed, Elena," he said as she stepped out of the
circle of light from his lantern, letting the darkness and
smoke swallow her as she ran.

This time she wouldn't stop… She wouldn't stop
until she'd gotten as far away as she could. And even
then, she wouldn't ever stop running…

From who and what she was.

Armaya, Michigan, 1986

The candlelight flickered as the wind danced through
the open windows of the camper, carrying with it the

scent of lavender and sandalwood incense. Myra Cooper dragged in the first breath she'd taken since she'd begun telling her family's legend; it caught in her lungs, burning, as she studied her daughters' beautiful faces.

Irina snuggled between her bigger sisters, her big dark eyes luminous in the candlelight. She *heard* everything but, at four, was too young to understand.

Elena, named for that long-ago ancestor, tightened her arm protectively around her sister's narrow shoulders. Her hair was pale and straight, a contrast to Myra's and Irina's dark curls. Her eyes were a vivid icy blue that *saw* everything. But at twelve, she was too old to believe.

Ariel kept an arm around her sister, too, while her gaze was intent on Myra's face as she waited for more of the story. The candlelight reflected in her auburn hair like flames, and her green eyes glowed. She listened. But Myra worried that she did not hear.

She worried that none of them understood that they were gifted with special abilities. The girls had never spoken of them to her or one another, but maybe that was better. Maybe they would be safer if they denied their heritage. Yet they couldn't deny what they didn't know; that was why she had shared the legend. She wanted them to know their fate so they could run from it before they were destroyed.

"We are Durikken women," she told her daughters, "like that first Elena."

"You named me after her," her eldest said, not questioning. She already knew.

Myra nodded. "And I'm named for her mother." And sometimes, when she believed in reincarnation, she was sure she was that woman, with her memories as well as her special abilities.

However, most of the time, Myra believed in nothing; it hurt too much to accept *her* reality. But tonight she had to be responsible. She had one last chance to protect her children; she'd already failed them in so many ways. They didn't have to live the hardscrabble life she had. They didn't have to be what she was—a woman whose fears had driven her to desperation.

"Our last name is Cooper," Elena reminded her.

"Papa's name," she said, referring to her own father. None of their fathers had given his child his name, either because the man had refused or she hadn't told him he was a father. "We are Durikken, and Durikken women are special. They know things are going to happen before they do."

Pain lanced through Myra, stealing her breath as images rolled through her mind like a black-and-white movie. She couldn't keep running and she couldn't make *them* keep running, either.

She forced herself to continue. "They see things or people that no one else can see. This ability, like the charms on my bracelet—" she raised her arm, the silver jewelry absorbing the firelight as it dangled from her wrist "—has been passed from generation to generation."

But Myra was more powerful than her sisters, had inherited more abilities as a woman and a witch. That was why she had been given the bracelet—because her mother had known she would be the only one of her three daughters to continue the Durikken legacy.

Myra's fingers trembled as she unclasped the bracelet. She'd never taken it off, not once since her mother had put it on her wrist, until tonight. Her daughters had admired it many times, running their fingers over the crude pewter charms, and she knew which was each one's favorite.

Elena had always admired the star, the sharp tips now dulled with age. Irina loved the crescent moon, easily transformed—like Irina's moods—from a smile to a frown, depending on the angle from which it dangled. Ariel favored the sun, its rays circling a small smooth disk. Despite its age, this charm seemed to shine brighter than the others. Like Ariel.

Even now, in the dingy little camper, an aura surrounded the child, glowing around her head as spirits hovered close. Did Ariel know what her gift was? Did either of her sisters? Her daughters needed Myra's guidance so they could understand and use their abilities. They were too young to be without their mother, but she couldn't put them at risk. All Myra could hope was that the charms would keep them safe.

Myra knelt before her children where they huddled in their little makeshift bed in the back of the pickup camper, their home for their sporadic travels. This was all she'd been able to give them. Until now. Until she'd shared the legend.

Now she'd given them their heritage, and with the help of the charms, they would remember it always. No matter how much time passed. No matter how much they might want to forget or ignore it.

She reached for Elena's hand first. It was nearly as big as hers, strong and capable, like the girl. She could handle anything...Myra hoped. She dropped the star into Elena's palm and closed her fingers over the pewter charm. The girl's blue gaze caught hers, held. No questions filled her eyes, only knowledge. She'd already seen too much in visions like her mother's. The girl had never admitted it, but Myra knew.

She then reached for the smallest—and weakest—hand, Irina's. Myra worried most about this child. She'd had so little time with her. She closed Irina's hand around the moon. *Hang on tight, child.* She didn't say it aloud. For Irina she didn't need to—the child could hear unspoken thoughts.

Myra swallowed down a sob before reaching for Ariel. But the girl's hand was outstretched already. She was open and trusting, and because of that might be hurt the worst.

"Don't lose these," she beseeched them. Without the protection of the little pewter charms, none of them would be strong enough to survive.

"We won't, Mama," Elena answered for herself and her younger sisters as she attached her charm to her bracelet and helped Irina with hers.

Despite her trembling fingers, Myra secured the sun charm on Ariel's bracelet, but when she pulled back, the girl caught her hand. "Mama?"

"Yes, child?"

"You called it a curse…this special ability," Ariel reminded her, her voice tremulous. She had been listening.

Myra nodded. "Yes, it is a curse, my sweetheart. People don't understand. They thought our ancestors were witches who cast evil spells."

And they had been witches, but ones who'd tried to help and heal. Her family had never been about evil; that was what had pursued them and persecuted them through the ages.

"But that was long ago," Elena said, ever practical. "People don't believe in witches anymore."

Myra knew better than to warn them, to make them aware of the dangers. She'd shown them the locket earlier, the one nestled between her breasts, the metal cold against her skin. It was the one Thomas had pressed upon Elena all those years ago. Inside were faded pictures, drawn by Thomas's young hand, of his sisters, who had died in the fire. Their deaths could have been prevented if only they'd listened and fought their fate. "Some still believe."

"Mama, I'm cursed?" Ariel asked, her turquoise eyes wide with fear. Her hand shook as she clutched the sun.

No more than I. Myra had lost so much in her life. Her one great love—Elena's father. And now…

"Mama, there are lights coming across the field!" Ariel whispered, as if thinking that if she spoke softly they wouldn't find her. Maybe she didn't hear as much as her sisters, but she understood.

Myra didn't glance out the window. She'd already seen the lights coming, in a vision, and so she'd hidden the camper in the middle of a cornfield. But still they'd found her; they'd found *them*. She stared at her children, memorizing their faces, praying for their futures. Each would know a great love as she had, and all she could hope was that theirs lasted. That they fought against their fate, against the evil stalking them, as she would have fought had she been stronger.

She just stood there next to the camper, in the middle of the cornfield, as the child protective services, who'd already declared her unfit, took her children away. The girls screamed and reached for her, tears cascading down their beautiful faces like rain against windows.

This wasn't Myra's final fate; her death would come much later. But as her heart bled and her soul withered, this was the night she really died.

But the authorities didn't take them all. Her hands clasped her swollen belly. Soon she would have another little girl. This child would need her even more than the others, for she would have more abilities than they had. She would be more powerful a witch even than Myra. But yet she would be even more cursed. The witch hunt would end for the others. But for her fourth child, whom she would call Maria, the witch hunt would never end…

Energy flowed from the cards up the tips of Maria Cooper's tingling fingers. Warmth spread through her as the energy enveloped her. *This will be a clear reading...*

Chapter 1

Energy flowed from the cards up the tips of Maria Cooper's tingling fingers. Warmth spread through her as the energy enveloped her. *This will be a clear reading...*

She had been blocking her special abilities for so long that she'd worried she might have lost them. But maybe that wouldn't have been such a bad thing. In the past they had proved more destructive than special—more curse than gift.

"What do you see?" the young woman asked, her voice quavering with excitement.

"I haven't turned the first card," Maria pointed out. Only the Significator, the fair-haired Queen of Cups, lay faceup on the table between them. The card didn't represent the young woman's physical appearance—not since the girl had dyed her hair black, tattooed a crow on her face and renamed herself Raven. But the card represented the wistfulness of the young woman's nature, so Maria had chosen it for her.

"But you see stuff—that's what people say about you," the girl continued. "That's why I wanted to learn from you—how to read the cards and how to make the potions and amulets. I know that you have a real gift."

A gift. Or a curse? She used to think it was the first and had grown up embracing her heritage. But then everything had gone so wrong, and she had begun to believe what others had—that she was cursed. That was why she had refused the girl's previous requests to learn to read. Maria had taught her about the crystals and herbs she sold in her shop but she'd resisted the cards—afraid of what she herself might see.

"I have it, too," Raven confided. "I get that sense of déjà vu all the time. I know I've already dreamed what's happening. I saw it…like you see stuff."

I hope you don't see the stuff I've seen…

"That's why I want to learn tarot," the girl said. "Because I know I'll be good at it."

Raven had been saying the same thing ever since she had first started hanging around the Magik Shoppe. The twenty-two-year-old had spent so much time there that Maria had finally given her a job, and now she had given in on teaching her tarot. She hoped like hell that she didn't come to regret caving in to the girl's pleas.

Maybe Raven had a gift. Or maybe, like so many others, she only wished she did because she had glamorized the supernatural ability into something that it wasn't. Into something powerful, when having these abilities actually made Maria feel powerless, helpless to stop what she might see.

"Thank you," Raven said, "for helping me."

I hope it helps and doesn't hurt…

"To teach you how to read the cards, I have to show you how I do a reading," Maria said. That was how her mother had taught her, having Maria watch her do readings for other people. But Mama hadn't always told the truth of the cards. Instead of telling people what she saw, she had told them what they'd wanted to see.

The old gypsy proverb that her mother had always recited echoed in Maria's head. *There are such things as false truths and honest lies.*

But there was no one but she and Raven in the old barn on Michigan's Upper Peninsula that Maria had converted into her shop. She had only the girl's cards to read. And she had already told Raven the meaning of each card, so she wouldn't be able to lie to her—even if it would be the kinder thing to do.

This is a mistake...

Her fingers stilled against the deck, which was the size of a paperback novel. She preferred the big cards because of the greater detail. She had always used them, ever since she had first started reading—at the age of four. She had read cards before she'd been able to read words.

"I've been working here almost since you opened a few months ago, but I've never seen you do a reading," Raven remarked.

And she shouldn't be doing one now. She shouldn't risk it...but it had been so long. She had missed it. Surely it couldn't happen again. The cards wouldn't come up the way they had before...

"I haven't done one in a while," she admitted. But she hadn't lost the ability. Energy continued to tingle up Maria's fingertips, spreading into her arms and chest. Before the girl could ask her why she hadn't, Maria shuffled the cards again and eased one off the top of the deck. "This first card will represent your environment."

Maria turned over the card atop the Significator, and dread knotted her stomach as she stared down at it. The moon shone down upon snarling dogs and a deadly scorpion.

A gasp slipped through the girl's painted black lips. "That's not good."

Maria's temple throbbed, and her pulse beat heavily in her throat. "No. The moon represents hidden enemies. Danger."

The girl's eyes, heavily lined with black, widened with fear. "You're saying I'm in danger."

Not again...

"That's what that means, right?" Raven persisted, her voice rising into hysteria.

Since Maria had already taught the girl the meaning of each card, she couldn't deny what Raven already knew. So she nodded. "Danger. Deceit. A dark aura..."

Maria saw it now, enveloping Raven like a starless night sky—cold and eerie, untold dangers hiding in the darkness. Goose bumps lifted on her skin beneath her heavy knit sweater, and she shivered.

"Turn over the next card," the girl urged. "That's what's coming up—that's what's going to be my obstacle, right?"

Maria shook her head. She wouldn't do it; she wouldn't turn that card. "No. We need to stop. We can't continue." She shouldn't have even begun; she shouldn't have risked the cards coming up the way they had before. But it had been more than a year...

She had thought that she might have reversed the curse, that her fortunes might have finally changed.

She'd been using the crystals, herbs and incense that she used for healing to treat herself.

"Turn the card!" The girl's voice had gone shrill, and her face flushed with anger despite her pale pancake makeup. "Turn it!"

"No." Her heart beating fast, she could feel the girl's panic and fear as if it were her own. But she also felt her desperation and determination.

"I have to know!" Raven shouted.

Maybe she did. Maybe they both needed to know. Maria's fingers trembled as she fumbled with the next card. Then she flipped it over to reveal the skeleton knight.

Raven screamed. "That's the death card."

"It has other meanings," Maria reminded her. "You've been studying the tarot with me. You know that it might just mean the end of something."

"What is it the end of? You see more than the cards. You see the future."

As Maria stared across the table at the young woman, an image flashed through her mind. *The girl—her face pale not with makeup but with death—her fearful eyes closed forever.*

Raven demanded, "What is my future?"

You won't have one.

"I don't see anything," Maria claimed.

"You're lying!"

Maybe the girl actually had a gift—because Maria was a very good liar. Like reading the cards, she had learned at a very young age how to lie from her mother. "Raven…"

"You were looking at me, but you weren't really looking at me. You saw something. Tell me what you saw!"

"Raven…"

"Oh, God, it's bad." The girl's breath shuddered out, and tears welled in her eyes. "It's really bad."

"It doesn't have to be," Maria assured her. "We can stop it from happening. I'll make you an amulet of special herbs and crystals…" And maybe this time it would work.

The girl shook her head, and her tears spilled over, running down her face in black streaks of eyeliner. "Even you can't change the future!" She jumped up with such force she knocked over her chair.

Maria jumped up, too, and grabbed the girl's arms. "Don't panic." But she felt it—the fear that had her heart hammering in her chest and her breathing coming fast and shallow in her lungs.

"Stay here," she implored the girl. "Stay with me, and I'll make sure nothing happens to you."

Blind with terror, Raven clawed at Maria's hands and jerked free of her grasp. Then she shoved Maria away from her, sending her stumbling back from the table.

"No. It's you," the girl said, her eyes reflecting horror. "I've seen it—the dark aura around you."

That was what Maria had been trying to remove. But she had failed. As Raven had said, even *she* couldn't change the future—no matter how hard she tried.

"It's you!" Raven shouted, her voice rising as she continued her accusation. "You're the moon!"

She hurled the table at Maria, knocking it over like the chair. The cards scattered across the old brick pavers of the barn.

Raven was right: even she, with all the knowledge of her witch ancestor, could not change what she had seen of the future. Like that witch ancestor, who had burned at the stake centuries ago, Maria was helpless to fight the evil that followed her no matter how far and how fast she had tried to outrun it.

The girl turned now and ran for the door, leaving it gaping open behind her as she fled. Just like Maria, Raven wouldn't be able to escape her fate: death.

The night breeze drifted through the bedroom window and across the bed, cooling Seth Hughes's naked skin and rousing him from sleep. He didn't know how long he'd been out. But it couldn't have been long, because his heart pounded hard yet, his chest rising and falling with harsh breaths. The breeze stirred a scent from his tangled sheets, of sandalwood and lavender, sweat and sex.

He splayed his hands, reaching across the bed. But she was gone even though he could still feel her in his arms and how he'd felt buried deep inside her body. He could taste her yet on his lips and on his tongue.

With a ragged sigh, he opened his eyes and peered around the room. Moonlight, slanting through the blinds at the window, streaked across the bed and across the naked woman sitting on the foot of it, turned away from him. She leaned forward, and her long black curls skimmed over her shoulders, leaving her back completely bare but for a silver chain and the trio of tattoos a few inches below the chain that circled her neck. There was a sun, a star and a crescent moon.

"I thought you'd left," he murmured, his voice rough with sleep and the desire that surged through him again. She was so damned beautiful with that sexy gypsy hair and all that honey-toned skin.

"I couldn't just leave," she replied as she rose from the bed.

Not after what they'd done? His pulse leaped as the desire surged harder, making him hard. Making love with her had been the most powerful experience of his life. And even though he wasn't certain he could survive it, it was an experience he wanted again. And again...

"I'm glad," he said.

She shook her head. "You won't be."

"Maria?" he asked, wondering about her ominous tone.

"You're going to be dead." Finally, she turned toward him, and the moonlight glinted off the barrel of the gun she held. He glanced toward the bedside table, where the small holster he clamped to the back of his belt lay empty. She held his gun.

"You don't want to do this," he said, holding his hand out for the weapon. But as he reached for it, it fired. The gunshot shattered the quiet of the night and...

The peal of his cell phone pulled him, fighting and kicking, from the grasp of the dark dream. Seth awoke clutching his heart, which pounded out a frantic rhythm. Pulling his hand away, he expected it to be covered with blood. His blood.

But his palm was dry. The room was too dark for him to see anything but the blinking light on his phone. No moonlight shone through the worn blinds at the window of the motel room. The only scent was dust and the grease from the burger and fries he'd brought back from the diner down the street.

"It was just a dream," Seth said, but no relief eased the tension from his shoulders or loosened the knot in his gut. Nothing was ever just a dream with him.

Drawing a breath into his strained lungs, he reached for the persistently ringing phone. His holstered gun sat on the nightstand next to the cell. His fingers skimmed over the cold barrel before he grabbed up the phone.

Just a dream...

"Hughes," he said gruffly into the phone.

"Agent Hughes?"

"Yes."

"You were right!" The girl's voice cracked with fear as it rose with hysteria. "It's her! She's here."

"Maria Cooper?"

"I lied to you when you were here earlier. I didn't believe what you said about her, but you're right. You're right about everything!" A sob rattled the phone. "I never should have trusted her. Now I'm in danger."

"Where are you?" An image flashed into his mind of the young woman with the bird tattooed on her face. "Raven?"

"I'm at the Magik Shoppe," she replied.

The old round red barn was hardly a store. But that was another reason he'd known it was *her* shop even though he hadn't found her there, just the girl.

"Why?" he asked. He had no doubt that she was right; she was in danger. So why was she at the barn?

"I came back here to get you proof that she's the one," Raven said. "I found it. I have the evidence you need. But you have to come quickly!"

He kicked back the tangled sheets. "I'm coming."

"How far away are you?"

"I stayed in town." Although calling Copper Creek, Michigan, a town was stretching the description since it had only a gas station, a diner, a bar and this one ram-shackle motel. Despite the girl's denial, he had known the shop belonged to Maria Cooper. Finally, he'd come across one of her witchcraft stores before it—and she—was gone.

He'd stayed in Copper Creek with the intent to keep returning to the store until he caught her there. Hell, if not for the long drive up north having worn him out, he would have staked out the place until she came back. But if he had fallen asleep and she'd discovered him, the least she would have done was run again.

Maybe he should have risked staying; at least he would have been closer when Raven called and he wouldn't have to traverse the winding, rutted gravel road in the dead of night. "I'll be right there."

"You're going to be too late..."

Oh, shit. The girl must have warned her boss about him. Maria Cooper was already on the run again. "Stay there. And keep her there if you can."

Another sob rattled the phone. "No. I don't want her to find me. I don't want her to kill me, too."

Seth reached for his gun again. Maybe it would be fired tonight. "I'll protect you," he promised. "I won't let her hurt you. Just wait for me."

Her breath hitched, and he could almost see her nodding in acquiescence. "Please hurry. She read my cards. She told me I'm going to die."

He shuddered. Every time Maria Cooper had read someone's future, they had wound up not having one anymore. They'd wound up dead.

Just as he had in his *dream*...

"She's dead," Ariel Cooper-Koster said. Goose bumps of dread and cold lifted on her skin as she stood outside in the night breeze.

"You've seen her ghost, then," Elena Cooper-Dolce replied, her pale blond hair glowing in the lights spilling out of the stately house in front of which they stood. There was no surprise in Elena's voice. As she'd previously admitted to Ariel, she had already witnessed their youngest sister's murder in a vision.

Ariel stared at the ghost of a woman with big brown eyes and long curly dark hair. Caught between two worlds, her image wavered in and out of a cloud of sandalwood-and-lavender-scented smoke.

"I haven't seen her yet," she admitted. "But Mama's back..." And she hadn't seen her in years. "She wouldn't have left her if Maria were still alive." After child protective services had taken Ariel, Elena and Irina from their mother, they had been separated and hadn't been reunited until twenty years later. Once they had all found each other and saved themselves from the evil force stalking them, their mother's ghost had left them. She had stayed with the daughter who'd needed her most— the one who'd been alone. Maria, whom her sisters hadn't even known existed until those twenty years had passed. It was Irina who'd figured out that her roommate, at the time their mother had died, was actually their sister. But once they'd learned of her existence, they hadn't been able to find her.

Elena shuddered. "I hope you're wrong. For her sake and for Irina's."

"She can't know," Ariel agreed. Their younger sister was in a fragile state; eight months pregnant with twins, she had been confined to bed rest and absolutely no stress.

"She does," a raspy male voice said as Ty McIntyre opened his front door to his sisters-in-law. He was a muscular man with dark hair, dark blue eyes and a jagged scar running through one eyebrow.

"Maria is not dead," Ty said as he gestured them inside the two-story foyer of his grand house. "She knows what the two of you are thinking, though. She *hears* you."

Ariel's face heated, and Elena's flushed bright red in the glow of the chandelier hanging over their heads. "Of course…" Irina could hear the thoughts of others—especially those with whom she was connected. "We can't block her like *she* can…"

"Maria isn't blocking her right now," he said, and a muscle twitched along his clenched jaw.

"But you wish she was," Elena said as she reached out and squeezed his arm, offering support and comfort.

"Maria can't block her when she's really upset," he said. "When she's really scared. Her emotions are so strong that Irina feels them, too."

Ariel's heart rate quickened. "Maria is upset and scared?"

Maybe that was why Mama had come back to her—to get her other children to help her youngest. While Ariel had always been able to see ghosts, she couldn't always hear them. She had struggled the most with her mother's ghost—probably because of all the emotions her mother's appearance always summoned in Ariel. The pain and regret and resentment.

Ty grimly nodded. "That's why I asked you both to come over tonight," he said. "Irina wants me to go find Maria."

"You've been looking for her for eight years," Ariel said with frustration and resignation. "We all have." And with the six of them working together, they had more resources than most—financially and supernaturally.

"So you're giving up?" It wasn't Ty asking; it was Irina, standing precariously at the top of the stairwell—her legs wobbling.

Ty vaulted up the steps and caught his wife up in his arms, lifting her as easily as if she were one of their seven-year-old twins. "You're not supposed to be out of bed."

"I could hear you all," she said. But probably only in her mind, since they hadn't awakened either one of the twins.

Ariel and Elena hurried up the stairs and followed Ty down the hall as he carried Irina back to their bedroom. "We didn't mean to upset you," Ariel said.

"We came to help," Elena said, her usually soft voice heavy with guilt and regret.

Ty gently settled his wife back onto their king-size bed. Irina sat up against the pillows and stared at them all, her brown eyes even darker with hurt and accusation.

She looked so much like the ghost of their mother—so much like the picture she'd shown them of their sister Maria. The three of them looked like gypsies—like witches—while Ariel and Elena didn't look related to any of them or even to each other. But their abilities united them—the Durikken blood that flowed in all their veins. Or had once flowed in their mother's...

She hovered near Irina. Maybe she had come back because Irina needed her more than Maria did.

"We're going to find her," Irina insisted.

Or maybe Maria would find them—after she died.

"Ty will bring her back."

It might not be possible. All they had found of their mother's remains had been her ashes.

"She's not dead," Irina said. "I can sense her feelings. I can hear her thoughts. She's anxious and scared. And very much alive."

For now. But if she was anxious and scared, she must be in the danger that Elena kept envisioning. And none of those visions had ended well for Maria...

She was gone. Maria couldn't even feel her anymore. There had been so much panic and fear and now...

Nothing. Maybe she was just too far away. Maybe she wasn't dead...

The wipers swished the streaks of rain from Maria's windshield, but still she could barely see—the headlamps of her old pickup truck were not strong enough to penetrate the thick black curtain of night in the Upper Peninsula of Michigan. The tires bounced over the ruts of the drive leading to Maria's little round barn at the end of the gravel lane. No cars were parked next to the shop.

Maria should have known that the girl wouldn't come back here. But she'd checked for Raven's car at the motel in town where the girl had been staying since her move to Copper Creek. She had also checked at the house of the guy Raven sometimes dated. But his windows had been dark, the driveway empty of any cars—even his.

Maybe they'd left together. Maybe he could protect the girl since she didn't trust Maria to do that.

I don't blame her, though. I don't trust myself.

That was why she rarely stayed anywhere for long— why she kept running, as Mama had always been running. It was why Maria tried to not get too close to anyone or let *anyone* get too close to her...

She never should have hired the young woman, and she definitely never should have agreed to teach Raven to read. Her fingertips tingling from the energy from the cards, Maria regretted ever touching them again. Why hadn't she left them behind…as she had so much else in her life?

Like Raven, she needed to run now. The girl had been right about the aura of darkness hovering over Maria. But besides the cards, Maria had left something else behind in the shop—something that she couldn't leave without. Her fingers trembled as she lifted her hand to her bare neck. During her scuffle with Raven, the chain must have broken.

Her lungs burned as she breathed hard, fighting the panic at the thought of what she'd lost. It had to be here. It couldn't be gone…

The hinges of the old pickup truck squeaked in protest as she flung open the driver's door. She jerked the keys from the ignition and tried to determine by touch which one would open the door to the shop. But as she stumbled in the dark, across the gravel, she noticed the faint glow spilling out of the barn—through the open door. She had locked it behind herself when she'd left to search for Raven. And the only other person with a key to it was her employee.

"Raven!" she called out as she hurried through the door. "I'm so glad you came back!"

She reached in her pocket for the amulet of dried alyssum, rosemary and ivy, and anise and caraway seeds, eucalyptus and huckleberry leaves, and a thistle blossom. She'd cinched the sachet with a leather thong on which she'd fastened a jet stone, a piece of obsidian and a tiger's eye. "I made something for you— something to keep you safe."

Then her eyes adjusted to the faint candlelight, which wavered back and forth—not because the flames flickered but because a shadow swung back and forth in front of them. Like the herbs, Raven hung from the rafters.

Maria was too late. Again.

Or was she? She glanced around, searching the shadows for another image—an orb or mist, some field of energy that indicated Raven's ghost. But nothing manifested from the shadows.

And the girl's body swung yet. "You're still alive. Stay with me. I'll help you." *But how?*

Panic pressed on Maria's lungs, stealing her breath. She righted a chair and clamored on top of it, but then jumped down again when she realized she had nothing to cut the rope that wound tight around the girl's throat. She fumbled for a knife and scrambled onto the chair again. Summoning all her strength, she hacked at the rope until the girl fell, her body hitting the worn wood floor with a soft thud.

"Please be alive," Maria murmured as she scrambled down beside her. She'd seen others do CPR on television, so she tried breathing into Raven's mouth and pushing on her chest. But the girl didn't breathe. She didn't move. Probably because Maria didn't know what she was doing. She knew how to heal with herbs and crystals, though. But she had never pulled anyone back from the brink of death before. What could she use? What would it take?

She ran back to the table where she cut herbs and grabbed up some dried hyssop and licorice. Both were used to treat asthma because of their anti-inflammatory powers. Maybe they could reduce the swelling in the girl's throat. She added some tincture of arnica that was used for bruising. Her hands shook as she mixed it together. Then she hurried back to where the girl lay limply on the floor of the old barn.

She pressed the mixture to the girl's swollen throat and slipped some between her open lips. Then she chanted a prayer, begging the higher power to heal the wounded, to reverse her cruel fate.

"Raven?" She leaned over the girl, listening for breathing. No air emanated from the girl's black-painted lips as her mouth lay open. Maria looked to her chest to see if any breaths lifted it, but a shadow fell across the room—blocking the light from the candles.

"Don't move!" a deep voice ordered.

Maria glanced up at the hulking shadow blocking the door. Only his eyes glinted in the dark—and the metal of the gun he held. Was he who had done this to Raven? Who had killed all of the other ones?

She tightened her grip on the handle of the knife and slid it beneath the folds of her long skirt. If he came close enough...

"What the hell," he murmured, his voice a low rumble in his muscular chest. He glanced from her to the body on the floor. His brow furrowed in concern and confusion as he stared down at Raven. "What did you do to her?"

Maybe he wasn't the one who had hurt the girl.

"I tried to help her," she told him. But her herbs weren't working. "Please, do something! Save her!"

The man knelt beside Raven, and his fingers probed her wrist. "She's dead."

"No, not yet." If Raven were dead, Maria would have seen her ghost because she always saw the souls of the recently departed. And sometimes of the not-so-recently departed. "She needs a doctor."

He shook his head.

"Why won't you help her?" The answer was obvious. He had tried killing the girl; he had no intention of saving her. Or of letting Maria live...

If she had any hope of surviving—and getting help for Raven—she had to act. Just as she had swung the knife at the rope noose with all of her strength, she pulled it from beneath her skirt and swung it at the man leaning over Raven's body. She didn't want to kill him; she just wanted to hurt him badly enough that he dropped the gun.

But as she neared his body, her momentum slowed—and she hesitated before burying the blade. She closed her eyes and pushed the knife down, then gasped as strong fingers locked around her wrist. Something cold and shaped like a circle pressed against her chin.

She drew in an unsteady breath, and the gun barrel pinched her skin. Maybe she should have read her own cards. Maybe then she would have seen this—would have seen this man. She opened her eyes to study him because his was the last face she would probably ever see.

He stared at her, his grayish-blue eyes as cold and hard as his gun. The candlelight flickered, picking up red glints in his thick brown hair. Even kneeling on the floor, he towered over her, broad shouldered and square jawed.

She tugged at her wrist, but his grasp tightened. And the knife dropped from her numb fingers onto the floor. "Let go of me..."

His mouth curved into a faint grin. "I've spent too long tracking you down to let you get away now."

Her heart slammed against her ribs. He was the *one*. The person who'd been hunting her for all these years and had taken all those other lives...

A gasp broke the eerie silence of the room. But it hadn't slipped through her lips. Or his.

She glanced down at Raven as the girl's eyes fluttered open and she stared up at them, her eyes wide with shock and horror. The girl had survived a hanging—maybe because of Maria's healing, maybe because she was stronger than she looked. But Maria doubted Raven was strong enough to survive whatever else the man had planned for her. For them.

She should have driven the knife deep in his chest while she'd had the chance. So that she wouldn't die as the others had—as Raven nearly had.

Like a witch...

Chapter 2

Red-and-blue lights flashed and sirens wailed as the ambulance pulled away from the Magik Shoppe. Rain streaked down Maria's face and soaked her sweater and skirt as she stood in the gravel drive, watching the ambulance speed away with Raven. That gasp for breath had been her only one, and then the man had done CPR on her.

Except for opening her eyes once, the young woman hadn't regained consciousness again. She hadn't been able to tell them who had hung her from the rafters.

Had it been him?

Maria turned her head to where he stood with the Copper Creek sheriff near the police cruiser. Even though he talked to the older man, his gaze was fixed on her, his steely blue eyes just as hard and cold as they'd been when he had pressed the gun to her chin.

The sheriff jerked his balding head in a couple of

quick nods, as if obeying the younger man's orders. Tall and broad shouldered, the stranger held himself with a confidence and authority born of power.

Despite the water running down his leather jacket and darkening the denim of his jeans, he seemed oblivious to the rain—focused only on her. As it had from the cards, energy flowed from him and spread through Maria so that her skin tingled with awareness and fear. She had never felt such a connection to another human being.

He had to be the one.

His conversation with the sheriff ended with the lawman hurrying back inside the open doors of the barn. So he approached her alone.

Her heart pounded with the urge to run, but before her feet could move, he was in front of her, his long legs needing only a couple of strides before he stepped close to her. So close that Maria had to tip back her head to hold his gaze as her heart continued to pound out a frantic rhythm.

"Who are you?" she asked.

His hand slipped inside his leather jacket, and she tensed, expecting him to withdraw the gun he'd put there before he'd begun CPR on Raven. But instead he took out a wallet and flashed it open to an FBI badge.

She blinked back the raindrops clinging to her lashes and read his name. Seth Hughes. And he was a special agent. But it didn't matter that he had an FBI badge; he could still be the one she'd run from in fear all these years. He could be the witch-hunter.

Anyone could be the witch-hunter.

"I've been looking for you for a long time," he said.

Tracking her down, he'd said earlier. The ominous words turned her colder than the rain that seeped through her clothes to her skin, and she shivered. "Not me." She shook her head. "You must have me confused with someone else."

"No," he said with absolute certainty. "You're Maria Cooper." He reached for her now, his big hand clasping her wrist as he turned her around.

That flow of energy between them grew more intense, her skin heating beneath his hand. Despite her empathetic gifts, she'd never reacted to anyone's touch the way she did to his. It had to be a warning...

"I'll scream," she threatened him. "Sheriff Moore is just inside the barn. He'll hear me. You won't get away with it."

"You're the one who won't get away," he said as cold metal clamped around her wrists. "Maria Cooper, you are under arrest. You have the right to remain silent—"

"Under arrest?" She jerked around to face him. "What are the charges? Assault?" She grimaced over having almost stabbed him. "You never identified yourself. You just pulled that gun on me."

A muscle twitched along his jaw. "I didn't have a chance to identify myself. I had to assess the situation."

"You can't arrest me for trying to defend myself," she pointed out.

"I'm not arresting you for trying to kill me."

"I didn't..." Until tonight she had never raised a hand, let alone a weapon, to another human being. She was all about healing—not hurting.

Had her potion or her prayer worked on Raven, bringing that gasp of breath to her lungs? Had she done enough for the girl to survive?

Agent Hughes ignored her denial and led her toward the dark SUV parked behind her pickup truck. After opening the back door, he put his hand over her head and guided her onto the seat.

Hating that even her hair tingled from his touch, she pushed against his hand. Then she twisted around on the seat, keeping her legs out so that he couldn't lock her inside the vehicle. She was afraid to get into a SUV with him, afraid of where he might take her.

Of what he might do to her...

"If not for assault, why are you arresting me?" she asked. "What are the charges?"

"Murder." That muscle twitched again along his jaw as he stared down at her.

"I didn't hurt Raven," she said. But it must not have looked like it when he walked into the barn and found her alone with the unconscious girl. "And she's going to live."

She has to...

"Your arrest has nothing to do with her," Agent Hughes said. "Yet. You're under arrest for multiple counts of first-degree murder."

She would have laughed—had he not looked so deadly serious. So instead she shook her head. "I'm not a killer."

"You're not just a killer, Maria Cooper—you're a se-rial killer. And while Michigan doesn't have the death penalty, some of the other states where you've killed do have it. You won't be able to hurt anyone else where you're going."

She didn't need any special gifts to know he was talking about sending her straight to hell.

Seth had promised to call them when he found her. But breaking his promise would probably be a bigger favor to them than keeping it. Maria Cooper was a dangerous woman.

And he had locked himself inside the tiny interrogation room at the local jail—with her. Just the two of them. The table between them was so small that every time he moved, his knees bumped against hers. That contact, however slight, sent blood rushing through his veins, roaring in his ears. What the hell was wrong with him?

Over the years, he had connected with victims… through evidence left behind at the crime scenes. And he'd had those damn vivid dreams ever since he was a kid. But never before had he had such a reaction to a suspect, as if inexplicably drawn to her no matter the atrocities she'd committed.

He pushed back his chair, but it bumped up against the cement-block wall behind him. And she was still so close he could feel her. To slow his pulse, he drew in a deep breath, and her scent filled his lungs—that sweet, smoky mixture of lavender and sandalwood that had his stomach knotting with desire…and apprehension.

He closed his eyes, but then the images from that damn dream—*that wasn't a dream*—flashed through his head. Her hair skimming across her slender shoulders. Her naked back, turned toward him, the moonlight playing across her honey skin and that trio of tattoos. She stood and faced him, the gun in her hand. The shot echoed inside his head, and he winced and opened his eyes.

"The caffeine's giving you a headache," she murmured, gesturing toward the paper cup of sludge sitting between them.

His stomach roiled at the thought of how long it had been sitting in the bottom of the pot in the sheriff's office.

"You should drink herbal tea."

"I need the caffeine." To stay alert. To keep his wits about him. "You sure you don't want some? It's going to be a long night."

"It already has been," she remarked with a wince of her own. "You finished reading me my rights." She gestured at the paper she'd signed acknowledging that he had. "Why haven't you locked me in a cell yet?"

Because while he'd put her under arrest and read her the Miranda rights, she wasn't really under arrest. He had a warrant only to bring her in to question as a material witness in all those murders—not for committing the actual murders. Seth really didn't have enough to arrest her for murder yet, even though she was his prime—his only—suspect. He had enough only to question her involvement. Fortunately, she'd waived her right to legal representation during this interview, so whatever she said he would be able to use against her.

"I have some questions for you," he said.

"About Raven?"

"About all of them." He picked up the leather briefcase he'd taken from his car and laid it on the table between them. He unlocked it and withdrew a thick folder. "These are the people you were more successful at killing over the past eight years."

He flipped open the folder and fanned out the crime scene photos across the surface of the table as she probably did her tarot cards. He didn't need to look at the pictures. All he had to do was close his eyes, and like that dream, the images played through his mind. The first girl had been drowned. A young man had been crushed beneath a board weighted down with bricks. Another girl had been hung...as someone had tried to hang Raven tonight. And the worst, the fire…had left behind little of its victim.

Of *her* victim.

She didn't look at the photos, either. Instead she held his gaze. The color drained from her face, making her wide almond-shaped eyes look even bigger and her high cheekbones and heart-shaped chin even more delicate. "I don't know anything about any murders. I don't even know why you keep calling me Maria Cooper."

"Because that's your name. That's who you are." Now that he had found her, he had a feeling that he would never be free of her…that this eerie connection that had haunted him would always bind him to her.

She shook her head, tumbling her glossy black hair around her shoulders as she had in his dream. "No. No. I'm not her."

"Who are you, then?" he asked, humoring her. "You have no ID. No driver's license. No birth certificate."

"Is there a driver's license or birth certificate on file—anywhere—for Maria Cooper?" she asked.

"You know there's not. There is no evidence you ever existed." He tapped the photos. "But these. You're the one person every single victim had in common. You're the last person every single victim saw…when you read their tarot cards." In most of the crime scene photos, the cards were still strewn across the table.

She closed her eyes, as if trying to shut out the images before her. But was she like him? Did they live on inside her head, haunting her just as they—and she—haunted him? Then, closing her eyes would give her no reprieve. In fact, sometimes it only made the images more real for him, like those dreams that weren't just dreams.

She opened her eyes, just a little, and studied him thoughtfully. "That's why you took my fingerprints."

He glanced down at her hands, which were slightly stained on the front and slightly scratched on the back. He'd already requested that the sheriff have Raven's fingernails scraped—to see if DNA could be matched to the woman who denied she was Maria Cooper.

She narrowed her eyes more. "I may have read their cards, but that doesn't mean I killed them. You have no evidence that I hurt any of them. There's no way that a judge really issued a warrant for my arrest."

"No," he admitted.

She stood up. And so did he, reaching across the narrow table to grab her wrist again. Like every other time he'd touched her, his fingers tingled and images flashed through his mind like a slide show.

His hands cupped her shoulders, and he pulled her closer. Her chin tipped up, her lips parting on a gasp of desire. She dragged in a deep breath that lifted her breasts against his chest. His head lowered, closer and closer to hers...

He hesitated, his mouth just a breath away from her full lips. Hunger burned in his gut; he'd never wanted to kiss anyone more. Never needed to kiss anyone the way he needed to kiss her...

"Let me go!" she said, tugging at her wrist. "You have no right to keep me here."

"I have every right to keep you here," he said. Just no right—or reason—to want to kiss her. Hell, she was the last woman he should be tempted to kiss. He knew exactly how dangerous she was.

"You're a person of interest," he explained, "and I do have a warrant to pick you up for questioning." Ignoring the desire that hardened his body, he slid his hand up her arm to her shoulder and gently but firmly shoved her back into her chair. "You're going to stay here and answer all my questions."

"You have the wrong person," she said, stubbornly sticking with her lie. "I'm not Maria Cooper."

"DNA would prove who you are."

Fear widened her dark eyes. "You can't take my DNA without my permission."

"Unless I get a warrant for it," he warned her. Since he'd finally found her, he would be able to ask for one— especially since the attack on Raven. But it would be faster than waking a judge in this godforsaken county in the Upper Peninsula if she freely offered it. "If you're not her, why won't you provide a sample of your DNA to prove it? To clear yourself?"

"You forget—it's innocent until proved guilty," she said, her lips lifting in a slight smile. But it was grim— not taunting.

He had been taunted by other killers, ones who had sat across the table from him, laughing at him during the interrogation. Proud of their crimes. She didn't act that way. But then, nothing about her was completely what he had expected except for her beauty.

She was so damned beautiful.

But he reminded himself and her, "We both know you're not innocent. Your name—your description— comes up in police reports across the country going back nearly two decades. Since you were ten years old, you helped your mother run cons on desperate, gullible people."

And because of that, he doubted she was the real deal. Like so many other self-proclaimed *psychics*, she was nothing more than a con artist.

She shook her head. "You have the wrong person."

For a con artist, she wasn't a very good liar. Then again, most suspects had trouble lying to him. "So prove it."

She shook her head again.

"You won't give up your DNA, because you know it's going to be at every one of these murder scenes." He tapped the photos again as he settled back onto the chair across from her. He needed to look at those photos, to remind himself what happened to people who got too close to Maria Cooper.

The tip of her tongue slid out and flicked across her lower lip. Was she manipulating him? Did she know how that simple action had his guts constricting with desire? With *need*?

"Just—just because someone was at the crime scenes," she stammered, "*before* the crimes happened, doesn't mean they were involved in the crimes."

"Once," he allowed, "maybe even twice. But four times—five, including tonight? That's more than coincidence. That's means and opportunity. The only person who'd be at every one of these crime scenes is the killer."

"And you," she said. "You've been at every scene."

First in his mind and then in person. He nodded. "I've been looking for you for a long time. Catching you has been my number one priority."

She shivered—maybe it was because her clothes were wet from the rain. Maybe it was because his determination scared her.

"Number one priority?" she repeated. "Why? Nobody's died in over a year."

He cocked his head at her significant slip. "How would you know that unless…?"

"The dates on the pictures." She pointed toward the corner of one of the photos. "The most recent one is over a year old."

"Yes, no one's died in over a year," he admitted. Most of his colleagues had considered the case cold. That was why he had made the trek to the UP alone, on his own time. He'd been chasing down a lead no one else had considered worthwhile, working a case no one else cared about anymore. "Until tonight…"

She shuddered. "No. Not Raven…"

"It shouldn't have been any of them, either," he said. "No one should have died. Why? Why did you kill them?" Especially as gruesomely as she had. Was it because they'd had real gifts and she had resented them for it?

"I didn't kill anyone," she insisted. And maybe she was a better con artist than he'd thought, because she actually sounded sincere. "I would never hurt anyone."

He snorted in derision of her claim—not because of the dream but because of the reality of her swinging that knife toward his back. If the flash of the blade hadn't caught the candlelight and reflected it into his eyes… If he hadn't stopped her…

"That's not what Raven said when she called me tonight," Seth informed her. "She was afraid of you."

"She called you?" she asked, surprise flickering through her dark eyes. "Why—how—did you contact you?"

"I gave her my card when I stopped by your shop earlier today," he said.

Her golden skin paled. "You were there earlier today? She never said…"

"That an FBI agent had tracked you down," he finished for her. "She covered for you earlier—with me, denying that you are who you are." Much as Maria herself was trying to deny her identity.

"That's because you're wrong about me," she insisted.

Seth had never been more certain of anyone's identity than he was of hers. He didn't need DNA to prove she was Maria Cooper. But he did need her DNA to link her to those other crime scenes.

"I'm not wrong," he replied. He could have added that he rarely was—because it was true and well-known in the agency. "And Raven realized I was right about you, too. She called me because you scared her."

Color returned to her face as her skin flushed. "I—I didn't mean to scare her. She shouldn't have been afraid of *me*."

"You threatened her," he reminded her. "You told her she was going to die."

Maria shook her head. "It wasn't me. It was the cards. It was what I saw."

"What you *saw*?" Did she really see things, the way he did, or was she like so many other *psychics*, a crackpot looking for money and attention? Those old police reports from people who had given up their money to her and her mother claimed that she was a fake. But maybe she'd just been faking with them...

"When I read the cards," she said, "I saw that she was in danger. I wanted to protect her. I tried to get her to stay with me—"

"She stayed," he said. "She called me from the shop. And that's where I found her—with you." If only he had been able to get there in time, the girl might not be fighting for her life at that very moment.

"She left," Maria argued, "right after I read her cards. I tried to stop her."

"Was that when you struggled?"

"Struggled?"

"The table was overturned, the cards scattered across the floor." He caught her hands in his and stroked his thumbs over the scratches on the backs of them. As if she felt the same jolt he did, she jerked her hands from his. "Is that when she scratched you, or was it when you tied the noose around her neck?"

She shook her head. "No. I found her like that...when I came back to the shop."

"So you left the shop, too? You chased after her?"

"Not right away," she said. "I made her the amulet first. Then I tried to find her—to give it to her."

"Amulet?" The dried plants hanging, like the rope, from the rafters, and the crystals and candles hadn't been just for ambiance. She used them, as witches had centuries ago, to cast spells.

"I made it of herbs and crystals to ward off the evil and protect her from harm."

"It didn't work." Harm had befallen Raven. And from the last words the girl had said to him, he had his prime suspect sitting across the table from him. Their knees touched again, his sliding between hers. The warmth of her body emanated through their rain-damp clothes, and heat rushed through him.

Another image flashed through his mind.

Her hair tangled across his pillow. Her nails digging into his shoulders, then clawing down his back. She clutched at him, her body tensing beneath his. She cried out his name. "Seth!"

He blinked, forcing the thoughts from his brain. He had been focused on the case—and on finding her—for too long. Had he—as some of his colleagues had suggested—become obsessed? His obsession needed to be justice. Not her. He coughed, clearing the thickness of desire from his throat, and asked, "What were you saying?"

Her brow furrowed with confusion, but then she repeated, "I couldn't find her—to give the amulet to her."

"You did find her," he pointed out. "Or had you stayed at the shop the whole time, waiting for her?"

Had Maria been there already when Raven had called him? After hearing the terror in the girl's voice, he'd driven as fast as he could and also had called Sheriff Moore as he had left the motel, hoping the older lawman had been closer. Still, Seth had beaten him to the Magik Shoppe.

She shook her head again, making her wild curls cascade around the shoulders of her worn sweater. "It wasn't me. Someone else must have been there. Someone else hurt her. I tried to help her. That's why I had the knife. I cut her down." She shivered. "You'll see—when she wakes up, Raven will tell you everything."

"I hope like hell she can," he said. The girl had mentioned having evidence to prove that Maria was the one he had been looking for, the killer he was determined to stop. That was why she'd gone back to the shop, to find him that evidence. She'd risked her life for it. But what he'd found on her didn't prove that Maria was a murderer, just that she was Maria Cooper. There must have been something else...

He pulled his cell from the inside pocket of his leather jacket, checking to see if he had missed any calls. "I left a message for the hospital to call me as soon as she regained consciousness."

"And they haven't called."

Regret trapped his breath in his lungs. Had he been

too late? Had his efforts at reviving her been unsuccessful? "No. They haven't."

"She's not dead."

"I wouldn't be so sure," he replied. "What the hell did you put on her throat and in her mouth?"

"Those were herbs that I use for healing," she said. "The mixture should have restored her breathing and reduced the swelling in her throat."

He held up his cell phone. "I don't think it worked," he said. "Or I would have a call by now."

Maria gazed around the small room as if searching the corners for something. For what? And she insisted, "She can't be dead."

"You better hope like hell she isn't, because I can put you at the scene. In addition to your DNA that I'm sure was under her fingernails, I'm an eyewitness." He had her. He finally had her. And now the senseless killing would stop.

"I didn't hurt her. It wasn't me." She gestured at the photos. "I didn't hurt any of them."

"You're the one. Raven confirmed it to me on the phone." Even without that confirmation, he had been certain. She was the only thing all the victims had had in common; she was the last person every one of them had seen. "Raven also said she had proof." And he needed to find out what that proof was. He needed to talk to the girl—needed her to live—so that he could officially close all those other cold-.case files. "I should call the hospital again."

But a call wouldn't be good enough. If she regained consciousness, even for just a second as she had at the barn, he needed to be there to question her. "Actually, I should go to the hospital."

She nodded and stood up again. "I want to go with you. I want to see her."

"I can't let you go," he said. "I have a material witness order for you. I don't have to release you until you answer my questions."

Or until she called a lawyer who could get her released. He could question her for only so long without charging her. And he didn't have enough to charge her. Yet.

He hoped Maria was right and that the girl wasn't dead. But he wasn't sure how anyone could have survived a hanging. He doubted that the herbs put in her mouth and on her throat had actually been a healing potion. They were more likely to have been poison.

Maria settled back onto the chair. "I'll stay," she said as if she had a choice. "Please check on her."

He slid his phone back into his pocket and reached for his keys. "I'm going to lock you in here." Because he had no doubt that if he didn't, she would be long gone by the time he returned.

But he waited for her protest. Maybe she would even ask for that lawyer now.

Instead she nodded in agreement. "That's fine with me. I want to stay until you get back anyway. I have to know how she's doing."

Seth studied her beautiful face and wished he could read her mind. Did she want the girl alive or dead? Did she really believe the girl would exonerate her? Or was she afraid that Raven would implicate her, and she wanted the young woman as dead as her other victims?

It was so much easier than he had thought it would be—easier even than killing them in Maria Cooper's little magic shops. Maybe a big-city hospital would have had better security, but here in Copper Creek he had no problem moving freely around the building, which was more urgent-care center than actual hospital. The lights low, as patients slept, he hovered in the shadows, as he had earlier that night in the barn.

He had been there when the girl had placed her hysterical phone call to the FBI agent. For him that call had confirmed that she really was a witch. How else would she have known, just as she'd told the FBI agent, that he would be too late to save her?

She had seen her future. Her fate. At *his* hands. And since she could see the future, she was definitely a witch.

But the girl hadn't seen that Maria would come back to the shop. Neither had he.

Usually when the cards came up as they had, Maria Cooper took off—leaving everything and everyone behind her. Except him. She would never be able to leave *him* behind. He always knew where she was—unlike the FBI agent who'd been trying to track her down for years.

But Seth Hughes couldn't save her—just as he hadn't been able to save the girl with that hideous tattoo painted on what must have once been a pretty face.

Maria had been the one to cut her down—just seconds after he had strung up the girl and knocked the chair from under her. He would have grabbed Maria then, but he'd known the FBI agent was on his way. He couldn't risk getting caught before he'd completed his mission.

Before he killed the most powerful witch…

And he'd thought the girl was dead—that surely her neck would have broken when she hung. But Maria had used one of her potions and some mystical spell to save her life. Or to steal her death from *him*.

Sticking to the shadows, he now crept into a room the farthest down the hall from Raven's. Then, after tripping the alarm on the machine connected to the patient in that room, he slipped deeper into the shadows. He waited for the medical staff to rush to the elderly man's aid before he stole, unseen, into Raven's room.

Acting quickly, he disconnected the air hose from the machine and poured in the water he carried in a cup. It slid down the tube and directly into the girl's airway. Her eyes opened, big with terror, and she stared up at him, a question in her gaze.

Why?

She wanted to know why he was so determined to take her life.

"Because you're a witch," he whispered. "And I'm a witch-hunter." He didn't know if she heard him, because with one last gurgling gasp, she was gone.

Another witch dead...

But he felt none of the satisfaction of his earlier kills; his joy in the hunt was waning. Yet he couldn't leave his mission undone. He couldn't allow witches to live— to work their craft and mess with people's minds and hearts and livelihoods. He had to save the world from their evil ways.

The alarm sounded on Raven's machine now, signaling with a flat line that she was really gone this time. He disappeared again into the shadows behind a tall cart in the hall as the nurses hurried back toward the girl's room.

"What the hell happened?" one of them asked as she grabbed up the disconnected tube.

"Could she have done it?" the other nurse asked. "She's in here because she tried hanging herself."

Curses rang out, the voice deep and masculine, as the FBI agent joined the nurses at the bedside of the dead witch. He was getting close, too. Not just to Maria but to *him*.

He had been saving Maria until last, using her as bait to draw out the other witches. But she seldom shared her knowledge of witchcraft now.

While she sold the herbs and talismans and amulets, she didn't teach the craft of spells and potions. It had taken Raven a long time to get close to her, and probably no one would get that close again.

Except for him.

It was time for Maria Cooper to die.

Chapter 3

Blood and water leaked out as the scalpel sliced through the flesh and tissue of the victim's lungs. Seth didn't even flinch; he had already seen so much horror in his job.

And in his dreams.

"I don't understand it," the coroner murmured as he stared down at the water spilled on the stainless steel table.

Bright light shone onto the table and the body of the young woman lying on it. Seth stood just outside the light, in the shadows, where he felt he'd spent so much of his life.

"With the trauma to the neck and the lack of oxygen that would have caused to her brain," the doctor said, "I figured it might have been a stroke that caused her death."

"She was drowned," Seth said. He'd had the sheriff

wake up the coroner to perform the autopsy to confirm it. But he'd already known.

He had seen the water that had spilled on the floor and had condensed on the inside of her breathing tube. When he'd stepped off the elevator, he had heard the alarm beeping.

And he'd known. He was too late.

Raven had told him that he would be too late to save her. And she'd been right. He had failed her twice.

"How the hell did she drown?" the coroner asked. The older man shook his head as if befuddled. The sheriff had assured Seth that despite Dr. Kohler's age, the man was sharp. With his years of experience and the expansive county he worked, he had seen everything before.

Apparently he hadn't seen anything like this—like a woman being drowned in her hospital bed.

"I'm pretty sure someone poured water into her breathing tube," Seth said. While waiting for Sheriff Moore and the coroner to arrive at the hospital, he had investigated the scene and interviewed all the possible witnesses.

The coroner gasped but nodded his gray head. "That would have done it."

"But how?" the sheriff asked. He had joined Seth in the morgue in the basement of the county hospital, but he'd stayed even farther from that brightly lit table than Seth had. So he hadn't witnessed much of the autopsy. He wasn't asking about the medical aspects, though.

He was asking the same question that Seth had been asking himself when he'd found Raven dead. How?

Maria was in custody. Wasn't she?

"You have someone watching the suspect?" he asked Sheriff Moore. Again. It had been the first thing he had asked the man when he'd called him from Raven's bedside.

The older lawman nodded. "Yes." Now he glanced at the body on the autopsy table. "But it looks as if we should have had someone watching *her* instead."

Seth silently cursed himself. He should have had a protection detail on Raven. But he'd thought he had the right person in custody.

He could feel his suspect slipping away now, though. This death would give her reasonable doubt. A grand jury might not even indict her now. And then she would be free again.

And if Maria was free, he was certain that more people would die—since everyone around her kept dying...

If only he had been able to talk to Raven...

Frustration eating at him, Seth grumbled, "I can't believe this hospital doesn't have security."

"We've never needed it," the coroner said. "This is Copper Creek."

"But no cameras—"

"Never needed them," the doctor interjected.

"Tonight you needed them," Seth said. Because all of the nurses he'd questioned had claimed that they had seen no stranger—no one suspicious at all—lurking around the place. But they'd shivered as he'd talked to them—as if some cold spirit had crossed their paths.

Or some heartless killer...

Despite his leather jacket, goose bumps lifted on Seth's skin. Maybe it was the coldness of the morgue. Or maybe it was something else that chilled his skin and his blood. He refused to believe in spirits.

Evil.

Hell, he knew evil existed. He had already seen so

much of it. More likely what had chilled his skin was the thought that had just occurred to him.

If Maria really was at the station, then someone else was out there. Not acting instead of her but maybe in collusion with her. He should have considered before that she wasn't working alone. The gruesome ways all the other victims had died would have been hard for her to pull off alone—unless she really was a witch. Or she'd had someone stronger helping her. Probably some hapless male who had fallen for her undeniable sexy charms...

Seth swallowed nervously as he realized he could be that hapless male—that he had been distracted so much by her looks that he hadn't thought to put protective duty on Raven. His distraction had cost the girl her life. Along with the frustration, guilt ate at him, clenching his stomach into knots.

"I need to get back to the station," he said. To make certain that Maria was still there—that whoever had just killed Raven for her wasn't trying to break her out of the room in which he'd locked her.

As if he'd read his mind, the sheriff assured him, "Your suspect is still there."

Where Maria Cooper was concerned, Seth would accept no assurances. He had to see for himself. But he didn't want to just see her. He wanted to touch her, too.

"I'll drive Dr. Kohler back to his house and meet you at the station," the sheriff said.

"I have to finish up the autopsy," the doctor said. "I can't leave her like this..." He stared grimly down at the body.

"That'll give you time to finish up the investigation here," Seth suggested to Sheriff Moore. "Maybe you'll have better luck talking to the nurses than I did."

They might talk more freely to the local lawman than the stranger he was to them. They might admit to seeing something or someone tonight that would explain how Raven had died.

And maybe now that Seth knew Maria wasn't working alone, he might have better luck getting her to talk. Maybe she would implicate her accomplice in order to save herself. If her accomplice hadn't already managed to free her...

The security at the sheriff's office wasn't much better than at the county hospital. So Seth worried that he would find her as he had found Raven: already gone.

"She's gone..."

"Who?" Elena asked as she glanced over her shoulder at her sister Ariel, who'd spoken so softly that she'd barely heard her whisper.

"Mama," Ariel murmured. She was probably being quiet so she wouldn't wake Irina. She was sleeping, finally, and hopefully so deeply that she wasn't able to *hear* them.

When they were kids, the three of them had slept together on that lumpy mattress in the camper on the back of Mama's old pickup truck. As they had then, the three of them slept together now—on the soft mattress of Irina's king-size bed, though. Elena lay in the middle, as she had all those years ago, a younger sister under each arm as if she could keep them safe from all those horrible dreams she'd had. All those horrible things she had *seen* each of them endure...

As she thought of those twenty years without her sisters, Elena's pain increased. And now she knew there was still one sister out there—still alone, as they had each been alone for so long.

Because, eventually, Mama had abandoned Maria, too.

Ariel's husband, David Koster, had discovered that as he and his best friend, Ty, had tried tracking down Maria. Elena's husband, Joseph, had other sources who had discovered other things about Maria.

Like her criminal past…

Or was it actually in the past…?

Elena closed her eyes and played out the vision she'd had days earlier.

Candlelight flickered, casting shadows about the interior of a barn. Dried herbs hung from the rafters. But they weren't the only things dangling from the worn boards. A noose swung in the cool night air blowing in through the open door.

A man crouched on the floor, leaning over a woman—trying to save her. The candlelight glinted in his auburn hair.

The first time she'd had the vision, Elena had awakened screaming. As always Joseph had comforted her, pulling her tightly against his hard chest. His strong arms had held her close, and he'd reassured her that she was safe. But she had known she wasn't the one in danger. She had thought that the woman lying lifelessly on the ground was Maria. But then she'd had the vision again and she hadn't awakened that time until later. And then she had been even more horrified.

A woman crouched behind him. Long curly black hair hung down her back. She wore an old gray sweater and a long skirt. And from the folds of the long skirt she pulled a knife. The backs of her hands were gouged, as if she'd already fought with someone. And then she swung the blade of that long knife toward the man's back…

That woman was Maria. Not the one lying on the floor. Joseph's contacts had confirmed that Elena's youngest sister had been a con artist. Elena remembered helping her mother run cons—before she, Ariel and Irina had been taken away from her. But Maria had kept running those cons—by herself—after their mother abandoned her. So she'd chosen to be a con artist. Was she now a killer?

Or had she always been?

Elena had had other visions. She had *seen* other bodies. Was Maria so damaged—so evil—that she had taken those lives?

"No…" Irina murmured the word in her sleep as she shifted restlessly on the bed.

"She can hear you," Ariel warned her. "What are you thinking?"

"I'm remembering a vision."

Ariel's turquoise eyes widened and glowed in the darkened bedroom. She knew about the visions—knew that Elena wasn't as convinced as she and Irina that it was a good idea to find Maria.

They were desperate to find the youngest Cooper sister because they were worried that Maria was in danger. Elena was worried that Maria *was* the danger.

Maybe to them all…

Ariel settled closer to Elena's side, as if seeking comfort. She softly murmured, "I hope you're wrong."

Elena shrugged so that her shoulder rubbed against Ariel's—offering comfort as she had when they were kids. "I can't help what I see."

And if Maria was what Elena was afraid she was, then they wouldn't be able to help her, either.

Maria fought to breathe as she waited in the cell, opening her mouth to suck in deep breaths—to fill her aching lungs.

Was it her fear? Or someone else's?

Shortly after Seth Hughes had locked her in the room and left, she'd felt that choking sensation. It wasn't the too-close walls that were shrinking the already small room. It was the mist that filtered in beneath the door.

"No," she murmured around the sob choking her throat. She felt as though that noose were around her neck, pulling tight, cutting off her breath. Off *her* life…

Raven had been such a sweet girl. She had never done anything wrong except for trying to be Maria's friend…and for being a witch. Raven had wanted to be a witch. That was why she'd sought out the shop. Not for the healing cures or love potions that Maria could sell her. Like learning to read the cards, Raven had wanted to learn to make the potions and cures herself.

Maria glanced down at the photos Agent Hughes had left strewn across the small table. Every one of them had wanted the same thing. To practice witchcraft…

Even the two guys. And one of them had been crushed to death, the other burned. But had becoming a witch been their real wish…or was it just because they'd wanted to be close to her?

She had been told that she was that kind of person— the kind who drew other people to her. Apparently even when she didn't want to…

Like Raven…

Her breath shuddered out with the sob that she couldn't restrain. Nobody could get close to her without losing everything.

Nobody…

She reached out for the briefcase Agent Hughes had left on the table to see what else he had inside—like maybe the keys to the door. But the case was empty; he'd only had those crime scene photos in it. No keys. She needed the keys. She had to get out of here—before she suffocated or strangled. But as soon as her fingers touched the leather, images flashed through her mind... like when she read cards or touched a crystal ball.

His smoky blue eyes stared down at her, his gaze intense. Not with anger or suspicion now but with passion. Moonlight gleamed on the bare skin of his broad shoulders and heavily muscled chest. Then his face, so handsome with his square jaw and sharp cheekbones, got closer as he lowered his body. His legs, naked but for soft hair, parted hers. And his chest covered her breasts, crushing them so that her nipples hardened and pressed against his skin.

She moaned at the exquisite sensation. But it wasn't enough. She wanted more, wanted his mouth...everywhere. On her lips, on her breasts and...

He must have read her mind because he chuckled and his chest rumbled against hers. "I can't believe this..."

She shook her head, shaking off the image. "I can't believe it, either." It couldn't be a vision; making love with Seth Hughes would *not* happen. Not just because he thought she was a killer, and she wasn't entirely convinced he wasn't one, too, but also because she would never, ever make the mistake of getting close to anyone else.

Ever again.

Even though she didn't need reminders of what happened to people who got too close to her, she tried to focus on those pictures. Maybe she could see something in the crime scene photos that would help her figure out who was doing this. Who was the dark aura following her...

But even in her visions, she never saw a person, never saw who was hurting these victims. She saw only the darkness. The evil.

And then these images that the crime scene photos had captured. She had seen them before they had even happened—in her mind as she'd read their cards. The same cards that had turned up tonight. For Raven. The mist thickened so that she couldn't see the photos. Or anything in the room.

Then the mist shifted into a human form. She expected Raven's tall thin body, so she gasped in surprise at the small stature and long curly black hair of the ghost. "No…"

She shoved back her chair, as far as the wall would allow, and jumped up. Then she turned toward the door, clawing at the handle and hammering at the wood. "Let me out! Let me out!"

"I'm not going to hurt you," that all-too-familiar soft voice assured her.

The scent of sandalwood and lavender, mixing with her own, overwhelmed her. And smoke. She always smelled smoke now whenever this ghost visited her. Tears burned her eyes. Seeing her always hurt. "I don't want to see you. I told you to leave me alone!"

Her voice cracked with so many emotions as the ghost whispered her name: "Maria…"

"Go away!" she screamed.

"I can't leave you, child."

"Why not? You had no problem leaving me before!" she lashed out.

"I did it for you," her mama's ghost insisted. "To keep you safe."

"You left a fifteen-year-old to fend for herself. How was that keeping me safe?" She had been lucky to survive on her own, driving without a license, continuing the scams so that she could put gas in the truck Mama had left her. So she could eat…

She had done it just so she could survive. But she felt sick with guilt and self-loathing as she remembered turning those cards and telling so many lies to the people who'd paid her to tell their real futures.

But that wasn't all she'd done...

There had been the fake séances her mother had taught her to run. The way of projecting her voice so the *ghost* said what the person wanted to hear. She hadn't charged as much as her mother had to summon the people's lost loved ones, but she shouldn't have charged at all for a *lie*.

Unlike her mother, most people passed from one world to the next without ever coming back. So no matter how much she had actually tried, she hadn't often been able to summon the real spirit for her mark. And then the times she had, the real spirit hadn't always said what they had wanted to hear. So she'd lied.

And people had paid more for her lies, tipping her generously as they'd cried with relief.

"My leaving you was my way of keeping you safe." Mama's reply was one that Maria had heard before. "I knew *I* was in danger."

Even though it hadn't happened until five years after she had abandoned Maria, Mama's witch-hunter had eventually caught her. He had burned her alive. And that was the first time her ghost had appeared to Maria, warning her to run for her life—that he was coming for her, too.

"I thought that no one knew about you," Mama said. "So I thought that if I left you alone, I could keep you safe...from my demons."

Maria closed her eyes, trying to shut out the ghostly image.

But Mama's voice wrapped around her, filling her

head as she continued, "But you always had your own demons, hovering like that dark aura around you, putting you and anyone who would ever get close to you in danger. You were always…"

"Cursed," Maria said, bitterness filling her with the warning her mother had given her. Too many times. A child shouldn't have to grow up knowing that she would never know true happiness, that she would always be hunted.

"I should have left you sooner," Mama said, "like I did the others." The others were the sisters Maria had never known. "Or I should have given you to your father."

The father Maria hadn't even known about until she'd read about him in the letter her mother had left her, along with the locket. She was supposed to go to him if she needed anything. She had needed her mother—not some stranger she'd never met.

"But he wasn't equipped to deal with you," Mama continued, "because I saw *this* in your future."

In the same cards Maria kept turning over for the others, Mama had seen her youngest daughter's future, too. Had seen all the tragedy and loss…

"So I had to teach you how to run," Mama explained. "How to stay ahead of the danger that surrounds you, that goes after anyone who ever gets close to you…"

Was that why Mama hadn't wanted Maria to have anything to do with her sisters? To keep *them* safe? Maria believed that Mama had always loved them more than she had the child she had actually kept.

Hurt, because Mama always hurt her, Maria opened her eyes and lashed out. "Were you the right one to teach me…when you weren't able to run fast enough yourself?"

"I always knew he would catch me one day," Mama said. "But the witch-hunter didn't know about you. No one did."

Not her mama's killer, and not even her sisters.

She turned away from the door and gestured at the pictures spread across the table over which FBI special agent Seth Hughes had interrogated her. "Your killer couldn't have done that. He's dead. My sisters worked together to end his reign of terror. They took care of him."

And he would never hurt anyone again.

Elena, Ariel and Irina hadn't known about her, but Maria had always known about them. Mama had talked about them incessantly—about how beautiful, how smart, how sweet they were. And Maria had never felt as beautiful, as smart or as sweet. She had never felt as if she'd been worthy enough to replace everything that Mama had lost, everything that the woman had missed so much that there had been a hole in her heart. A hole that Maria had never been quite enough to fill.

"But the witch-hunter had a son." Maria remembered what she had learned from all the media coverage of the ordeal her family had barely survived eight years ago. "Could *he* be carrying on the legacy?" While Maria's family legacy was witchcraft, his was witch-hunting.

"He may not even know about it," Mama replied. "Donovan Roarke hadn't learned about the legacy until long after he lost contact with his son, when he came across the journal of his long-dead ancestor Eli McGregor, who'd begun the witch hunt centuries ago."

Eli McGregor had chased the first Elena for years. Thanks to his son, Thomas, he had never found her. But eventually Eli's descendants had found hers and killed so very many of them…

"If it's not Donovan Roarke's son, then who's after *me*, Mama?" Who hated her so much that he killed anyone who got close to her?

Sadness filled the hollow eyes of her mother's ghost. "I don't know, child."

"Then why are you here?" Maria asked. "I told you to stay away from me. I don't need you." Just as Mama hadn't needed her, hadn't loved her—not the way she had loved her three older children. "Go away! And stay away from me!"

Mama's arms reached out, as if she wanted to hold Maria. But her image faded…even as the mist thickened and took another shape: the tall thin figure of Raven.

"She led me here," the young woman explained. "When I first saw her ghost, I thought she was you. I thought he killed you, too. You look so much alike. She's your mother?"

"She's nothing to me," Maria replied. "She wasn't there for me when I needed her, like I wasn't there for you." Tears stung her eyes and filled her throat. "I didn't protect you like I promised. I am so sorry…"

Raven's ghost stepped closer, the energy of her spirit warming Maria. "I'm the one who's sorry."

"No." Maria reached out, trying to envelop the girl, but her hands and arms passed through the mist. "It's my fault. I never should have hired you. I never should have let you get close to me. Everyone who does winds up dead. It's all my fault."

"It's not you," the girl said, her eyes shimmering with tears she would never be able to shed now. "You're not the killer. I'm sorry that I thought you were. If I hadn't run from you…"

"You would probably still be dead," Maria said as regret filled her. "We would probably both be dead because we would've been together when he came to the shop. Did you see him?"

Raven's image wavered as she shook her head. "I never saw him at the Magik Shoppe. He came up behind me and started strangling me. Then I thought it might have been you. But at the hospital I saw *him*."

Maria gasped as realization struck her. "He was at the hospital?" Why would he have gone there...unless to finish what he'd started?

"He killed me there," Raven explained. "He drowned me..."

Maria shuddered in horror. She could have asked how. But she had a more important question. "Who is he? Is it Agent Hughes?"

Raven's ghostly brow furrowed. "I don't know who he is. His face was in the shadows, but I could see the outline of his jaw and his hair. And his voice..." The ghostly image flickered, as if she was trembling with terror. "Something about him was familiar..."

So it might have been the FBI agent...

Maria wanted to ask more questions about the killer, but her heart ached over the senseless loss of her young friend. And guilt overwhelmed her. "It should have been me. I'm the one he's after. I just wish I knew why..."

Was it as simple as Mama had always said? Because she was cursed?

"Because he's a witch-hunter," Raven replied. "That's what he calls himself."

"Did you recognize his voice?"

"No, it was just this weird whisper. He said that he thought I was a witch." The ghost's lips curved into a faint smile of satisfaction.

That was all she had ever wanted—to be a witch like the older sister she had told Maria about—the older sister she had felt she would never be as smart or as beautiful as. Her sister had refused to teach Raven the craft. Maria should have refused, too, but she had identified too much with the girl.

"You are a *real* witch, Maria," Raven continued. "Your knowledge and powers are legendary. I heard about you before I ever met you. That's why I came up here. It's why I wanted to learn from you."

Maria would never forgive herself for hiring the girl. Even though it had been a year since a murder, she should have known the hunter was still out there, still watching her.

She shivered as the girl's image grew fainter. Maria reached for her again, trying to hold her in the room. "Don't leave…"

Her voice a mere whisper, her image just a wisp, Raven warned her, "You're in the most danger from him now. He's going to try to kill you."

"Don't leave me!" she begged. She had to apologize more, had to try to make amends, to assuage the guilt that cramped her stomach in knots. "Come back!" she cried.

Keys rattled in the lock, startling her into shocked silence. She should have been relieved that the door was opening, but terror gripped her.

Even without Raven's warning, she'd known *he* would be coming for her. Soon.

The door opened, and a deep voice asked, "Who are you talking to?"

"You're back," she said, turning to where Agent Hughes filled the doorway; he was so tall, his shoulders so broad. His square jaw was clenched, his handsome face grim. Was his the face Raven had seen in the shadows of her hospital room?

"You weren't begging me to come back," he surmised. "The deputy said you were in here yelling."

"Because I wanted to get out," she said, rubbing her hands over her arms. Her sweater had dried from the rain earlier in the evening. But she was still so cold—even her blood chilled and pumped slowly and heavily through her veins. And that pressure was back in her chest, squeezing her lungs and heart with panic. "I need to get out of here."

"The deputy was watching you through the mirror and listening through the intercom," Agent Hughes divulged. "He said you were telling someone *else* to get out, that you were talking to someone in here."

She lifted her hands and gestured around the tiny room. "Do you see anyone else in here?"

"I don't see anyone," he said, glancing around the small space. "But do you?"

She drew in a ragged breath. Even without the DNA, he already knew who and what she was. She had already admitted to trying to heal Raven, so she might as well admit to the rest of her abilities. "Raven's ghost. She's dead."

That muscle twitched along his jaw. "How could you *know* that?" His gray-blue eyes narrowed with suspicion. He obviously had some ideas...

Some ideas that cast his suspicion on her again...

"I just told you that I saw her ghost." Hers wasn't the only ghost she had seen, but she wasn't about to tell him about Mama. That brought out even more pain and vulnerability than seeing Raven's ghost had.

"She was here," Maria replied honestly even though he would probably think she was lying. Or trying to con him. "Her *ghost* was here...until you came in."

Was he the reason that Raven had slipped away so quickly? Because she didn't want to see her killer again?

"Why was she here?" he asked, speaking slowly and softly as if Maria were a young child…or mentally unstable, which was probably what that poor deputy thought of her, too.

"She came here to warn me. I'm in danger, too. That's what all this is about," she said, gesturing at those photos he'd left on the table.

He cocked his head as he continued to scrutinize her through narrowed eyes. He was probably trying to determine if she'd lost her mind. "What is all this?"

"All these murders," she said impatiently. Why wasn't he following her? "*This* is about me. Someone's trying to kill *me*." Because she was the real witch.

Images flashed through her head of the murders of everyone who'd gotten close to her. But in her mind she was now the victim. It was her head being held underwater, her neck the noose wound tightly around, her body the brick-laden board crushed…her skin the flames burned.

Not only could she see a vision of what would happen to someone, she experienced every feeling that person did when it happened. Every moment of terror. Every stab of pain. When they died, it was as if she died, too.

She gasped for breath, fighting to get air into her lungs—fighting to slow her racing heart. "I need…I need…"

She reached out and grasped his arm, digging her fingers into the leather sleeve—afraid that she might pass out as she had before when pummeled with all those horrible feelings. But she couldn't count on Agent Hughes to hold her up. She had learned long ago that she couldn't count on anyone but herself.

So she pleaded, "Let me go…"

She could run. She could protect herself. She had been doing it for so many years…

"No," he said, his gaze dropping to her hand clutching his arm. "I can't let you go…"

She pulled back and twined her fingers together to still their trembling and that crazy tingling she felt whenever they touched.

"Just let me go to the restroom," she said. "I—I need to splash water on my face. I need a minute to…"

His brow creased, he studied her face for a long moment before finally nodding his agreement. "Okay." Maybe he'd seen that she was about to pass out, because his hand closed around her elbow.

She gasped again, at the jolt of recognition. That damn connection. His touch was familiar and exciting and frightening as hell. Who the hell was he really? She tried to pull her arm away from his grasp, but he held her easily—tightly.

"I won't run," she said. "Just show me to the door."

Instead he walked her down the hall, past the courtroom and the city hall office, to the door at the end. The town was so small that they made the most of their one city building.

"I won't run," she repeated as she stopped outside the door.

"No, you won't," he agreed. "I already checked the bathroom. No window. No other way out but this door." He turned back, but he walked only a few strides away—keeping the door in sight of his smoky blue gaze.

Dread tightened the knots in her stomach. She had hoped for a window, had hoped she would be able to find an escape route. But the splash of water on her face would have to suffice. With a sigh, she shoved open the door and stepped inside the dark room. She slapped her hand against the wall until she fumbled across the light switch and pushed it up. The fluorescent bulbs crackled and buzzed and then illuminated the small space, chasing away the shadows.

Except for one.

A noose swung from the ceiling, the rope casting a shadow on the floor. It converged with the shadow of Maria's body, as if the noose were already wound around her neck. She could feel the scratchy fibers digging into her skin, could feel the rope squeezing...

A scream tore from Maria's throat. Even before Mama's and Raven's ghostly warnings, she'd known.

She was going to be the next witch to die...

Chapter 4

The scream jerked Irina awake. But it must have been just inside her head, since her sisters slept peacefully on, their breathing deep and steady. They hadn't even stirred.

But one of her sisters wasn't with her, and she wasn't sleeping. Maria's heart was hammering, her pulse racing with fear. She was terrified. And Irina was feeling all those emotions. She reached out—not for either of her sleeping sisters. She didn't want to disturb them. She already knew what they were thinking about Maria. She reached out for her husband. Ty had left earlier—at her urging. But as always, he knew when she needed him, and he was back. His strong arms closed around her as he drew her close to his chest.

"It's okay," he murmured in that raspy voice she always found so sexy. She found everything sexy about him—his thick black hair, his eyes that were so dark a

blue they were nearly black. She even loved the jagged
scar that ran through one of his eyebrows. The story
behind it wasn't pretty, but it had made him the man he
was. The man she loved...

She shook her head. "No..."

He placed a hand on her belly. "Are they okay?"

She put her hand on the back of his big one. "They're
okay."

With sudden understanding, he murmured, "Maria..."

"You need to find her now," she urged him. "She's
in danger. I can feel her fear. It's more intense than it's
ever been. She knows he's coming for her. He might
already be there—close to her..."

Ty gestured toward a bag he'd packed and left on the
bedroom floor next to the bed he usually shared with
her. But tonight he had asked her sisters to stay with her
while he met with his best friend and brother-in-law,
David Koster. David was a computer genius; he could
find out things few other people could. Maybe David
had finally found something to lead them to Maria.

"I don't want to leave you," he said, "but...we have
to..." They were so close, so connected that he always
felt what she felt. He always knew when she needed
him, and right now she needed him to find Maria before it was too late.

"Thank you," she whispered, and leaned closer to
brush her lips over his. Tears leaked from her eyes and
trailed down her cheeks. "You always know. You always believe..."

Her own sisters doubted Maria. But then, they didn't
know her the way Irina did. She had lived with her
briefly while they'd been in college; she hadn't known
then that Maria was her sister. But Maria had known.

But even if Irina hadn't lived with her, she would

have known her. She felt her emotions, so she knew her heart. It was good—like the witch.

But she was still a witch. And the witch hunt had resumed. Maria was the hunter's next target. Because of her powers, probably his ultimate prize.

"I know I promised you before," Ty said, "eight years ago, that I would find her. And I haven't kept that promise…"

"You will," she assured him. "You will find her." She just hoped that it would be in time. Before she died…

He nodded. "I will, and I'll be back before our babies come."

As he knew and believed in her, Irina knew and believed in her husband. He was a man of his word. A man of honor and determination.

But still she couldn't help but worry that she would be bringing her children into a world that her younger sister had just left.

Maria's scream coursed through Seth as if her terror were his. His heart hammering, he ran the few feet down the hall and shouldered open the bathroom door. While he didn't remember withdrawing it from its holster, he held his gun, his finger along the barrel, ready to squeeze the trigger should he need to fire.

Maria Cooper whirled toward him, anger replacing her fear as color flushed her beautiful face. "Did you do this? It's you, isn't it? You're the witch-hunter."

He sucked in a breath at the accusation. "Why—why would you say that?"

"You just admitted you'd been in here. If you were, you must have seen this." She raised her hand toward the ceiling. "You must have done *this*."

He glanced up at the noose hanging from a joist

over her head. And he couldn't control the grimace as he remembered the marks on the pale skin of Raven's throat. But that wasn't how the girl had died. The water dripping from the unattached end of her breathing tube was how she'd died tonight. Drowned. Like a witch…

Maria Cooper couldn't have done that; she had been locked in the tiny interrogation room under the deputy's watchful gaze. She hadn't escaped him. But she hadn't escaped the killer, either.

Maybe she didn't want to, though—if she was working with him. Then, what was the noose about? Was it a diversion or a threat?

"I didn't do that," he said. "I checked out the room before I left for the hospital…in case you needed to use it when I was gone. That wasn't in here then."

She shuddered. "So he was here when you were gone…"

After killing Raven, the man had come here from the hospital. And Seth had stayed behind, waiting for the autopsy to confirm what he'd already known—that someone had disconnected the girl's breathing tube and filled it with water. He had worried that the guy would come to the police station. But he'd figured that the man was her accomplice and would try to break Maria out—not threaten her with a noose. But maybe he was threatening her not to talk.

Now Seth knew for certain that there was some sick, dangerous bastard who was still one step ahead of him.

"Son of a bitch," he murmured.

How the hell had the bastard gotten in here? He scanned the small room and noticed the displaced ceiling tiles. Reaching up, he pushed aside more of them, knocking them loose from the grids holding them up.

Then he leaned out the door. "Deputy! Search the building. Someone's been in here!"

He should have called for a helicopter and brought Maria back to the bureau tonight. Bringing her here—to this unsecured city building—had been a mistake. He was damned lucky that the man hadn't been waiting in the bathroom for her—that he hadn't pulled her up into the ceiling and helped her escape Seth.

"You should go, too, and search the building," she urged him. "You need to find him. You have to stop him…before he kills anyone else."

He stepped closer to her and touched her, just his fingers on her chin, tipping her face up so that she had to meet his gaze. But his skin tingled as if electrified. What the hell was it between them that whenever they touched, it felt so intense? So *important*…?

Her throat moved as if she was struggling to swallow—or breathe. She was scared. She hadn't faked the terror in that scream. And it was in her eyes now, dark and haunting. It was almost as if she feared him, too.

"Who is he?" he asked.

She shook her head—maybe because she didn't know. Maybe because she was trying to remove his hand. His touch…

She felt that connection between them, too. Her eyes darkened even more with the awareness. With the undeniable attraction…

"I don't know…"

He heard the frustration in her voice, the anger and aggravation that she had no idea who had placed that noose where she would find it—as she had found that other noose just hours ago with Raven still swinging from it.

"Don't *you* know?" she asked him. "You've been chasing after me all these years, so don't you know?"

He searched his mind, his memory, for everything he knew about her—for everyone who knew her. And he shook his head. "All the people who've gotten close to you have died."

She trembled. "I know…"

There was no one left to be her accomplice. The person had to be someone else—someone who was close to her not emotionally but physically. A stalker?

Was that noose left as a threat to her life? Indicating that she would be next?

"You should go," she said. "Help them search…" Now there was desperation in her eyes along with the fear.

Seth had seen that look before—before he'd joined the bureau. Back when he'd been just a beat cop, he had seen that look in the eyes of a deer who'd accidentally crashed through a sliding door and gotten trapped inside the sunroom of a house. In that deer's eyes, he had seen sheer panic and desperation to escape—to run.

That was why Maria wanted him to leave her. So that she could run, too.

But the deer had never run again. The older cop who'd been training Seth had shot and killed the animal. He'd claimed it was so the deer wouldn't do any more damage to the house—or to itself. It had been hurt.

But Seth thought it could have survived if it had been given a chance. The old cop hadn't given it a chance. Neither could Seth…

"I'm not going anywhere," he said. "I'm not leaving you alone."

She shuddered with fear. "You don't want to be close to me. You've seen what has happened to everyone who's gotten close to me in the past. They've been murdered." Apparently her fear was for him—not for herself.

He glanced up at the noose again and barely restrained a shudder of his own. "Protecting you is my job. You're a material witness. I have to keep you alive." That was all it was; he wasn't feeling protective of her for any other reason.

She nodded. "Yes. Of course," she agreed. Too quickly, as if embarrassed over implying they might become closer than agent and witness. "I know that you're only doing your job."

Finding her had never been just a job to him. She was so much more than that...

So much more than he had ever realized before meeting her. Was she really what she claimed? What everyone else had claimed she was? Was she really a witch?

And if she was, how could she not know who was after her, who had killed all those people who had been close to her?

If Raven's ghost had really visited her, wouldn't she have told her who'd killed her?

"I could do my job more easily if you stopped lying to me and told me everything you know." He touched her again, tipping up her chin to meet his gaze.

Her thick black lashes fluttered as she blinked—as if trying to shield her thoughts and feelings from him. Could she sense what he was feeling?

Could she feel his desire for her? His madness...

He had to be crazy—after those dreams—to want anything to do with her besides arresting her. But he doubted that either of them would be safe, even with her locked up.

Her voice low and raspy, as if that noose were around

her neck, tightening, she whispered, "What do you mean?"

"You told me Raven's ghost visited you," he reminded her.

"And you thought I was crazy," she accused him.

He shrugged and answered honestly, "I don't know what to think about you, Maria…"

Her lips, sensually full and tempting lips, curved into a slight smile. "You don't know if I'm crazy or…"

"Or if you're the real deal," he said. "So if you are the real deal, how can you *not* know who he is?"

Her frustration was back, knitting her brow. "I don't know…"

"Why didn't Raven's ghost tell you who he is?" he persisted. If she was telling the truth, she'd had a chance to question the ultimate eyewitness. The victim.

"She didn't see him," Maria replied. "He came up behind her at the Magik Shoppe. And his face was in the shadows at the hospital."

The room had been dark. The nurses had confirmed that. Maybe she hadn't seen him.

Or maybe Maria was making it all up.

She must have seen the skepticism on his face, because she continued, "I really saw her ghost."

"Why?" he asked. "If she didn't see him, why did she come to you?"

She looked up at that dangling noose and shivered. "To warn me that I would be next."

Instinctively he reached for her, pulling her into his arms to protect her. But instead of reassuring her or himself, touching her rattled him. His nerves jangled and his skin tingled.

Maybe it wasn't because of touching her. Maybe

it was because of the threat. He couldn't imagine her hanging. Or drowning…

Or dying in any of the gruesome ways those other victims had died. He couldn't lose her.

Yet she wasn't his to lose.

He should have released her, should have stepped back. But he continued to hold her as he asked, "Why would he want to kill you? Or any of the others?"

"I don't know who he is," she replied. "But I know what he does. He kills witches, or people he thinks have special abilities."

She clutched at him, maybe in fear, maybe because she felt what he felt: that connection, that desire, that gut-wrenching *need*…

Her breath shuddered out, warming his skin even as it made it tingle. "You'll be safe, then."

If his dream was real, he wasn't safe. But it wasn't the witch-hunter he had to fear. It was *her*.

He had been so close to her. When she'd stepped inside the restroom and shut the door, he had felt the vibration in the ceiling—through which he had crawled, right above the head of the FBI agent.

Excitement pulsed in his blood, pumping hot and heavy through his body. He had outsmarted them both—the witch and the special agent. Neither of them had suspected that he was close—until she had seen the noose he had left for her and screamed in surprise and fear.

Why hadn't she known that it would be there?

She saw other people's futures, but she must not have seen her own. So then she probably had no idea what he had planned for her. The noose was only the beginning. He had wanted to torture her for years—killing everyone stupid enough to get close to her and her witchcraft ways so that he isolated her from everyone. So that she was completely alone. But the FBI agent's presence had forced him to act sooner than he'd planned.

Nevertheless, he still intended to take his time with this witch. He would use every method of witch-hunting to kill her: hanging, drowning, crushing and burning.

"Agent Hughes! Agent Hughes!" The young deputy's shout of excitement carried back from the reception area. "We've got him!"

Maria's heart thumped against her ribs. Then she rushed forward, but Seth Hughes was there, his big body blocking the doorway to the restroom.

"I have to see him." She shoved against Hughes, but the lawman was all hard muscle—like in her vision— and he didn't budge. "I have to see who he is!"

"I don't know if they've searched him. I can't let you see him until I've made certain he's not armed," Seth explained. But he led her out into the hall, to the open door of that little room where she had already spent too much time. "I want you to go back in the interrogation room and wait for me."

She shook her head as the panic pressed on her lungs again with that feeling that she would suffocate. "You're not locking me back in there."

If the man had dropped through that ceiling instead of the bathroom one with his noose…

But then the deputy who'd been behind the mirror would have seen him. And the witch-hunter was too smart to be seen. Or caught…

"It's not him," she said with sudden realization, and now disappointment settled heavily on her chest. "It's not him…"

Seth Hughes's smoky gray-blue eyes closed for a second, and his nostrils flared as he dragged in a ragged breath. "Probably not."

"Then you can't leave me alone," she pointed out. "Not if you really want to protect me."

But could she trust him to protect her and not hurt her? Was he really not the hunter? She couldn't be certain. If only she could read minds, as one of her sisters could...

Irina would know what he was thinking. Maria knew only what he was feeling—that same damn overwhelming attraction she felt for him.

"I'm not the killer," he said.

And she wondered...could *he* read minds? But if he could, he would have already known that she had not killed her friends. No, as an FBI agent, he could probably just read people's expressions, as her mother had been able to. While Seth used his abilities for interrogations, Mama had used hers to determine what her mark had wanted to hear.

Was that simply what Seth Hughes was telling her now? What she wanted to hear?

"Is that her?" a male voice asked.

The man stood next to the young deputy. While the deputy held the guy's arm with one hand, he had drawn his weapon on him with the other. "This is him, Agent Hughes."

Seth shook his head. "No, it's not."

"Is that her?" the strange man repeated, tugging free of the deputy's loose grasp. Like Seth, he was tall, but lean where the FBI agent was muscular. His features more refined where Seth's were more masculine. His hair was lighter, almost golden, and his eyes a clear green.

Maria had never seen the man before, and yet he was familiar to her. Eerily familiar. She had to have seen him before. Maybe she and Seth were wrong; maybe he was the witch-hunter and he had become so arrogant that he'd gotten sloppy.

"Mr. Waverly, you shouldn't be here," Seth said, his voice rough with an odd mixture of disapproval, irritation and sensitivity.

"You're here," Mr. Waverly said, as if Seth's presence justified his. "You're following a lead—to her."

Seth stiffened and stepped closer to her, as if he really intended to keep his promise to protect her. "How do you know that?"

"Someone in the bureau told me where you were," Mr. Waverly explained, "and what you were doing."

Seth cursed beneath his breath. "Damn, Curtis, how much did you pay for that information?"

Information could be bought from the FBI? That thought unsettled Maria even more than she had been. But then, she'd already known she couldn't trust anyone. Especially not Seth Hughes…

Mr. Waverly ignored his question and asked his own. "Is she the woman you think killed my sister?"

Maria turned to Seth, waiting for his reply, wondering if he had completely changed his mind about her involvement in the murders.

But instead of answering the question, he told the other man, "You shouldn't be here, Curtis. You're interfering in my investigation."

"I had to know—" the guy's throat rippled as he swallowed hard "—what you've found."

"And I promised that I would keep you apprised of my progress," Seth said.

"You don't think this is progress?" the man scoffed.

"Finally finding the last person who saw my sister alive?"

Maria's stomach tensed at the hollow echo of loss in his deep voice. She'd never known her sisters—except for the one closest to her in age and that for only a short time—and she missed them. She couldn't imagine this man's pain.

But she didn't have to. She could *feel* it. Usually with living people, she was able to block it, and out of self-preservation she had to. But she was too exhausted to fight the feelings. His pain and regret rolled over her with his words.

"It's been so long," he said, his voice cracking, "so long with no justice for Felicia."

The name struck Maria like a hard slap. "Felicia…"

After her mother's first ghostly visit, Maria had been forced to abandon the normal life she'd been building for herself. Going to college, sharing an off-campus apartment with the sister she'd managed to find. She'd been attending undergrad classes while Irina had been going for her doctorate. Maria'd had to leave it all behind and start over—alone. She had never felt so alone, not even when her mother had taken off in the middle of the night, leaving behind only a note and a locket.

But then she had found Felicia, and in the young woman she'd found a friend who had felt like a sister. They had been so close…until Maria had found the girl drowned—in the bathtub of the little house they had been converting into a magic shop.

She hadn't been surprised when she'd found her, though. She had already seen it—when she'd read Felicia's cards earlier that day. And she had already felt it…as it had happened…

Air caught in her lungs as she struggled to breathe. But

every breath she drew brought more water into her mouth and nose, sending it down her throat so that she choked and sputtered. Her eyes burned like her lungs. She couldn't see anything, could only feel one large hand at the back of her head and the other wrapped around the nape of her neck, pushing her down—pushing her underwater.

Her arms flailed as she tried to fight him off, but her strength ebbed along with her breath. She had none left—no air. No energy...

It was easier to stop fighting. Easier to just give up. And once she stopped fighting, a strange peace settled over her, eradicating her fear and horror.

And she welcomed death...

Maybe Maria should do the same. Maybe she should just stop running and let the witch-hunter catch her. Maybe once he killed her, he would stop killing the others.

But then she saw her mother's ghost again as mist and smoke filled the hallway.

"No!" Myra Cooper yelled—so loudly that Maria was surprised the men couldn't hear her. The mist and smoke thickened as her image took shape. And she wondered why they couldn't see her. She had never been as clear to Maria as she was then.

"You can't stop running, child," Mama urged her. "You can't let him win!"

"Who is he?" she asked.

Mama had to know...

Seth knit his brows, confused, but he answered the question as if she'd asked him. "His name is Curtis Waverly. He's the brother of the first victim."

Felicia's brother. She knew who he was now and why he looked familiar. Felicia had shown her pictures of him; he'd also been on the news after her murder, offering a reward for her killer. He wasn't the witch-hunter.

Mama shook her head in response to Maria's question. "I wish I knew..."

But like Raven, she didn't know. She hadn't seen him. This witch-hunter wasn't her killer.

He would be Maria's killer, though.

"No!" Mama yelled again. Like Irina, she could hear thoughts. "You can't give up. You have to keep running..."

But what was the point of running when she was cursed? When she would never know happiness anyway? And if she could save other lives...

"You really think he will stop?" Mama asked. "He has killed so many already."

But Maria was the one he wanted. Why else would he have killed everyone close to her?

"Not everyone," Mama reminded her. "Your sisters are alive. Your niece. Stacia is more powerful than you are. You think he'll stop if you're gone. But he won't. If he's like Eli McGregor, he won't rest until every Durikken descendant is dead..."

"I—I have to go," Maria told Seth Hughes as panic filled her. "I have to get out of here." Not just the police station. She had to get out of Copper Creek.

Now.

Mama was right. He wouldn't stop with her. He would kill the others. Elena, Ariel and Irina...

And Elena's daughter.

Did the others have daughters, too?

Would more innocent lives be lost because of her?

"You can't let her go," Mr. Waverly protested. "You need to arrest her!"

"For what?" Maria asked. "I've done nothing wrong."

It wasn't her fault that she'd been born cursed. That she had been doomed to a life on the run.

The person who'd taken all those lives—he was the one responsible. The one Seth Hughes needed to catch.

If the killer wasn't Seth…

She hoped like hell it wasn't him. She wanted someone she could trust, someone to protect her and her family. But maybe she would have to do as her sisters had—maybe she would have to take out the witch-hunter herself.

"There is no evidence to prove she committed the murders," Seth said. "There is evidence that she didn't commit the last one. So I have no reason to arrest her."

No reason to hold her. So she slipped free of his grasp. She needed to leave. Needed to put some distance between herself and that noose hanging in the restroom…

But then her throat constricted, choking off her breath, as big hands closed around her neck and squeezed. She heard a scream, but it couldn't have been hers. She couldn't speak. She couldn't breathe. So it must have been Mama's…

There was just a buzzing in her ears—the sound of her blood pumping weakly through her veins. She couldn't even see who was choking her as her vision blurred. Then everything went black as she slipped into unconsciousness.

She suspected that the next ghost she'd see would be her own…

Chapter 5

They met in darkness. The three men. And they kept their voices low as if someone might overhear them. But the person they worried about eavesdropping wasn't anywhere within normal hearing distance.

But then they weren't married to normal women. They were married to the Cooper sisters.

David Koster considered them all damn lucky. His best friend, Ty McIntyre, didn't look happy, though. He looked grim. "You sure you want to do this?" David asked him. He'd asked him the same thing when he had seen Ty earlier that night. Now the night was nearly over. "You can stay with Irina, and Joe and I can go check out this lead."

Ty shook his head. "No. I promised my wife that I would do this for *her*." He pushed his hand through his short black hair. "Hell, I promised her I would find her younger sister eight years ago."

"You've worked hard on this," David said. "We all have. But it's hard to find someone who's desperate to never be found."

"That's because she might have a damn good reason to never be found," Joseph Dolce remarked. Given his questionable past, his comment was no surprise.

"There's a statute of limitation on those cons she ran," David pointed out. And there was a damn good reason she'd had to run them: survival.

Joseph should understand that; he had grown up on the streets. But even as a kid, Joseph had probably been intimidating. Despite the fact he had as much silver as black in his hair, he was even more intimidating now. Because of everything he had seen and done...

"There's no statute of limitation on murder," Joseph said.

David had seen and done a lot in his life, too, so he used to be as cynical as Joseph. But then he had met and fallen in love with and then married Ariel Cooper. She had brought sunshine and hope and love into his life. "She's just a person of interest in those murders."

"Just?" Joseph repeated. "That's a lot. And then there're Elena's visions—"

"Which aren't always clearly interpreted until after the vision has become a reality," David reminded him. "Ariel is afraid those visions indicate that someone's after Maria. She thinks she may not live long enough to be reunited with them." And that scared her. She didn't want her first meeting with her sister to be with the woman's ghost.

David would do anything within his power to keep his wife happy. And while he had millions of dollars and contacts, he hadn't had the right kind of power to save Ariel before.

She and her sisters were the powerful ones. But even they hadn't been able to find or help Maria.

"Someone is after Maria," Ty said. "Irina feels her fear. She's scared." He turned toward Joseph. "That's why I asked you here, Joseph. You need to watch them while we're gone. You need to keep them safe."

Joseph's green eyes widened with surprise, but then he nodded in acceptance.

"You think they're in danger?" David asked, his heart beating faster.

Ty nodded. "The witch hunt has started again."

Panic and dread filled David that the nightmare had returned. He had promised that he would pilot the helicopter for Ty to follow his lead. But now he was torn. He wanted to stay. He wanted to protect his family. While his kids might be safe, since he and Ariel had adopted their children, his wife would not be safe from a witch hunt.

"I'll keep them safe," Joseph vowed.

While David hadn't known this brother-in-law as long as he'd known Ty, he trusted him. Joseph Dolce would do whatever necessary to keep the family safe from harm. But still he hesitated to leave them...

"What about that FBI agent—Seth Hughes?" he asked Ty. "Don't you trust him to keep Maria safe?" And then they could protect their wives.

"He thinks she's the prime suspect in those murders," Joseph said. "Would he protect a suspect?"

They both turned to Ty to answer the question. Ty was the former lawman among them. While he had loved his job protecting and serving the public, he loved what he did now more—finding lost loved ones. He had found everyone's but his wife's.

David understood his friend's frustration and determination. What he didn't understand now was his hesitation. And then he realized, "You don't trust Seth Hughes."

"No, I don't," Ty admitted.

He and Ty had learned at a young age to trust no one, so they had thoroughly checked out the FBI agent. "The guy doesn't need to work. He's richer than we are." And that was pretty damn rich. "He went into law enforcement because he loves it—because he wants to help people."

So why didn't Ty trust him?

Joseph snorted derisively. "You can't trust rich people." He was probably including himself. "And you can't trust that he just wants to help people. He could have another agenda entirely."

"Maria could be his agenda," Ty murmured.

"You think he's the witch-hunter?" David asked.

"He's the one who's been hunting her for almost a decade," Ty said. "And now that he's found her, she's more scared than she's ever been."

"Damn it," David said as Ty's mistrust and unease became his. "Let's get this bird in the air." He didn't want Ariel seeing her sister for the first time as a ghost. And he didn't want it to be his fault for trusting someone he shouldn't have. He turned back to Joseph, who just nodded as if David had asked his question.

He didn't need to ask. Joseph would give up his life to protect their family. But if Joseph died, then there would be no one to save the Cooper sisters from another witch hunt.

She was going to die—right before his eyes. Seth slammed his fist into Curtis Waverly's jaw. The man staggered back, but he didn't release her, his hands locked tightly around her throat.

The deputy raised the gun he held, the barrel bouncing around as his hands shook uncontrollably. The young man had probably never drawn his weapon before tonight, let alone shot someone.

Seth didn't want to be the one he shot, and he certainly didn't want Maria to get hit, either. "Put that down!" he shouted.

Then he struck Curtis again, this time driving his first hard into his throat. The man gasped as Maria gasped for breath, and he dropped to the floor, clutching at his neck.

Maria, pushed against the wall, slid down it onto the floor. Her dark eyes had already closed. Hopefully in unconsciousness—not death.

Seth dropped to his knees beside her. He didn't dare touch her neck, which was already red and swelling. He felt her wrist instead. And it was as if her pulse leaped at his touch. She was alive!

"Are you breathing?" he asked. He dipped his head close to hers. Her lips were slightly open, but he could hear no air passing through them. So he pressed his lips to hers and breathed for her. And as their mouths met, images played through his mind of other kisses. Hungry, passionate kisses...

She gasped and pushed against his shoulders, shoving him back. Her eyes were open now and wide with shock.

"You can breathe?" he asked, as he struggled for air himself. Maybe it was nearly losing her. Maybe it was the shock of touching her lips...

She nodded, but her hands lifted to her neck. And he knew she wasn't all right.

"Call an ambulance," he told the deputy.

She grabbed his arm and in a raspy whisper protested, "No…"

But maybe the young deputy had already called in reinforcements, because a door opened and footsteps echoed from down the hall.

"What the hell's going on?" the sheriff asked as he stared down at them all. Nervous of his deputy, too, he took the gun from the kid's shaking hands.

Fortunately, he wasn't alone, since the coroner stood beside him. "Is everyone okay?" Dr. Kohler asked.

"He nearly strangled her," Seth said with a glance back at Curtis Waverly.

The man lay on the floor, his body curled into a ball of pain and misery. Sympathy tugged slightly at Seth. He knew Waverly was hurting, and not from Seth's blows.

"Then why the hell haven't you cuffed him?" Sheriff Moore asked his deputy as he shoved the kid forward.

Maria's grip on Seth's arm tightened. "No," she whispered.

She didn't want the man who had attacked her arrested?

"We should get her to the hospital," Dr. Kohler said from where he knelt on the other side of her. "If this swelling gets worse, it could cut off her breathing again."

She shook her head, then flinched and touched her neck again. "I—I need my herbs…"

"You're going to the hospital," Seth said. "Not back to that barn…" It was already a crime scene. And usually the crime scenes in this case were eventually destroyed.

That was why he'd made certain the sheriff had collected as much evidence as he could without waiting for the bureau techs to show up. Sometimes they were too late.

"I brought those herbs in," Sheriff Moore told him. "I have them in evidence."

"Are those the herbs she used on that other girl's throat?" Dr. Kohler asked his friend. When the sheriff nodded, he ordered him, "Bring them over here!"

Seth shook his head, disgusted with the other men's behavior. "She needs medical attention, not some spell…"

"Those herbs worked," Dr. Kohler said. "If someone hadn't put that water in the girl's breathing tube, she would have recovered." His voice quavered with excitement. "She would have recovered from a *hanging*! It had to be those herbs…" The doctor sounded as befuddled as Seth was.

Why would Maria have saved the girl if she'd been the one who had hurt her? None of it made sense—except that Seth had been wrong about her. Maria Cooper was not a killer. She was a healer.

Seth's dream the night before had been just that—a dream born of his suspicion and mistrust of her. Nothing more. It wouldn't come true—even though most of his other dreams had.

The sheriff hurried back with an evidence bag clenched in his hand. He handed it to the doctor, but the doctor handed it to Maria. Her hands trembled as she tore open the seal and reached into the bag.

He couldn't tell one dried weed from another. But she sorted through them quickly and pulled out a poultice. Instead of pressing it to her own throat, though, she crawled across the hall to Curtis Waverly.

He tensed when she touched him, as if he thought her

touch alone could kill him. But all she did was press that poultice against his throat where Seth had slugged him.

She murmured something beneath her breath—like some weird chant. Then she told him, again in a weak whisper, "Hold that…"

Curtis's fingers trembled, but he held it. Dr. Kohler followed her across the hall and checked the man's neck. "The swelling's already going down…"

"Treat yourself," Seth implored her.

She was already reaching back into that evidence bag, already concocting another potion, which she pressed against her own throat. Only her lips moved as she chanted again. She had no voice—no breath or strength to actually utter the words.

"This is crazy," he said. "I need to take her to the hospital."

"No," she said, and now her voice was clear and loud. "I don't need medical attention."

The doctor gasped and shook his head. "I had Maurice bring me back here so I could take a look at those herbs. But I probably still wouldn't have believed it…"

If he hadn't seen it—as Seth had.

"My wife's been going to her," Sheriff Moore admitted. "She's helped Katherine with her MS." He rubbed his knuckles. "Hell, I've seen her myself. She's helped me with my arthritis."

"Have you all gone crazy?" Curtis Waverly asked. "She's a killer."

"You nearly killed her," Seth said. "Arrest him, Sheriff, for assault with intent—"

"You were going to let her go!" Curtis protested. "After all these years of looking for her, you were going to let her just walk away."

"Curtis—"

Waverly whirled toward him. "You told me that once you found her, you would lock her up for the rest of her life. That she would never get away again."

Maria turned to him, too, her eyes wide with fear. She looked the way she had when Curtis had been choking her—as if she couldn't breathe.

"You promised me justice for my sister's murder," Curtis said, his eyes hard with accusation. He obviously felt as though Seth had betrayed him.

"Justice isn't killing the wrong person," Seth admonished him as he helped the man to his feet.

"I didn't mean to...hurt her," he said, and his voice broke with sobs. "I didn't mean to... I just wanted to stop her from leaving..."

"Don't arrest him," Maria said. And her hand was on Seth's arm again, squeezing, as she stood up, too. Her strength was back.

Seth shook his head. "He has to be booked for assault."

"What about her?" Curtis asked. "Are you going to arrest her? Or are you just going to let her walk away? She'll disappear and you will never see her again. This time you'll never find her."

Seth was afraid that Curtis was right, but for the wrong reasons. He was certain that whoever had killed Raven intended to kill Maria—just as the girl's ghost had warned her.

"I'm not letting her go," Seth vowed. "I'm going to hold her..."

Seth was holding her, all right—but not in that unsecured jail where she had nearly been killed by a man he had trusted.

Maybe Curtis hadn't meant to hurt her. Maybe he

had only been overwhelmed with emotion at finally seeing her and thinking she was about to escape again. But Curtis was the one in jail now—at least until he hired an expensive lawyer to get him out on bail.

Maria was in custody, too. *His* custody. Despite her protests, he had brought her to the room he had rented at the little motel in Copper Creek.

While he stood watch near the window and door, Maria slept peacefully in his bed. Even though her potion had healed her neck so that she bore no bruises or swelling anymore, she must have been exhausted from the ordeal. The minute her curly-haired head had hit his pillow, she'd fallen asleep. The sunlight shining through the blinds and across her beautiful face hadn't bothered her at all.

But then, Curtis Waverly strangling her hadn't been her only ordeal. She had lost a friend—another one. And she'd been threatened with that noose.

Had Curtis done that?

Seth doubted it. It wasn't the man's style. Then again, Seth wouldn't have thought strangling a woman was his style, either. Was his opinion of anyone right? He'd thought Curtis harmless and he'd considered Maria Cooper a killer.

But she was a healer. She was a victim, too. Or she would be if the killer had his way. If his threat became reality…

Seth flinched at the image in his mind of her swinging from that noose. She wouldn't be able to heal herself if she was dead.

"Damn…" He pushed a hand through his hair, pulling at the strands. He welcomed the brief jolt of pain to his scalp because it helped him fight the weariness dragging down his eyelids. They were so heavy, his eyes so gritty with the sleep he'd been denied.

After Raven's call, he had checked in with the bureau and told them what had happened and that the case was now hot. But who had given up his whereabouts to Waverly? His superior hadn't mentioned the man being around the office. Curtis must have called or met his source elsewhere. Seth needed to know who among his coworkers could be bought. Because Curtis might not have been the only one who'd learned of Maria's location through this person. Instead of protecting her, as Seth had promised he would, he might be putting her in more danger. He might have led the killer right to her.

"Hell," he murmured. He should know better than to make any promises when he had never managed to keep a damn one of them.

The bedsprings creaked softly as Maria shifted beneath the blankets he had pulled over her. He stepped away from the window, closer to the bed, to check on her. Her lips parted, and a quiet moan slipped out. That damn image flashed through his mind, of her naked beneath him as he buried himself inside her. And his body ached with desire.

He bit back a curse, disgusted with himself. He was thirty-six years old, not thirteen; he should have better control over his hormones by now. He had never before been attracted to anyone involved in an investigation. His work life had never spilled over into his private life...until Maria.

He should have called for a helicopter and brought her straight back to the bureau. For questioning. And for protection. He shouldn't have brought her back to his motel room.

But he couldn't leave Copper Creek until he had thoroughly investigated Raven's murder. And he couldn't trust anyone else, including the Copper Creek sheriff, to keep Maria safe.

She moaned again, and her body wriggled under the blankets. "Seth…"

Desire jolted his heart. "I'm right here."

She lifted her arms, as if reaching for him. "I need you…"

"You're okay," he assured her, stepping closer yet to the bed.

She grabbed at his hand and tugged him toward her. "Seth…"

He sat on the edge of the bed, trying not to touch her any more. Just her hand on his had his pulse racing with that strange energy that flowed between them. "You're safe." He patted her hand before pulling his away.

Her thick lashes lifted as her eyes opened. She gasped and sat up and stared around her as if she'd never seen the room before. Or maybe as if she had seen it before…in a dream. "Where am I?"

"My motel room. I brought you here to keep you safe," he reminded her. "I should have probably brought you to the hospital, though—after Waverly attacked you." The herbs had obviously helped her. But had they really healed her completely? After she'd slept so long, he wondered. He worried.

"He got to Raven there," she said with a shiver. "And he'd nearly gotten to me at the jail. Do you really think anyplace is safe from him?"

"I won't let him get to you," he said, inwardly groaning as he heard the promise slip through his lips again. What the hell was he thinking?

"What about you?" she asked. She stared at him intensely, as if her dark eyes could see inside his heart and soul.

"It's not me," he said, trying to make her feel safe with him. If only he could feel the same with her... "I'm not a witch-hunter."

Had she really seen Raven's ghost? Had the girl really claimed that was what her killer had called himself? After watching Maria use those herbs and that indiscernible chant to heal, he was finding it harder to doubt her abilities.

"You have been hunting me," she reminded him. "You said so yourself—that you've spent the past several years tracking me down, just like he has."

"I thought you were the killer. I wanted to bring you to justice," Seth explained.

"Like you promised Curtis Waverly," she murmured. Instead of saying the man's name with anger or fear, she said it as if she pitied him. "You really shouldn't have had him arrested."

"He assaulted you," Seth said. And he felt the anger she should have over how the man had hurt her, how he might have killed her if Seth hadn't finally reacted and stopped him. "And he has enough money to hire a lawyer to reduce his charges." Or get them thrown out. He had enough money that he'd bought an informant in the bureau. "I'm not worried about Curtis Waverly. I'm worried about you."

"You said you thought I was the killer," she said. "You don't think so anymore?"

Now that he'd met her, he knew she was too petite and slender to have committed those brutal murders... alone. If she'd had help, though, the person had never turned up in his investigation. Neither had another suspect besides her, though.

"You weren't at the hospital," he said. "You couldn't have drowned Raven."

She shook her head and tumbled her hair across his pillow, making his stomach tighten with desire. "But you accused me of having an accomplice, of working with someone else…"

"You would have had to have help," he said, "to overpower the victims. You would have had to have been working with someone else." He sighed. "But in everything I've learned about you, I've found no evidence of you ever working with anyone but your mother."

"Mama…" she murmured, and so many emotions passed through her dark eyes. So much loss and regret and resentment…

It was almost as if he could feel what she felt, his heart growing heavy with it. "I know how you lost your mother," he said. "I'm sorry."

"I lost my mother years before she was killed," she said.

"It was a witch-hunter who killed her," he said with a shudder over the horrible way she'd died. "But he's gone. He can't hurt anyone else."

"It's another one who's killing these people," she said. "Another witch-hunter."

Seth should have realized that long ago—from the horrific way all her friends had died. A witch wouldn't kill using those means. But a hunter would.

"Maybe he thinks he's doling out justice, too," she said, "by killing witches."

"You think that's his motivation?"

She lifted her slender shoulders in a slight shrug. "I don't know. I don't know what would make someone kill."

He opened his mouth, tempted to tell her about his dream—about her shooting him.

But then she continued, "When I asked about you, I wasn't asking if you were the killer. I was actually worrying about him getting to *you*. Anyone who gets close to me winds up dead."

He shook his head. "That's not going to happen."

"I just had a vision…" She drew in a shaky breath. "I saw something happening…"

Had she seen what he had—the two of them making love? Maybe that was why she'd moaned and reached for him. His body hardened as desire and tension filled him. He had to know. "What did you see?"

"You…" She reached for him now, grasping his arms with hands that trembled. The heat of her palms penetrated the thin material of his shirt.

He touched her, too, sliding closer on the bed so that his thigh rubbed up against hers. And he slid his fingertips along her jaw. "It's okay. Tell me…"

"I saw you dead," she whispered, her eyes wide with horror. "You had been shot in the chest." She moved her hand there, pressing her palm over his heart. "There was so much blood…"

"It was just a dream." One that they'd eerily both had.

"It doesn't make sense," she said, her brow creased. "The witch-hunter has never shot anyone."

"None of the victims had gunshot wounds," he confirmed. Probably because it would have been too quick and humane for the sadistic bastard.

"Maybe he shoots you because you're not a witch and, by protecting me, you're in his way."

"Maybe it's not him."

Her lips parted on a soft gasp. "Of course. You have other cases. But…"

"But what?"

"*I* was there," she said, her hands gripping him tighter. "I saw you bleeding."

"How did you feel about that?" he wondered. Since in his dream, she had been the one who'd shot him.

"I hurt for you." Her voice cracked with emotion as her eyes shimmered. "I know we just met, but there's something between us. Something I can't explain."

"Neither can I," he admitted. Even knowing what he did, he was surprised by the inexplicable bond between them.

"You feel it, too?"

He stroked his fingers along her jaw. "I don't want to feel it."

"You don't still think I had something to do with those deaths…"

She had something to do with his death—if his dream was real. And unfortunately, she could still have something to do with the other murders—if she had someone helping her. But she was a healer. Not a killer. Or so he hoped.

"I don't know what to think right now," he admitted, wanting to blame his weariness. But with her touching him, the last thing he felt was tired. He was tense, on edge. "I need to stay focused. But you…"

"What about me?" she asked, leaning closer to him.

"You are so beautiful…"

She shook her head. "No, I'm not."

He stared into her eyes and realized she believed that; she wasn't just being coy or modest. She really had no idea how beautiful she was. "You are."

"Not enough…"

"Not enough for what?" With her honey-toned skin,

curly black hair and delicate features, she was hauntingly beautiful.

"I'm just not enough...anything."

Her vulnerability hurt his heart more than the bullet from his dream. Not being able to stand her pain, he leaned forward and closed the distance between them. His lips followed the path of his fingers, along her jaw, then across her cheek until his mouth covered hers.

She kissed him back, her lips moving beneath his, parting for the exploration of his tongue. She tasted as sweet and exotic as her beauty and her sandalwood and lavender scent. Her tongue met his, boldly slipping inside his mouth.

He groaned as desire pummeled him, hitting him low in his gut so that his every muscle tensed. A car engine on the street drew his attention away from her for a moment, and he lifted his head from hers. He couldn't lose his focus. But hell, with her touching him, kissing him, he was losing his mind.

Her fingers grasped his hair, pulling him back for another kiss. A deeper kiss. She sucked his tongue into her mouth, pulling him deep—as he ached to bury himself inside her.

Her hands slid from his hair down his nape to his shoulders and she tugged him onto the bed with her, on top of her. Her curves cradled him, her hips rubbing against his erection. Her breasts pushed into his chest.

Panting for breath, he pulled back. "We can't do this," he said. She was at the most a suspect, at the least a material witness. He couldn't compromise his investigation or his integrity—no matter how much he wanted her.

Maria's eyes sparkled with desire—and something deeper—as she stared up at him. "I don't think we can *not* do this. If I read your cards, I would see this—I would see *us*. I know I can't change what I see in the cards—what I see in my head. I've seen you and me."

Me, too. But he couldn't admit that to her. She thought him safe from the witch-hunter only because she didn't realize he had the same gifts she had.

"You've seen me dead," he reminded her.

"Shot," she said. "Not dead. You'll survive. You have to survive."

He allowed a grin to lift his mouth. "And if I don't…"

"Then you may not have another chance to do this… with me."

And that was a risk he couldn't take—even if it killed him. He would rather die after making love with her than die wishing that he had.

Maria held her breath while she waited for his response. Her skin flushed with embarrassment over how brazen she had been. But she wanted him. As she'd said as she had awakened, she *needed* him.

It was too soon. He was a stranger. All those arguments ran through her head, but none of them cooled her desire for him. Because everyone who got close to her got killed, she didn't have time to form a relationship. She didn't want a relationship. She just wanted one night with this man. And he really wasn't a stranger. They had a connection she'd never had before—not with her mother, the sister she'd met or any of the friends she'd lost.

She wanted to explore this deep connection before she lost it—and him, too. She closed her eyes, unable to watch his face when he rejected her. And that image flashed behind her lids, the blood spreading across his skin from the dark hole in his chest. She swallowed the sob burning in her throat.

Kisses pressed gently against her closed lids, then slid down her cheek to her lips. She opened her eyes to his face, his smoky blue eyes dark with desire. For her.

"You're sure?" he asked.

For her response, she lifted his shirt, pulling it up over his head. Then she reached for his belt. But he pulled back and stood up, unbuckling his belt and the holster that attached to the back of it. He put aside his gun.

Maria shuddered at the sight of it and forced her focus back to him. To his heavily muscled chest. There was no hole, no blood, nothing but a dusting of reddish-brown hair. She rose from the bed and pressed a kiss to his chest, sliding her lips over a flat male nipple until it pebbled.

His fingers tangled in her hair, holding her mouth to him. His heart beat hard beneath her lips. Hard and fast and strong. He was alive.

And so was she. And for now Maria wanted to celebrate life. She skimmed her lips up his throat and over his square jaw to his ear. "I want you..."

"You have me," he said wearily, as if resigned to his fate. "You had me before we ever met..."

She shivered at his words. He felt it, too—that it was fate that they would be together. That they belonged together. But it wasn't possible for her to stay close to anyone, to keep anyone, so they had only tonight. She would have to make it enough.

She kissed him again, stroking her tongue inside his mouth. And he kissed her back—really kissed her now. But he didn't touch her with just his lips.

His hands were everywhere. They ran down her back and tugged up her sweater. As she had with his, he pulled it up and over her head. She wore only a lacy camisole beneath—for a moment. Then it was gone, too, leaving her breasts bare to his gaze.

And his mouth. It skimmed down her throat, over her collarbone to the curve of each breast. His lips closed over a taut nipple, tugging and teasing until she moaned.

He treated the other nipple to the same sweet torture, making her wriggle and squirm on the bed as a pressure built inside her. Even as his mouth stalled on her breast, his hands kept moving. He pushed her skirt and panties down over her hips, skimming his palms along the length of her legs.

It was as if they had made love before. Many times. He knew her body well. He knew exactly where to touch her and what to taste.

He bit the outer slope of her breasts, lapped the indentation of her navel, trailed his tongue down the inside of her thighs.

She gasped and moaned, clutching at his hair as he settled between her legs, making love to her with his mouth. He slid his tongue deep, then withdrew and teased the center of her femininity until her world shattered and she screamed his name. "Seth!"

It was as if her saying his name snapped his control, because he shucked off his pants and boxers. Then he was inside her, the impressive length of his erection sliding deep.

She wrapped her legs around his waist, meeting his thrusts. She grabbed his shoulders, then drew her nails down his back, holding him tight as the pressure built inside her before a deep thrust shattered it again.

As she panted for breath, he withdrew and lifted her boneless body from the mattress. He turned her over so that she knelt before him. And his cock slid inside her again, where she was wet and pulsing for him. His hands cupped her breasts, teasing the taut nipples.

She grabbed the headboard, holding it tight in shaking hands as he thrust again and again into her. Her hair fell forward and his lips skimmed across her nape—and lower across the trio of tattoos she had conned an artist into giving her when she'd been just fifteen.

All her rational thoughts vanished when one of his hands skimmed down from her breasts to touch where their bodies joined. And she came apart—this orgasm more powerful than the ones he'd already given her. Unconsciousness threatened again, her world shattering as she wept at the intensity of their lovemaking. She had never felt anything like this—not even in her dreams.

She had never even known such passion existed.

Then he held her tight against him, and a groan tore from his throat, stirring her damp curls from her temple. His body tensed as he came, filling her. He cradled her close, rolling so that she sprawled atop him. Both gasped for breath, their hearts racing in frantic unison.

"That was…" He swallowed hard. "That was…"

"Beyond explanation." As so much of her life was, like the strange connection between them.

He didn't try to explain it or apologize or rationalize. Instead he just held her, as if he never intended to let her go. But eventually, after several moments of silence, his breathing slowed, his arms relaxed around her.

And Maria's panic grew.

What the hell have I done?

While she knew he was an FBI agent, she had no idea of his true intentions toward her. To protect her? Or kill her? She had already given him more than she ever had anyone else. She couldn't give him her life, too.

But that was the least of her worries. She didn't really believe he would hurt her, or she wouldn't have slept so peacefully in his bed for most of the day. Or at least, her sleep had been peaceful until she'd had that horrible dream…

That was her real fear—that the killer would take Seth's life. Everybody who got close to her died.

She pulled free of his arms and quickly grabbed up her clothes from the floor. She had just put them on when mist seeped under the door. Not Mama. Not now. She didn't need to be reminded how much she was like her mother, how she never chose the right men.

"Go away," she whispered.

But the shape that formed was Raven's, the bird tattoo stark against her ghostly pale face. "You have to leave," the girl warned. "The witch-hunter is close."

Maria glanced to the bed, to where Agent Hughes slept fitfully, his muscular chest rising and falling with jerky, uneven breaths.

How close was the hunter? Was the man who'd just given her the greatest pleasure of her life the very same man who had made her life a living hell?

She turned away from him, her gaze falling on the nightstand where he had left his holster and cell phone. She reached out, but she passed over the gun and the phone in favor of his keys. No matter what he was, they would both be safer if they weren't together.

"Quickly," Raven murmured as her ghost began to fade. "He's coming for you…"

Maria opened the door, her breath held in burning lungs as the hinges creaked. But Seth didn't wake up. Hopefully, he wouldn't until she was gone. She stepped outside and drew the door shut. Cool autumn air rushed over her, chilling the skin that had been hot and flushed just moments ago.

She ached to crawl back in bed with him, to wake him with kisses and caresses so they could make love again. So she could prove to herself that it had really happened. That it had been real, because she had never believed passion that powerful was possible.

She ignored the ache and forced herself away from the door. The motel was a two-story cement-block-and-vinyl structure with an outside stairwell. Maria hurried down the steel steps to the parking lot.

As the mist had filled the room moments ago, it now filled the lot. But it was thick and dark and close to the ground, nature's fog as night began to fall instead of supernatural beings.

She moved through it toward the vehicles, trying to distinguish which one was his. But she had made it only a few feet when a big hand reached out of the mist and wrapped tightly around her arm.

The witch-hunter was close. Very close...

Chapter 6

A scream—albeit muffled—jerked Seth awake as the terror in it reached deep inside him, squeezing his heart. "Maria!" He reached for her, but like in his dream, she wasn't lying next to him anymore.

But when he opened his eyes, he didn't find her sitting at the end of the bed. Or inside the tiny bathroom that he could see through the open door. She was gone. He jumped up and stepped into his boxers and pants while reaching for his gun.

The Glock was there, cold and heavy in its holster. He drew it out and ran from the room. Where was she?

Night was beginning to fall again and the fog that rolled in with it hid her from him, as well. Another scream, this one even more muffled, as if someone covered her mouth, drew him toward where he had parked the SUV. He moved quickly but silently, keeping low so as to not alert her attacker to his presence.

Just as he had been with Raven, would he be too late to save Maria? Damn him for losing focus, for making love with someone he'd sworn to protect. And he hadn't made that promise to just her...

As he neared where the scream had emanated from, he spied two dark shadows, taller than the cars, grappling. Maria was too delicately built to ward off the muscular man who held her tightly against his body. The fog distorted their images, overlapping their shadows; Seth didn't trust himself to take a shot.

He shouldn't have trusted her, either. She had probably just made love with him so that he would drop his guard and allow her to slip away. All those old police reports called her a con artist, but he had another, better reason than other people's claims to mistrust her. He had his dream...

Then he had her attacker, as Seth vaulted toward the shadows and knocked the man to the ground. Maria fell back against a car, out of the way of their scuffle. But she screamed his name, her fear seemingly for him now. She had reason to be afraid.

And so, probably, did Seth. The guy was strong, wrestling free of him. So Seth swung his fist, catching the guy across the jaw and knocking him down again.

The man landed with an oath. "Son of a bitch..."

"Oh, shit," Seth said with a sigh as he recognized the man's distinctively raspy voice. "I'm sorry..."

"You're apologizing to *him*?" Maria asked, her dark eyes wide with shock and anger.

He extended his hand and helped the dark-haired man to his feet. "This is Ty McIntyre," he explained.

"Someone else who bribed one of your coworkers to find out where you are?" she asked. It was a fair question, given that was how Curtis Waverly had found them.

Seth shook his head. "No. I called him." Not as early as he had promised Ty that he would—the minute he'd found her. He'd thought he'd been doing the man and his family a favor—keeping them away from a killer. But after Curtis Waverly had attacked her, Seth had realized that he'd almost waited too long. He had called Ty then.

"Why? Who is he?" she asked, stepping closer and grabbing Seth's arm as if she still wanted his protection. Fear and dread radiated from her.

"Ty isn't one of the victims' family members," he assured her.

"Your partner, then?"

McIntyre laughed, either at the thought of his being an FBI agent or his working with Seth. "I'm one of *your* family members," Ty answered for himself. "I'm your brother-in-law."

Her breath audibly caught. "Irina's husband?"

"Yes," Ty replied with a big grin of husbandly pride.

"You're the knight of swords," Maria said in breathless awe.

"I'm the who?" the man asked with a deep chuckle.

"Before I left the apartment I shared with Irina, I read her cards," she explained. "I saw you coming to protect her. I knew she would be safe with you—that you'd fight for her. She could trust you."

Seth caught the wistfulness in her voice, as if she, too, yearned for someone she could trust. *He* wasn't that someone; he had too many secrets. If she learned any of them, she would never be able to trust him. In fact, she might act out his dream and shoot him dead.

Even more wistfully she added, "She could love you."

"She does," Ty said, his raspy voice cracking with emotion. "And I love her more than I had thought it possible to love anyone. That's why I had to come here first. I had to make sure you were really you. We've been looking for you for so long. We've had so many disappointments. She couldn't handle another one right now."

"Right now?" Maria asked, her beautiful face tense with concern. "Is Irina okay?"

"Great—but she's very pregnant with our second set of twins. The doctor has ordered her to bed rest. And Irina has ordered me," he said, "to bring you home—to Barrett, Michigan."

Maria shook her head, looking nearly as panicked as she had when she had seen that noose dangling from the ceiling of the restroom. "That's not my home. I can't go back there."

"You lived there—with Irina," Ty reminded her. "But it's not your home because you shared an apartment there. It's your home because of your family. All your sisters live there—and your nieces and nephews and brothers-in-law."

"They only *live*," Maria said, her voice shaking, "because I'm not there. I have to stay away from them—to keep them safe." The longing was in her voice and the pinched expression on her face. She wanted to be with her family, but she had sacrificed what she wanted for the safety of the ones she loved.

If she had anything to do with the murders, she wouldn't believe her family needed protecting. She wouldn't have had to make any sacrifices...

Ty McIntyre had been right when he'd told Seth that Maria was as much a victim as those who had died. He had been so certain that she couldn't have had anything to do with the murders. But Seth hadn't been able to put aside his suspicion. Even now he struggled more with his doubts than he had physically struggled with Ty McIntyre.

Ty's brow furrowed, and his eyes warmed with compassion. "Maria, you're wrong. You need to be with your family."

She shook her head, tangling her hair around her shoulders like the long spiral curls had tangled when she'd made love with Seth. "No," she argued. "I'm *cursed.*"

She said it with the same conviction that she had insisted that she wasn't beautiful, that she wasn't enough. And, just as it had when she'd made those claims, her vulnerability reached inside Seth and squeezed his heart.

"Whoever gets close to me dies," she continued. "Ariel can see ghosts. Have her talk to Mama. She'll tell her that I'm cursed. She knew it even before I was born. She didn't want me to be around my sisters."

Seth's heart hurt even more with her pain. He understood this pain all too well. Family could hurt you the most.

"Myra said and did a lot of things she shouldn't have," Ty said. "She was wrong about you. You need to be with your sisters—with our family."

But she shook her head. "I can't—I can't come around them. I can't risk any harm coming to my family because of me."

"Maria." Ty reached out, but she shrank back and tightly clutched Seth's arm.

"Show him the pictures—the crime scene photos," she urged Seth. "Show him what happens to anyone who gets close to me."

"I already showed him," he admitted. He had shown the private investigator the photos and the case files when he'd tried to convince McIntyre that he didn't want to find Maria Cooper. Ty McIntyre had tracked him down because they'd both been looking for her—just for very different reasons.

"Then you know why I can't go with you," she told her brother-in-law. "You don't want me anywhere near your family."

"They're your family, too. We all want you to be with us, to get to know you and to keep you safe." He speared Seth with a hard stare full of his disdain and disapproval for how the FBI agent had been protecting her. Apparently he'd heard about Waverly attacking her at the police station.

"I can't release her to you," Seth said. "There's been another murder."

Ty's gaze traveled up and down him, from his bare feet to his bare chest. And Seth suspected the guy was tempted to commit one himself. "You can't still suspect that she's responsible."

No. He couldn't, but he would still be a fool to trust her, given the way she had sneaked out after making love with him. While Seth was beginning to believe she had genuine special abilities, as Ty had sworn her sisters possessed, Maria was also a con artist.

"I am responsible," she insisted, guilt quavering in her voice and lower lip. "If those people hadn't gotten close to me, they would still be alive."

"The murders do have something to do with her," Seth told Ty. "She's involved somehow. I need to keep her here so that she can help me stop the killer. I've barely had a chance to interview her since I found her."

Ty glanced at his state of undress again. "Really? Did you get sidetracked?"

"Yes, by my friend Raven's murder," Maria said, defending him.

Seth had no defense for how he'd lost control. It was almost as if Maria had put a spell on him. Or her beauty and passion had bewitched him.

"I need to stay here and answer all his questions," she continued. "I want to help him find the killer. It's time for this to end. And when the killer's caught, I'll come home. I promise."

Ty stared hard at Seth and warned him, "You better keep her safe."

Seth nodded.

He would keep Maria safe, but who would keep him safe? He had totally lost perspective with her; he'd let her con him. Would his dream come true? Would he wind up letting her kill him, too?

Seeing Maria for the first time in person should have brought Ty McIntyre triumph. But she was so much like his wife that she made him miss Irina even more.

She was also so much like his wife that he'd known he wouldn't be able to change her mind. She was convinced that she was a danger to her family. That was why she had stayed away from them all.

To protect them...

David turned toward him as he climbed into the chopper next to him. "Are you sure you want to leave?" He had found an old airstrip to use, but they could have landed several places in the remote area.

"No," Ty admitted. "But I have to get back to my wife." Irina probably wouldn't be happy to see him. But his gut was telling him that she needed him. And he had promised that he would always be there for her. She would always come first with him.

"Of course," David said with complete understanding. He loved Ariel the way Ty loved Irina—completely. But because he loved Ariel so much, he hesitated. "What about Maria? How can we just leave her here?"

"Seth will protect her."

"What changed?" David asked. "You didn't trust him when we came up here. But now you do? Was it what the sheriff and deputy said about him?"

Ty hadn't heard much of their praise of the FBI agent firsthand. David had stayed behind at the station, talking to the local lawmen, while Ty had gone to Seth's motel alone. He hadn't wanted to overwhelm Maria.

Guilt and regret tugged at him for how he had scared her in the parking lot. But she had nearly disappeared into the fog—as she had kept disappearing into thin air anytime he had gotten close to finding her. So instinct had had him grabbing and holding on to her.

Until Seth had rescued her.

A grin tugged at his mouth, but he flinched as his slightly bruised skin stung with pain. He didn't mind that the FBI agent had struck him. Instead he respected him more for having done it.

"Oh," David said with the instant understanding born of their years and years of friendship. "Your instincts…"

"It's more than that," Ty admitted. "Because at first my instincts were saying I shouldn't have trusted him. I had the lead she was here, and so was Seth Hughes, yet he didn't call me right away…"

David's brown eyes narrowed with renewed suspicion. "You wanted to make sure everything was all right."

"Yeah," he said. "But now we can go home."

"But everything's not all right," David said. "Another

woman was killed and Maria was attacked while in police custody—while in Hughes's presence."

Ty chuckled. "And I grabbed her in the motel parking lot."

David shook his head, disgusted. "We should stay. Your earlier instincts were right. We can't trust Seth Hughes to protect her."

"He saved her from that attack," Ty reminded his friend. "And there was no way I would have gotten out of the parking lot with her. He would have killed me first."

David laughed. "And that makes you happy."

"Oh, yeah," Ty said. "There's no way Seth Hughes will let anyone hurt her. And she won't be able to run away from him again."

David nodded again with that sudden understanding. "She's not just a case to him anymore."

Ty wondered if she had ever been just a case. "She's his *Irina*."

"His *Ariel...*" David sighed. "Poor bastard. I almost feel sorry for him."

If she was in as much danger as Irina thought, then Ty felt very sorry for him, too. Because Seth Hughes wouldn't just kill to protect her—he would die, as well.

The urge to run burned in Maria's stomach...along with her desire for the FBI agent who was insistent on keeping her in protective custody. She had almost gotten away from him. She would have if not for her brother-in-law showing up, wanting to bring her "home."

She had never had a home, just the old pickup truck with the camper on the back that was still parked in the driveway next to the Magik Shoppe. That would be home enough until the killer was caught—only then would she keep her promise to meet up with her sisters.

But she doubted she could help catch him, no matter how many of Seth's questions she had spent the night answering when he'd questioned her. She'd told him how she'd come to know each victim. She had met Felicia and one of the young men in a class on parapsychology at Barrett University. The others had sought out her.

He'd already known most of what she told him. So none of it was likely to lead him to the killer.

"Thanks for bringing me back here," Maria told Seth. She had convinced him that coming back to the Magik Shoppe just might help them find a clue to the killer.

He had refused to make the trip down the treacherous dirt road until morning. Neither of them had slept that night, though. He had stood watch at the window, and she'd lain in the bed where they had made love watching him, wanting him...

She had never felt this way about anyone—had never felt so connected. So *consumed*...

She'd had boyfriends in the past, but the relationships had been brief, and she'd never let herself get too attached because she'd known she would have to leave them and keep running. Or they would wind up leaving her...

She was already too attached to Seth. She didn't want to lose him like she had the others. She had to get away from him. For his protection and hers... The other night when she had driven back and found the barn door open and Raven swinging from that noose, Maria had left the keys in the truck ignition. Maybe if she could distract Seth, she could get away from him. Then she could do what she had after every other murder. Someday she might run far enough and fast enough that *it*, the killer and Seth wouldn't catch up with her again.

But trying to get away in the truck wasn't why she had asked to come back here. She needed to find what she had been looking for the night she had found Raven hanging. She lifted trembling fingers to her throat. It had healed from Felicia Waverly's brother strangling her. But her neck felt naked. She hadn't been without the chain and locket since Mama had left it with her...

"You shouldn't be here," he said as he pulled his SUV behind the truck. "This is a crime scene. I shouldn't let you back in there." His hands, which had done such incredible things to her body, clenched the steering wheel.

"I won't touch anything." But the locket. Even though her fingers itched to touch him again, to caress those muscles so that they rippled beneath her fingertips, she had to resist her desire for him. Because it wasn't just desire...

After they had made love, the connection between them had grown stronger; that was partly why she had run from him.

For his sake as much as hers, she needed to get away from him. She threw open the passenger's door, but he caught her arm and held her inside...with him. Her skin tingled from the heat of his palm, and she wanted him touching her the way he had. She wanted him.

"Are you conning me again?" he asked.

"Again?" She had tried conning him into thinking she wasn't Maria Cooper. But she suspected that he was talking about something else.

"Yesterday...when we...when—whatever happened in that motel room..."

Dread gripped her stomach as she worried he couldn't even acknowledge what had been the most powerful experience of her life. The connection was all on her side. She wasn't enough for him, just as she hadn't been enough for her own mother.

"*Whatever? Whatever* happened?" She tugged on her arm, trying to wrest free from his grasp. But his fingers didn't budge.

His other hand cupped her cheek, turning her face toward his. As he leaned across the console separating their bodies, his pupils dilated, swallowing the smoky blue irises. "I know *what* happened. It was amazing—unreal…"

Despite the damp air of the cold autumn morning, heat suffused Maria, and her pulse quickened. Images flashed through her mind. Not of the future but of the past. Of the two of them in bed, naked skin sliding over naked skin…as they made love frantically. Desperate for release from the feelings building inside them.

His throat rippled as he swallowed hard. "I just don't know *why* it happened."

"What do you mean?"

"I've never crossed that line before…with *anyone* involved in a case. I've never lost control like that. *Ever.*" He leaned closer, his lips just a breath away from hers. "What did you do to me?"

"You think that I…" She struggled to spit out the insult as she understood exactly how he thought she had conned him. "You think that I…purposely seduced you?"

"Didn't you?" he asked, his voice a husky whisper that raised goose bumps on her skin. "Wasn't it part of your plan to distract me so that you could escape?"

Offended that he thought she would whore herself, she lifted her chin and glared at him. "I hadn't planned that—any of *that*."

"You didn't use some of your—" he gestured toward the sign above the double doors of the barn that proclaimed it the Magik Shoppe "—special potions to make me fall under your spell?"

"My spell?" she scoffed. She'd seen his disbelief earlier. "I didn't think you believed that I am a real witch. I thought those old police reports had you convinced that I'm just a con artist."

He skimmed his fingers across her throat. "I saw you heal yourself and Curtis Waverly. There was redness and swelling and then you concocted those herbs and chanted something…"

"A prayer," she said. No one was more spiritual than a witch. "I chanted a prayer."

"I don't know what you are," he said, leaning so close now that his lips brushed across hers in a whisper-soft kiss.

Her breath caught in her lungs as desire overwhelmed her. Everything else disappeared like the mist. She saw only Seth—*wanted* only Seth. Her lips clung to his, and he deepened the kiss. As his tongue slid inside her mouth, she moaned. A kiss wasn't enough—not when she knew intimately the pleasure he could give her.

She leaned across the console, pressing her breasts into his chest—silently begging for his touch. Now she ached just for him. His heart pounded hard against hers in perfect, frantic rhythm. She reached for his shirt, wanting to open the buttons and press skin to skin. But he caught her hand, manacling his fingers around both wrists like handcuffs. His touch wasn't cold like the metal cuffs had been; it was hot, setting her aflame with desire and that curious tingling sensation that spread throughout her body every time they touched.

"Maybe you are a witch," he said with a ragged

groan. "I wasn't going to do that again. I wasn't going to touch you, let alone kiss you. But every time I get close to you, I can't resist you."

"I am a witch," she admitted. But who had put the spell on whom? "But the last thing I would ever make for myself would be a *love* potion. I don't want anyone falling for me. I don't want anyone getting hurt because of me again."

She had tried other spells on herself, other cures to reverse the curse, to remove the dark aura that hung over her. But all she had ever needed to protect her from harm was the locket; she'd felt as though that had kept her safe all these years—as it had kept Elena Durikken safe from Eli McGregor. But now the locket was gone…and so was her common sense.

She had no business kissing—making *love*—with a man she couldn't trust. Despite all the promises he'd made her, or maybe because of them, she couldn't trust Seth Hughes. "I didn't plan what happened last night."

"Then why did you sneak out the minute I closed my eyes?" he asked, his distrust apparent in the question and the cooling of the passion in his eyes.

He might be beginning to believe in her special abilities, but he obviously still thought she was a con.

"I just panicked," she replied. "The witch-hunter is out there." She peered through the windshield but dark fog had wrapped around the car, blanketing it like night. Maybe a storm was coming, or maybe another spirit. "He's going to keep killing." She didn't want Seth getting killed, as she'd seen in her vision, because he had gotten too close to her.

"Your running isn't going to stop him," Seth pointed out, his hands still wrapped tight around her wrists. "Every time you run away, he finds you. Then he kills again. The only way to stop him is to turn this around. Instead of him chasing and catching you, we need to chase and catch him."

"We," she repeated. "If you mean that—if you're going to let me help—you have to let me go inside the Magik Shoppe."

He, too, peered out the window toward the fog-enshrouded barn. "Crime scene," he corrected her with a gruff murmur.

"If you let me into the *crime scene*, maybe I can read it," she said, "like I do tarot cards. Maybe I can pick up some clues about his identity."

That muscle twitching along his jaw, he remained stoic, staring straight out the windshield as if he hadn't heard what she'd said. Or didn't care...

"You really think I'm a con," she said. He wasn't the first to call her that, but it bothered her that he didn't believe in her. Even though they had just met, she felt as if she'd known him longer—her whole life, and maybe even longer than that, maybe other lives. "Is it just me, or do you think that anyone who claims psychic abilities is lying?"

"You've conned people," he reminded her.

"There are such things as false truths and honest lies," she said, quoting her mother's favorite gypsy proverb.

"What?"

"That was what Mama always said. She believed she was making people happier by telling them what they wanted to hear rather than what she really saw." Maria sighed. "She lied so much I think the lines became blurred to her. I think she lost sight of what was real and what she'd made up."

And because she'd realized that about her mother,

Maria had hoped that she wasn't really cursed. For a while she'd believed that it was just another of her mother's wild stories. That was why she'd sought out her sisters and found Irina. But then Mama's ghost had appeared to her. And she'd known then that Mama had never lied to her. Maria was cursed—to lose everyone she cared about.

"You don't tell people what they really want to hear," Seth said. "You tell them what they *least* want to hear. When you read their cards, you tell them that bad things will happen to them."

"I tell them what I see." And because of the witch-hunter, it had been bad more often than it'd been good. That was why she hadn't read in over a year—and before that, she had tried to read for only strangers. "After Mama died, I promised myself no more lies." If only that were a promise she had been able to keep. To herself. To him.

"So you're not running cons anymore?" he asked.

She shook her head.

"Then how do you get the money to set up your shops? No banks have ever loaned you money."

She had eventually taken the advice in her mother's letter. She had sought out her father. But he wasn't just her father. "I have a benefactor—someone who gives me the start-up money."

Actually, it was his creepy assistant who sent the money orders. She shivered as she thought of the intense young man.

"I've never traced a benefactor to you," he said. "And you didn't mention him when I was questioning you last night. Who is it?"

She had already brought her father enough embarrassment. She didn't want to bring him any more. "My parapsychology professor," she said. "He believes in what I do."

He narrowed his eyes in suspicion. Maybe of the professor. Or probably because he thought she'd conned or seduced the professor. But that wasn't the case at all.

"We're wasting time," she said. "I need to go inside the shop." She had to get inside the barn to search it for her locket.

Before Mama had lost them to social services, she had given each of her three older daughters an antique charm. Maria had had an image of each tattooed on her back. So Mama had had only the locket left to give when she deserted Maria. She had left it in that letter. Maybe the locket was not as powerful as the three-hundred-and-fifty-year-old charms that were rumored to have special powers, but it was the only thing Maria had left of her family. Of her heritage.

Without it, she was not a Cooper. She was nothing. The child with no birth certificate. With no driver's license. With no record that she had ever existed...

"How old were you when she took off?" he asked, his deep voice gentle with sympathy.

"Fifteen."

That muscle jumped along his jaw again. "Me, too."

"What?"

"I was fifteen the last time I saw my dad."

"I'm sorry."

"I'm not," he replied, the sympathy gone now, replaced by a coldness that raised goose bumps on Maria's skin. "My dad was a son of a bitch. And we actually left him. I never saw him again. How about you? Did you see your mom again?"

She nodded. "Like Raven, after she died, I saw her

ghost. That was when I started running." Like Elena Durikken...

"And you haven't stopped for more than a few months or, at the most, a year anyplace," he said. He had done a good job of tracking down her whereabouts. Her past. "Don't you think it's time?"

"I will...once the killer is caught," she said. The promise she had made to her brother-in-law was one she intended to keep—if she lived to keep it. "You don't have to believe in what I do. Just let me do it. Let me see what I can read from the scene." She tugged on her wrists, trying to shake off his hands, but his grasp tightened. "Seth—"

"No, don't get out of the car," he warned her. "Something's not right."

She studied his face. A glaze had settled over his smoky eyes, as if he was seeing something else—something no one else could see, as the vision was only inside his head. She furrowed her brow. "Do you—?"

"The sheriff told me he would post a deputy at the scene until FBI techs could get here—to make sure nothing happens to this crime scene like it's happened to the other ones."

She hadn't realized anything had happened to the other crime scenes.

She peered through the fog and noticed a police car with a light bar on the roof parked next to the barn. "The car is there..."

"But where's the officer?" he wondered. "He should have come up to us before now."

Dread tied knots in her stomach as she noticed the empty driver's seat. "I don't see anyone..."

"Stay here. And lock the doors."

"No." Now she clutched his arm, her fingers grasping the sleeve of his leather jacket as she tried keeping him inside the car. "You can't go out there alone." That image flashed through her mind again—of his heart pumping blood through the hole in his chest. "Call the sheriff."

"There's no time," he told her. "That officer could be in trouble." He shook off her hand and stepped onto the gravel drive. Reaching beneath his jacket, he pulled his gun from its holster. "I have to make sure he's okay."

"He's probably sleeping." She glanced back to the police car, which was parked beside her old truck, which she had pulled up next to the barn that night. An eerie glow illuminated the truck interior and glinted off the metal. Uttering a gasp, she turned toward the barn just as flames burst through the roof with a whoosh of air that sounded like a clap of thunder.

Even as far away as he'd parked, the explosion rocked the SUV and sent flames and debris hurtling toward the windshield. She closed her eyes, as a reflex, to avoid any flying glass. When she opened them again, dust poured down on the SUV like rain. The police car and her mama's old truck were both ablaze—like the barn.

"Seth!" she screamed.

But he was gone.

Choking and gasping for breath, she jumped out of the car and ran toward the burning barn.

Chapter 7

Some of the most violent men Joseph Dolce had ever met—and he'd met some violent men during the course of his long and sometimes ill-spent life—surrounded the estate. They carried guns and the kind of couldn't-care-less attitude that got people killed.

The witch-hunter wouldn't get past them—not these men that Joseph had hired. They were working for his money, but they were also working for his respect. They would give up their lives to protect his family.

He and David and Ty had gathered them all at the McIntyre estate—to support Irina and so that they could keep everyone safe. Halfway home David had had to land his helicopter because of the fog; they'd sworn it was following them from Copper Creek, as if they were bringing Maria's darkness home to Barrett.

He'd once been a cynical man—a man who believed in nothing. Who had no soul…

But then he'd fallen for Elena and he'd started believing in everything. In good as well as evil. In love as well as hate. In witchcraft and spirits and things that couldn't be explained...

She had stolen his heart but given him back his soul.

He was almost relieved that David and Ty hadn't made it back yet. He didn't want Maria's darkness falling over *his* family.

Then he heard it—a scream of such terror and agony that his blood chilled. He shoved open the front door and vaulted up the stairs to the master bedroom. Irina was sitting up, as much as her swollen belly would allow, in bed. And she was screaming uncontrollably.

"Shh," Ariel said, patting her back as Elena held her tightly in her arms. "This isn't good for the babies. You have to settle down."

"It's so hot and smoky," Irina said. "So hot..."

The room was actually cold. Icy cold—which probably meant that Joseph's mother-in-law had joined them. Or maybe another ghost had. He shivered with revulsion and regret.

"It's like I'm burning," Irina said, her voice breaking into sobs. "It's like *she's* burning..."

Over her younger sister's head, Elena met his gaze. Her blue eyes were bright with unshed tears—of dread and fear.

"Ty," Irina gasped. "I need Ty."

She had no more than asked for her husband before the bedroom door opened again and he rushed through it.

"I'm here," he assured her. "I'm here!"

Elena stepped away from the bed so that Ty could take her place. He enfolded his wife in his arms. "I'm sorry I'm late. I shouldn't have left you."

Even though Irina clung to him, she said, "You shouldn't have come back. You should have stayed with her."

Elena tugged Joseph into the hall with her and closed the bedroom door. Then she stepped into his arms, clinging as tightly to him as Irina had Ty. And her slender body trembled with silent weeping.

"What's wrong, sweetheart?" he asked. "What's going on?"

"Irina could feel her burning," Elena said, her voice cracking with emotion.

She was the strongest woman he'd ever known—usually so strong that she refused to betray a flicker of emotion.

"Maria?"

She nodded, and her silky hair brushed against his chin. "I was wrong about her," she said, her voice heavy with regret and guilt. "Just like I was once so wrong about you…"

"You weren't wrong about me," he reminded her. He held her so closely that he could feel her heart beating in his chest. "I was the man you thought I was. But loving you made me a different man—a better man."

She looked up at him, and love radiated from her eyes. "The best," she murmured.

But he hadn't always been. He'd grown up on the streets and had cared only about money and power… until he'd fallen for her and her daughter. They had brought out a side of him he hadn't known he'd possessed—a loving and tender side.

She shed her tears silently, but they streaked down her face. He wiped them away with his thumbs, trailing them across her silky skin. As usual, her beauty had his breath catching with surprise and appreciation. She was so damn beautiful...

And he was so damn lucky that she'd taken a chance on a man like him—that she'd trusted him when half the time he barely trusted himself.

"I was wrong about Maria, though," she insisted. "She was never the danger. She was only in danger."

"Was?" He remembered that cold chill in Irina and Ty's room and wondered...

"If she's burning..."

It was too late. The witch-hunter had claimed another victim; he had burned Maria Cooper at the stake.

Smoke filled the barn with the heavy scent of sandalwood and lavender. The dried herbs hanging from the rafters caught fire, showering sparks down onto the floor of the barn. It was already burning, the fire rising higher from the source of oxygen through the hole blown into the side wall.

The hole and the fire illuminated the interior as the light flickered across the face of the unconscious deputy. At least, Seth hoped he was just unconscious. He lifted the young man into his arms and headed toward the double doors just as Maria ran inside—right past him as if she didn't even see him.

"Get out!" he yelled at her. But the crackling fire drowned out his voice.

He quickly carried the deputy away from the barn and laid him on the ground. Then he rushed back inside, shouting, "Maria! Maria!"

She had disappeared into the shower of burning herbs and rising flames—as if they'd consumed her.

His heart slammed against his ribs and panic overwhelmed him. He couldn't have lost her. Not like this...

Ignoring the heat and the flames, he stepped into the fire. "Maria!" Through the smoke he glimpsed her, kneeling on the ground near the toppled-over table and the tarot cards. Was she trying to do a reading now?

He didn't need the cards to tell him what would happen if they stayed any longer inside the fire. As the fire rose and the structure weakened, the old barn groaned and shook. And the old rafters began to give...

"Maria!" He reached for her, grabbing her up from the floor just as the roof shuddered and imploded, collapsing onto them. Holding her tightly, Seth ran through the falling rafters and crumbling plywood and burning shingles. He ran for those open doors just as the wall began to crumble, the opening closing. He ducked low, beneath the burning beam, and carried her out of the barn.

Or was he out? The smoke enveloped them yet, wrapping close around them with that overwhelming scent of sandalwood and lavender.

"Are you okay?" he asked in a raspy whisper. His throat was burning and raw from the smoke and the heat.

Maybe that was why she didn't hear it. Maybe it was because she was unconscious. Her body was limp in his arms.

Soot streaked her beautiful face and blood trickled from a small cut on her forehead. The sight of her, disheveled and hurt, reached inside Seth, squeezing his heart in a tight vise of fear. He wasn't doing a very damn good job of keeping her safe.

As he'd rushed into the barn, he'd pushed the button on his phone that connected him with the sheriff. He probably hadn't even disconnected before he shoved it back into his pocket. The sheriff would send help. An ambulance…

But Maria and the deputy needed help now. If only she were conscious…

But how would she heal herself when all her herbs were gone? Burned to ashes…

He carried her to his SUV. He would drive her and the deputy to the hospital himself.

Just as he turned back for the deputy, he heard the sirens. The sheriff had sent help. He helped them load the deputy into the ambulance, then drove Maria to the hospital himself.

And he stood watch while the ER physician cleaned her wound and affixed a butterfly bandage to the injury. His fists curled at his sides; he hated another man touching her almost as much as he hated that she'd been hurt. He had never been the possessive type, but with the killer determined to get close to her, Seth was looking at everyone as a possible suspect.

As if Seth's scrutiny made the man uneasy, he stepped back with a sigh of relief. "She's fine," he said.

At least she was conscious now. She had regained consciousness in the SUV—with a scream on her lips. She'd thought they were still in the fire. But Seth had reassured her and continued to hold her hand.

"But you should be checked out," the doctor persisted. "You inhaled a lot of smoke, and you have cuts that appear deeper than hers. The skin on your hands and forearms looks to be burned, too."

"I'm fine," Seth said, dismissing his own injuries. He felt none of his own pain. Only hers. She had been so terrified.

The young guy swallowed nervously. "Okay, then. Well, you can get dressed now," he told Maria. He opened the door to the private room Seth had insisted she have, and he held it open, waiting.

Seth shook his head. He wasn't leaving her alone in the very hospital where her friend had been murdered. When the door finally closed behind the nervous doctor, he walked over and locked it.

"Well, this is awkward," she murmured, glancing down at the paper gown she wore.

"I've seen you in less," he reminded her. And himself. His body tensed with a desire all the more intense for them having made love. Now he knew the reality of being with her, of being buried deep inside her body. He felt closer to her than he ever had to anyone.

"He didn't have to know that," she said as she rose from the exam table.

"You care what he thinks?"

She shook her head. "No."

"What the hell were *you* thinking?" he asked, anger overwhelming him at the danger in which she'd put herself. "Running into a burning building? You could have been killed."

"You could have been, too," she replied, anger flashing in her dark eyes. "You ran in there first."

"I was looking for the deputy," he reminded her. He suspected she had been looking for something else— something that she wouldn't find in the ashes of her magic shop.

"I was looking for you," she said, her voice cracking with emotion as her eyes sparkled with a hint of tears. "I thought for sure you were dead…" Her breath hitched.

"I'm fine," he assured her. He stepped away from the locked door and moved closer.

"You should have let the doctor examine *you*," she said. "You could be seriously hurt."

"I'm seriously hurting," he admitted.

She gasped and reached for him, running her palms over his chest. "Where? What happened?"

"My heart stopped beating when you walked into that burning barn. And I don't think it's started back up yet." His relief that she was all right cooled his temper even while his passion caught flame. He cupped her gorgeous, soot-streaked face in his palms and lowered his mouth to hers.

Her lips parted on a soft sigh, and he deepened the kiss, sliding his tongue inside her mouth—tasting her unique flavor of sweetness and erotica. She must have put a spell on him, because he'd never wanted anyone the way he wanted her. He forgot everything else—what had happened, what he'd seen would happen—and he thought only of her and his all-consuming desire for her.

She pulled back, panting for breath. "It's beating now," she said, her palm pressed over his furiously pounding heart.

A grin tugged at his lips. "See? I don't need a doctor. I just need you." His grin fled as he realized the truth in what he'd just said. He *needed* her.

"Seth…" She wound her arms around his neck and pulled his head down to hers. She kissed him with all her passion, her lips moving voraciously over his. Then she slid her tongue inside his mouth, tasting him as he had tasted her.

Did she taste the bitterness of the secrets he kept from her? Did she know that he hadn't told her everything about himself?

She pulled back and studied his face. "Are you really all right?"

He shook his head. "No."

She uttered a wistful sigh. "I wish I had some of my herbs so I could heal your injuries."

"I'm not hurt," he said, unconcerned about whatever wounds he had.

"Then what is it?" she asked. There was tentativeness in her voice, almost as if she was afraid to know.

A lifetime of lying about who and what he was. But she was the last person he could tell the truth. She would never trust him if he did. And if she didn't trust him, he wouldn't be able to keep her safe.

Her arms around his neck, she waited for his reply, her eyes wide and vulnerable. Had she already made the mistake of beginning to trust him?

"Maria, I…" Couldn't share his secrets with her. But he had to tell her something that was true, at least. "I can't let you keep distracting me from doing my job."

Her wide mouth lifted into a sexy smile. "I really haven't put a spell on you."

"I'm bewitched all the same." He hoped like hell that was all he was.

Her teeth scraped over the full curve of her lower lip. Then she soothed the hurt with the tip of her tongue, teasing him as she stared up at him through her lashes. "Is that such a bad thing?"

Her flirting affected him, predictably, his body tensing with the need to take hers again. He released a heavy sigh. "My being distracted could have gotten us both killed."

"We're alive. We should celebrate that." She pressed her breasts against his chest. Her hardened nipples penetrated through her paper gown and his thin sweater.

He groaned as desire shot straight to his groin. As if wanting to torture him more, she arched her hips and rubbed against him. Unable to resist her, he lowered his head and kissed that sexy smile. But he pulled back before she could slip her tongue between his lips, before she could push him beyond the limits of his control.

"I need to check on the deputy and find out if he's going to make it." The explosion, or more likely a blow to the head, had knocked the young man unconscious, but Seth had managed to get him out of the fire before it had burned him too badly. The guy had been breathing when the ambulance had taken him. But then, Raven had been breathing, too, when the ambulance had taken her away from the barn.

However, if the killer was, as Maria was convinced, a witch-hunter, then he had no reason to kill the young deputy. The lawman had only been in the killer's way when he'd done what he had after each of the other murders, gone back and destroyed the crime scene.

In the past he'd thought the person had been trying to destroy evidence as well as any trace that she had even been there. Now he realized that the killer might have been trying to eradicate all trace of her—all evidence that she had ever existed.

Maria stepped away from him and nodded. "Of course. You need to go."

Seth needed to leave, and not just to check on the deputy but also to get away from her for a few minutes. He needed to shake off the spell she'd put him under before he got burned worse than he'd already been.

Seth had said he was leaving, but he didn't take a step toward the door. Instead he kept staring at her, his blue gaze intent on her face, on her body, which the paper gown did little to cover.

"You can leave me alone," she assured him. But she

didn't want him to leave. His kisses had wound that pressure tight inside her so that she ached for release.

"That's the problem," he said with a ragged sigh. "I can't leave you alone…"

"The sheriff is here and all of his deputies and several state police officers," she reminded him. "I'm probably safer here than I've been anywhere else." The witch-hunter wouldn't risk trying to grab her around so much law enforcement.

"That's not what I meant. I can't leave you alone." And he dragged her against him again, his hands clenching the back of her gown as he wound his arms tight around her. The paper parted, and his palms slid down her bare back to her hips, which he pulled tight against the erection straining the fly of his jeans.

She moaned and rubbed her hips against him, seeking release. But he lifted her away from him, setting her on the edge of the exam table. He dragged the paper away from her, leaving her naked but for the flush of desire on her skin. Like the first time they'd made love, his hands caressed her with the intimate knowledge of a longtime lover.

Why was their connection so strong? As if they'd known each other forever…as if they had loved each other before?

His palms cupped her breasts, his thumbs stroking back and forth across her pebbled nipples. And he kissed her again, deeply, his tongue thrusting through her lips as it stroked over her tongue. Tunneling her fingers in his soft hair, she clutched his nape. But he pulled back, his mouth sliding down her cheek and her throat.

"I must taste awful," she murmured. Like smoke and dust and whatever else had gone up in the explosion. All of the herbs she'd spent the summer growing. All of the candles and oils she'd spent so much time making. The crystals that she'd collected over the years might have survived if the fire hadn't gotten too hot. She might be able to clean and recover their luster. But they would never be the same, their energies forever altered by the violence that had taken place in her magic shop. Maybe it was better that it was all gone.

Except the locket. Her heart ached for losing that.

"You taste sweet," he assured her. "And you still smell like sandalwood and lavender."

Her mother's scent. Like the locket, she wore it to remind herself of who and what she was. A Cooper. A witch. Now she had only the scent, as the locket was probably forever lost in the fire. But maybe it hadn't been there anymore. Maybe the witch-hunter had it. Maybe he'd found it when he'd hung Raven or when he'd set the fire.

She had no doubt that he had set it.

But she couldn't think of him now. Couldn't think of what he had done or would do. She couldn't think at all as Seth touched her…with his hands and with his mouth.

His lips traced the curve of her collarbone, and his hands skimmed from her breasts over her hips to her legs. He parted them and stroked his fingers up and down the sensitive skin of her inner thighs. His head dipped lower, his tongue laving a nipple, and his fingers slipped inside her.

She arched her neck and writhed against his hand, unable to stand the pressure building inside her. A moan burned in her throat. Then his hands and mouth switched places, his fingers teasing her nipples as his tongue stroked inside her. Pleasure rushed through her, blinding her with its intensity as she came apart. She tangled her fingers in his hair, holding him to her as he lapped and teased another orgasm from her.

Then she pulled him up, wanting him buried inside her. She reached for his belt, but he stepped back and shook his head.

His voice hoarse with passion, he said, "I can't. I can't lose my focus again." His hands shaking slightly, he grabbed up her clothes from the end of the exam table and handed them to her. "While you get dressed, I'll check on the deputy. Hopefully, he's all right and has regained consciousness. Lock the door behind me and wait for me here."

He had that look in his eyes again—that glazed-over seeing-something-else look that reminded her of Mama when the gypsy fortune-teller had really been seeing the future in her crystal ball.

"Before the explosion—how did you know something wasn't right?" she asked. "Was it really just because you didn't see the deputy?"

He nodded. "In every crime scene for these murders, the killer has come back later and set a fire."

Maria's heart tightened with fear and regret. The witch-hunter had to destroy everything and everyone that mattered to her.

If he had the locket, it was lost to her.

"That's why I had the sheriff post an officer at the scene," Seth continued. "I thought that if the killer came back, he might get caught this time. But I should have guarded it myself instead of putting some young deputy at risk."

Instead he'd been guarding her from harm. Did he resent her for that?

"You risked your life to save him," she pointed out. "I'm sure you got to him in time."

He glanced to the closed door. "I hope he's okay and has regained consciousness. He might be the only one who can give us a lead to the killer. Unless you know more than you've told me…"

She knew she was cursed to the same fate as the first witch in her family, who'd been burned at the stake over three hundred and fifty years ago. But if Seth didn't believe in her special abilities, he wasn't going to believe in legends and more-than-three-century-old curses. So she just shook her head and reached for her clothes.

He stopped at the door and turned back, his gaze holding hers. "I'm trusting you to stay here and wait for me."

She didn't lie to him or make any false promises. She just gave a noncommittal nod. Then she finished dressing. As soon as the door closed behind him, she reached for it—but not to lock it.

Instead she held the knob while she waited for him to have walked the length of the hall. Hoping he hadn't turned back to check on her, she opened the door. She needed to leave now—before the next ghost she saw was his.

He had been lucky to escape the explosion with minor injuries. But Maria didn't count on his luck holding—not when he was getting too close to someone who had only ever had bad luck in her life.

She couldn't put him at risk again.

Growing up on the run with a paranoid mother had honed more than Maria's supernatural abilities. She had learned other things—like how to slip undetected through a crowd. So she bound her hair into a braid and slipped into some scrubs in the staff locker room. Disguised, she moved easily through the hospital and out of the employee entrance/exit doors.

As soon as she stepped out of the building, her shoes scraping against the asphalt of the parking lot, she breathed a sigh of relief.

She shivered, and wished she'd kept her sweater or had stolen someone's coat. She hurried through the parking lot.

During those years she had been on her own, she'd also learned to pickpocket. She opened her fingers, which were growing numb from the cold, to the keys she had lifted from Seth.

Guilt overwhelmed her, extinguishing that brief flicker of relief. When he found her gone, he would be furious. He would think that she had tricked him—that she'd seduced him just so she could escape him.

But she was the one who'd been seduced, not him. He hadn't let her touch him—hadn't let her distract him. But he'd given her pleasure.

And he'd promised her protection.

Should she trust him? So far he'd kept his word to her. But in keeping his word, he was putting his life at risk—for hers. She wasn't worth it. Even her own mother hadn't thought so.

And Maria would never forgive herself if he died as all the others had—violently, senselessly...

No, it was better to deceive him and run than to put him at risk any longer.

And really, after all the years he'd been chasing her and learning about her, he should have known better than to trust her.

By the time he realized his mistake, hopefully she would be gone. But she'd just neared his SUV when strong arms wrapped around her, trapping her arms against her sides.

It wasn't Seth. Her skin would have tingled; her

blood would have heated with desire and awareness. While this man seemed familiar, too, he didn't set her pulse racing with anything but fear. She opened her mouth to scream, but his hand covered it.

"I just want to talk to you," a cultured-sounding voice said.

It wasn't her brother-in-law who had that distinctly raspy tone. She almost wished it had been—but then he'd bring her back to her family and put them all in danger.

"I'm not going to hurt you," the stranger assured her.

Yet. He didn't say it but the word hung in the air.

She stilled her struggles, and he lifted his hand from her mouth. She recognized his hands more than his voice—since those hands had recently been wound tightly around her neck.

"What do you want to know?" she asked Curtis Waverly.

"I want to know the truth about you."

She had no truths he wanted to hear. He wanted a confession that she couldn't give him.

"Were you my sister's friend like you claimed?" he asked, his already beady eyes narrowed with suspicion. "Or are you my sister's killer?"

She shook her head. "I would have never hurt Felicia. She was my friend. My very dear friend. I miss her so very much…"

His throat convulsed as if he was choking on emotion. Or as if Seth's blow had done more damage than she'd been able to heal…

Finally, he murmured, "Me, too. I miss her…"

He was suffering. That was why she hadn't wanted him arrested for attacking her. While Seth had done it anyway, he had known that Curtis Waverly would hire a lawyer to get him out.

He probably hadn't expected it to be so quickly, though.

But she was glad. She did owe this man the truth. The whole truth.

"I didn't kill her," she said, "but I am responsible for her death."

His arms tightened around her—painfully so.

Just like when he'd strangled her, she would not easily escape him. And now she didn't have Seth to save her.

His voice eerily low and hollow, he murmured, "Then you'll have to pay…"

Chapter 8

By the time Seth had noticed his keys were gone, so was Maria. He had known he couldn't trust her. So he'd asked the sheriff to watch for her and make sure she didn't get away.

His heart pounded with fear as he ran from the building and out into the parking lot. Evening came early this far north, so the light was already fading behind the all-encompassing fog. The whole damn town seemed like the set of a horror movie—eerie and otherworldly, a place he wouldn't have thought existed outside a movie screen. A place he wished like hell he'd never had to visit.

Just like at the hotel, he spied two shadows grappling in the fog. And then her scream rang out again. Even though he'd heard it twice before, it still reached inside him—still squeezed his heart with fear.

"This is getting to be a bad habit," he murmured as

he approached them. But this man had already proved a far greater threat to her than the brother-in-law who had grabbed her in the motel parking lot. This man had already hurt her once. He drew his weapon and pointed it at him. "Curtis, let her go!"

And this time, if he didn't, Seth would shoot him. He had known the guy wasn't going to stay behind bars long. According to the sheriff, he'd been released only that morning, and he'd already come after Maria again. If only he'd been locked up longer...

"I can't." The guy shook his head, his eyes wild with grief and desperation.

"Curtis, the sheriff told me the conditions of your bail. Coming anywhere near Ms. Cooper violates the number one condition," Seth said. At least he would be going back to jail for a while. "You have to let her go!"

"I can't!" he shouted. "Just like I can't let Felicia go." Tears shimmered in those wild eyes. "She haunts me—the way she died..." His voice cracked with grief. "Someone held her down until her lungs filled with water. She was gasping. Fighting for air..."

"Stop torturing yourself," Seth told him. But Curtis wasn't torturing just himself. Tears streaked down Maria's face, almost as if she relived what her friend had endured. And maybe she did. He couldn't deny that she had supernatural abilities; he'd seen her heal herself.

So maybe she saw ghosts and the future and...

What other abilities did she have?

Ty McIntyre had said that his wife, her sister, was empathetic in addition to being telepathic. Seth didn't think Maria was telepathic, or she would have tried a lot harder to get away from him. And she never would have made love with him. But he suspected she was empathetic, that she felt what all the victims had felt.

No wonder she had left town right after the murders. She hadn't been scared just of the killer coming for her; she had been scared of the pain she'd felt when her friends had died.

"Who would do something like that?" Curtis asked between sobs, his arms constricting around Maria. His nose ran as he completely lost it. He looked nothing like the debonair sole heir to a textile fortune who regularly graced tabloid and fashion-magazine covers. He was lucky the media hadn't followed him to Copper Creek to report his current condition.

How completely had Waverly lost it? Was he beyond reason, as he'd been when he'd strangled her? Would Seth need to pull the trigger? He trained the barrel on the man's head. If it was Waverly's life or hers, it was no choice for Seth. He had promised to protect her.

"Who would do something like that to a girl as sweet and beautiful as my little sister?" Curtis asked, one of his arms sliding up and around Maria's throat.

She didn't speak or fight. She just stood perfectly still, but her eyes talked to Seth, telegraphing her fear and vulnerability. And trust. She wasn't talking or fighting, because she trusted Seth to get her out of the situation. Alive.

Waverly was a pretty big guy. A strong guy, too. If he wanted, he could easily snap her neck.

He moved his finger from the barrel of the Glock to the trigger. Then he peered down the scope, getting his target in focus. "Maria didn't do that to Felicia," he said. "She was your sister's friend."

"You told me she was your number one suspect," Curtis reminded him.

And Seth had been careless when he'd shared his suspicions with a victim's family member. But the guy's grief had gotten to him; Waverly had been blaming himself for his younger sister's death. He had been filled with guilt that he hadn't been able to protect Felicia from her killer. So Seth had assured him that there was nothing he could have done to save his sister.

"Maria is not a suspect at all anymore," he said—as he had at the police station. "She has nothing to do with any of the murders."

Her gaze had never left his face, but now her eyes widened with surprise. And relief. She was still in danger, but she was relieved that he finally believed in her. Was it too late, though?

"Why?" Curtis asked. "Did she get to you? Did she mess with your head like she did Felicia's?" His arm tightened around Maria's throat.

Finally, she made a noise, a soft gasp for breath as her almond-shaped eyes got bigger with fear.

"You don't want to hurt her," Seth said. "You need to let her go…" Or Seth would have no choice but to shoot him. He had killed before in the line of duty, but never someone with whom he'd sympathized. "C'mon, Curtis, you don't want to do this…"

The young man's arm didn't loosen, and her face began to turn red. "I have to do this. I have to stop her. She turned my sister into a witch."

If what defined a witch was having supernatural abilities, then Seth was one, too.

"Maria's innocent," he insisted. "She could not have killed the most recent victim. She was locked up in jail at the time. And there's no way she could have caused the explosion at the crime scene today. She was with me."

"Maybe she's not working alone," Curtis said. "Did

you think about that? Have you considered every explanation, Agent Hughes?"

"I considered that," Seth admitted. He had even questioned her about it. But everyone she'd been close to the past eight years had died. "I wasn't certain that she would be physically capable of having killed the victims as they were killed. But I can't find anyone connected to her—anyone who would have helped her—and she couldn't have acted alone."

"If she's really a witch," Curtis said, his voice rising with his temper, "like my sister thought, she could have managed it. Maybe she puts a spell on people and forces them to do her bidding."

Seth definitely felt as though she had put a spell on him, but she hadn't forced him to do anything he hadn't really, really wanted to do. "Curtis, you must hear how ridiculous that sounds…"

"It's possible!" the man hysterically insisted. "She's a witch! You saw what she did at the jail—the herbs, the chanting. She's a witch!"

Seth couldn't deny that she was. "But she's not a killer." He stepped closer. "I don't want to have to shoot you." But he would.

Maria tried to shake her head, but Curtis held her neck too tightly. But she murmured, "No…"

"You need to let her go," Seth said. "Now." He had tried to reason with the man, but he feared that Curtis Waverly was beyond reason.

"You promised me that you would stop her," Curtis said, his voice rough with outrage and betrayal.

"I promised you that I would find and stop your sister's killer," Seth said. "And I will."

"She's right here," Curtis said, his arm squeezing harder so that Maria's face grew redder still as she fought for breath. "And I can end it now."

Seth shook his head. "I can't let you do that. You can't be jury, judge and executioner." But would he be able to stop him before the man took Maria's life?

All the stares were on her—as they had been so many times before. Back then it might have been because she'd been locked up in an observation room in some psych ward. Eventually she had learned to hide the fact that she could see what no one else could. Eventually she had learned to pass for normal.

But with these people, she didn't have to be normal. She could be who she was—especially with David's arms wrapped tightly around her, offering his unconditional support and love as he had from the minute they'd met. She had never loved or been loved as much as with her husband.

"Ariel?" Elena called her name—the way she used to when they were kids. And Ariel snapped out of it and focused again on her family.

"Can you see her?" Irina asked. "Is she dead?"

She shook her head.

"But there are ghosts here," said Joseph with such certainty and dread that she wondered if he could see, too. He shivered and said, "I can feel *her*..." He wasn't talking about Maria, whom he'd never met. Fortunately, neither had Ariel.

"Mama is here," she said. And while she might have been able to block out her ghostly voice as she often had, the other woman spoke for them both.

"But she's not alone," Irina said. "I can feel another spirit. And she's endured terrible fear and pain…and has so much guilt and regret."

Ariel leaned on her husband and focused on the other ghost. When she had first seen her hovering over Irina's bed as the pregnant woman had awakened screaming, Ariel had thought it was Maria. Her hair was black. But she was tall and thin, and when she'd turned toward the one who could see her, Ariel had seen her face—which had looked as if a bird were flying out of the side of it.

What the hell had happened to her?

"I was hung and drowned," the girl answered, almost with pride. But then, it had taken the witch-hunter two attempts to kill her; maybe that was a source of pride.

"Maria saved me from the hanging," she said.

"Maria—is she alive?" Ariel asked the spirits. "Is she okay?"

"The FBI agent saved her from the fire," Raven said.

Irina had been feeling heat and smothering from smoke—of course there had been a fire. As she'd felt that heat, she'd grabbed her charm. And Ariel and Elena had held their charms as well, praying for Maria's protection. Seth was Maria's protection.

"Seth Hughes saved Maria," Ariel told the others, who couldn't hear the ghosts. Except for Irina. She could hear, but she was completely exhausted—from her pregnancy and from her stress.

Would Ariel lose two sisters? She worried that she might, and as if David felt her worry, he kissed her cheek and whispered, "It'll be all right…"

"We can trust Seth," Ty said. "He will protect her."

"But who will protect him?" It was Raven who asked the question. "Everyone who gets close to her dies…"

The mist began to fade as the spirit slipped from the room. But Mama turned back, her mouth open. She was speaking, or trying to—as if she was warning them again.

Were they all in danger? Or only Maria and Seth?

Maria shuddered as she wiped the blood from her face. "I can't believe you shot him!"

Waverly lay on the asphalt, writhing and groaning. Obviously he couldn't believe it, either.

"I just hit his shoulder," Seth said, as if shooting a man were of no consequence to him.

But he was an FBI agent. He had probably shot many more people than Curtis Waverly. He had probably even killed before.

His hands were gentle, though, as he wiped the blood from her face. "Are you okay?" he asked.

She jerked her head in a quick nod that had her wincing in pain. Her throat was sore from how tightly the man had held her. He could have broken her neck. Maybe he would have if Seth hadn't shot him.

But still it bothered her that he was hurting. She dropped onto the asphalt next to him. "Are you okay?" she asked.

Blood oozed from the gunshot wound in his shoulder. Her palms itched for her herbs—for the poultice she could make to press to the hole in his flesh. The bullet had probably passed through, so she could heal the wound quite easily. If she had her herbs…

"Stay away from me!" the man yelled at her. "Stay away!"

He was afraid of her?

But then, he was convinced that she was a killer—no matter that she had told him that she hadn't directly hurt his sister. Even Seth had vouched for her. Did he really believe now that she'd had nothing to do with the killings?

She had worried when she'd run *from* him that he might think she was running out of guilt. But she was really running *for* him—to protect him.

"You're the one who needs to stay away from her," Seth told Waverly. "You've violated the terms of your bail, so you'll have to go back to jail."

"I need a doctor!" the man wailed. "I need medical attention."

"I could help you," she offered. But when she reached toward him, he shrank away from her. She had healed him once. Why couldn't he trust her?

Seth shook his head and stared at her in disbelief. "Why would you want to help him after he's attacked you—twice?"

"He's Felicia's brother," she said. So he had already lost so much. She didn't blame him for wanting justice.

"See," Curtis said, "she feels guilty. She has to be her killer."

"I feel guilty because I shouldn't have let her get close to me." And that was why she shouldn't have let Seth get close, either. But he had. Too close…

"I knew I was in danger," she added.

"That's why you can't go running off alone," Seth told her. He gestured toward the hospital, and the sheriff and two deputies rushed forward.

"We heard a gunshot," Sheriff Moore said. "Is everything all right?"

"No!" Curtis wailed. "He shot me!"

"He was about to break Ms. Cooper's neck," Seth explained.

Despite the man's injury, the sheriff grabbed his

shoulders and hauled him to his feet. "You're under arrest—"

Curtis yelled and swore. "I need a doctor!"

"Please, get him medical attention," Maria implored them.

The sheriff turned to Seth, who nodded in reluctant agreement. "But don't let him slip away from you. As soon as he's treated, he needs to go back to jail. And hopefully, he won't get released on bail again."

The sheriff passed Waverly off to a couple of the deputies who'd run up behind him. "You heard Agent Hughes. Once the doctor's done with him, bring him back to the station. He violated his bail."

As the two men led him off, Curtis Waverly stared back at Maria, his eyes dark with a mixture of fear and hatred that made her shiver.

"What about you, Agent Hughes?" the sheriff asked.

"What about me?"

"Has the doctor seen you yet?"

Seth shook his head. "I'm fine."

"You should be treated, too," Maria said. Soot coated his scratches and burns, but they were still red and as angry looking as Curtis Waverly had been.

Seth snorted. "And give you a chance to run again? I'm not letting you out of my sight."

He had defended her to Waverly, so she hadn't been able to tell if he was mad at her. But now she heard the anger in his voice. He was furious with her for taking off on him.

Why couldn't he understand that she'd done it for him?

"I brought the herbs," the sheriff said, his face reddening slightly as if he was embarrassed that he believed in her healing. "I thought you might need them."

"How is your deputy?" she asked.

"Mostly just embarrassed," the sheriff said. "He never saw who hit him."

Seth muttered a curse. "How did he not see the guy?"

The sheriff sighed and admitted, "I think he might have fallen asleep."

"If you bring me the herbs, I can put together something for the deputy's headache," Maria offered. She was grateful that not all her herbs had been lost in the fire.

The sheriff quickly retrieved the bag from his car and watched in fascination as she put together a poultice. She chanted a brief prayer over the packet and passed it to him. "Thank you, Ms. Cooper," Sheriff Moore said. "He will appreciate the help."

"Bring it to him," Seth said. "And make sure Waverly gets back to the jail."

The sheriff nodded. "Of course. What about that other matter, of Ms. Cooper's assistant? We haven't made a death notification yet."

The night that Waverly had attacked her at the police station, they had briefly discussed the death notification. "You haven't told her sister yet?" Maria asked.

The sheriff shook his head. "We only have your assistant's first name."

And Raven wasn't even her real name. The girl had rejected her given name for one she'd chosen herself.

"What about her boyfriend?" Maria asked.

"The address you gave me—nobody's lived there for years," the sheriff said.

Maria shook her head. "Maybe I got the address wrong. But I know where I dropped her off. I can show Agent Hughes."

With another thankful smile at Maria, the older lawman hurried back toward the hospital.

Maria was grateful to the sheriff for bringing her
herbs. She held tightly to the evidence bag with the
broken seal. Would Seth let her use any of the herbs
on him?

"I can help you, too," she offered. "I can make something for your scratches and burns."

"We need to get out of here," Seth said. He reached
for her, holding her arm as if worried that she might
try to run off again. As he led her toward his SUV, he
glanced around the hospital parking lot. His long body
was tense; it was as if he felt there was someone else
there.

There was.

The mist rolled in, thickening the fog. Maria already
smelled the familiar scents, which now clung to her
hair and her skin and hung in the air around her. Then
Mama's ghostly shape became apparent—only to
Maria, though.

Seth walked right through her as he opened the passenger's door for Maria. But then he shivered—as if
he felt her presence. Maria couldn't step forward—she
couldn't walk through her mother. It was as if Mama
was blocking her from getting into the SUV with Seth.

*Why are you here? Why do you keep coming back?
You're in danger, child.*

Seth was angry with her, but Maria couldn't believe
that he would hurt her. If he had meant her any harm,
he could have let her die in the fire—or he could have
let Waverly break her neck. But he kept saving her,
again and again.

So Maria sucked in a breath to brace herself, and she
stepped through her mother. As he had when he had ar-

rested her after Raven's hanging, Seth covered her head with his palm and guided her down onto the seat. He was always protecting her. "Thank you…"

"Don't thank me," he said. "I'm not letting you go." He stepped back from the SUV but carefully, as if he sensed Mama there. He skirted her spectral image and then crossed around the front of the SUV, never taking his gaze from Maria. He was serious about not letting her out of his sight.

Maria wanted Mama out of her sight. She wanted to block out the ghost. But she hovered yet by her window.

He's no danger, Mama…

You're the danger, child.

That was why she'd tried to run.

Seth held out his hand for the keys she'd stolen from him. She pulled them from her pocket and dropped them into his palm. Her skin tingled at the briefest of contact with his.

"We can't leave Copper Creek yet," Seth said with a shudder as he glanced around at the thick fog. Maybe he could see Mama, still looming. "The FBI techs are coming tomorrow."

"For what? There's nothing left of the crime scene." Not even her locket.

"There could still be evidence there," Seth stubbornly insisted. "This case is hot—it's our best chance to catch him."

"What happens once it goes cold?" she asked. As all the other cases had.

A muscle twitched along his tightly clenched jaw, and he said with grim determination, "I'm not going to let that happen."

"Just like you haven't let anything happen to me." If not for Seth's interference, Curtis Waverly might have seriously hurt or even killed her. He was out of his mind with grief.

"You make it hard for me to protect you," he pointed out as he started the SUV and pulled out of the parking lot, "with the way you keep running off every time I turn my back on you."

"What happens when you're done here in Copper Creek?" she asked. "Where will you take me then? Some FBI safe house? Witness relocation?" Except that she really hadn't witnessed anything.

While she had seen the victims murdered when she'd read their cards, she had never seen their murderer. She was pretty damn certain she knew who the witch-hunter was: the son of her mother's killer, Donovan Roarke. But she had no idea what he looked like. No clue what identity he might have assumed.

Seth drew in a deep breath, as if bracing himself, and replied, "Home."

Maria tried to open the passenger's door. But it was locked. The handle wouldn't budge. She couldn't escape. But she couldn't go "home." She couldn't even call it that. "I can't go back to Barrett."

"Don't you think it's time?"

"I thought you—of all people—understood," she said. "I can't be close to my family—not when someone is determined to kill everyone who gets close to me."

"Then don't you think it's time we catch this killer and stop him?" he asked. "You told Ty that's why you wouldn't go home with him, that you intended to help me find your friends' killer. But then you tried running from me again. If not for the explosion, you probably would have taken off at your shop. Isn't that why you wanted to go back there—to try to get your truck?"

If she wanted him to believe in her, she needed to

start telling him the truth. "Yes," she admitted. "But that wasn't the only reason I wanted to go back to the shop."

"You really think you would have been able to read the crime scene—that you would have been able to pick up some clue to the killer?" he asked as if he was open to the idea.

"I don't know," she admitted. "I have these visions—see bad things happen to people I care about—but I've never been able to see who the killer is."

"You can't see, or you're scared to look?" he challenged her.

"I am scared," she admitted with a shiver. Mama was gone now, but her warnings rang yet in her head. "He's a ruthless, sadistic killer."

"And you've let him control your life all these years," he said with another weary sigh of disappointment.

That disappointment stung her pride.

"You've let him keep you away from your family," Seth said. "You've let him take everything away that you've built—again and again."

Anger surged through Maria as she realized the veracity of Seth's claim. She'd been so intent on following her mother's advice to run that she hadn't realized that she had never escaped the witch-hunter. She had let this monster control her—destroy her. "Son of a bitch…"

"Yes," he agreed. "Don't you think it's time you stop running away from him and you stand and fight him?"

"You're right." She had agreed with him earlier, but now she really meant it. After seeing and feeling Waverly's despair, she understood that it wasn't just about staying ahead of the killer. Or even about stopping him. He needed to be brought to justice—for his victims and their families. "But I don't know how to stop running. It's how I grew up. It's all I've ever known."

"Why?" he asked. He reached across the console and grasped her hand, his fingers entwining with hers.

Her skin tingled at the contact between them, and her pulse quickened—as it always did—when he touched her.

"Was your mom running from the police or from social services?" he asked. "Ty told me how they took away your older sisters."

"Mama was running from the witch-hunter. She saw, in a vision, that he would come for her—that he would kill her—just as horribly as she died." A chill ran through her as she thought of the vision that had haunted her mother, the vision she'd had herself when she'd read her mother's cards. "She was burned at the stake."

He grimaced and tightened his grip on her hand. "I'm sorry."

"It happened nine years ago. You must have heard the story," she said. "If you didn't see it on the news, then Irina's husband must have told you."

He nodded. "Ty told me everything that happened. But he assured me that the witch hunt is over. That the witch-hunter died back then—eight or nine years ago— before Felicia Waverly was murdered."

"Just because that witch-hunter died doesn't mean that it's over," she pointed out. "The first witch hunt began over three hundred years ago when my witch ancestor was burned at the stake like my mother. Like my mother, she saw her fate and forced her daughter to run away." Elena, for whom Maria's eldest sister had been named, had been only thirteen when she'd lost her mother and had been forced to figure out how to survive on her own. As Maria had.

He squeezed her fingers gently, as if he understood

how much the legend upset her, even though it had happened so many centuries before she was born.

Her breath hitching, she steadied her voice and continued, "The daughter got caught by the witch-hunter's son. But instead of killing her, he let her go, giving her a locket that he'd made for his mother, who'd died in a lightning strike that my ancestor had warned her about. His father swore to track down that girl and kill all her descendants."

"He wasn't very successful," Seth pointed out as he lifted her hand to his mouth. He brushed a gentle kiss across her knuckles. "You're alive. Your sisters are all alive—all their children."

"The guy who killed my mother was a descendant of Eli McGregor," she explained. "That first witch-hunter."

"Your mother's killer is dead," Seth said again, his voice suddenly as cold as the evening air that the heat blowing out the vents had yet to dispel.

"But he had a son," she shared. Even though she'd stayed away from them, she had kept apprised of her sisters' lives. She'd read about everything that had happened to them and had learned everything she could about the man who had hunted them. "That son has to have taken over his father's witch hunt. He's the only one who can be the witch-hunter."

"The only one?" Seth asked. He released her hand and gripped the steering wheel with both of his. "Why hasn't he killed you already, then, since you're the witch he's really after? Why hasn't he gone after your sisters? They're the ones he would probably hold responsible for his father's death, aren't they?"

"I don't know. His father was crazy. He undoubtedly is, too." She shuddered at the evil inherent to the witch-hunter. "I can't imagine what goes through his mind."

"No, you can't," he said. "You may be able to see things—when you read cards—but you're not telepathic."

"No, I'm not," she admitted. "But I do have special abilities. I wish you would believe me."

"It's not that I don't believe you," he said, "but I don't believe he's the killer. I believe it's someone else, probably someone you know. A stalker who resents anyone else getting close to you. Did you jilt a lover who wouldn't leave you alone afterward?"

"Who's asking?" she wondered. "The FBI agent or the man I *seduced*?"

His intent expression cracked as a slight grin curved his lips. "The FBI agent—who's finally asking the questions he should have been asking."

"You thought you had your man—uh, woman," she said, reminding him of his suspicions. Not that he needed the reminder. No matter what he said, she was worried that Curtis Waverly had raised Seth's doubts about her again. "You were convinced I was the killer."

He reached across the console and stroked his fingers along her jaw. "I wasn't totally convinced. I had my doubts. But I wanted it to be you."

"Why?" she asked, lifting her chin away from his touch. He'd stung her pride again.

"Since you knew and had had the last known contact with every victim, it made sense that you were the killer," he pointed out.

She couldn't argue with him. Put like that, she would have suspected herself, too.

"And that makes more sense than some dead man's son coming after everyone close to you."

"You don't understand." That made perfect sense to her, but she'd had her whole life to accept and fear the witch hunt. "It's the fulfillment of that legacy, of that old curse."

"Curse?" he asked.

"I'm cursed." And because of that, she shouldn't have let Seth close, and she certainly shouldn't have begun to fall for him herself. "I'm cursed…"

The witch-hunter stayed back, far behind the FBI agent's SUV. There was something about Seth Hughes—something uncanny, something supernatural.

He hadn't just become bewitched by Maria Cooper. It was more than that. The way he'd stared at the barn and then started toward it, he seemed to have anticipated the explosion even before the candle had burned low enough to ignite the gasoline he'd poured around the propane tanks.

How could the agent have known? Unless he saw things before they happened, as Maria did when she read the cards. But it was more than card reading with Agent Hughes, something even more instinctive and powerful.

That was probably why, even though he followed them at a distance, the agent's SUV sped up. It was as if Hughes already knew he was there. As if he sensed his presence.

Did the FBI agent have visions of the future? Did Seth Hughes know what was coming next?

His death.

The agent obviously had some special abilities, some witchcraft powers of his own. So he would have to die like the others—like a witch…

The agent wasn't heading toward town but taking a road that led away from it—away from the barn. Maybe the hunter had some psychic abilities of his own, because he realized where they were heading. They were taking the long way there, though. And he knew a short-cut that only he, in his four-wheel drive, could take. He would beat them there and set up another trap for them—like at the barn.

And hopefully, Agent Hughes wouldn't sense this one. Until it was too late...

Chapter 9

Pain throbbed in Stacia Dolce's head. It wasn't just the babysitting that was bothering her. She actually didn't mind watching her younger brother and cousins. The house was alive with emotions, and like Aunt Irina, she felt them all.

They pummeled her. Exhausted her.

Mom told her to block them.

As if...

Just as Mom couldn't block her visions, Stacia couldn't block *any* of it. She saw, heard and felt *everything*. And there was just *too much* in the house right now.

Usually she loved having the gifts she had, and she enjoyed being a witch. But then there were times, like today, that she just wanted to be a regular teenager.

The door to the attic playroom creaked open and Mom stepped inside the space. She glanced over to where the younger kids played the virtual computer game Uncle David had set up on a big screen for them. It was cool having a techie uncle.

Stacia's whole family was cool, though. Even her mom...

Most of her friends complained about their mothers. But Stacia had a bond with hers that nobody else had with theirs. She and Mom had nearly died together. But her dad had saved them. He'd been just Joseph then. But after that he had become her dad.

He called Stacia her mother's mini-me since she looked so much like her. That was cool, too, since her mom was really pretty with pale blond hair and light blue eyes. But Stacia was nearly taller than her now, so Dad wouldn't be able to call her mini-Mom much longer.

After she'd made sure the younger kids were all right, Mom walked over to Stacia. She touched her hair. "Headache, sweetheart?"

Her mom wasn't telepathic with anyone else, but it was as if she could read Stacia's mind. And Dad's.

Stacia nodded.

"I'm sorry," Mom said. "I know this must be overwhelming for you. Everyone's so scared and upset."

Stacia nodded again. "Even Grandma."

"She's here?"

"She was earlier. She's worried about Aunt Maria." She reached out and squeezed her mom's hand, which was shaking a little. "You are, too."

"Have you seen what I have?" her mom wondered.

Tears stung Stacia's eyes. "Yes." Like the tears, the vision burned her eyes. And the pain overwhelmed her. She didn't want to start crying and scare the younger kids. But Mom pulled her into her arms, and the tears slipped out. "I don't want them to die."

But she had seen death. And she worried that the only way she would ever meet her aunt Maria was as a ghost—like Grandma.

Seth glanced in the rearview mirror. If there had been a vehicle behind them, he had lost it around one of the hairpin turns in the backcountry road. Even though he couldn't see the lights anymore, he pressed harder on the accelerator.

With one hand Maria grasped the console and with the other the armrest on the passenger's door. "Slow down or you'll miss the driveway. It's coming up around the next turn."

An image flashed through Seth's mind of what could be coming up: *metal crunching, gravel flying, the car spinning end over end as it bounced down the side of a steep, dark ravine...*

He lifted his foot from the accelerator and touched the brake. But his pulse didn't slow with the SUV; it quickened to a frenetic pace.

"It's a little farther up, I think," Maria said. "It's hard to see—it's so dark."

And foggy.

The damn stuff wrapped around the SUV, hiding the edges of the road—hiding where the road ended and dropped off into that ravine. And maybe it hid the lights of the vehicle Seth suspected had followed him from the hospital parking lot. He glanced again into the rearview, but there wasn't even a glimmer of headlamps burning through the fog behind them. He hadn't actually seen a vehicle behind them. Maybe he had only imagined that someone was following them. Or maybe it was back there yet—just fully concealed by the fog.

"This is a bad idea," he murmured. "The sheriff

should be the one making the death notification anyway."

"I thought that after what happened with Curtis Waverly, you understood why I want to do this," she said, her voice quavering with guilt.

"Because of what happened with Curtis Waverly, you should absolutely not be with me when I do this." In case this next of kin also blamed her for his loved one's death. Maybe he would attack her as Curtis had.

"I'm the only one who knows where Raven's boyfriend lives," she argued. "The sheriff didn't even know his name."

"Neither do you," Seth reminded her.

"No," Maria admitted. "Raven was pretty secretive about him. She had confided to me that her elder sister had always stolen her boyfriends, so she liked to keep her relationships private until she was certain she could trust the guy."

"Since she didn't introduce you to him, she must have decided not to trust the guy." Foreboding lifted the hairs on his nape. He should have listened to the instincts that had warned him this was a bad idea.

"Or she decided not to trust *me*," Maria said. "She had some special abilities. She saw the aura that hangs over me. I don't blame her for not trusting me."

"But you know where he lives," Seth pointed out. "So she trusted you with that information."

"I only know where he lives because I dropped Raven off here a couple of times." She straightened in her seat and pointed to a break in the trees lining the road. "Here. Turn here."

Seth touched the brake again and turned the wheel. The tires bounced along the ruts of a nearly overgrown driveway. "You're sure someone lives here?" he asked as his lights shone on a dark house. "The sheriff didn't think that anyone had for quite a few years."

"I probably gave him the wrong address," she said, but then insisted, "I know this is the place."

"It doesn't look like anyone's home now," he pointed out as he parked the car in front of the old log cabin. Boards had been nailed across one of the windows. "Were those boards there before?"

She nodded. "I think the glass must be broken. There wasn't anyone here when I came by looking for Raven that night I found her in the barn..."

His instincts were screaming now as his pulse quickened even more. This was it. A real lead. "Do you remember anything about him? Anything she said?"

"I told you she was really private about him."

"According to the sheriff, no one knows anything about him," Seth mused aloud. Was the mysterious boyfriend a real lead or just a story Raven—or Maria—had invented? "Hell, no one knows anything about her," Seth said. "Not even her real name. Did you get anything from her when you hired her? Her full name and Social Security number?"

"It's not as though I was going to fill out tax forms for her. I paid her cash when she worked—or in herbs and crystals," she admitted, and then sighed. "There's another crime you can arrest me for."

"Tax evasion?" He chuckled. "That is what tripped up some of the most notorious gangsters."

"I'm not a gangster."

He had known gangsters. None of them would have healed someone who'd tried to kill them. She was amazing. She was good—in a way that he hadn't realized she would be. Selfless and loving...

"No, you're not a gangster," Seth agreed. "But you're not an employer, either."

She flinched with pain. "Not now. All my employees wind up dead."

He regretted the comment. "I meant because you didn't get any emergency contact information for her. She might've given you her sister's information. Or her boyfriend's."

"I wouldn't put down a boyfriend's name as my emergency contact information," Maria replied.

"Why's that?" he asked, and then remembered something. "You never answered my question earlier about jilted lovers."

"Like Raven, I never had any boyfriends that lasted," she said.

"Why was that?" he asked. "Because you never stayed in one place for long?"

She turned to him, and the dashboard lights illuminated her beautiful face and the pain and loss in her dark eyes. "Because anyone who gets close to me dies."

That image flashed into his mind again: *the flash of gunfire as she fired his own weapon at him...hitting his heart...*

He flinched. "The two male victims…" One crushed. One burned.

She nodded, and tears glistened in her eyes. "Yes."

"They weren't witches, then. You're wrong about the witch-hunter." For so many reasons…

"They had special abilities," she said. "They wanted to learn the craft from me."

"I doubt that was all they wanted from you." He reached across the console again and traced his thumb along the line of her delicate jaw. "You're so damn beautiful." But it was more than her beauty that had him ignoring all his suspicions and doubts about her.

Had she cast a spell on him?

Just touching her face had his pulse tripping and his skin tingling. To control his desire, he turned away from her—and noticed the glimmer of light inside the deserted-looking house. "Someone's inside."

She reached for the door handle, but Seth leaned over and caught her wrist, keeping her from opening the door. "You're not going in there. It's a trap."

He didn't need the images flashing through his mind—of fire and debris blowing toward his face—to know that it was. His gut instincts were screaming at him, as they'd been on the drive here. This was definitely a trap.

The question was, who had set it? The killer? Or Maria? She was the one who had lured him out to the middle of nowhere. God, he was such a fool. Would she have to actually kill him before he was finally able to resist her?

The suspicion was back; Maria saw it in the way he studied her face, as if he were trying to read her mind.

"What's the trap?" she asked. "You going inside the house? Or you leaving me out here where he can grab me?"

"Depends on who the trap is for," Seth replied. "Me? Or you?"

"I don't know if I should be flattered or offended that you think I'd be able to trick you." Not that she hadn't given him reason, every time she'd tried to slip away from him, to doubt her.

"I wouldn't be flattered," he said. "Since I don't seem

to be able to think at all around you, I'm easy to trick right now—as you know."

Her stomach flipped with regret. Did he still think she'd purposely seduced him just to try to get away? But maybe she couldn't blame him for doubting her. Given how recently they'd met, he was really a stranger but that hadn't stopped her from throwing herself at him. But then, to her, because of the connection that reached so deeply inside her, he didn't seem like a stranger. It seemed as though she'd known him her whole life and longer.

And if something happened to him, she would never forgive herself, but she would also want to know about it. She wouldn't want to be wondering where he was— if he'd just left her as her mother had.

"What if it's not a trap?" she wondered. "What if Raven's boyfriend is in there?"

And what about Raven? She hadn't seen the girl's ghost since that day she'd awakened Maria in the motel, when she'd warned her that the witch-hunter was close.

Raven...

She peered around the car, trying to discern if the fog was just fog or that eerie mist that precipitated the arrival of an apparition. The girl knew this house, knew who'd lived here. She could tell Maria if it was a trap. But none of the mist formed into her image. It remained just fog.

Mama...

Where was she now—when Maria needed her? Where she'd always been when Maria needed her.

Gone.

Of course, Maria kept ignoring her and sending her away. Ever since she had awakened alone in the camper, she had wanted nothing more from her mother but what she'd left her. Her fingers lifted, out of habit, to her neck. But it was bare, the chain broken—the locket forever gone.

Seth reached inside his leather jacket. Instead of bringing out his gun, he held his cell. "I'm going to call the sheriff. Have him send out a deputy."

"To check out the house or babysit me while *you* do it?" she asked, flinching as she remembered the barn exploding and his just being gone—running into the flames to find the missing deputy.

He glanced down at the cell phone and shook his head. "Neither."

"No signal," she guessed. "The reception is horrible up here."

"Everything's horrible up here," he said. And he reached inside his coat again, returning the cell to an inside pocket. But when he withdrew his hand, he held his gun now.

She shuddered at the sight of it as the image from her vision flitted through her mind. *Blood pumping out of the hole in his chest...*

"You're not going to go in there alone," she insisted. "I'm going with you."

"No." He peered through the windshield at the house to where that faint light flickered through one of the windows that hadn't been boarded up. A strange look crossed his handsome face, his eyes glazed over yet intense.

"What is it?" she asked. "Do you see something that I don't?" She glanced from his face to the house, trying to figure out what had made him so tense. "Seth, what is it?"

In reply he slammed the SUV into Reverse and stomped on the accelerator. Gravel spewed from the

wheel wells as he backed haphazardly down the driveway. Like earlier, when he'd been driving too fast
around those sharp turns, she grasped the console and
the armrest.

"What the hell are you—?" A boom louder than
thunder rattled the SUV windows, and a burst of flames
illuminated the woods and lifted the fog as the deserted
house exploded. Fire and debris spiraled toward the
windshield, but Seth turned the wheel, backing them
onto the street.

"I guess we have our answer," he remarked, almost
casually, as if he were nearly blown up every day. But
today it had almost happened twice in less than twelve
hours. "It was a trap."

"For you?" Did he think she had set it up with the
partner first he and then Curtis Waverly had suggested
she had? "Why would he want to kill you? You have no
special abilities."

Or did he?

His broad shoulders lifted in a slight shrug. "Maybe
because I'm in his way."

An engine revved and lights broke through the trees
as a truck followed them out onto the road.

"And he intends to get me the hell out of his way,"
Seth continued. He jerked the SUV from Reverse to
Drive and pressed hard on the accelerator so that it
shot forward.

Her neck snapped back. "His way?"

"I'm keeping him from getting to you. And I'm going
to do my damnedest to make sure he never gets to you."
He reached across and squeezed her hand before returning both of his to the steering wheel.

Maria's heart constricted with fear, but she wasn't
worried about the witch-hunter getting to her. She was

more worried about what the witch-hunter would do to Seth so that he could get to her.

The truck's lights illuminated the SUV interior. Its engine rumbled as it drew ominously close. Then her neck snapped forward as the truck connected hard with the back bumper of their vehicle.

"Son of a bitch," Seth cursed, and gripped the wheel. Then he pressed harder on the accelerator.

"Hurry, hurry," she urged him. "You can lose him."

Seth shook his head. "No. I can't. He knows these roads. I don't—especially in this god-awful fog. I can't even tell where the road ends." The truck bumped the rear end again, sending the SUV into a tailspin. Rubber burned; gravel sprayed.

Seth yanked the wheel, steering the vehicle back to the center of the road. The headlight beams glanced off the tops of trees as the road gave way to one of the deep ravines in the Upper Peninsula.

"Where's your gun?" she asked.

He'd had it in his hand a little while ago. Now he clutched the wheel with both hands, his knuckles turning white in the dashboard lights.

"I can't shoot at him and keep the car on the road," he said, with another curse as the truck bumped them.

"Give *me* the gun," she offered. "I can shoot at him."

"No." He sped up, the wheels squealing as he steered around a sharp curve in the road.

"I can shoot," she said, then admitted, "Not well. But I might be able to get him to back off."

"He's backing off." But even as he said it, the truck closed the distance between them—the lights illuminating the interior of the SUV again. That muscle twitched along Seth's strong jaw. He maneuvered around another turn as he accelerated—too fast—and the tires squealed again.

"Give me the gun," she urged him.

"No."

And she realized why he wouldn't. He didn't trust her any more than he trusted the person who was trying to run them off the road.

"You have to let me help," she said. "Or we're both going to die."

The truck hit the SUV again. Hard. And the tires dropped off the pavement and onto the gravel shoulder, spewing loose pebbles. The vehicle began to slide down—toward the trees. And Maria screamed.

Her scream echoed inside the close interior of the car and inside Seth's mind. Outside, he saw nothing but fog and treetops, and he struggled to get the tires back on the road. Inside his head, he saw *the car turned over, lying atop its roof, the driver's side crushed, his body trapped inside as he lay unconscious. Or worse. Dead.*

But Maria wasn't dead. Blood trickled from the reopened cut on her forehead, but her eyes were open—wide with terror as big hands reached through the passenger's window. He dragged her from the car—dragged her up the road to his truck.

Other images flitted through his mind.

She gasped for breath, water streaming from her face and soaking her hair as her head popped up from a wooden vat. Then the big hands closed over the top of her head and pushed her under again. But she didn't drown, because moments later—her hair still wet—she lay on a cement floor, her wrists and ankles tethered to steel posts anchored to the floor. Those same big hands lifted a rock onto her, pressing it onto her chest—stealing away her breath as the water had.

He had promised to protect her. He could not fail her. Wrenching the wheel in sweat-dampened hands, he steered back onto the road just as the truck drew alongside. The driver was only a shadow in the dim glow of the dashboard lights. As if scared that he might be recognized, the driver turned off the headlamps. He and the truck nearly disappeared.

But Seth knew where it was as metal crunched against metal. The jacked-up truck was bigger than the SUV and, with its roaring engine, faster. He couldn't outrun it. He leaned forward slightly and directed Maria, "Grab my gun."

If not for that damn vision—the one of her shooting him—he would have handed it over sooner, would have let her fire at their attacker. But his gut had tightened at the thought of putting in her hands the gun he had envisioned killing him.

She reached for it, her hands sliding under his jacket and over his belt to the holster. But before she could withdraw the weapon, the truck struck harder. The SUV lurched, knocking Maria away from him—against the passenger's door—as the wheels fell off the road and then the shoulder.

Metal scraped against metal, the truck catching on the driver's side of the SUV. Rubber squealed as the truck braked. Metal twisted and tore as the truck broke free. But the SUV spun out.

Seth jerked the wheel, but he couldn't regain the road. The tires slipped and metal crunched—on the passenger's side—as the vehicle began to turn. Then the wheels were in the air, spinning uselessly. The lights glanced off trees and then black sky.

And in Seth's head, everything went black.

* * *

Maria's throat burned from the screams she had uttered as the SUV had turned over and skidded on its roof down the steep ravine. With a groan of metal, it caught against the trees, its descent drawn to a shaky, tremulous stop. She drew in a deep breath, trying to refill her aching lungs.

Growing up with the horrible visions she'd had, her life hadn't been easy, but she had never screamed about anything until she'd met Agent Seth Hughes. She wasn't screaming because of him, though. She was screaming for him.

"Seth…" she murmured, struggling to turn her head in the space between the seat and the crumpled roof. He didn't answer her, not with so much as a moan. She couldn't even hear his breathing—just her own labored pants for air.

Finally, she crooked her head enough that she could peer through the gap between the roof and console toward the driver's side. But she could barely see through the moisture running in her eyes. She lifted a trembling hand to her forehead, and her fingers came away sticky with blood. Blinking back the blood that trickled into her eyes, she tried to focus. The dim glow from the dash lit some of the interior, but fog seeped eerily in through the broken windows, swirling around Seth.

He was bleeding, too. But instead of trickling, blood flowed from a gash on his head—which was jammed at a horrible angle against the post between the doors on the driver's side. Was his neck broken?

She didn't think she could heal a broken neck. But she could stop the bleeding. If she could find the bag of herbs… It had catapulted around inside the SUV as it spun over and over and could be anywhere…

"Seth!"

He didn't stir at her shout. His closed lids didn't even flicker in response. Along with the blood draining from his wound, the color drained from his skin, leaving him as ghostly pale as the apparitions that visited her.

"Seth!"

She pulled her arm from where it was trapped between the console and her seat and reached over to him. She pressed her scraped and swollen fingers to his throat, trying to detect a pulse. Her skin tingled at the contact, but his was as cold as it was pale.

"Seth, wake up." Tears rushed to her eyes, washing away the blood. "Please wake up…" She ran her fingers over his chin, over his lips, hoping to feel a breath. But his lips were cold, too.

She needed her herbs—needed to try to restore his breathing. She caught sight of the bag; it was wedged between his seat and door. She reached over him and grabbed at it. The plastic snagged and ripped, spilling herbs over him. Her hands shaking, she pulled out lavender and turmeric and licorice. Chanting a prayer, she mashed them together in her fingers and pressed them to his lips.

"Please, sweetheart, don't leave me. I need you…"

More than she had ever needed anyone.

Especially now. Branches snapped, gravel and dirt flying, as someone hurried down the steep slope. A flashlight beam danced around the ravine, then shone through the broken window, bouncing off Seth's bleeding face before shining in her eyes. She squinted, blinded, but she didn't need to see to know that the witch-hunter was coming for her.

Her heart pounded furiously with fear and dread. She moved her hand from Seth's face down his neck again to his chest. But she couldn't feel his heart beating. She twisted in her seat, trying to reach farther down his body. But his back was pressed tight against the seat, too tight for her to squeeze her hand between and pull out his gun.

The snapping noises grew louder as the hunter neared his prey. Then his feet must have slipped on the treacherous slope, because he bumped against the wreck. The SUV rocked, as if about to slip again.

Maria gasped and clutched at Seth. She couldn't let him go; she couldn't lose him. "Go away!" she screamed. "Leave us alone!"

"I can't do that," a deep voice rasped.

Shattered glass tinkled as it fell out of the metal frames. Then big hands reached through the broken window, grabbing for Maria…

Chapter 10

She welcomed the darkness—the blindness of it. And for once she saw no images—no visions. Elena breathed a deep sigh of relief—even though she knew it wouldn't last. The visions would return.

There had already been so many. So many deaths…

Elena wanted life. She wanted her sister's babies safely born. But no matter how many powers she and her sisters shared, they couldn't control their lives.

But once…they had united and killed. Could they do it again? She lifted her wrist and stared at the star-shaped charm that dangled from it. Each of the charms had powers.

They had united them to protect Maria—to save her from the danger Elena kept envisioning. But Irina was so weak that maybe uniting the charms and chanting their prayer hadn't worked.

Elena lowered her wrist—because she worried that

it was probably too late. That was why she had no more visions…

All those horrible things may have already happened. To Maria.

The gunshot jolted Seth awake, his chest burning. He clutched his hands against his heart. It pounded beneath his palm, fast and furious. He hadn't been shot; he had only dreamed it again when he'd passed out after the crash.

The crash! Remembering it cleared his mind and quickened his pulse. Had she been hurt when the vehicle went down the ravine? Or had the killer gotten to her?

"Maria!"

"I'm here," she said, the mattress shifting beneath him as she joined him on the bed.

He blinked his eyes open to find out where *here* was. His room—not at the motel in creepy Copper Creek but in his house in Barrett, Michigan. Light streaked through the wooden blinds at the windows, falling across the hardwood floor and four-poster bed.

"How…are we here?" he asked.

"You don't remember?"

Like his heart, his head pounded—with the echo of metal crunching and her screaming. "I remember the crash. He forced us off the road…"

But that was the only part of his vision that had come true…since she was here with him, instead of at the mercy of a killer.

"I thought you were dead," she said, her voice hoarse—either from screaming or with emotion. "Your head was bleeding so much, and I couldn't feel a pulse. And your skin was cold, so cold…" She shivered as if reliving a nightmare.

It had been a nightmare…when he had awakened to those big hands reaching through the window for her, just like in his vision. Whatever she'd pressed against his lips must have revived his consciousness and his strength. He had tried to fight off the attacker despite the other man's strength. To protect her, though, Seth would have killed him. Until he had recognized him…

"Ty," he remembered. "It was Ty McIntyre who helped us out of the wreck, who got us up the ravine."

She expelled a soft sigh of relief. "Yes. He said Irina made him return to Copper Creek. They knew about the fire, so he had David fly him right to the hospital. The sheriff told him where we were going, and he happened upon the truck just as it was forcing us off the road."

"Thank God for that…" Or both Seth and Maria might have been dead by now. After the truck had raced away, Ty had helped them from the wreckage, and then, instead of waiting for an ambulance, he'd brought them to the hospital himself. Then there had been another ride, in a helicopter, that had brought them back to Barrett.

"My sisters used their special abilities to help us," Maria said as if awed by the women even though she had met only Irina. Not the others…

"Have you talked to them?" he wondered.

She shook her head. "No. Ty talked to them. He told them that we were all right. Elena had warned them about the crash. Both she and her daughter, Stacia, had seen it. They used their charms together and chanted a prayer for our protection—over the fire and the crash." There was such longing in her voice when she talked about her family. Why wasn't she with them?

"He wanted to bring you to them." Seth remembered the argument at the hospital. And after what had happened, Seth had accepted that she would probably be safer with her family than with him, so he had willingly released his material witness into Ty McIntyre's custody. "But you're here…"

With him. In his house. In his room. In his bed. Her hair hung in damp curls around her face; she must have used his shower, because sunshine, not rain, streaked the windows. And she had helped herself to his clothes, too, because she wore one of his old T-shirts and a pair of cotton boxers that sagged low on her hips.

"I needed to stay with you," she said, her skin flushing with embarrassment. "You left the hospital against doctor's orders. You have a concussion. You needed someone to watch over you, to make sure you don't start bleeding in the brain…or swelling…"

Her sitting in bed with him, so close, had something swelling. His body tensed with desire for her. "You missed your chance," he said as he reached for her.

"What chance?" she asked, her eyes widening as his hands clasped her shoulders, pulling her close to him.

"To run away again."

"You convinced me that I need to stop running." She lifted her arms, her fingertips brushing lightly across the bandage on his forehead before sliding down his face. "I need to stay here…with you."

If she knew who he was, she wouldn't stay. She would run faster than she ever had. He needed to tell her his real identity but not now. Not yet. Not until the real killer was caught. It wasn't Curtis Waverly—he'd been either in the hospital or the jail when the truck had come after them.

But he would find out who the killer was. He had already figured out another suspect—one he should have discovered before. Once the killer was caught, maybe she would accept that Seth was no threat to her life. Only, hopefully, her heart—as she was to his. Her fingers stroked down his throat, back and forth over his leaping pulse.

"I thought you were dead," she whispered, her voice choked with emotion. "I couldn't feel you breathe. I couldn't feel your heart beating…"

"I'm alive," he said, "which I have a feeling is thanks to you and your magic potions."

She shivered. "I wasn't sure what I was doing. Or if it would work."

"It worked," he said. "I'm fine."

She pressed her hands, which trembled now, against his chest and pushed back, nearly breaking the hold of his arms around her. "I should leave."

"You just said that you need to stay with me," he reminded her.

"I need to stay with you," she repeated. "But you need me to leave. I'm putting you at risk."

"You care about me?" he asked, his heart warming with hope. If she cared enough, she might forgive him for keeping secrets from her.

Her eyes glistening with unshed tears, she nodded. "I shouldn't. I don't really even know you."

She had no idea how little she knew about him.

"But you've been there for me," she said, "saving me again and again, when no one else in my life has ever been there for me."

"Because you won't let them," he pointed out. "You keep pushing them away, like you're trying to push me away now."

"I can't be selfish," she said. "I can't stay just because I want to…"

"Then stay because I want you to." He leaned forward, closing the distance between them. He brushed his lips across hers. "Stay because I want you…"

Those tears caught on her thick lashes now, quivering before dropping onto her delicate cheekbones. He wiped them away with his thumbs.

"I can't risk your life," she said. "I can't…"

"You're not. This place is like Fort Knox." That was probably the only reason Ty had let her stay with Seth— his security system was high-tech. He also remembered something about McIntyre posting guards outside to watch the house, and probably to make sure Maria didn't try to slip away again. "No one can get in here," he assured her. "You're safe here. You're safe with me."

But she kept her palms pressed against his chest, holding him away from her. Then she pushed, forcing him to lie back down. He grimaced as pain radiated from his bruised ribs.

"I'm sorry," she said, her eyes going wide with horror and regret. "All I do is hurt you."

"You won't hurt me," he said, ignoring the image that flashed through his mind—of her firing that gun. "Unless you leave…because I ache for you."

"I can't leave you," she said, her breath catching. "I want to. I know I should, but something binds us together. Something I can't explain. I'm so connected to you."

He opened his mouth, wanting to tell her why. But then she kissed him. Not his lips but his chest, her mouth gently caressing his bruised skin.

"I'm sorry you got hurt because of me," she said, her usual guilt apparent in her throaty voice.

"It's not your fault."

"Do you believe that?" she asked, her dark eyes large with hope and vulnerability as she stared up at him.

"Do you really believe I have nothing to do with the murders?"

The crash had killed whatever doubts he'd been hanging on to about her. If she'd been working with the killer, the man wouldn't have risked her life to take Seth's. "I really believe."

She released a shaky sigh. "I wish I did. But I still feel responsible for those murders and for you getting hurt."

"You're not—"

She pressed her fingers across his lips. "I want to make it up to you," she said. "I want to make you feel better." She dipped her head again, her hair brushing softly across his skin as she moved down his body. Her lips skimmed across his chest, where she teased first one nipple, then the other with the tip of her tongue. Then she trailed that tongue down his stomach.

Her fingers were unsteady as they slid beneath the waistband of his boxers and pushed them down his hips. Then she kissed him, intimately. Her lips closing around the tip of his pulsing erection, she sucked him into the moist heat of her mouth.

He tangled his hands in her hair. But instead of pulling her away, he held her against him as she continued to torture him. Her lips slid up and down as she sucked his cock even deeper. He groaned.

And she lifted her head. "Am I hurting you?"

"I'm hurting," he admitted as he sat up again.

"The doctor prescribed pain pills. Do you need one?" She reached toward the nightstand, where his holstered gun lay next to his cell phone and a brown bottle.

Ignoring the pain that pounded at the base of his skull, he shook his head. "I'm hurting for you."

Her lips quirked into a slight smile as she turned back to him. "Then let me make you feel better…"

Before she could lower her head again, he caught her shoulders, holding her back. "You didn't ask if you could borrow my clothes."

"Do you mind?" she asked, glancing down at the T-shirt and boxers. "I used your shower, too."

He minded that he hadn't been in it with her, soaping her naked skin. "Yes. I want my clothes back." He reached for his T-shirt, pulled it up and over her head. Then he eased his borrowed boxers over her hips.

He kissed all the skin he'd exposed, sliding his lips down her throat and over the curve of each breast. As she had done with him, he teased her nipples with the tip of his tongue…until she moaned. Her legs shifted restlessly, so he parted them and slid his fingers inside. She was wet and ready for him.

He pulled her astride his hips. Her fingers wrapped around his throbbing erection, and she guided him inside her as she settled on top of him. He bucked, thrusting deep, as he gripped her hips, pulling her up and pushing her back down.

She matched his rhythm, her nails digging into his shoulders as she bobbed up and down. He leaned forward, kissing her deeply. He thrust his tongue between her lips as he thrust his cock deep inside her body.

Her inner muscles squeezed him, stroking his erection more tightly than her mouth had. He thrust harder, a groan tearing from his throat. He pulled his mouth from hers, slid it across her cheek, down her throat to the taut nipple of one breast. His teeth nipped, and then his tongue laved the sensitive point.

She threw back her head and released a keening cry as she came, her orgasm flowing hot over him. His body tensed, every muscle tight, until finally he found release, his cock pumping out an orgasm that filled her.

She collapsed onto his chest, panting for breath. "That—that was incredible…"

"You're incredible." He had never met anyone like her—so self-sacrificing, so generous. So strong…

Was it any wonder that he was falling for her…even though he knew they had no future? Because of their past, they had no future…

"I'm stupid," she berated herself as she quickly rolled off him. "I could have hurt your ribs."

"You didn't," he assured her, catching her close to his side. "You didn't hurt me."

But how badly would she be hurt when she learned the truth about him? He pressed kisses against her temple. Her lashes fluttered down, as if her lids were heavy. She had stayed awake, keeping watch over him. Now it was his turn to watch her while she slept.

But instead of seeing her delicate face in peaceful slumber, he saw her in pain—fighting to draw a breath into her lungs as the big hands continued to pile rocks onto her body, crushing her beneath the weight.

His head pounded with frustration that he couldn't see to whom those hands belonged. Who was it who was hurting the woman he loved? And why wasn't he there in this vision?

He hadn't died in the vehicle crash. So where was he? Why was he breaking his promise to protect her? Because he was already dead?

"Maria!"

The urgency in her mother's voice jolted her awake. She opened her eyes to a thick mist and the overpowering scent of smoke and sandalwood and lavender. Sunlight glowed behind the mist like flames.

"Mama…"

The mist formed into the image of her mother—the delicate-featured face with the big dark eyes that had haunted Maria since Myra Cooper's tragic, prophetic murder. Those eyes brimmed with fear. Not for herself anymore, but for her youngest daughter.

"Child," she said, her voice soft with concern and disappointment. "You are too much your mother's daughter, too much like me. Don't make the mistakes I've made."

Maria glanced to the bed, which was empty but for her, the sheets tangled around her naked body. "Seth…?" She called his name but she also questioned if her mother referred to her choice in men. Did she think Maria had made a mistake getting involved with the FBI agent?

But Seth wasn't like the men Mama had been with. Seth was honorable and protective. He didn't run from his responsibilities and try to ignore them. He took on responsibilities that weren't even his—like her.

"You need to keep running," Mama warned. "Don't stop. Don't ever stop…"

Weariness overwhelmed Maria at her mother's words so that every bone and muscle ached with it. "I can't. I can't run anymore."

"You don't want to leave *him*," Mama said, and those haunted eyes filled with disapproval.

"I can't," she repeated. "I'm not like you. I can't keep leaving the people that I…"

"The people that you what?" Mama asked. "Do you love him? You don't even know him."

"I know that he's been there for me when I needed

him," Maria said. "Even when I thought he was dead, he came back to me—to keep me safe."

Relief flooded her again as she remembered him regaining consciousness and fighting off the hands reaching through the car window for her. If it hadn't been Ty, she knew that Seth would have defended her until he was really dead. She had never had anyone fight for her like that.

"Then where is he now?" Mama asked.

Maria bolted upright in bed and peered through the mist to the open door of the master bathroom with its black-and-white marble and shiny platinum fixtures. It was dark and empty. "Seth?"

"And *who* is he, child?" Mama asked.

She regretted now that she had wanted to see Mama's ghost the night before…because all Mama ever gave her was self-doubt and disappointment.

"Who is he?" the ghost prodded.

"Seth Hughes," Maria replied. "He's an FBI agent." And the only man she'd ever loved.

"With this house? With this security system?" Mama scoffed. "He's more than you think he is." The mist began to fade, as did the smell of smoke. Only the scent remained, along with her mother's last whispered warning. "He's much more…"

Mama was right about the house, because it wasn't just a house. It was a mansion within a brick-walled estate. How could an FBI agent afford such a place?

She crawled out of the four-poster bed, leaving the warmth of its rumpled silk sheets. But she might need to drag one off the mattress to wear since she couldn't find the boxer shorts and T-shirt Seth had taken off her that morning. His cell phone and gun were gone, too.

Just the bottle of prescription painkillers remained on the bedside table—unopened.

Had he left her? Naked and alone in his estate. He probably thought she would be safer here, given his security system, than wherever he had gone. But his leaving her—sneaking out while she slept—reminded her of how Mama had left her sleeping alone in that little camper they had shared for fifteen years. Her heart ached with old pain and new pain.

Then she noticed the clothes: a red sweater and dark jeans folded at the foot of the bed. She grabbed the sweater and a bra and panties dropped to the floor. He had thought of everything. But a note...

After getting dressed, she opened the bedroom door and stepped into the hall. She had helped him to his room in the early-morning hours, but she hadn't paid that much attention to the house—except for its expansive size. Now she noticed the details: the expensive oriental carpet running the length of the hardwood floor, the ornate trim and crown moldings and the antique furniture. Seth Hughes wasn't just rich; he was didn't-need-a-real-job rich. Yet he worked—not in an office or a bank but in a dangerous career that had nearly killed him more than once in the past few days.

"Who are you, Seth Hughes?" she wondered. "And why do you do what you do?"

"Maria?" His deep voice emanated from the bottom of the stairwell.

She hurried, nearly skipping steps as she rushed to the first floor. And... "Seth?"

"In here." His voice drifted through French doors that opened off the wide marble-floored foyer.

Drawn to him, as she had been since the first moment they'd met, she stepped into his den. Here was more ornate trim, more polished hardwoods, more antiques and his reason for doing what he did despite all that wealth.

A huge portable whiteboard crowded the desk, leather couch and chairs. Pictures, of every one of the witch-hunter's victims, were taped up, with notes scribbled beneath them. Her picture was there, too, with lines drawn from it to each of the victims.

She stopped in front of the board and stared up at all his evidence. Confronted with what led him to her, she remarked, "No wonder you thought it was me. I'm the one connection between all of them."

"There is another one," he said. His thick reddish-brown hair was tousled, as if he'd been running his hands through it. "The killer. We just have to find him."

A chuckle bubbled out of her with all her bitterness and anger. "We don't have to find him. He finds me. No matter how far or how fast I run, he always finds me. Even here, in this secure estate, I know he'll find me."

"Probably," Seth agreed.

And she appreciated his honesty. She didn't want the false truths and honest lies. She wanted him again—even after last night. But he was back to being the focused FBI agent—even with all his scratches and bruises, or maybe because of them.

"How does he find you?" Seth asked. "How does he always find you?"

"It's the witchcraft," she realized.

"He's not a witch-hunter," he said with a weary sigh. "You have to let that angle go. He's no descendant from some centuries-old madman."

"No. It's the witchcraft because I can't stop practicing. I always set up a shop—wherever I land. I can give up a lot, but I can't give up trying to help people." It was what kept her sane. It was what made all the running and loneliness worthwhile—if she could provide some relief for someone else. Some peace…since she would never have any of her own.

"You do always set up a shop," he murmured as he stared up at the board. "With the help of your old professor…"

Every one of her friends had died in one of her shops, after hours, after she'd left because of the cards she had read. She hadn't come across the bodies, but she'd already known what was going to happen to them…before it had happened.

"Is that how you found me?" she asked. "Through the shops?" Or through the professor?

Or had he used another method—the one that caused his eyes to glaze over while he got that blank inward stare?

He nodded again. "Of course. The witchcraft. They're drawn to it. It's the one thing that links them all. He's not the only one who's finding you. They're finding you, too. How?"

She reached out and touched Felicia's picture. "I found her," she reminded Seth. "We took that class together at Barrett University." She smiled. "A parapsychology class. Her brother made her drop it, though, and convinced her to move back home." Her lips curved. "Salem. She lived in Salem."

"Massachusetts?"

"No. Utah. It was perfect irony," she said, smiling as she remembered how much fun she and Felicia had had about that. "When…when my mother was murdered, and I started running again, I ran there. I found her."

"And the others?"

"Kevin." She touched the picture of the boy buried

beneath the rocks. He had been such a sweet and funny young man. "Kevin found me. He was in that class, too."

"Two of the five victims took the class with you," he mused. "Did any of the others?"

"Not with me."

"At another time?"

She shrugged. "They didn't mention it, and neither did I. I didn't ask them about themselves." Seth had been the only one she hadn't kept at arm's length.

"Maybe it's time we find out." He glanced at his phone. "I need to stop by the bureau office and check in. I can use the computers there to find out if any of the others took that class."

"Are you going to leave me here?" she asked, nerves fluttering in her stomach. She wasn't afraid of being alone—but she was afraid that she was getting too used to being with him.

He shook his head.

"You don't think I'm safe?" Hadn't he promised her that she was?

His lips lifted into a slight grin. "I don't quite trust you to stay here and wait for me."

"I'm done running," she promised—no matter what her mother's ghost advised.

"That worries me even more," he said, "because I think that you're going to try to find him on your own."

Staring at the bandage on his head, among the other cuts and bruises, she realized that might be the safest thing for Seth—if she found the killer herself. It wouldn't be safest for the killer, though. She was still angry—so angry—over how she had let the madman control her life all these years.

"Don't even think about it," he said, pulling her into his arms.

"Can you read minds?" she wondered.

He laughed. "If only that were possible…"

"It's possible. My sister can." That was why Maria was always so careful to block her thoughts, to try to keep Irina out of her head. She hoped Seth couldn't really read minds; she didn't want him to know how she felt about him. She wasn't sure she was ready to admit it to herself yet. That she was falling for him…

Seth ignored the pounding in his head, which increased in intensity with the volume of his superior's voice.

"She should be in the interrogation room," the guy yelled, "not sitting at your desk. She's the one link to all the victims."

"No. She's not."

Agent Ames leaned back in his chair, the metal frame creaking beneath his substantial weight. "Well, you've changed your tune. You're the one who was so convinced she's the killer that you started looking for her on your own time."

"I was wrong," he admitted with a heavy sigh of regret. "Given what's happened the past few days, I think we have proof that she can't be responsible."

"She can't be solely responsible," Special Agent Ames agreed. "But she can definitely be partially responsible. She can even be the one manipulating someone else into doing her killing."

"You've been talking to Curtis Waverly," Seth said. The man had interfered in the investigation from the beginning, throwing around his money and connections to learn what he wanted. Seth had overlooked the guy's manipulations because he'd seen his grief and loss. Now he resented it.

"He had the sheriff call me," Ames admitted. "You shouldn't have arrested him."

"He attacked Maria."

"Maria? Sounds like he's right—that she's gotten to you." The gray-haired man shook his head. "I didn't think it was possible for anyone to get you to lose focus."

Seth wouldn't have thought it possible, either. "I'm more focused than ever."

"So is Waverly. He's determined to get justice for his sister's murder. That's why I had Sheriff Moore release him."

"When?"

Ames shrugged. "Shortly after you had the sheriff arrest him the second time. They were still at the hospital. I wasn't going to be responsible for Curtis Waverly spending the night in some small hick jail."

Had Waverly paid off the bureau chief himself? Seth worried that he had, but at the moment his supervisor's integrity was the least of his concerns.

After Waverly had been released, would he have had enough time to beat them to the cabin? If he knew the area well enough, he could have. There were all kinds of back roads and snowmobile trails around the cabin. Had Waverly been staying in Copper Creek all that time, plotting Raven's murder? "Are you sure that justice is all he wants?"

"What else could he want that the rich kid doesn't already have?" Ames asked.

"Vengeance," Seth said, anger coursing through him as he remembered the man's arm wound so tightly around Maria's delicate throat that she'd gasped for breath. "Curtis Waverly could have been the one driving the truck that ran us off the road last night."

"The sheriff is investigating the accident," Ames said.

"It was no accident."

"According to the sheriff, it was foggy out and you were unfamiliar with the roads," Ames said with a faint twinkle in his eyes. He knew Seth was a better driver than to let weather and road conditions get the best of him.

"And a truck drove me off the road. You'll find its paint on the wreckage of my SUV, and you'll probably find the truck burned out somewhere. That's what this guy does to whatever evidence might be left behind to link him to his crimes. It could be Curtis Waverly."

Ames shook his head. "Doubtful. I think he really just wants justice."

Seth snorted.

"What do *you* want, Hughes?" his boss asked. "You've gotten too personally involved with this case. If you didn't have…whatever the hell it is that you have, I'd take you off it. But you're the one hope we have of finally catching this killer as long as you aren't falling for the number one suspect."

He wasn't falling for Maria, not anymore. He had already fallen—deeply in love with her self-sacrificing nature and her beauty and sensitivity. Now he could only hope like hell that he was right—that she had nothing to do with the murders.

Maria twirled the chair, which creaked beneath her weight. She leaned back and scanned the walls of Seth's small office. It was half the size of the den at his estate, the chair painfully underpadded and uncomfortable. "Why would you work here, Seth?" she mused aloud.

"I ask myself that," a male voice replied.

But it wasn't Seth. He'd gone inside another office

with a gray-haired man. This guy had thin hair and a cheap suit that barely contained the belly that spilled over his belt as he leaned against the open jamb of Seth's door.

"You ask yourself why you're here?" she asked, wanting clarification of his comment.

"I ask myself why moneybags Hughes wants to work here," the man explained.

She gestured to the framed awards and certificates that covered the walls and sat atop Seth's cluttered desk. Maybe those answered her question. "Because of those?"

Seth's coworker snorted in derision. "Who the hell knows why he does anything? Do you?" he asked. "Have you known Hughes long?"

It felt like her whole life…and inexplicably longer. She shook her head. "I didn't even know the FBI had an office in Barrett."

"Some important people live in this town," he replied, his voice sharp with envy. "That computer guy— you know, Michigan's answer to Bill Gates—David Koster."

Her middle sister's husband.

"Elena and Joseph Dolce. They own most of the town."

Her oldest sister and her husband. That witch hunt eight years ago had been all over the news—even national media outlets had picked it up and ran coverage on it.

"And Ty McIntyre and his wife, Dr. Irina Cooper-McIntyre. They own a lot of properties around here, too."

Ty hadn't been mentioned as much in the news since he hadn't had as high a profile as David Koster and Joseph Dolce. That was why Maria hadn't recognized him at the motel in Copper Creek. He'd always been the Knight of Swords to her, though.

She barely suppressed a smile of pride. These wildly successful, influential people were her family. But they were also strangers to her. She didn't know them the way she knew Seth. Or did she know Seth?

"Of course, compared to Hughes," the man continued, "they seem about as poor as I am."

"Why is he so rich?" she asked, curiosity getting the better of her. Was it inherited money? From his family?

She hadn't noticed any family portraits or photographs hanging around his house. But then, she had been too concerned about him to really check out the place. He had mentioned his father being a bastard, though, so he wasn't likely to have his picture in his house. Would he have accepted an inheritance from the man, or had he made his own money?

"He probably got his money the same way he got those," the man replied, gesturing at the awards. "With his damn psychobabble voodoo shit."

"Voodoo?" Her breath caught in her lungs. "What do you mean?"

"That psychic mumbo jumbo he spews." He put his hand to his balding head in what must have been an imitation of Seth. "Oh, he's seen this—he's seen that. And it always breaks the damn case."

"He has visions…"

"He probably got so rich because he sees what numbers are going to hit for the lottery. Or what stocks will skyrocket. But will he share that information with anyone else? Hell, no." Bitterness twisted the man's face into a grotesque grimace. "Not ethical or some other garbage…"

And now she knew whom Curtis Waverly had paid to learn Seth's whereabouts. She also knew why she and Seth had had such an immediate and deep connection. They were more alike than she had ever imagined. He was psychic.

He had as many special abilities as she had—or maybe more. And if the witch-hunter realized that, he would have a motive to kill Seth other than just to get to her. He had another witch to kill…

Chapter 11

Seth stared at the computer screen, but he didn't see the college transcripts. Instead he saw that image in his head: *those big hands holding Maria's head underwater as bubbles rushed to the surface, where her hair billowed like a wet black cloud.*

"What do you see?" she asked.

He shook his head, clearing away the image. "I can only verify that you, Felicia and Kevin took the parapsychology class at Barrett University."

"I don't want to know what you see on the computer," she said, her hands gripping his shoulders as she leaned over the back of his chair. Her face was so close, her gaze so watchful. She had been studying him intently ever since he had come back from his meeting with Ames. "I want to know what you just saw inside your head."

Nothing she wanted to see.

He groaned with sudden realization. "Culpepper was in here. He talked to you."

"Yes. He told me what you didn't," she said, hurt flashing in her dark eyes. "That you have psychic powers, too."

He shrugged, unwilling to accept any labels. "I don't know what I have."

"You see things."

He nodded but clarified, "Not all the time. But sometimes I see…things."

"Bad things? That's why you do this, why you work in law enforcement," she surmised, "even though you're rich."

Rich. He didn't think about the money anymore, which was funny given how much it had meant to him when he and his mom had been trying to make ends meet. Then they had met his stepfather. He had been rich, but more important than that, he had been kind. And that had meant much more to Seth than his money.

"I want to stop the bad things from happening," he admitted. Especially to her.

"Do you?" she asked. "Can you…once you've seen it happen? Are you able to interfere and change the future?"

"It's the future," he pointed out. "So it hasn't happened yet. Sometimes I can interfere. Sometimes I can change what I've seen."

"Often?" she asked, her voice breathless with hope.

"No," he said, hating that he had to dash her hopes. "Not often enough." But this time he would have to change pretty much every vision he'd had since meeting her. Or he would lose her and his own life.

She expelled a shaky sigh of disappointment. "I was afraid you'd say that."

"But I have interfered," he said. "I saved a boy that I saw die. I found him in time. He's still alive."

"Anyone else?" she asked, narrowing her eyes as if skeptical now of his claims.

He probably deserved her doubt, since he had doubted her abilities and had called her a con artist. "I stopped a killer before he claimed three more victims that I watched him kill in a vision."

"You see more than I do," she said with a wistful trace of envy. "I can read the cards. I can see people's fate through the cards."

"You see ghosts, too," he reminded her with a shudder of gratitude that he couldn't.

"But it's too late then," she said. "I can't help them. I can't do what you can."

"Your herbs have healed—I've seen that myself. Then I've heard and read that your amulets have protected. Your talismans have brought good fortune." He brought up the blog he'd found, the one that had helped lead him to her. "They talk about you—the healing witch. A lot of people want your sachets and amulets, your candles and potions. A few of those people want to be you. That's how you're found no matter where you go. You're a legend."

She shivered. "The only legends I've known are of killing and curses. I don't want to be a legend."

"Maria…"

She sniffled and shook her head. "I need a minute. Where's the restroom?"

The memory of the noose hanging from the ceiling flashed through his mind. And from the way the color drained from her face, she remembered, too. "You're safe here, Maria. No one will hurt you."

"No?"

Then he realized that he already had. By not telling her about his visions, he had hurt her. She would never forgive what other secrets he kept from her.

Pain struck sharply, low and deep in her back—as if someone had shoved in the blade of a knife. This time the pain Irina felt was hers. Not anyone else's.

She sucked in a breath. She couldn't be in labor. It was too early. She covered her belly with her hands and felt the strong kicks of little feet.

"Are you all right?" Ty asked as he settled onto the bed next to her. His hand covered hers on her belly. "Are they all right?"

She waited, but no other pain stabbed her. "Yes, I'm fine," she said, "now that you've brought Maria home."

"She's not home," Ty said with regret in his raspy voice.

"She's home," Irina said as she leaned closer and kissed Ty—right on his scarred eyebrow. He was still the sexiest man she'd ever met. So she skimmed her lips down the side of his face to his chin. Then his lips…

He chuckled—that deep, throaty chuckle that made her weak in the knees. "You are supposed to be taking it easy, Mrs. McIntyre."

"I will," she promised. "Everything's going to be fine now."

His brow furrowed, buckling that scarred eyebrow she loved so much. "The new witch-hunter is still out there," he warned her. "We haven't caught him."

"But Maria isn't scared anymore." Irina smiled as her younger sister's emotions washed over her. "She's in love."

"With Seth Hughes?" Ty asked, and his raspy voice was even gruffer with concern.

Irina nodded. "Must be—since she's with him." And from the feelings of Maria's that Irina had felt, she had really been with him. Intimately. "She loves him."

Ty blew out a ragged breath.

"Why does that worry you?" she asked. "You left her with him. You must trust him."

"David's going to check him out more thoroughly," he said. "We don't think he's exactly who or what he says he is."

Irina shivered as fear rushed over her. Again that feeling was her own. Maria was blissfully unaware and would remain blissfully unaware until it was too late. Given that she loved him, it already was too late.

He would never forgive her for running away again. But she had no choice—not if she wanted to keep him safe. She didn't need Irina's telepathic gift to know that his visions were not any better than hers. The way he had clenched his jaw so tightly that a muscle twitched in his cheek betrayed his tension and his fear.

Her hand trembling, she pushed the button for the elevator, then gasped as the doors opened to Raven.

But there was no forewarning mist, no raspy whispers. No tattoo on her face. Instead of dyed black hair, hers looked naturally black—even the streaks of violet in it looked natural as they matched her eerie violet-colored eyes. And her name: Violet.

Maria remembered now what Raven had said about her sister: she had respected her as much as she'd resented her. She had wanted to be exactly like her. That was how she'd gotten to Maria, because Maria had been able to identify with the young woman's envy and admiration. Commiserating over older, better sisters had drawn them close, closer than Maria should have allowed anyone to get.

"I'm supposed to meet with Special Agent Seth Hughes," the woman said. "But I think you're the one I really need to talk to about my sister. You're Maria."

She nodded. Guilt and regret overwhelming her, she could only whisper, "I'm sorry."

"It wasn't your fault," the young woman assured her. "It was hers. She knows that now."

"You can see her ghost?"

Tears glittered in those mysterious violet eyes as Violet nodded. Maria identified with the woman and the history Raven had given of her. Violet had been gifted since childhood, able to see things no one else had. Like Maria, she had embraced her witchcraft and made the most of it. But she hadn't wanted Raven to be part of the life that had chosen her.

"I can't see her anymore," Maria admitted, feeling the loss of Raven's ghost almost as acutely as she had felt the loss of the girl herself.

"She's embarrassed and regretful. She thinks that she brought him to you," Violet explained. "She feels it's all her fault."

"It's mine," Maria insisted. "He's been after me all this time. I never should have let her close to me. I never should have agreed to teach her."

"You wouldn't have had to...if I had. I saw that something bad would happen to her," Violet explained. "I saw that she would be murdered if she became what I am. What *you* are..."

"A witch," Maria murmured. But she knew who and what she was. She asked the girl what she really wanted to know. "Who's the witch-hunter? Did she tell you?"

The woman's gaze shifted away from Maria, beyond

her. She turned, expecting the mist and maybe Raven's image. Instead she saw Seth leaning against the door-jamb of his office as if he had been there for a while.

Had he been watching her ever since she'd left him? Had he known she was going to break her promise and run again? Of course he knew... Even if he couldn't read other people's minds, he could read hers because of that connection between them.

The woman spoke to them both now. "Raven hasn't told me who the man is. She doesn't know his real name."

"I need to talk to her," Maria said. "She needs to come to me again. I'm not mad at her."

Violet shook her head as more tears glistened in her eyes. "She's passed over. She's gone now."

And so were whatever leads Raven's ghost might have given them to the witch-hunter.

The hunter watched as they walked from the building. The agent kept his hand on the witch's arm, as if he didn't trust her not to run away again. He was a fool to try to hang on to her. His chivalry in trying to protect her was just going to get him killed.

He would do it now, with the gun he'd purchased off the street, but he wasn't the only one who watched them. He was more patient than the others knew. He had been watching Maria Cooper for years; he could watch her awhile longer...until he found his opportunity to kill her.

He'd had other opportunities over the years. But he hadn't been ready to end it then. He hadn't been ready to end her.

Instead he had used her—her ability to draw people to her—to draw out the other witches. She had already drawn out another one, the one with the purple eyes and streaks in her hair.

Then there were her sisters and nieces. They were all witches, too.

So much killing to do…

So little time…

He had to get busy. But first he had to get rid of Special Agent Seth Hughes, and not just because the guy stood between him and Maria. He had to get rid of Hughes because, just like the others, Hughes was a witch, too.

Seth watched her—as he had at the bureau. Maybe he had more abilities than just seeing the future. Maybe he could read minds, because he'd known that the moment she had learned what he had kept secret from her, she would take off. And she didn't even know it all. But realizing that he had kept one secret from her had shattered that fragile trust she'd begun to feel for him.

When she learned the rest, he would never be able to rebuild what he'd just destroyed. "I'm sorry," he said, because he should have told her but couldn't. Sorry, too, because he couldn't let her go.

He had spent too long looking for her to let her slip easily away from him. Especially as a killer waited somewhere out there, probably close by, to get her alone, waited to kill her.

"You should have told me," she said as she hesitated outside the door he held open for her.

To his bedroom. Would she share it with him again? Or had he destroyed not only her trust but also whatever else she had begun to feel for him?

"I don't tell people," he said.

"You're embarrassed?" she asked, her voice sharp

with accusation. Apparently it offended her if he denied his abilities.

"I would feel like a fraud if I claimed to be a psychic," he explained. "I'm not sure it's even real. It comes and goes. I can't do it on command, like other people think. I'm not a psychic. I just have…psychic moments."

She glanced to the bed and then to his face. "Have you had any about us?"

"Yes." He couldn't tell her about the shooting, not without making her even angrier with him. "I knew you and I would make love."

She stepped farther into the room, closer to the bed. "It was inevitable."

"It was incredible," he said as he followed her, moving close enough that his chest brushed her back. Then he lowered his head so his lips brushed across her ear when he added, "I knew it would be…from the dream. But yet, it—you—surpassed whatever I could have envisioned."

"What do you envision now?"

Horrible things. Her drowning. Her being crushed. He flinched and shut out the images. "You forgiving me for not telling you," he said.

She chuckled, recognizing his lie. "Why should I forgive you?" she challenged him. "What are you going to do for me?"

"I got that box of stuff you wanted," he told her. "It's in my den."

She nodded. "That's a start."

"But it's not enough?"

Hurt flashed through her eyes, and he remembered that she had once referred to herself as that—as not enough. Instead of waiting for a reply, he turned her in his arms and pressed his lips to hers. Determined to prove to her that she was more than enough for him, more than he deserved, he deepened the kiss. His tongue stroked in and out of her mouth, driving deep.

Her fingers tunneled into the hair at his nape. Instead of tugging him away, she clutched him closer. She tangled her tongue with his, sucking it deeper into her mouth.

At least she still wanted him—even if she couldn't trust him. He wanted her trust, too. But he had no way of earning it—not with the secret he was keeping.

She pulled back from him and stared up into his eyes, as if she knew he was keeping more from her and she searched for the secret. "Why do I react this way to your touch?"

"What way?" he asked.

"I tingle," she replied, "all over."

"Here?" he asked, sliding his lips across her cheek to her ear. He blew lightly on her lobe and she shivered. He moved his mouth down her throat, flicking his tongue across the point where her pulse pounded quickly beneath her skin. "Here?"

She moaned and leaned against him, as if her knees had weakened. Instead of supporting her, he pushed her back—onto his bed. Then he unsnapped and dragged her jeans down her legs and pulled her sweater over her head.

"I didn't thank you for the clothes," she murmured, her face flushing with embarrassment.

"You lost everything last night," he reminded her. "I bought you some other things." Actually he'd ordered them from a nearby boutique and had them delivered. "They're in the closet." Hanging next to his clothes, lying in drawers next to his. He had never lived with anyone before, always more focused on his professional life than his personal one. But he liked the idea of her living with him.

"I didn't lose everything," she said.

"No," he agreed as he stood up and shrugged out of his own clothes. "You still have your family."

"I still have you," she said, her eyes wide with awe as she stared at him.

She had seen him naked before, so he doubted his nudity accounted for her reaction. Was she just surprised that he'd stuck around?

"I'm not going anywhere," he assured her as he joined her on the bed. "Except here…" He kissed her shoulder, then skimmed his lips down her arm to the curve of her elbow. "And here…" He ran his tongue along the crease. Then lower to her hand, where he licked her fingers.

Her breath shuddered out. "Seth…" She tried to sit up, but he pushed her back onto the pillows, as she had pushed him last night.

And as she had made love to him, he made love to her. Kissing every inch of her, stroking his tongue and then his thumbs across her nipples. Then he moved down her body, licking his way across her navel, through the curls between her legs. And he buried his tongue inside her, lapping and thrusting, until she tensed and screamed his name.

Unlike at the hospital, he couldn't hang on to control and think only of her pleasure. He had to take his own, so he thrust his throbbing erection into her wet heat. She locked her legs around his waist and her arms around his shoulders, and she arched her hips, meeting his every thrust. Her fingers dug into his shoulders and her inner muscles clenched him, pulling him deep, and she came again.

And so did he. A groan tore from his soul as pleasure shattered his world. He wanted her clothes in his closet and her body in his bed—every night. But she was already wriggling free of his arms and out of his bed.

He relaxed when water ran in the bathroom, but then moments later another door opened. He opened his eyes as she was stepping into the hall. "Where are you going?"

"You said that box is in your den," she replied as if that were answer enough.

He didn't really think she was running, but still he hurriedly dressed and followed her downstairs. "What are you doing?" he asked as she opened that box of things he'd had one of his staff purchase for her.

She lifted out some candles and sat them on his desk. Crystals and sachets of herbs joined the candles. And then, her hand shaking, she lifted out the package of tarot cards. "I didn't ask for these," she said, her gaze going to his face. "I won't read anymore."

"You will," he said, "once the killer is caught. You'll be able to read again."

She dropped the cards back into the box. "I don't want to read."

Given what she saw when she did, he didn't blame her. But he also knew from experience that it was impossible to ignore a psychic ability. "What do you intend to do with all this stuff?"

"I'm going to hold a séance," she replied matter-of-factly, as if he should have known.

"Raven's sister said it was too late," he reminded her. "That Raven is gone. She's passed over." He hoped that the sister was wrong, though, because Raven could give them information no one else could—if she could speak from beyond the grave.

Maria turned toward his whiteboard and the photos taped to it. "Not all of them have passed over, not with the violent ways they died. I'll be able to bring at least one of them back to talk to me."

He shuddered at the thought of a ghost in his house. But he knew it wouldn't be the first time. He had felt other presences; he just wasn't able to see them clearly as Maria and Raven's sister were able.

"You don't see ghosts," she said.

"Sometimes when I handle a victim's personal effects, I see what they saw…when they died." Too bad it wasn't admissible in court or grounds for a search warrant that could lead him to evidence that would be admissible.

"Did you do that with them?" she asked as she stared up at the whiteboard.

He nodded, swallowed the lump in his throat and replied, "Yes."

"And what did you see?"

"You."

She whirled back to him. "What?"

"Not killing them," he clarified. "But you were the one person they all saw before they died." Just as he had in his dream.

Chapter 12

*Mc*Gregor...

David Koster grimaced as the name came up on the screen of his tablet. Unable to sleep in the guest suite of Ty's house, he'd resumed his online investigation.

"What is it?" Ariel asked as she leaned over his shoulder, her breasts soft and full and naked against his back. She gasped as she saw the name, too, and her warm breath tickled his neck.

He shivered—more at her closeness than at what he saw. The woman excited him as no one and nothing else ever had.

"You found him," she said. "You found Donovan Roarke's son."

He had done what Donovan Roarke had been unable to do. The crazy private investigator had tracked down Myra Cooper and three of her daughters. But he hadn't been able to find the wife and the son who had been hiding from him.

David shook his head. "I didn't find him. He found us."

"Why?" Ariel asked. "Do you think he wants vengeance for what Elena, Irina and I did to his father?"

David shrugged. He knew about abusive fathers. His own hadn't been, but Ty's father had—until David had stopped him. "Or maybe he wants to thank you…"

Maybe that was what motivated him. Or maybe it was what Irina had told Ty…

"We need to tell everyone else," Ariel said. "We need to warn them."

David hesitated.

"You don't think we should tell them?"

"We will," he said. In their family it was impossible to keep a secret. But he wanted to do a little more digging first—into the past of Donovan Roarke's son.

And he wanted to make love to his wife. He set the tablet down and turned toward her. Her hair, so red and vibrant, was tousled around her naked shoulders. Her skin shimmered in the faint light of the bedside lamp.

He pushed her back onto the pillows and covered her mouth with his—her body with his. She shifted beneath him, arching into him, taking him deep into her body as she had already taken him deep into her heart.

Passion and love burned between them with an intensity that humbled and awed David. He wasn't worried about McGregor having found them. He wouldn't let anyone hurt his family. He had killed once to protect someone he loved; he would have no qualms about killing again.

Maria stared into the flickering flame of the sandalwood candle. Seth had stepped out of his den to take a call on his cell, leaving her alone with the candles and incense and the ghosts. He might have been skeptical about the séance, but it was working. Along with the scent of sandalwood, the den filled with mist.

"I'm so sorry," she murmured. For all their deaths.

"It wasn't your fault," a soft voice whispered.

"Raven?" Maybe her sister had been wrong; maybe she hadn't passed over.

The mist formed into a tall, athletic shape. But the wispy hair was blond and short. The spirit was of Felicia Waverly. "No, my friend…"

"Licia." She reached out, wanting to wrap her arms around the girl she had loved like a sister. "I'm sorry." Most sorry about her death because, after her mother's ghost had warned her to run, Maria had sought out Felicia, tracking down her former classmate at her home in Utah. "I never should have gone to see you."

"I still would have died."

Maria squinted, trying to see Felicia's image more clearly. "Why?"

"Because this is all about me," Felicia said. "I'm the reason for the killing, not you."

"Felicia, is that why I never saw your ghost?" Not as she had seen the others. She had figured that Felicia had been mad at her, that she had blamed her for bringing the danger—the evil—with her and hadn't wanted to see her again.

"I wanted to warn you," the girl replied. "But I didn't know how to explain…what I can't understand myself."

Excitement quickened Maria's pulse. "You know who killed you?"

The ghostly image wavered as she nodded. "I didn't actually see him. He came up behind me. But I know who he is."

"Who?" Maria asked.

"My brother. My brother killed me."

"What?" Maria asked. He had seemed so grief stricken, so determined to find justice for Felicia's murder.

"Actually, he's not my real brother—only a step-brother," she explained with a shudder of revulsion, as if she couldn't stand anyone thinking they might have been really related. "He's my stepmother's eldest child. He's an evil, violent man…just like his father was. That was why he took my father's name instead of his own."

Maybe that was why Curtis Waverly had seemed so familiar to Maria. He had changed his name to hide his identity. But she knew who he was now. He was the witch-hunter—the son of the man who had killed her mother and had tried to kill her sisters and niece.

"He killed me for the inheritance," Felicia said. "All that money he uses to get what he wants—that was *my* money. He never would have gotten his hands on it if I had lived." The ghost began to fade. "He only wanted to kill me. But he keeps killing to cover his tracks…"

"No," Maria assured her friend, but the ghost was gone. "He keeps killing because of who he is…" A Mc-Gregor—he had to be a McGregor.

"Who's who?" a deep voice asked.

"Curtis Waverly," she answered Seth. "That's not his real name. He took his stepfather's name—Felicia's dad's name. He's the son of the witch-hunter. He's taken over and is witch-hunting now."

"No, he's not." But Seth couldn't explain how he knew it. "None of these murders have to do with that legend. I think it has more to do with the professor of that class you took."

"But only three of us took it here at Barrett University," she argued. "You couldn't even find out if the other victims had ever been in Barrett."

"It doesn't matter if they came here," Seth said. "Professor Chandler teaches it online and travels around the country lecturing about his novel on parapsychology. Every one of the victims has had contact with him. That phone call just confirmed it. Raven's sister confirmed Raven attended one of his lectures and had an autographed copy of his book."

"But why would he do it?" Maria asked. "He teaches parapsychology. He believes in—even reveres—psychic abilities. That's why he gives me money for the magic shops."

"Exactly," he said. "He gives you money so he knows where you are—before anyone else does." Resentment gripped him.

"He's not the only one," she said. "His assistant sends me the money orders."

"Then we need to talk to them both," he said. "The professor first, though."

"He wouldn't be a witch-hunter," she said, dismissing his suspicions. "It doesn't make sense."

"But it makes more sense that the estranged son of some guy your sisters killed would be killing everyone close to *you*?"

"Yes," she stubbornly persisted. "You have to admit that he has the most motive. Vengeance. And if he's half as crazy as his father…" She shuddered.

"Then wouldn't he be going after your sisters? Or their kids? Why you? You haven't had any contact with them. Why go after the people close to you?"

She shrugged. "Maybe it's like how lions take down the zebra that gets separated from the herd. I'm an easier target than they are. They're together. They're strong."

"Why do you think it's Curtis?" He glanced around the room. The air in it was heavy with her scent and smoke from the candles. He squinted his eyes as he peered around, but he could make out no celestial images.

"The ghost is gone."

"Who was it?" One of the boys who had loved her and died for her? Inexplicably, jealousy coursed through him. But those guys were gone—physically and spiritually. Yet they had a better chance of being with her again than he did...once she learned the truth about him.

"Felicia Waverly," she replied. "She told me that Curtis is the killer."

"She saw him?" How the hell would he bring this new information to his supervisor? Or a judge? He couldn't—without risking his career and his freedom. They would probably commit him. There were already too many rumors flying around the bureau about him.

With a sigh of disappointment, she replied, "No. But that's the only way he inherited his money—by killing her."

"He had an alibi for her murder," Seth pointed out. "And no reason to commit the other murders."

"You don't think he could have bought the alibi—like he bought your whereabouts?"

"He could have," he admitted. Initially he had suspected Curtis of the murder, so he had thoroughly investigated the man. But several people had seen Curtis the night his sister had drowned.

Or so they had claimed...

A shiver of unease raced down his spine as he remembered that, on the bureau chief's orders, the sheriff had released Curtis. He was free again—free to attack Maria again as he had already.

"But why would he kill the others? To cover his tracks? It's been years since Felicia died." He shook his head. "It doesn't make sense that he would keep killing." That he would keep torturing Maria, cutting her off from everyone she cared about.

If he had killed his stepsister, he had gotten away with murder. Why would he have kept risking getting caught?

But then, why had he attacked Maria not once but twice in front of a federal agent?

Maybe he was just so arrogant that he thought no one would catch him. Or that if he was caught, he could buy his way out of trouble—as he'd been buying his way out of the arrest for attacking Maria.

Was the bureau chief the one who'd given him Seth's whereabouts? Could he trust anyone but himself?

Maria's fingers touched her throat—as if she was remembering those attacks. "Curtis Waverly makes more sense than Professor Chandler killing anyone."

"He's another link between the victims," Seth pointed out. A link he probably would have discovered earlier if he hadn't been so convinced Maria was the killer. "So I'm going to talk to him."

She leaned over his desk and blew out the flames, sending spirals of smoke into the air. "I'm going with you."

"No, you're going to your sisters," he said. "Ty keeps calling. They're dying to see you."

"They'll be dying if they do see me," she insisted. "It's bad enough that I'm here."

"In my house?" Did she regret coming home with him—regret forgiving him for keeping the visions from her?

"In Barrett. I swore I was never coming back here. I

was never even going to return to Michigan again, but Copper Creek called to me."

As she had called to him before they had ever met, beckoning him to fall for her. "I can't leave you alone here," he said. "I can't trust you to not take off again." And probably confront Curtis Waverly with the allegations of his sister's ghost.

"So take me with you."

"I can't do that, either." He shook his head. "If Chandler is the killer, then I would be delivering you right to him."

"He's not the killer." She uttered a ragged sigh of resignation and reluctantly admitted, "He's my father..."

"I see your mother from time to time," Dr. Chandler said as he led them through the foyer of his Tudor house, which was just off the campus of Barrett University. "Even in death, she's beautiful."

"You loved her." And that was probably why he had convinced himself that he saw her, even though Mama had said that the self-proclaimed expert of parapsychology actually had no psychic abilities himself.

In only his early fifties, the professor was a handsome man with his black hair and unlined face. His mouth lifted in a self-deprecating grin. "I was a besotted kid when I met your mom."

Maria turned to Seth, who stood protectively next to her in the professor's living room, as if he was ready to defend her should her father try to hurt her. "Dr. Chandler was working on his thesis when he met my mother," she explained. "He interviewed her and included her in his research."

"That was thirty years ago," the professor added. "She was raising three daughters alone. She was an amazing woman. I couldn't help but fall for her." He winked at Seth. "You understand…"

Heat flushed Maria's face. "No, it's not like that," she said. She had fallen for Seth, but she knew better than to think he had fallen for her, too. Sure, he was attracted to her, but as he'd told her before, he was just doing his job. "Agent Hughes is investigating the murders."

"Your mother's murder was solved eight years ago." The professor shivered despite the thick cardigan sweater he wore. "It happened just as she had seen it. At the hands of the man she knew was coming for her."

Because she had always known how she would die, Mama had lived in fear, taking little pleasure in life. Maria didn't want to live her life the way her mother had. She wanted to stay with Seth, but until the witch-hunter was caught, it wasn't possible for her to stay anywhere.

"It happened—" Maria turned to Seth and held his gaze, trying to make him understand that it was the curse "—just as the legacy foretold, with one of the McGregor descendants determined to kill all the descendants of that first witch, Myra Durikken."

"That has nothing to do with this," Seth said. "It has to do with you, Professor. Over the past eight years, there have been five murders—"

Maria interrupted to detail how they had died. "Drowning, hanging, crushing, burning…"

"Witch-trial murders." The professor sucked in a breath of surprise and nodded. "There must be another witch-hunter."

"Yes," Maria said, relieved that someone else agreed with her. Maybe now Seth would realize that it wasn't just a silly legend. This was her reality.

"These murders have more in common than the way

the victims were murdered," Seth persisted. "Dr. Chandler, they have you in common. Every one of these victims took one of your classes, here in Barrett or online, or they listened to your lecture or had a copy of your book."

The professor, whose face had grown pale and whose eyes had widened behind his glasses, was clearly shocked—as Maria had been when Seth had told her. Even though he had been protecting and making love with her, he hadn't become as distracted as he'd claimed he was. He had been working the case, trying to find a link between the victims other than just her.

But given the interest in witchcraft of each of the victims, and her reading their deaths in their cards, she was still the stronger link.

"They also have me in common," Maria assured her father. "I doubt their deaths have anything to do with you. They were all interested in the supernatural, so of course they might have attended one of your classes or lectures or bought your books. It doesn't implicate you. You're not the one responsible." Too old to be Donovan Roarke's son, he was not the witch-hunter.

Dr. Chandler lifted a shaking hand to his face and rubbed it along his jaw. "Their deaths might have everything to do with me."

Maria gasped. "That can't be…"

"What do you mean?" Seth asked, his smoky blue gaze intense as he studied the professor.

"During my lectures I've been going into great detail about the witch hunts, about the ways that witches are killed," he explained.

"But why?" Maria asked. "The class I took from you focused on psychic abilities. So did your book. You've never talked about witches or witchcraft."

"I'm working on another book," he replied, "about your mother dying at the hands of a witch-hunter." He reached out to her, caught her hands in his and squeezed. "I'm sorry, honey, if this brings up all the pain again. But there were so many reports about what happened eight years ago. I wanted to go into more detail than those sound bites on the evening news. Your mother deserved having her story told in its entirety."

Maria squeezed his hands back as emotion rushed over her. "Thank you." He had loved her mother so much, maybe more than Maria had. "Thank you for honoring her this way."

"Honoring or taking advantage?" Seth asked, his voice heavy with cynicism. "Given the sensationalism of the story, you're sure to make a lot of money off the book and the lectures you're apparently already giving about it."

"Seth!" she admonished him.

But Dr. Chandler nodded. "Agent Hughes is right," her father admitted. "I do stand to make a lot of money off your mother's tragedy. At least, that's what my agent and editor think after reading the draft."

"I'll need their names," Seth said, ever the FBI agent. "And besides them, who else might have seen this book?"

The professor lifted his shoulders in a shrug. "I don't know who else at their offices might have read it."

"What about your office? Did you give anyone else a copy of it?" Seth asked.

He shook his head. "I should have given you a copy," he told Maria. "Or at least discussed it with you before I sold the book."

She smiled. "It's fine. I haven't been in contact with you all that often over the years." Her face flushed with embarrassment when she realized it had usually been only when she'd needed something from him. Not support or comfort. They didn't have that kind of relationship, since they hadn't even known about each other until Maria had brought her mother's last letter to him. Despite the DNA they shared, she had never felt the connection with him that she had with any of her other family members.

Or with Seth.

But Dr. Chandler had promised he would make it up to her that he hadn't been in her life. But his way of doing that had been to write checks. Without his financial support, Maria wouldn't have been able to set up her magic shops every time she started over.

"So no one else has seen the book?" Seth asked.

"Nobody that I know about," the professor replied.

"What about your assistant?" Maria asked. "Does Ethan still work for you?"

He shook his head. "He left me a few months ago. He needed some time off. But he'll be back." He grinned. "He always comes back."

Goose bumps lifted on Maria's skin as she remembered the creepy young man. "He does?"

"He'll be gone for a few months. Then he comes back—helps me with my correspondence and my research—before he needs to leave again." A sad smile lifted his handsome face. "It reminds me of your mother. Of you…"

"Have you seen him recently?" Seth asked.

"No," her father replied. "But he called, sounded as though he was working on something important. But he said he was almost done and then he would come by and talk to me."

"Don't meet with him," she warned, worried about

her father's safety. While he wasn't a witch, and his young assistant had always seemed to idolize him, he was closer to her than anyone else right now. Except Seth. "Don't let him anywhere near you!"

Seth was already on the phone, giving orders to the police officers who had followed them to her father's home. It hadn't mattered to him that Dr. Chandler was her biological dad; he had still suspected the man was capable of killing everyone she had cared about.

Maria hadn't believed it. She hadn't believed, either, when her mother had told her the professor was her dad. But after Mama had taken off, Maria had struggled alone for a few years before eventually seeking him out. Then he, and a DNA test, had confirmed the claim her mother had made in her goodbye letter. He hadn't resented finding out that he had a daughter. He had wanted to make up for the years they had missed. He had wanted to take care of her, had given her money and a scholarship to the school where he taught. But Maria had always felt more like a science experiment he wanted to study than a daughter to him.

When Seth hung up his call, he turned to her father. "I need to know everything about your assistant, including where we might be able to find him."

Near. Maria was certain of it. If Ethan O'Donnell was the witch-hunter, then he was close. Always watching her. Always waiting to kill those she cared about before, eventually, he killed her.

Ethan O'Donnell was not the witch-hunter that Maria thought he was. Given everything Seth had learned about the young man, the professor's assistant was probably the killer who had been stalking Maria. But he wasn't the descendant of the first witch-hunter from over three hundred and fifty years ago. He wasn't the son of the man who had killed Maria's mother and aunts and had tried to kill her sisters.

Seth stood back in the foyer near the door as she and the professor hugged. They didn't look like father and daughter, but they had a connection—one that had compelled Maria to let him know where she was when she had finally stopped running long enough to set up one of her magic shops.

But Ethan O'Donnell had also seen the postcards she had sent to her father, so he had also learned where she was. And he had sent other people to her—to learn her ways of witchcraft.

Then he killed them.

Seth knew now *how* the murders had happened. He just didn't know why. He waited until he and Maria were in the car, driving back toward his estate, before he asked, "What made you think about your father's assistant?"

She shivered despite the warm air blowing from the SUV vents with such force that it stirred her curls, tangling them around her shoulders. "He was my father's teaching aide at the time Felicia, Kevin and I attended that class. And he was just always—" she shivered again "—a little too intense."

"But what made you think he might be the killer?" he wondered. Maybe it was investigative curiosity or maybe it was jealousy that had him asking, "Had you ever had a relationship with him?"

Now she shuddered with disgust. "God, no!"

Her admission gave him some relief. "Then he's not a jilted lover who might be stalking you."

"Definitely not," she replied.

"He could still be obsessed with you. Maybe he

wanted something to happen between you and him."
Seth couldn't blame the guy for that, but he could blame
him for how he had handled her rejection.

"He never even talked to me," Maria said.

Seth sighed. "Then I don't understand why he would
have become a killer."

"There's only one explanation," Maria replied. "He's
a descendant of that first witch-hunter. He must be the
son of the man who killed my mother."

"You don't know that." But Seth did. And maybe
it was time he finally told her the truth, no matter the
consequences. "Maria…"

But before he could say more, the wheel jerked, rubber slapping against asphalt. He had been vigilant about
other cars on the road and had made certain the same
one hadn't stayed near them—on the way to the professor's brick-and-stucco Tudor and since they had left
the college campus. Had he just driven over something
that had blown the tire?

Then the windshield shattered, glass spiraling out
from a hole in the middle. He reached across and
grabbed the back of Maria's head and pushed her lower
than the dashboard. "Get down!"

Then he ducked himself and gripped the wheel,
keeping the SUV on the road. There were no steep ravines here, but he didn't want to swerve out of control.
Even though the bare rim rumbled against the road,
he couldn't stop the SUV. That was what the shooter
wanted. He was out there somewhere, determined to
kill Seth.

So determined to get to Maria that he would kill an
FBI agent to get to her. Could it be Ethan O'Donnell?
Had he been watching the professor's house, waiting
for them to show up?

"He's going to kill you," she said, her voice shaking with horror. "He's going to kill you just to get to me."

"He's not going to get you," Seth vowed. But even as he made the promise, those images flashed through his head.

Her being drowned, sputtering and choking for breath as the water filled her nose and mouth and slid down her throat to her lungs. And once she had passed out, he tied her to the stakes anchored in the cement floor. And he began piling those rocks atop her body, snapping her bones, crushing her organs until she breathed her last...

"I'll die before I let him hurt you," he swore, cursing as the driver's-side window shattered, too.

"I'm afraid that's what's going to happen," she murmured, tears of fear streaking down her face. "Right now..."

Chapter 13

Ty had been a good cop. But he was an even better private investigator. He was good at finding people who didn't want to be found—well, good with everyone but Maria. And he was damn good at following someone without their being aware that he followed them.

Apparently even an FBI agent…

He'd been trailing Seth Hughes since he and Maria had left Hughes's impressive estate. While they had been visiting with the professor, he'd noticed someone else parked outside Chandler's house. Maybe the person had noticed him, because he'd taken off. But it was clear now he'd been leaving only so he could ambush the FBI agent.

Ty flinched as each shot rang out. One struck the tire. Another bullet shattered the windshield and the last one the driver's-side window as Seth drove past where the other car had been waiting for him—pulled off into a tree-lined driveway.

The SUV rolled to a stop against the curb across from the driveway, the horn blaring as a body slumped over the wheel.

"Damn it!" Ty cursed as he braked hard and threw his vehicle into Park. He should have reacted faster. Seth was hurt, but maybe he could protect Maria. The passenger's door of the SUV opened. But it wasn't her who dropped to the ground. As the horn continued to blare, Seth slipped from the vehicle and sneaked around it, his gun drawn.

Ty expelled a breath of relief. He was alive. And if he'd been hurt, he wasn't seriously injured—because he moved quickly. He circled around to that vehicle concealed in the driveway.

Ty hurried across the street to back him up, his gun drawn, too. Seth, blood trailing from cuts on his face, nodded at him, and Ty pulled open the passenger's door as the FBI agent dragged open the driver's door. "Drop the gun! Drop the gun!" he shouted.

The man's hands trembled on the gun he held, but he didn't drop it. He continued to hold it, but he didn't point it at either Seth or Ty. He pointed it through the windshield at the woman who hurried up to the vehicle.

"I told you to stay put," Seth told Maria.

"And let him kill you when it's me he wants?" She shook her head. "No…"

And Ty realized that his wife was right. It was too late for Maria. She already loved the FBI agent.

Seth ignored her and shouted again at the man in the car, "Put the damn gun down!"

Ty cocked his gun, too. "Do as the agent says."

"I saw Felicia," Maria told the man. "Her ghost came to me."

The gun trembled more in the man's hands—so much that Seth reached out and easily snapped it out of his grasp. Then he dragged the suspect from the car and hooked him up. "Curtis Waverly, you're under arrest for attempted murder. Again…"

"For murder," Maria corrected him. "Arrest him for murder. He killed Felicia. She told me you killed her."

Curtis shook his head. "No. No, I would never kill her. I *loved* her."

"You love her money—money you wouldn't have gotten if you hadn't killed her," Maria accused him. "You only inherited it because she's dead."

The cuffed man began to sob, his muscular body shaking with grief. "I would give up all that money for her—to bring her back. I loved her. She wasn't really my sister, you know. We could have been together. We could have been…if she hadn't died."

Maybe loving Irina as long and as deeply as Ty had had given him some of her power of empathy. Because he felt the other man's pain and inconsolable loss.

Ty met Maria's gaze and realized she felt it, too. While this man had just tried to kill her and Seth, he wasn't the killer. He wasn't the witch-hunter.

"We should have gone to the hospital," Maria said as she lifted her fingertips to Seth's handsome face. She gently applied some lavender oil to the scratches on his skin. "You're cut again." Hurt again—because of her.

"I'm fine," he assured her, and he stepped back so that her hand fell to her side.

She couldn't blame him if he didn't want her to touch

him—if he didn't want her healing. Cursed as she was, she was bad luck for anyone who got close to her.

He paced around his bedroom, as if the adrenaline had yet to leave his system. "I should have let Ty McIntyre take you to your sisters, though—where you would be safe."

That was why Ty had been following them—to protect her. To make sure she stayed safe. But as usual, Seth had kept her safe. He had also been right about Curtis Waverly; he wasn't the witch-hunter.

Ty had confirmed that he and David Koster had searched for Donovan Roarke's son, and it wasn't Curtis Waverly. He was a few years too young and not the same coloring as either Roarke or his wife. So it had to be Ethan O'Donnell.

"You should have gone with Ty," Seth repeated.

She couldn't blame him if he didn't want her anywhere near him anymore. She had brought him nothing but danger and pain. "If you want me to leave…"

She would, even though it would be the hardest thing she had ever done, harder even than when she had left the apartment she had shared with her sister Irina. As much as she had loved her sister, she loved Seth so much more.

"No!" He rubbed his hand over his face, wiping away traces of blood. "No. I should take you to your family, but I don't want you to leave." His throat rippled as he swallowed hard. *"Ever…"*

She shivered at his intensity even as his admission warmed her, chasing away her doubts and fears. Maybe he wouldn't reject her. Maybe she was enough for him. "Seth…"

He wrapped his arms around her. "You're cold. I'm

sorry that we had to stay at the scene so long. That's another reason you should have left with Ty."

"He had to stay, too. We both had to talk to the police," she reminded him. "We were eyewitnesses to the shooting." But that shooting and those earlier attacks on her were all that Curtis Waverly had done. He hadn't killed his stepsister. He had loved her, and his grief had driven him to insanity.

She could understand love driving one beyond reason. She was afraid that she loved Seth like that. And if something happened to him…

Seth shook his head. "I didn't think he killed her or the others. But he kept trying to kill you."

"You saved my life." And had nearly lost his own. She wrapped her arms around his waist, the holster at the small of his back digging into her forearm. "You saved my life again."

"Always," he said. "I will always keep you safe. Please believe that—that you're safe with me."

Growing up as she had, always on the run, always knowing she was cursed, she had never felt safe. Until now, until Seth Hughes held her tight.

Her heart shifted in her chest, warming and swelling, as love for him filled her. She had never felt like this. None of anyone else's emotions or even her own had been as intense as what she felt for Special Agent Seth Hughes. She opened her mouth, wanting to share her feelings with him as their intensity overwhelmed her.

But he lowered his head and took her open lips in a deep kiss. His tongue slid over hers, tasting—teasing.

She slid her hands up his back to his broad shoulders. Then she pushed off his jacket. He released her—just long enough to strip the sleeves from his arms. Then he grabbed her again, clutching her close to him.

But she pressed her hands against his chest and pulled free. Just long enough to drag off her sweater and kick off her jeans...until she stood before him naked. It wasn't just her body she bared to him, though. She bared her heart, too, as she made love with him, kissing every bruised and scratched inch of his skin she exposed as she stripped off his clothes. She stroked her fingertips over every sculpted muscle, which rippled beneath her touch.

He made love to her, too, kissing and touching her everywhere she loved: her lips, the side of her neck, the curve of her collarbone. Then his mouth closed over a nipple, his teeth scraping gently across the point before he stroked his tongue over it.

She moaned and lifted her legs, wrapping them around his waist, holding tight as he carried her to the bed. He laid her on the edge of the mattress. Then he kissed her some more, his mouth skimming down her body. His tongue stroked over her clit now, back and forth before dipping inside her.

"Seth!" She came, her body trembling.

But before the pleasure ebbed away, he was there— thrusting inside her. The pressure built again, winding tighter and tighter. She locked her legs around his waist once more, matching his every thrust.

He leaned down, kissing her deeply. His tongue stroked in and out of her mouth, across hers. Then his lips skimmed down her throat, his tongue teasing her pulse—making it jump wildly as the pressure broke free.

She clutched at him, holding him close as the orgasm slammed through her. Overwhelmed with pleasure, Maria could not hold in her feelings any longer. "I love you! I love you, Seth!"

He didn't return the declaration. He just held her closely, wrapping her tightly in his arms, as if he had meant what he'd said, as if he never intended to let her go.

Maybe that would have to be enough for her—since she had never been enough for anyone else. She hadn't actually expected him to return her feelings. She hadn't actually expected him to love her when no one else had.

Once he fell asleep beside her, she tugged free of his arms. She pulled on his shirt and buttoned just a couple of buttons, then headed down to his den.

Instead of turning on the lights, she lit the candles that sat on his desk. And in the flickering glow, she studied the whiteboard and the pictures of all those poor victims.

"I know who killed you all," she said. If it wasn't Curtis Waverly, it had to be Ethan O'Donnell. "It's time to stop him. To make sure he doesn't kill anyone else."

Especially not Seth.

"Help me," she implored their spirits. "Tell me where your killer is."

But no mist formed. It was so late that even the spirits must be tired. Restlessness filled Maria so that she couldn't relax. She couldn't sleep. Now that she knew who the killer was, she just wanted him stopped. Before he killed again…

Before he killed Seth.

She settled into the chair behind his desk. Unlike the one at the bureau, the leather was supple, the cushions thick and comfortable. But she couldn't relax, not even in the chair. Maybe Seth had something she could drink, something to ease her tension.

She opened a drawer and peered inside. Something

glinted in the dim light, but it wasn't a bottle. It was metal—ancient pewter—from a locket.

Her heart slammed into her ribs. Her fingers shaking, she fumbled around for the chain and pulled it from the drawer. The big oval locket dangled from the chain. The clasp had been replaced.

He'd fixed her chain. Why did he have it?

When had he found it?

And what else did he have? A book lay beneath the locket, the leather cover probably as old as the locket. Why wasn't it on the shelves in here or in the library, which was next to his den? Why was it hidden away like the locket?

She lifted it out. And as she did, an envelope slipped from between the cover and the brittle pages. The letter wasn't that old, maybe just a few years. The sender was a law firm, the addressee, Seth McGregor Roarke.

Dread clenched her stomach, so tightly that she doubled over with pain. She didn't even need to open the book to know to whom it belonged. It was the journal of Eli McGregor—the first witch-hunter. The man who had started all the killing over three hundred years ago.

Her fingers trembling, she pulled the letter from the envelope. The first sheet was from the law firm; it discussed his inheritance as the only heir of Donovan Roarke. The next sheet was from his father:

Mac,
If you're receiving this letter, it's because my vision came true and the witches killed me, burning me at the stake like I burned their mother. I haven't seen you in many years, but no matter how your mother tried to change you, I know that you

are a McGregor through and through. You have
the special abilities—the visions.

You won't be like Thomas, who let the witch
go instead of making certain her lineage ended
by killing her. You will be like Eli, like me. You'll
avenge my death. You won't rest until all the
witches are gone.

Seth awoke with a start, angry that he had fallen
asleep. Again. He reached across the bed. The sheets
were still warm from her body. The scent of sandalwood
and lavender hung yet in the air, filling his senses. But
she was gone.

He jerked upright. He had to find her—before Ethan
O'Donnell did. The image flashed through his mind—
that first one.

Maria sat at the foot of his bed, her naked back
to him. She leaned down, her hair falling forward—
swirling around her shoulders. Leaving her back completely bare but for that trio of tattoos. And the thin
chain of her locket.

Or was the image inside his head? It seemed so
real—as though he could reach out and stroke his fingers across her silky soft skin. "Maria?"

She stood up then and turned toward him…and just
like in his vision, she held his gun. Instead of staring
down the barrel of the gun, he stared at the locket nestled between her naked breasts.

"You found it." He had intended to give it back to her.
Eventually. After he had explained everything to her.

"How did you get it?" she asked.

"It was in Raven's hand," he replied. "I found it when
I gave her CPR at the barn."

"And you took it?" she asked. "Why did you take it?"

"I thought it was evidence," he explained. "More proof that the two of you had struggled before her death."

"But you didn't put it in an evidence bag."

He had wanted to, but he hadn't been able to seal the locket away in plastic. To him it wasn't just a piece of jewelry. It was a piece of history—his history as much as or more than Maria's—and proof that all his descendants hadn't been as evil as Eli McGregor or his father.

"You brought it home with you," she pointed out. "You fixed the clasp. Why?" Her voice shook with anger and fear, and the gun shook in her hands.

He glanced at it, then met her gaze. "I brought it home for me," he admitted. "Because it belonged to my family."

The pictures still inside had been drawn by Thomas McGregor, of his little sisters, who had died in the lightning fire of which Maria's ancestor had warned them. "But then, after getting to know you and realizing you weren't responsible for the murders, I accepted that it's yours. That's why I fixed the clasp, so you could wear it again. I wanted to give it back to you."

"Why?" she asked. "Like you said, it belongs to your family. It's yours, Mac."

His gut tensed with dread and regret. She had found the journal, too. His sad and sinister inheritance from his father. "Don't call me that," he snapped, and he began to shake, as he had every time his father had called him that—usually after he'd beat the crap out of him or his mother. "Don't *ever* call me that."

"Where did the *Hughes* come from?"

"My stepfather—my *real* father, the man who protected and hid us from the madman who used to abuse my mother and me."

She nodded. "That was how you knew the witch-hunter wasn't Curtis Waverly. That's probably also why you identified with Curtis—you shared similar pasts and both took your stepfathers' names."

"You were right about my biological father," he said. "He was crazy." Seth leaned forward, tempted to reach for the gun. But that other image flashed through his mind, of her firing the weapon. "You're wrong about *me*, though. I want nothing to do with that sick legacy. I am *not* my father's son. I'm not a McGregor."

"You're the last one."

"Your eldest sister is one, too. She's a descendant somehow. So are your niece and your four-year-old nephew. They're McGregors," he reminded her. "Do you think they'll automatically become witch-hunters just because of their genetics? It doesn't work that way."

"Why not? We're all witches just because we're Durikken descendants. You are what you are." She raised that gun, pointing the barrel directly at his heart. "And I can never trust you because of it, but most of all because you lied to me about it!"

He shook his head. "I didn't lie." He was not a liar. "I just didn't tell you."

"Because you knew I would never trust you if you told me the truth," she said. "You knew I would never fall in love with you."

His heart ached with the intensity of his love for her, the love he had known he couldn't declare until she knew his true identity. He held out his hand—not for the gun but for her. "Maria…"

"Was that all part of your plan?" she asked as tears streaked down her face.

"Plan?" he asked, his head pounding with confusion.

"Are you working with Ethan O'Donnell? Or maybe

even Curtis Waverly—you two share a common past. Maybe you convinced him that I'm the one who killed his sister so that he would kill me," she said, her eyes dark with mistrust.

If she had been falling in love with him, it wasn't apparent now. She stared at him, her expression hard with hatred.

"Neither of them is smart enough or evil enough to pull this off on their own. As I suspected all along, there had to be a McGregor behind it."

He sucked in a breath of pain. After all they had shared, how could she think him evil just because of who his father had been?

"You might as well shoot me," he suggested, pointing toward the gun, "just like I saw in my vision. It would probably hurt less than hearing your opinion of me." And having all his fears confirmed—she would never trust him. Never love him as he loved her.

The barrel trembled, the gun shaking in her grasp. "What? It was me? You saw *me* shoot you?"

"I saw this," he confirmed. "You with the gun, you firing that gun into my chest when you found out who I was." He swallowed hard. "Was. I got rid of his name. I wanted nothing to do with him and nothing to do with that damn legend."

She shook her head. "I'm not going to shoot you," she said, "unless you try to stop me."

"Stop you? From killing me?"

Since she was so fixated on the past, she probably thought that was the only way to end the witch hunt— kill the witch-hunter's son, no matter that he'd had nothing to do with the killing.

"From leaving," she clarified. She held the gun with

one hand while she grabbed up her clothes from the floor.

He lurched forward, hoping to disarm her. But she lifted the barrel to his chest again, to the heart that ached with fear over the thought of her out there without him, at the mercy of the real killer. "You can't leave."

"I swear I'll shoot you," she threatened. "You saw it, so you know that I will."

"I saw other things, too," he shared. "I saw you being drowned."

"You saw my death?"

Maybe if he told her what he'd seen, she wouldn't leave him; she would understand that the danger she was in wasn't from him.

"You don't die by drowning," he said. "He only holds you underwater until you pass out. Then he ties you up, holding you down while he piles rocks on top of you." She gasped, but he forced himself to continue—for her sake. "That's how you die—he crushes you to death."

Tears ran down her cheeks; he wasn't even sure she knew she was crying, though. She was so focused—on hating him. "You only saw that because it's you. That's what you want to do to me."

"I want to protect you, Maria." He swallowed hard, choking on the emotion overwhelming him. Now that she knew all his secrets, he could give her the words he had struggled to contain earlier.

When she'd told him she loved him, he had wanted to declare his feelings. But it wouldn't have been fair... until he'd told her the truth. Now, staring down the barrel of his own damn gun, he didn't care about fair.

"I love you, Maria," he said. "And I want to love you, Maria, for the rest of our lives."

"That'll be short if you try to stop me," she warned

him, clutching her clothes to her chest with one hand
while she held the gun with the other. She moved around
the bed, her gaze trained on him.

"And it'll be short if you leave me," he said. "We've
fought him off because we've been together. You won't
be able to fight him alone."

"I won't be alone," she assured him, "because I'm
keeping your gun." She ducked into the bathroom, the
lock snapping behind her.

He followed her and pounded lightly on the door.
He might have considered kicking it open, but then she
would no doubt believe he was trying to hurt her—and
she would hurt him by firing the gun.

"Maria, you have to know I would never hurt you.
I'm not the monster my father was. You have to know
that." He had struggled with his own doubts growing
up, and so had his mother. When he'd started having
visions, she had been so frightened that he was going
to be like his father. That was why he'd wanted to become an FBI agent, to use his gift for good—not to hurt
people as his father had.

"We have this connection," he reminded her. "I feel
as though I've known you forever. You have to feel the
same way about me. You wouldn't have made love with
me if you really believed I was a killer."

The door opened again, and he drew in a breath,
hopeful that he'd gotten through to her. But, dressed
now, she still held the gun. He would have grabbed it
from her if not for the vision taunting him. He had seen
her fire it, and from the cold glare she directed at him,
she no longer had any feelings for him.

"I don't know you at all," she said. "You made sure
of that—with all the secrets you've kept from me. Secrets I should have known…"

"You told me you loved me," he reminded her.

"I was wrong," she said. "I didn't even know who you were. Now that I know, there's no way I could ever love you. The hatred between our families runs too deep."

"It wasn't all hate," he reminded her. "Thomas gave Elena that locket. He loved her."

She glanced down at the locket. "He did love her, and he wanted to protect her. That's why he let her go."

"I can't let you go," he said, holding his hand out for the gun.

She shook her head, her eyes glistening with more tears and disappointment. "Then you don't love me, either."

He looked down the barrel. And he had no doubt now that she would shoot him.

But if he let her leave and something happened to her, he would die anyway. So he grabbed for the gun, and just like in his vision, it went off...

Chapter 14

She moved like a criminal—like Joseph used to move. He had once been able to go invisible—able to move around the most dangerous area of the city undetected. How did his men not notice her?

Was she real?

Or maybe he and his daughter Stacia were so close that he was getting like her, and he had begun to see ghosts, too. The two-way radio he held crackled in his hand. Finally they'd noticed her.

"Joe," Shorty said. "There's some scary chick coming up to your front door—dressed in some cape thing. And she's armed, man."

"She has a gun?" he asked with surprise. From everything her sisters had told him, Maria wasn't the type to go for weapons. With her powers, she didn't need them.

"Sorry, man, that she got past the guys," Shorty said. "You want me to send up some guards—"

"No," Joseph said as Ty headed down the stairs to the foyer. "We've been expecting her."

They had been anticipating her, actually, and for a long time.

Maria couldn't stop shaking, and it had nothing to do with the cold autumn air of the predawn hours. She had fired a gun—a gun she had stolen from an FBI agent. That wasn't all she'd taken from him, though.

She clasped the McGregor journal under one arm as she stood outside the door to her sister's estate. She had slipped past security and made it through the gates surrounding the estate, but not inside the mammoth stone-and-clapboard house. She waited on the porch, in the shadows, her heart pounding with fear and adrenaline.

What if Seth had chased her here? What if she had led the witch-hunter right to her family?

But he already knew Ty, so he probably knew where her sisters were. Why hadn't he tried to hurt them, then? They were the ones who'd killed his father, the ones on whom his father had asked that Seth—that *Mac*—seek vengeance.

Could she have been wrong about him?

She wished she was, but then his voice echoed inside her head, emotionlessly recounting his gruesome visions of her death. She shuddered and then gasped when the door finally drew open.

"Maria, are you okay?" Ty McIntyre asked as he ushered her inside and peered out into the darkness beyond her. "Where's Hughes?"

She glanced back into the darkness, too, in case he'd followed her. There were other men out there—security guards. But he wasn't there. If he were close, she would have felt it. She would have felt *him*.

"Hughes is not his name," she said, clasping the book

even tighter. She had kept the gun, too, in the pocket of the cape she'd pulled from his closet on her way out his door. He'd had the clothes she'd worn in the fire cleaned. "I need to warn my sisters. I know it's late—or early—but I need you to bring them together for me."

"They're all here," he said as he shut the door behind her.

Had they known she would need them?

"Ariel and Elena are staying to help out Irina while she's confined to bed rest." He led her to a wide stairwell. "They're all together in our room."

"And you don't mind?"

He grinned. "I'm a lucky man to have an amazing wife and the support of her incredible sisters. With seven-year-old twins, I could never manage on my own."

"You're busy," she said. "Maybe I shouldn't be here." Especially as there were children in the house, children she might be putting in danger.

"I'm glad you're here," he assured her. "Your sisters are, too."

"They already know?"

His grin widened. "They probably knew you were coming before you did." He led the way up the stairwell and to an open door off a wide hall. His arm extended, he waited for her to cross over the threshold.

But she hesitated, her stomach tight with nerves, and panic overwhelmed her. "I—I shouldn't be here." Her presence might still put them at risk. "It's not safe to be around me." She turned back to the stairs. "I need to leave…"

"No!" Ty's raspy voice wasn't the one that uttered the protest. This voice was soft and feminine yet strong and certain, too. "You're where you belong."

She didn't belong here; she had never belonged anywhere. Although for a little while, she had felt as though she'd belonged…with Seth. But he wasn't who she'd thought he was. And she needed to warn her family that he was the witch-hunter. She drew in a breath, bracing herself, before she turned back to that bedroom doorway.

A redhead stood next to Ty, her fingers gripping his forearm. "It's her—it's really her…" She blinked back a shimmer of tears and gazed intently at Maria. "You look so much like Mama…even more than Irina does. You look so much like her."

"You do," agreed the blonde who stood behind the taller redhead. She was petite with flaxen blond hair and pale blue eyes. "I'm so glad you're here." She stepped forward and stared at Maria, as if unable to believe that she was real. "I keep seeing horrible things."

Things like Seth had claimed he'd seen? But he probably saw those things only because he was doing them to her. It was his hands drowning her until she lost consciousness, his hands piling rocks on top of her until she lost her life.

"Don't torture the fat chick," a voice murmured from inside the room. "I can't get out of bed without these babies falling out. Please bring Maria in here."

Ariel and Elena laughed. Then they reached for Maria, each taking one of her arms. They pulled her into the bedroom with them. Tiffany lamps brightened the large master bedroom and shone across the face of the woman lying on the sleigh bed. Her palms cradled her belly, as if she were already holding her unborn children.

Since she could read minds, she probably knew that

she needed to protect them from Maria, from the dark aura that always hung over her.

Irina lifted her hands from her belly and held out her arms. "I'm so glad you're here."

From the first moment she had met Irina, Maria had felt the deep connection with her. Deeper than any connection she'd had with anyone…until she had met Seth Hughes. But that one hadn't been real, because he wasn't real.

"Maria," her sister called to her as if from a distance, bringing her back to them from her maudlin thoughts.

She moved closer to the bed, which Ariel and Elena had already settled onto, but she didn't embrace her sister. Irina was the one who looked like Mama, eerily so.

"We've been looking for you for so long," the dark-haired woman said.

"We've been so worried about you," Ariel added.

"There's no reason to worry anymore," she assured them. She had her life even though she'd lost her heart. "I know who the witch-hunter is."

"You don't," Irina said with a sad shake of her head. "You think you know, but you're wrong."

Maria had been so upset over what she'd learned that she must have stopped blocking her thoughts from her telepathic sister. But the others couldn't hear, so she had to explain. "I'm not wrong. And I have the proof right here."

She handed the journal and the letter over to her oldest sister. Elena's father had been a McGregor descendant, but like Thomas, he had fallen in love with their mother and hadn't been able to hurt her. So Elena's grandmother had carried on the McGregor curse, hurting Mama by having her children taken away.

Well, all the children she'd known about; she hadn't known about Maria.

"It's Eli McGregor's journal," Maria explained. "And that letter is from Mama's killer to his son. FBI Agent Seth Hughes is his son. He's the witch-hunter."

She waited for a reaction, for the shock and betrayal she had felt when she'd discovered her locket and the journal in his desk drawer. But they just stared at her. All of them—even Ty, who stood by the open door.

And the shock and betrayal was all hers again. "You knew!" she exclaimed as she backed away from the bed. "You all knew who he was!"

"My husband just found out," Ariel said. "Seth and his mother had changed all their records to hide from Roarke. They'd done a good job of changing his identity."

"So no one would know who and what he is," she said. "A killer. He intends to kill me." Instead he had made love with her and had made her fall in love with him. If only she had known the truth…

"No," Ty insisted. "He really thought *you* were the killer. That was why he's been chasing you all these years—to arrest you. Not to kill you. He would never hurt you."

Her brother-in-law was wrong about that. By keeping the truth from her, Seth had hurt her. The pain and betrayal she felt was worse than when Mama had left her.

Maria shook her head in denial of Ty's claim. "No…"

"I can *feel* his feelings," Irina said. "He's a good man. And he loves you."

Seth had claimed that he did, but Maria couldn't believe that he could love her. She couldn't believe that *anyone* could love her.

"We love you, too," Irina said, speaking again to Maria's thoughts.

Maria shook her head again, unable to accept their love. "You don't even know me."

Elena laughed. "I've had so many visions that I feel as if I've lived your life with you. And Irina has felt all your emotions. We know you."

"And we love you," Ariel added. Her heart shone from her eyes, the turquoise glowing. She was one of those women—one of those generous, loving women.

Maria had wanted to be that kind of woman, but she'd been too busy running all these years. From Seth?

"You can trust him," Irina assured her. "He's not his father."

"He's not the danger," Elena said, her pale eyes glazing over as she slipped into another vision. "He's the one in danger."

"What do you see?" Ariel asked, wrapping her arm around her older sister's tiny waist. "What do you see?"

Elena shook her head. "I don't know. The vision isn't clear…"

Ariel lifted the blonde's delicate wrist, adorned with a charm bracelet with only one charm. A star. And she pressed her own wrist, her own charm—a sun—against it. Irina reached over and joined her hand with theirs, metal glinting off her wrist and the tiny crescent moon that dangled from a bracelet.

The room warmed, alive with energy. Mama hadn't been lying or even exaggerating about the charms. They did have special powers.

And so did Maria's sisters.

That was how they'd stopped Seth's father. Forever. It was how they'd saved her. They were powerful women. Women she could trust…

Elena slipped into a trancelike state, her eyes locked in a blank inward stare. "He's bleeding," she murmured.

"I didn't shoot him," Maria said as she withdrew his gun from the pocket of the cape she had found in his closet. "I shot in the air—so that he would back off and let me leave. I didn't want him following me. I didn't want to lead him to all of you."

"He knows where we live," Ty said. "I've given him my address. I've invited him here."

"He loves you," Irina repeated insistently. "That's why he didn't dare tell you who his father was. He hated the man, too. His father abused him and his mother. They ran from him, hid from him. He grew up like you and Mama did, running from place to place. You were all running from the same monster."

He had told her the truth, then—about his childhood, about his hatred for his father.

"But the book." Her fingers trembling, she reached for her locket. "And the locket. He had the locket, too. He took it from Raven." She turned to Ty. "The girl who died in Copper Creek. I think he killed her."

"No." Ty shook his head. "You know he didn't. Look what he's done to protect you. He got run off the road. He nearly died. He's not the killer. And you know he's not."

She wrapped her fingers tightly around the locket. "No, he's not…"

And she had threatened him with a gun despite everything he had done for her. But she had been so stunned and so hurt to learn that he'd been keeping secrets from her—secrets that he knew would affect her. All those times she had brought up the witch-hunter, he should have told her the truth. But he'd kept silent.

Finding out the truth as she had, on her own by

accident, had devastated her. And she had been too emotional to think rationally. She had reacted like a wounded animal, lashing out at the person closest to her. And no one had ever been as close as Seth.

Elena grasped her sisters' hands and squeezed her eyes shut, focusing on the images in her head. "He's in danger. Extreme danger."

"Because of me?" Maria asked, her heart heavy with dread.

"He's found the real killer," Elena replied.

"He found Ethan O'Donnell?" And because of her, Seth didn't have his gun to defend himself from the madman.

Ariel shook her head. "No. It won't be possible for Seth to find O'Donnell."

"Why not?" Was Seth already dead?

Ariel could see ghosts, too. Maybe after the way Maria had treated him, he had gone to her sister instead of her. Tears stung her eyes. Had she lost the man she loved…forever?

"Ethan O'Donnell is dead," Ariel said. "Can't you see him?"

Maria blinked, trying to clear her eyes. When had the mist swept into the room?

"Mama brought him," Ariel murmured, her voice sounding far away. "She guided him here—to us."

"Ethan?" The mist shifted into a male form—tall, gawky, with slicked-back hair. "Ethan. What happened? Did Seth do this to you?" Maybe Ariel was wrong and the two men had already had a confrontation. Seth had promised to protect her—always.

"Seth?" the young man asked. "Who's Seth?"

"The FBI agent," she said. "Isn't that who killed you?"

The ghost's image blurred as he shook his head. "No.

I don't know the FBI agent. I know my killer. So do you."

"Oh, my God…" She closed her eyes on a wave of dread and fear. And an image flashed behind her lids.

Seth, clutching his chest, blood spurting between his splayed fingers. All the color draining from his face as his life ebbed away…

She hadn't shot Seth but someone else would—or already had. Had the killer confronted Seth at his house, or had Seth stumbled across the man when he had gone looking for her?

"Maria, do you know who the killer is?" Ty asked, his brows drawn together in confusion. He couldn't see or hear ghosts; he had no idea what Ethan had said. He must have just noticed the horror that gripped her.

She nodded and tightened her grasp around the gun. "I have to go. I have to get there before it's too late. Seth thinks Ethan is the killer. He won't realize he's in danger…"

Until he was dying.

"Send Seth a message," Irina suggested. "Warn him."

"He has visions, but he's not telepathic," Maria replied. "He's had visions of my death. He warned me. But I didn't listen to him. I didn't trust him. I told him that I would never trust him—that I would never love him." And now it might be too late for her to take those words back, for her to profess her love again.

"Tell him," Irina said. "You don't have to be telepathic. Not when you have the connection the two of you have. Ty has no special powers, but he can hear me…without my having to say a word. He can hear me because of our love."

Ty tensed, as if he was listening now. "You're going into labor."

"Tell him you love him—" A grimace twisted Irina's face as the labor pains began.

But she didn't need to finish what she had been about to say. *Tell him you love him...before it's too late.*

"I have to go," Maria said. "I have to save him." She headed toward the door, stopped and turned back. "I'm sorry. I want to be part of this family. But I'll be nothing if Seth dies. I'll be nothing…"

"You can't go alone. Wait for me," Ty said, but even as he said the words, he stepped closer to his wife, his arms reaching for her.

"I—I can't wait…"

Because Seth couldn't wait for help; he would be dead soon—because of her.

"I'm sorry to come by at this hour," Seth said as Professor Chandler opened the door. He glanced over his shoulder, looking for the police cars that were supposed to be stationed out front. "Where are the officers?"

The professor shook his head. "I sent them away. I'm fine. Perfectly safe. Ethan O'Donnell would never come after me."

"What about Maria?" he asked, his pulse racing with fear. "Has she been here?"

"She left your protection?"

"Yes." Because he'd lied to her, he had destroyed whatever trust she'd had in him. "This is the only place I could think that she would come."

"Really?" Dr. Chandler asked. "Doesn't she have sisters who live here in Barrett, too?"

"Yes, but she hasn't wanted to see them." Because she had thought Seth—the witch-hunter—would try to kill them, too. "You're the only person she's kept in touch with over the years. You're the only person she trusts."

"The only?" The professor lifted a dark brow. "When you were here earlier this evening, you two seemed quite close."

Seth flinched, remembering how close they had been—his body entwined with hers, buried deep inside her. Their hearts beating the same frantic rhythm.

"Maria doesn't let anyone close to her. Not anymore."

And certainly not him. Never again would Seth get close to her.

"She doesn't trust you? Why wouldn't she trust you?"

"I kept something from her," he admitted. "Something I should have told her when we first met."

"That you're a McGregor descendant."

Shock jarred Seth. "You know that?"

How? He and his mother had been careful to erase their past and any connection to Donovan Roarke. They'd wanted to make sure that he would never find them again. And that no one would ever associate them with the monster the man had been. But their new identity hadn't been foolproof, since Roarke's lawyer and executor had eventually tracked him down.

The professor nodded. "I've been researching that book, you know. About the Durikkens and the McGregors and the Coopers and the Roarkes. I tracked everyone down."

"I'm not a witch-hunter, like she believes," Seth assured her father. "I want nothing to do with that crazy legacy."

"I know. She will, too," the professor said. "Just like her sisters aren't really witches."

"No, they're not," he agreed with a sigh of relief. At

least her father understood. "They have some special abilities, though."

"But they don't practice witchcraft," Dr. Chandler said. "They don't cast spells and concoct magic potions. Not like Maria does. She's a real witch, like her long-dead ancestor. Your father shouldn't have gone after the other women at all."

"He was a crazy, sadistic bastard." And no one knew that better than Seth…except for Maria's mother, whom he had so brutally murdered.

How could Maria think, after all the times they had made love, that Seth was anything like his father?

I love you…

The thought popped into his head just as the visions usually did. Those horrifying visions…of Maria suffering. He had to find her.

I love you…

He flinched, his head pounding as if someone were knocking on it—trying to get inside, trying to read his mind.

"Uh, uh…" He pushed a hand through his hair. "So you never answered my question," he said. "Have you seen Maria tonight?"

"I was asleep," he said, gesturing at the robe he wore over flannel pajamas.

"And I'm sorry I woke you," Seth said. "I just really need to find her." Before any of those horrible visions became reality.

"She has her own key, you know," the professor remarked as if just now remembering. "Maybe we should check the house to see if she came in while I was sleeping."

"Thank you," Seth said. "I appreciate you letting me look around."

The professor nodded. "Sure. I want to make sure she's all right, too. I can check upstairs. I doubt she's up there, though. I would have heard her."

Seth nodded. "I'll look around down here. Thanks again." He hurried around the house, throwing open doors and turning on lights since the fog had come down with him from Copper Creek. The thick mist clung around the house, darkening the windows despite dawn's arrival.

"Professor." He paused at the bottom of the stairs. "Professor? Is she up there?"

"No," the older man called down. "Did you check the basement?"

He hadn't, but the door was there, just around the back of the steps that led up. It stood open, a bare bulb swinging over the stairs leading down. Each step creaked beneath his weight as Seth descended to the dimly lit cellar. When his foot hit the cement floor, he paused and listened.

Something shifted and dropped onto and then rolled across the floor. And someone moaned.

His heart slammed into his ribs, and he shouted her name. "Maria!"

Water stained the floor, overflowed from a wooden vat in the middle of the partial cellar. In front of a stone foundation wall, he saw another mound of rocks.

"Oh, my God! Maria!" Everything from his vision had happened just as he'd imagined it.

And just like in his vision, he couldn't see her face; her head was turned away, her long wet hair soaking the floor beneath her. He ran to her and began to lift the rocks from her body. She hadn't been completely covered yet. Maybe she wasn't crushed, just unconscious from the water in her lungs.

"Get away from her," a deep voice warned.

Seth reached for his gun, but the holster was not at the back of his belt. It was sitting empty on his bedside table. Still crouched next to her body, he lifted off another rock, his hands wrapped tightly around it.

"Put it down," the professor ordered, as authoritatively as he might have commanded one of his students to follow directions in class. He cocked the gun in his hand and trained the barrel right at Seth's chest.

If Maria was dead, it didn't matter if the madman shot him in the heart. He had already lost it...to her.

"You're going to have to shoot me," he told the professor, "because I'm not going to let her die."

"She's a witch," her father said. "She needs to die."

"She's your daughter."

"Maria Cooper is an evil sorceress," Professor Chandler insisted, "just like her mother. Myra Cooper tricked me and seduced me—with her magic potions and mind control."

"You can't blame Maria for what her mother did," Seth said. If only she hadn't held against him what his father had done...however horrible it had been.

"Maria tries to do the same," Chandler said. "She uses me for money—to open those little witchcraft shops of hers."

Seth asked the question he'd never understood. "Why do you give her the money?"

"She messes with my mind," he said. "She makes me feel as though I owe it to her. But I didn't know about her. I didn't know that I'd had a daughter—with the witch. Just like her mother, she deserves to die. It's the only way I'll be free of her."

While the professor was distracted, Seth knocked off another rock. Maria shifted and moaned. But still she faced away from Seth. He had to see her, had to look into her eyes and assure her that she would be okay. He would keep his promise to protect her.

He wouldn't betray her trust again.

I love you...

Was it just his thought—his love for her—echoing inside his head? Or was that her voice he heard? Hell, he could smell her—the sandalwood and lavender that always filled the air whenever she was near.

Wouldn't her fragrance have washed away in the water that soaked her hair and clothes?

"She's your daughter," he repeated. "You can't want to hurt her like this. You can't want to kill her as you have the others."

"She's a witch," the professor said with disgust. "She has to die. All witches have to die! You know this—because of who your father was."

Seth shook his head and rose from his crouch, a rock clutched behind his back. "I'm not going to let you kill her. I love her."

"Then I guess you'll have to die for her."

Before he could react, before he could hurl the rock he clenched, a gunshot rang out, echoing off the cement walls of the cellar. Pain exploded inside him.

He couldn't die. Because if he died, Maria was dead, too.

Chapter 15

Pain pressed down on Stacia, squeezing the breath from her lungs, the blood from her heart. There was pain…

So much pain.

She couldn't stand it anymore. It was tearing her apart. She had to stop it before it destroyed her—before it destroyed them all. She had to stop everyone's pain…

She opened her palm and stared down at the charms. They had been so preoccupied—her mom and her aunts—that they hadn't noticed her slipping them off their bracelets. Aunt Irina had gone into labor, so she'd taken hers off so as not to scratch her babies. Mom and Aunt Ariel had done the same, leaving them all on the dresser just inside the master bedroom.

They would understand. Maybe…

That she'd had to take them. She had to save them and everyone else. But the evil man…

The charms protected the pure and vanquished the evil. They had destroyed the bad man who'd taken away the innocence of her childhood. He hadn't physically harmed her. But he'd shown her an evil that had stolen her innocence. She had had to grow up too fast.

But because she was older than her thirteen years, she knew what she had to do—just as that ancestor for whom her mom had been named had known what she'd had to do. Run. Stacia refused to run. She had to be strong. It helped that Grandma Myra's ghost was embracing her, wrapping the mist and smoke and her ghostly arms around her.

Stacia squeezed the charms tightly in her palm. Her skin warmed as the pewter heated and glowed, shining right through the skin and bones of her hand, illuminating them like an X-ray. This was how her mom and sisters had stopped the witch-hunter.

She hoped that it would work now. She hoped she would save her aunt Maria. And stop her aunt Irina's pain...

And her own...

Because all the pain was tearing Stacia apart.

And then it wasn't just her and Grandma. Her father was there, too, wrapping his arms around them both. He shivered, as if he felt her grandmother's ghost. But he held Stacia tightly; he held her together as the magic flowed through her...

Maria fought to still the trembling in her hand. She had never tried to kill anyone before, had never fired a weapon at a person. She was all about healing with her herbs, protecting with her amulets and crystals. She wasn't about killing. But she would do whatever was necessary to defend the man she loved.

"Put down the gun!" she screamed at her father from where she stood behind him in the rickety stairwell. "Put it down, or my next shot will hit you."

The professor shook his head. "You didn't mean to hit me. You shot the right person. Agent Hughes—he's the one you hit. The one you should have hit..."

She gasped and ducked her head to see where Seth knelt next to a pile of rocks. He held his hand to his shoulder, where blood trickled down the sleeve of his jacket.

"Oh, my God..." She had done it, just like in his vision. She had shot the man she loved. The bullet she'd fired at the professor must have ricocheted off the stone walls or the stones piled beside Seth. Had her father been about to torture him?

"Maria?" Seth murmured, and his smoky blue eyes widened in shock—more over seeing her than her shooting him. He glanced from her to the pile of rocks. And then she noticed that the stones surrounded a body, one that had been tied down to stakes anchored in the floor.

Just as he had warned her that he'd seen in his visions. There was even the vat of water where a witch could be drowned.

She had been in this house before. But never in the cellar. Had this stuff always been down here?

"Who is that?" she asked, horrified that a body was beneath those stones. "Is it Ethan?"

"It's a woman," Seth replied. "I thought it was you."

"Of course he thought it was you," the professor said. "That's why he's trying to kill her. That's why I have the gun. I'm trying to stop him."

Maria's gaze traveled from Seth to her father. Had the man moved closer? She tightened her grip on the gun. "He was trying to stop you."

"No, I found him down here," the professor blatantly lied. She could see the untruth in his gaze. "I thought that woman was you," he continued. "I'm so glad you're all right, honey. Hand me the gun."

"No!" She backed up a step and nearly stumbled.

"He's the one," the professor insisted. "You know who he is. A McGregor. He's the witch-hunter. His father killed your mother and would have killed your sisters if they hadn't banded together."

Maria glanced over his head to where Seth crept closer to the bottom of the stairs. He widened his eyes as if he was trying to send her a telepathic message. She had been sending him one ever since she'd left her sisters.

Had he heard her? Did he know that she loved him? She needed him to know that, needed to connect with him so that they could work together, as her sisters had, to vanquish this killer.

But she didn't have the charms. All she had was her locket. And Seth's gun. He should have had his gun. He would have saved her already. He would have saved whoever lay beneath those rocks, too.

"If he's the witch-hunter, why hasn't he killed me?" she asked. "We've been alone together many times. He had opportunity." And so had her father. "Why kill other people? Why not just kill me?"

"All the witches have to die," Dr. Chandler replied— too quickly. Color rushed to his face as he hastened to add, "You know that's how the witch-hunter thinks."

And now she knew for certain who the witch-hunter was. Ethan O'Donnell hadn't had to say a name. She knew...

"If Seth was the killer, why wouldn't he have killed

my sisters?" she asked. "He's known where they are longer than he's known where I was. And they're the ones who killed his father."

"But they're not real witches," the professor said with disdain. "They don't practice like you do, like those other witches wanted to learn from you—how to manipulate people. They had to be stopped." Madness glowed in his eyes. How had she not noticed it before?

Of course, she hadn't seen him very often in the years since she'd discovered who he was. She had never felt comfortable around him, and now she knew why.

He was evil.

"Who's that?" she asked, using her shoulder to gesture toward the rocks and the water-stained cement. "Who's being stopped right now?"

"That last witch's sister. She's a real witch, too. More powerful even than you, Maria," he said with begrudging respect. "She figured it out."

"That you killed her sister." He must have been the man who Raven had been staying with—that was why she'd been so private about him. She'd probably been embarrassed that he was so much older.

He shook his head, but the insanity flashing in his eyes belied his action.

"No, it was him," he insisted. "He's the McGregor heir. He's the one who killed her sister. He's the one trying to kill her." He lifted the gun. "I was just trying to stop him. Let me stop him…because he's going to kill you next. He just let you live so you could lure the others. The ones who wanted to be like you, with the potions and amulets, those were the real witches."

"They're not hurting people," she said. "I don't hurt people."

He jerked his head in a quick nod of agreement. "You're right. Of course. But he does. He hurts people. So let me stop him before he hurts you." He turned back, his gun drawn, but Seth was there with the rock. He swung it at the professor's hand, knocking his weapon to the floor. It skittered across the cement.

But Dr. Chandler was too crazy to stop killing now. He launched himself off the steps, his fists flying at Seth. Grunts and groans emanated from the two men as they locked in combat, grappling together on the floor.

Maria didn't just hear the pain in Seth's voice. She felt it, felt the burning in his shoulder from where her bullet had struck him. She lifted the gun again, but she dared not shoot yet. They moved too fast, rolling across the cement. One of them reached out toward the gun Seth had knocked from her father's hand.

She needed to fire; she needed to stop the professor before he killed the man she loved. But she hesitated, finger on the trigger. What if she shot the wrong one... just like his vision...?

That stray bullet had struck his shoulder. But what if the next one struck his heart—as they'd both envisioned?

Tears burned her eyes, blurring the men so that she couldn't discern one from the other. She couldn't shoot. Footsteps pounded overhead, drawing her attention to the top of the stairs as two men burst through the door. One blond, one dark haired. She didn't need their names to know who they were: her brothers-in-law.

"Help!" she pleaded. "Please help!"

But before they could even join her on the stairs, a shot rang out—echoing again off those stone walls so that she cringed at the noise. And the pain...

So much pain...

* * *

Images flashed through his mind: those big hands holding Maria under water, her wet hair floating on the surface as the bubbles died. Then the rocks, piled atop her body, her hair dampening the cement on which it lay...

He jolted awake, shouting her name. "Maria!"

"I'm here, I'm right here," she assured him, her fingers gently stroking his damp hair back from his forehead. "I'm here..."

He blinked, trying to focus on the blurry image leaning over him. "It's not you..."

"It is," she said. "It's me. Here—this will prove it." She pressed something into his palm, worn metal that was warm yet from her body.

"It's your locket," he murmured.

"It's yours," she replied. "The locket really belongs to you."

He reached up and cupped her cheek as she leaned over him. "It wasn't you...in my visions. It wasn't you."

"No, it wasn't me," she confirmed. "It was Raven's sister. Violet figured out who was responsible for her sister's death and confronted him."

He flinched as he remembered the torture he had seen so many times in his head and then in the professor's cellar. "And she got herself killed."

"No," Maria said. "You saved her. You got to her in time...before the rocks did more than bruise her and crack a few ribs. She's actually the one who shot the professor. She worked free of the ropes binding her wrists, and she grabbed the gun you knocked out of his hand and killed him."

He was glad that she hadn't been forced to kill her own father. He was also glad that he hadn't killed him. If she couldn't forgive what his father had done to her mother, she would have probably never been able to forgive him for killing her father—even if it had been self-defense.

"I'm sorry," he said, stroking his fingers along her jaw to soothe the pain she was probably feeling. "I'm sorry…"

"What are you sorry about?" she asked, her brow furrowing.

"He was your father."

"He was a monster," she said with a shudder of revulsion. "He killed all those people, and I still don't understand why…"

He shrugged, then groaned as pain gripped his shoulder.

"I'm sorry," she said, pressing her hands to his chest to gently push him down onto the pillows piled behind his back. "Let me get you something to ease your pain."

"No." He shook his head—just slightly, though, so as not to jar his shoulder again. "I must have had too many painkillers. There's so much that I don't remember."

Tears of regret glistened in her eyes. "I shot you."

"I remember *that*." Though at the time he'd had to ignore the pain so that he would be able to save her from the professor.

But he hadn't saved her…

"I didn't mean to do it," she said. "I was shooting at my father."

"I thought you might have believed what he was saying about me," he admitted. "That I was the witch-hunter."

"I knew he was lying."

But she couldn't claim that she had never doubted him. His heart ached more than his shoulder as he remembered how devastated she had been when she'd learned who he was.

Instead of bringing all that up, he asked, "How did I get back home?"

She smiled. "Your stubbornness. After the doctors bandaged your shoulder, you refused to stay at the hospital. You insisted on coming home."

"I spent too much time in hospitals growing up— when my dad would hurt my mom or me. And he would find us there." He shuddered. And winced with pain. "He would always find us there."

She pressed something to his shoulder, some concoction of hers with the herbs and potions. And she chanted a prayer over him again.

And she healed him more than the doctor had been able to.

"I can take away your physical pain," she said. "But I wish that I could take away your emotional pain, too. That I could make you forget everything he did to you and your mother. He was a monster."

"He was," Seth agreed. "I can't help who my father was, Maria. Who I am…"

"You're a hero, Seth. My hero. I never should have doubted you. Never should have considered that you might be like your father." She leaned down and touched her lips to his, softly, as if she was afraid of hurting him.

He wrapped his uninjured arm around her back and pulled her down onto him. Cupping the back of her head in his hand, he held her mouth to his and deepened the kiss. Then, ignoring the pain in his injured shoulder, he lifted his other arm—and using both hands fastened the chain back around her neck.

She eased back and caught the locket in her palm.

"You were right to take this," she said. "It belongs in your family."

"It belongs to you," he said. "All those centuries ago Thomas gave it to Elena to keep her safe. He loved her, like I love you. I would never hurt you. I may be a McGregor, but I'm not a killer."

"I know that," she said. "I never should have doubted you. I was just so hurt that you hadn't told me. And I grew up with my mama making me run all the time because she was convinced that all McGregors were killers. But you're not a killer. You're a hero, just like Thomas was Elena's hero."

"But I didn't save you," he reminded her, guilt and remorse gripping him. He should have known, should have suspected that the professor had been the killer.

"That's because I had your gun," she said miserably. "Because I stole it from you…"

He glanced around the bedroom. "I don't remember if you gave my gun back to me…"

"David took it," she said.

"David?" He dimly remembered some other men coming down the stairs to that dungeon of witch-hunting horrors.

"Koster," Maria replied, "my sister Ariel's husband. Ty sent him and my sister Elena's husband, Joseph, with me."

"Where was Ty?" he wondered. The guy had been in Copper Creek when they needed him and had showed up when Waverly had been shooting at them.

"He needed to be with Irina," she replied. "She went into labor last night…when I was at their house."

"You went to your sisters when you left me?" he asked with surprise. She had been so adamant about staying away from them.

She nodded. "I felt as though I had to warn them about you."

He suspected that David Koster or Ty McIntyre had already figured out who he really was. "I'm sorry I didn't tell you sooner."

"I'm not," she said. "If I had known who you were, I wouldn't have let myself fall in love with you."

"You didn't really fall in love with me," he reminded her. "Because you didn't know who I was."

"I knew," she said with a smile full of confidence and certainty. "Your real name isn't who you are. You— the man who kept putting himself in danger to rescue me—are the real man. The man I love."

He expelled a ragged sigh. "Are you sure?"

"Irina was in labor," she reminded him, "but I left her and my other sisters because I was worried that you were in danger. I wanted to be with you."

"You can go now," he offered. "Chandler is dead. You should go—be with your sisters."

"I have the rest of my life to be with them," she said. "To talk to my sisters and play with my nieces and nephews. I want to be with you instead."

"You can spend the rest of your life with me, too."

She broke into a wide smile. "What are you suggesting?"

He lifted his fingers to the locket. "That I find you a ring to go with this. And you and I make this connection between us legal."

She knit her brow. "I'm still not sure what you're suggesting…"

"If you'd let me up, I'd get down on one knee and ask for your hand…and your heart…and every wonderful part of you…" He leaned forward and pressed his lips to hers. "Marry me, Maria. Become my wife."

She stared at him, her teeth nibbling her bottom lip. She'd said she loved him. But…

"Can you marry a McGregor?" Seth asked, his breath catching at her hesitation. "Can you marry the son of the man who murdered your mother? Or is it all too much for you?"

She shook her head. "I'm the daughter of the man who murdered my friends, who would have murdered the man I love. Who would have murdered me…"

"I don't think he would have," Seth said, trying to offer her hope. "I don't think he would have been able to hurt you…"

"No matter how much he resented me, how much he felt manipulated by me and my mother?"

"I'm not sure that was his motive, either." Or if he'd just gone crazy. "I think he started writing that book, and he got all mixed up in the legend. That's my fault— my ancestor started that first witch hunt."

"And you ended it," she pointed out. "The curse ends with us."

"What about *us*?" He had to know even as his heart tensed with dread. "Are we ended, too?" Before they'd ever really begun?

A smile curved her lips and brightened her dark eyes. "We'll tell our children how they wouldn't have even been here if not for Thomas McGregor letting Elena Durikken go."

"I can't let you go, Maria." He shook his head, trying to clear it of the painkiller fog, and realized what she'd just said. "*Our* children? As in yours and mine?"

"Of course. I'm not having children with anyone else. I want a lot of them," she warned him.

Joy filled his heart. "Good. I never liked being an only child."

"Irina just delivered her second set of twins," she said. "I don't think we'll have to worry about having an only child."

He kicked his legs from under the blanket and planted his feet on the floor.

"Where are you going?" She laughed. "Are you going to run away now?"

"No, I'm going to bring you to your family. I promised them that I would." And instead he had been selfish and kept her all to himself.

She wrapped her arms around him. "I'm with my family. You're my family, Seth. We'll go see the rest of them in a little while. But first I want to celebrate our engagement…if you're not in too much pain."

"With you as my bride, I'll never feel pain again." He turned and wrapped both arms around her. "I love you…"

"Prove it," she challenged him as she tugged him back onto the bed.

She didn't let him prove it, though. She kept him flat on his back as she bewitched him with her lips and her caresses. When she finally eased down onto his straining erection, he was out of his mind, groaning, as tension gripped his every muscle.

"I thought you weren't going to feel any more pain," she taunted as she slid up, teasing him until he clutched her hips in his hands and sped up her ride. Pulling her up. Pushing her down…until his world exploded with pleasure.

She screamed his name as her muscles caught him tight, held him deep, and her orgasm spilled over him. "I love you!"

"I love you."

Maybe he had loved her forever. Or at least three

and a half centuries. Their names were different now, but he had always felt the deepest connection with his ancestor Thomas McGregor, almost as if he had once been the man. But unlike Thomas, he would never let the love of his life go.

Pounding echoed throughout the shop as the man hammered in the nails to secure the sign above the door. Maria squeezed around the ladder and slipped out in the sunshine. He was up just high enough that she could admire his tight tush in his worn jeans. But staring at it wasn't enough; she had to reach up and squeeze.

"Maria..." a feminine voice admonished her. "Stop harassing the handyman."

She grinned at her sister Ariel as the redhead flitted around the store, helping her set out candles and crystals for the upcoming grand opening.

They'd already had an event at the new shop, though. They had held a séance to reunite Curtis Waverly with the woman he had loved and lost. Felicia had forgiven him and apologized for doubting him. And finally, Curtis had found relief and closure. That was what the shop was all about—helping and healing.

Elena, who worked at a computer on the counter, glanced up and tsked. "Maria can't keep her hands off that man."

"It's the hormones," Irina commiserated from where she nursed a baby on the couch. The other child slept in the bassinet next to her. There was a nursery in the back of the store, too, with a big playroom. The other kids were there—with Stacia babysitting.

They would be safe with her. At thirteen, Stacia was already the most powerful witch of all of them. Joseph had shared what she'd done with the charms; she had probably saved them all. Irina's difficult delivery might have taken her life if not for Stacia's interference.

And her magic with the charms had protected them from the evil in the professor's cellar—had stopped the bullet from hitting Seth's heart, as they had both envisioned.

"It's okay," Maria assured them with a wink. "My husband won't mind." She glanced down at the pewter wedding band, engraved with a sun, star and crescent moon. It matched the sign that the man nailed above the door of Charmed.

The last nail pounded in, he descended the ladder and wrapped his arms around her, pressing his palms over her protruding belly.

"Will your husband mind if I do this?" he asked as he lowered his head and kissed her lips.

She covered his hands with hers, and their baby kicked beneath their touch. "I don't know. Will you mind?" she asked him. "My wonderful husband…"

He kissed her again more deeply in response. When she pulled away, she was so flustered that she walked under the ladder when she waddled back into the store.

Her sisters all stared at her, their eyes—in shades of pale blue, turquoise green and dark brown—all widened with horror. "Maria, you just walked under a ladder."

She shrugged off the old superstition. "I spent too much of my life believing myself to be cursed. I'm not cursed." Or she wouldn't have found her sisters and developed deep relationships with them.

And if she were cursed, she most certainly wouldn't have met the man for whom she had unknowingly been waiting her whole life. The man fated to be her husband, the father to their children and her whole world.

"I'm not cursed," she repeated as he came up behind

her and wrapped his strong arms around her again—offering support and protection even though she no longer needed it. She needed only him and her family. "I'm blessed."

* * * * *

THE WORLD IS BETTER WITH

Romance

Harlequin has everything from contemporary, passionate and heartwarming to suspenseful and inspirational stories.

Whatever your mood, we have a romance just for you!

Connect with us to find your next great read, special offers and more.

f /HarlequinBooks

🐦 @HarlequinBooks

www.HarlequinBlog.com

www.Harlequin.com/Newsletters

⊞ HARLEQUIN®

A *Romance* FOR EVERY MOOD™

www.Harlequin.com

Love the Harlequin book you just read?

Your opinion matters.

Review this book on your favorite
book site, review site, blog or your own
social media properties and share
your opinion with other readers!

JUST CAN'T GET ENOUGH?

Join our social communities
and talk to us online.

You will have access to the latest
news on upcoming titles and special
promotions, but most importantly,
you can talk to other fans about your
favorite Harlequin reads.

Harlequin.com/Community

Facebook.com/HarlequinBooks

Twitter.com/HarlequinBooks

Pinterest.com/HarlequinBooks

HARLEQUIN®

A Romance FOR EVERY MOOD™

Stay up-to-date on all your
romance-reading news with the
Harlequin Shopping Guide,
featuring bestselling authors, exciting new
miniseries, books to watch and more!

The newest issue will be delivered right to you
with our compliments! There are 4 each year.

Signing up is easy.

EMAIL

ShoppingGuide@Harlequin.ca

WRITE TO US

HARLEQUIN BOOKS
Attention: Customer Service Department
P.O. Box 9057, Buffalo, NY 14269-9057

OR PHONE

1-800-873-8635 in the United States
1-888-343-9777 in Canada

Please allow 4-6 weeks for delivery of the first issue by mail.